Raughley, Sarah

Bones of Ruin: Book 2:
    The song of wrath

THE SONG OF WRATH

ALSO BY SARAH RAUGHLEY

Sarah Raughley

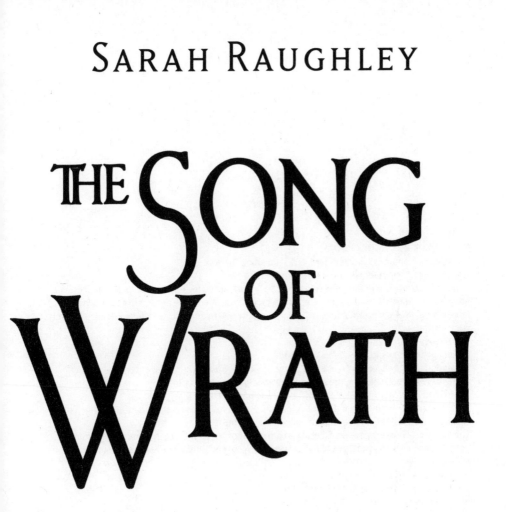

The Song
of
Wrath

MARGARET K. MCELDERRY BOOKS
NEW YORK LONDON TORONTO SYDNEY NEW DELHI

MARGARET K. McELDERRY BOOKS
An imprint of Simon & Schuster Children's Publishing Division
1230 Avenue of the Americas, New York, New York 10020
For information about special discounts for bulk purchases, please contact Simon & Schuster Spe-
cial Sales at 1-866-506-1949 or business@simonandschuster.com.
The Simon & Schuster Speakers Bureau can bring authors to your live event. For more information
or to book an event, contact the Simon & Schuster Speakers Bureau at 1-866-248-3049 or visit our
website at www.simonspeakers.com.
Interior design by Rebecca Syracuse
The text for this book was set in Matrix II OT.
Manufactured in the United States of America
First Edition
10 9 8 7 6 5 4 3 2 1
Library of Congress Cataloging-in-Publication Data
Names: Raughley, Sarah, author.
Title: The song of wrath / Sarah Raughley.
Description: First edition. | New York : Margaret K. McElderry Books,
[2023] | Series: Bones of ruin trilogy ; book 2 | Summary: Iris is on a
mission to stop herself from becoming the Hiva, a cataclysmic power that
can destroy the world.
Identifiers: LCCN 2022023228 (print) | LCCN 2022023229 (ebook) |
ISBN 9781534453593 (hardcover) | ISBN 9781534453616 (ebook)
Subjects: CYAC: Ability—Fiction. | Supernatural—Fiction. | End of the
world—Fiction. | Black people—England—Fiction. | Great
Britain—History—Victoria, 1837-1901—Fiction. | Fantasy. | LCGFT:
Fantasy fiction. | Novels.
Classification: LCC PZ7.1.R38 So 2021 (print) | LCC PZ7.1.R38 (ebook) |
DDC [Fic]—dc23
LC record available at https://lccn.loc.gov/2022023228
LC ebook record available at https://lccn.loc.gov/2022023229

FOR THOSE WHO RAISED ME
TO BE A DREAMER AND
TAUGHT ME TO NEVER GIVE UP

ON THE EDGE OF CATACLYSM

November 22, 1884
Strange fruit and the culling of the sowers

STRANGE FRUIT DANGLED FROM THE EVERGREEN trees.

"What you doing over *there*, boy?"

It was the sheriff who'd spoken. After one flick of his head, two men in plain shirts and short black ties grabbed Tom Fables around the neck and dragged him out from behind the tree that was hiding him. He had to run. The entire town was in this forest clearing with full bellies from their dinners. The dying rays of the evening light sifted through leaves onto the women's fine dresses and the jackets of their cherubic children.

"Don't be shy; join the fun!" taunted one of the men, carting Fables toward the crowd. As Fables tripped over his feet, he felt other hands touching him— his waist, his back, his buttocks—pulling him past policemen and city officials, housewives and laughing children, photographers and excited teenagers. All the way to the stage.

Fables liked stages. As a child, he'd make up his own stories and act them out in the parlor room, hoping the smile on his father's face meant he wouldn't get a drunken beating that night. It didn't. And later that night, when he was broken and bruised and alone in his room, Fables would create another story, one just for him. One where he had his own king to protect him. A king with an attack dog as big as Cerberus that would tear his father limb from limb at the slightest provocation. He'd act it out alone, making the room his stage.

This was not a stage. It was real. The trees, planted centuries before these townsfolk ever set foot on this soil, were *never* meant to bear this kind of fruit.

Fables didn't want to be here. He wanted to be with his king. After chancing upon him days ago in a lonely Kansas bar, the two had promptly left on their heroes' journey.

Hiva was a king not of this world.

Fables was less a damsel and more a dog, following his leader all week down to Oklahoma and then to this celebration in Okemah. Hiva was searching for someone. A woman. Someone important to him. And Fables? Fables was nothing more than his guide through this new, twisted world. The thought made Fables seethe with jealousy.

"I sense her," his king had said. "I can feel her. Smell her . . ." Then he stealthily disappeared into the trees to search for her, leaving Fables to contend with the townsfolk alone.

But what could Fables do alone? He was nothing. And when the gruff, stinking man forced him to the front of the crowd, telling him to stop being a little sissy and have fun, all Fables could do was look up helplessly and see the reason he'd been hiding.

It was an odd feeling, knowing that the only thing keeping him from suffering the same brutal death as the three corpses hanging from the Okemah trees was his light skin tone.

Come save me, Fables prayed, because somewhere deep inside he felt like his king could hear him. *I'm scared. Come save me!* He prayed like he'd always had as a child.

His mother had passed too, which was why his green-eyed father had married her without knowing. His grandmother, however, hadn't, causing her to flee West all those years ago. For this family of three, passing was not an option.

A mother, a father, and a young son. The photographer took their photos to sell as postcards later.

Fables fell to his knees, his heart pounding in his chest, his lungs heaving in air—but not too fast, because he was supposed to be one of the townsfolk, not one of *them.* His skin had saved him, his brown eyes and curly brown hair just neutral enough to keep him part of the crowd and not part of the evening's entertainment. Strange fruit these Southern trees were never meant to grow.

Behind him someone was talking. Charles Guthrie. Townsfolk called him "mister" with an emphasis, so he was probably one of those important types, like Fables's father. The officer was Alistair Griffith. The photographer, Johnny Ryals. Fables heard their names, but the three Black bodies swinging in the Southern breeze—what were *their* names? No one mentioned them.

Just make some up then, he figured: Tulip, Lily, and the young man could be Magnolia. Since their bodies would be returning to the earth.

This was just an evening in Okemah. Something to commemorate with photos and postcards. Fables often saw quite a few such postcards in shops for sale. WISH YOU WERE HERE.

All would return to the earth soon. It was the fate humankind deserved.

Fables's heart grew cold. Hiva was right. Humankind was wicked. Fables had always known it. Meeting his king only proved that he wasn't crazy for thinking it. That he had never been crazy, not even when secret dreams of bloodshed had slipped into his mind throughout his life: His father skewered on a long stake. The men and women he slept with for pennies, being stretched to pieces in torture chambers. His own body wasting away once this wicked world was done ravaging his soul.

This world was evil. But justice existed. Noah's flood. God's righteous vengeance. Fables just needed to see him one more time. Needed to hear his calm, steady voice amid the beautiful, sparkling laughter of these children who'd one day grow up to be killers themselves.

Please. Fables clasped his hands together and prayed. *Come back, Hiva....*

"Hey, we found the other one!"

Fables looked up quickly. Someone was pulling a horrified girl out from the gathering of trees behind her dead family. She couldn't have been more than ten years old.

Idiot! Why hadn't she run away? If his grandmother could run, why couldn't she? Indeed, Fables did see his grandmother in this girl's dark skin. He'd never seen her, but he imagined her in this girl's frightened doe eyes, in her black hair parted down the center, gathered in two big braids at the base of her neck. It bothered him. Made him want to stay far away from her.

Men mobbed her with rope, hands grabbing at her white dress.

Fables jumped to his feet but, as expected, did nothing as the rope went around her neck, as she pleaded for mercy and the crowd cheered. As they lifted her up while she screamed, staring at the corpses of her family, her sanity escaping through her red lips. The air was heavy with the taste of blood and evil sport. Had this girl been born just to die? Well, at least it wasn't him.

Do something. He couldn't. *Do something, you coward!* He wouldn't. He was too scared. He felt sorry for the girl, but Tom Fables was never supposed to be the hero of this story.

Where was his *king*?

"Tie her up *good!*" Guthrie cried again, the man's laugh too big for his body.

Fables was ready to run. But if he ran, they'd ask why.

They released the rope. The girl's body dropped. An excited hush fell over the crowd.

A gunshot rang out. A single bullet cut through the rope with expert precision. The girl fell to the ground, trembling but alive. The crowd turned behind themselves to the part of the forest where the shot had come from. They were given just a moment to be confused before trampling hooves brought a mighty horse out from behind the trees.

"Hiva?" Fables cried, hopeful.

Not a god, but a human. Not a man, but a girl in a black, wide-brimmed gambler's hat and a red bandana shielding half her face. Her leather gloves gripped the reins of the horse as she plunged into the crowd, her gun still smoking.

Nobody had expected a cowgirl with long, dark-brown curls to break up their celebration—especially one so fast and vicious, with seemingly no care about who she trampled over to get to the front of the stage. Black suspenders held up her pants over her white blouse, her long, half-buttoned blue coat fluttering open. The sheriff reached for his gun, but she shot him first, putting a hole in his head with barely a flinch. Then, with one slender but muscled arm, she picked the trembling girl up off the ground and threw her onto the horse.

It was like a play. Except in the plays Fables had seen when he was young, the savior would have been one of the sheriffs in the crowd and the evildoers the victims dangling from the tree. An offhand thought. Fables watched this new play, mouth agape in awe.

"Get that little bitch!" someone cried, but the ones not stomped on by horse hooves were staring at the spectacle, confused, terrified, even excited. Some ran.

The rest should have.

Fables's king finally emerged from the forest behind the hanging corpses, his bronze body cut like a statue. Golden, pupil-less eyes sparking with alertness. Beautiful and terrible as the falling dusk. The man had first appeared to Fables naked, with nothing but his curling brown hair to cover his manhood. Now he wore the shirt, pants, and worn smoking jacket that Fables had stolen for him. It was a shame. His body was glorious. But the straw hat upon his head was probably the most necessary for him to wear: it hid the band of sharp emerald-green laurels across his head, the white crystal shining at the center. A crown his king had once told him was imperative to completing his two missions. The first: to find "her"—whoever *she* was.

And the second: to wipe out humanity.

This was the Hiva.

The lynch mob stood affixed, baffled by this otherworldly creature, as they should be. Baffled by the weeds and flowers growing out of his glorious mane. But they were of no concern to Hiva. His golden eyes were trained on the girls riding away on the horse.

"I've found you," Hiva said. Before they could get too far, he lifted his hand.

And the horse vanished in a swirl of ashes.

The gunslinger and the girl she'd just rescued fell to the ground. Women and children were screaming. The photographer stumbled over his tripod trying to escape. Only one officer stepped forward to attack, pulling out his pistol and shooting Hiva in the neck. The bullet cut cleanly through his flesh and out the other side.

Then the bullet hole slowly closed.

The officer fell back in shock as a city official stepped forward and asked the question all were too terrified to ask.

"W-what the hell are you?" The officer's eyes were bulging in fear, as if he weren't a murderer himself. "What are you doing here? Answer me!"

"He's here to punish the wicked." It was Fables who answered—under his breath, of course, because even with his confidence suddenly skyrocketing in the presence of his king, he still didn't have the stones to draw attention to himself. It soon wouldn't matter.

Hiva lifted his hand.

It had only happened once before, at the Kansas bar Fables had met him in. But he hadn't gotten to witness it that time. This time he did. The sound of townsfolk screaming as they were burned from the inside out made Fables double over and throw up. He shut his eyes until he felt dust riding up his nostrils with each shaky breath. When he opened his eyes, he was surrounded by piles of ash. The townsfolk were gone. Only their toys, guns, and photography tools had been left behind. And the smell of burning flesh.

A sheen of black snow littered the grass. There was nothing left even for the crows to pluck. They really should have run when they had the chance.

Men, women, and children had vanished, their remains staining the earth as a reminder of the savage lives they had led. Justice. A beat of exhilaration electrified Fables.

But then he looked up. Three empty ropes hung silently from the trees, ashes flitting off the cords and into the wind. The weight of a life.

Fables shook his head. He'd decided long ago that everyone in the world could be divided into only one of two categories: perpetrators and victims. The perpetrators deserved punishment. The victims deserved release. Both led to death.

This family had already been killed. Maybe it was better this way.

But what about those two girls?

Several paces in front of Fables, they scrambled away from Hiva as he approached them. He was graceful and sure of each step, like a ballerina on stage. The red bandana slipped off the gunslinger's face just before she lurched over and threw up. Fables was shocked. She was so young. Not as young as the girl she'd saved, but young nonetheless. A face soft and round. A stubby nose and a pair of small lips. Mexican, perhaps. Her hands were small, but her eyes were hardened. Wiping her mouth, she jumped to her feet and smiled wickedly as if daring Hiva to come get her.

What a fool. But Fables recognized the look in that girl's eyes. The look of someone with nothing to lose. Maybe she'd saved the girl just for the thrill of it.

Hiva, three heads taller, walked up close enough to grab her. Without even blinking, she took out her gun and shot him in the chest. Smoke wafted from the barrel, but Hiva stood firm nonetheless. Fables could see the slight shiver of her body.

"You look like you're from hell," the gunslinger said, lowering her gun and cocking her head to the side. Her cowgirl accent was aggravating. She'd clearly spent years imitating it until every inflection came naturally to her. But Fables was an expert at telling tall tales to survive, so he could smell another fake from a mile away. "Don't know what to make of what you just did." She gestured to the ashes. "But since I seen it with my own eyes, guess it's true, so that's that." What a pragmatic girl. "Well, I've been to hell myself, so do your worst, El Diablo."

"It's 'Hiva'!" Fables cried before he could stop himself. Who did this girl think she was, talking to Hiva like that? Did she not see how beautiful he was? Did she not *feel* his divinity? Fables gripped his hands tight. He hated her.

But Hiva only shook his head. "You're not *her*. I can already sense that." His golden eyes glinted. "So why you have her scent, I'm not quite sure." Lightly, Hiva gripped the gunslinger's chin. "Have you met her? The Hiva of this earth?"

"Hiva of this earth"? Fables narrowed his eyes. But there was only one Hiva. There could only *be* one Hiva, *one* celestial savior to end humankind's wickedness. There couldn't be two.

The gunslinger yanked her chin out of his grip. "I don't know what the hell you're talking about. If you're going to kill me, do it. Who cares? I've killed enough deadbeats and bastards to deserve it. But the girl, she's innocent. Leave her alone. Let her go back home."

"Home . . . ," the brown girl behind her whispered—a word that must have sounded so suddenly alien to her. "But I don't have one."

She hadn't the strength to get to her feet, but she grabbed the cowgirl's legs and nuzzled her face into them. Then, with a feeble voice hoarse from screaming, she whispered, "Please. Please . . . please stop."

The gunslinger looked back, but the girl was already crawling on her knees, brown hands dirtied from the soil. Crawling toward Hiva.

"It's okay. I want to go to where Mama, Daddy, and Joey are," she said.

Her sweet voice was so serene, like the low notes of a flute. But when she smiled, Fables noticed something wrong. Her trembling smile was wide—too wide. Like her unfocused eyes.

"I've heard of you. Pastor Mike talked about you." She looked up, mumbling under her breath as if trying to remember her school lessons. Then she nodded, sure of herself. "You're one of the seven angels in the book of Revelation. I-I'm right, aren't I?"

Without standing, she gestured to shake his hand. "My name is Lulu. Lulu Jones. You're here to save me, right? Take me away?" She sounded hopeful.

Hiva quirked his head to the side. "I'm here to punish the wicked."

"And who's the wicked?" The gunslinger folded her arms, glaring at him. She put up a tough front, this girl, Fables had to admit. She *was* tough. And once again, he was jealous.

Hiva lifted his head. For a moment, it seemed like he would answer. But Lulu did instead.

"You saw it, didn't you?" She surveyed the ash-filled clearing. "The wicked. They're gone. They disappeared like dust. Like a bad dream. The Lord really does listen to our prayers." She looked up. "The Lord hasn't abandoned me." Lulu brought her praying hands up to her forehead, squeezed her eyes shut, and laughed while tears slipped down her cheeks. "You haven't abandoned me!"

"Lulu . . ." Fables saw this girl crumpled, praying and pleading on the ground, newly orphaned as the ashes of her family mixed with those of their killers and drifted up into the moon. She was hoping for solace. For someone that would give it to her. Anyone . . .

All would die soon. All were wicked. Humanity was a mistake. They all needed to disappear. But not now. Fables wasn't the giving type. But as a reward for this girl's suffering, at the very least, he thought it'd be kind if she survived long enough to understand just how glorious it would all be one day when it ended. How much sense Hiva's righteous dogma made. A reprieve from her grief . . .

"Uh . . ." Fables squirmed awkwardly, because he still didn't like being around this girl. "Hiva here's on a mission. I'm Fables, his guide."

"A mission." Lulu looked up at Hiva with hopeful eyes. "To punish the wicked and take the faithful?"

Hiva took off his hat. Lulu and the gunslinger both gasped. The emerald crown and white stone sparkled in the dying light. Lulu took to her feet and placed her hands on it so suddenly that Fables's heart jumped into his throat. For one moment, he thought she'd collapse, dead for the mere sin of touching him, but she didn't. Nor did Hiva move.

She felt his crown and cried tears of happiness.

"You really are an angel. . . . We're really not alone down here. . . ." She wept and fell to her knees again. "We deserve someone looking out for us too. Pastor said the Lord wouldn't forsake us, and he was right. He was right. . . . Mama, Daddy, Joey . . . you shoulda seen this. You should be here . . . you should be here!"

She screamed and wailed bitterly for what felt like days, inconsolable, while all looked on in silence. It pierced Fables's soul until he couldn't take it.

"W-why don't you come with us," Fables said all in one breath, giving a quick glance to Hiva to make sure he wouldn't object. He didn't. Fables supposed it was all the same to him. Everyone would have the same fate in the end. "This is a *movement*. A reckoning. The people who did this to you . . . there are people like that all over this country . . . all over the world. We're gonna punish 'em all. They're gonna get what's coming to 'em. And the faithful will be taken to a better place. It's all part of God's plan."

Whether it was part of God's plan or not didn't matter to Fables. It was an opportunity he needed to seize on, and it was enough to keep the girl going for now. The gunslinger looked skeptical as all get-out, but when she and Fables exchanged glances, she kept her mouth shut.

Meanwhile, Lulu nodded her head. "The faithful will be taken," she repeated. "They were just taken, that's all. . . ." And she continued sobbing on the ground.

"But before that, we need to find someone. . . ." Fables looked at Hiva.

"And you thought that someone was me?" The gunslinger picked up her bandana off the ground. "I smell like her or something? Guess she hasn't bathed in a few days either."

"Her anima is faint. It may be that you've met her . . . or have come into contact with someone who has."

Hiva's speech was measured and without feeling. He was as calculating as an abacus and had the same level of passion. He didn't seem emotional about his desire to find this person. He was like a machine built to check two items off the list. This just happened to be one of them. He was the complete opposite of Fables's father, who'd fly off the handle after hearing the wrong word. Fables didn't know how to feel about his king's empty coldness, but he had to admit—it did help him seem more trustworthy. What he said he would do, he did. When Hiva spoke, Fables believed him. And Fables had had enough of overemotional idiots for a lifetime. Hiva stood like a god who could not understand the preoccupations of human beings. He did not want to and did not need to. He was better off not knowing.

"That means you're a clue," said Fables helpfully, looking to Hiva for the kind of approval Fables knew he wouldn't get from someone like him. "Whoever Hiva wants to find, you're the clue to finding her." This "second" Hiva. "So you're coming with us."

The gunslinger laughed. "And if I don't? You gonna kill me?"

The girl seemed to welcome it. Behind the veneer of confidence was shattered glass. What this girl had been through, Fables had no idea. But it was the same for him. The gunslinger, Lulu, and himself. They'd all been broken by this vile world.

"Dunno," Fables said. "But if you do, you get to kill some assholes and get away with it."

"I've already been doing that," she answered, a wicked smile on her lips. "It's kind of my raison d'être."

He'd figured that would entice her, though, and he was right. After a moment of thinking, her hand twitched on her gun. "Sure. Why not. Nothing else to do."

Hiva wasn't listening. He was already peering through the treetops as if he'd seen something. When Fables's eyes followed Hiva's gaze, for a moment he thought he saw something too. Something that disappeared in a flash.

A grinning mask. But it couldn't have been.

"What?" the gunslinger said. "We being watched?"

"Perhaps," said Hiva. "By something not so human."

"Ironic of you to say that," she scoffed, and helped Lulu to her feet.

But Fables could have sworn he saw it. A harlequin mask covering a man's face. A black top hat. He shook his head. That didn't make sense. Then again, what about any of this made sense? He squeezed his eyes shut and looked again. Nothing.

"Looks like you killed half the town," said the gunslinger. "The place is going to be swarming with officers soon—I mean, the ones you didn't burn to a crisp. Wanted posters gonna go out. Newspaper articles." The gunslinger stretched her neck. "I know a place to hide if you're interested. A ranch a few miles west of here. Just gotta get on that road." She pointed to her right. "Could have gotten there sooner, but you killed my horse," she added with a sting of anger.

Hiva had already started off. "I guess we're going," Fables said. He hadn't intended on sharing his king with anyone else, but sometimes unexpected things happened.

Then, just for a second, Hiva stumbled. He regained his footing quickly, but that alone was enough to send Fables into a panic.

"Hiva!" He ran up to him but didn't dare touch him. "Are you okay?"

"Need a nap?" said the gunslinger, and Fables cast her a dirty look. Hiva continued as if nothing had happened.

His machinelike focus was truly something to behold. But what worried Fables was the fact that Hiva was walking a little slower than usual, his steps labored. After his massacre in the Kansas bar, Hiva had needed some time to recover. Fables had kept him hidden in the woods nearby while he went to steal clothes for him. Fables remembered returning to see him lying against a tree trunk, birds nesting in his hair, his long lashes fluttering as he slept. The most glorious sight Fables had ever seen. As if he were one with the earth.

But it made one thing clear to him: every time Hiva brought down the hammer of justice upon the evil, it sapped his energy. Even Hiva wasn't infallible.

Even gods had weaknesses.

Lulu didn't seem to notice. She wiped her face and cast one last look toward the ropes that had taken her family.

"A real, living *angel* sent by God. If only you could have seen it," she sniffed. "Mama, you always said things happen for a reason. Things happen for a reason." She nodded and repeated it a few times under her breath. "You're not really gone. You're all watching me, aren't you? Then watch me make things right." She nodded again, her eyes brightening. "I'll make things right." With a little smile, she sucked in a breath and followed behind Hiva, humming quietly to herself. "Battle Hymn of the Republic." Fables had played it enough times in saloons to recognize it.

"Mine eyes have seen the glory of the coming of the Lord. . . ."

That was when her little body gave out in exhaustion. The gunslinger wasted no time hoisting Lulu up on her back. Fables wasn't sure Lulu was ready for what was to come, but in her state, letting her believe what she wanted was the only humane thing he could do for her.

"You seem awfully nice," Fables said to the gunslinger. "What's your name?"

"Berta," she answered simply. "Berta Morales."

Lulu's weight didn't seem like it was much, but Berta did huff a bit as she bolstered her body a little higher on her back.

"Got any family?"

"Does it look like I got family, twiggy?" But there was an awkward pause before Berta's sharp response. Fables could only wonder.

"My turn. This person y'all want to find." Berta's question was for Hiva. "'The Hiva of this earth.' The girl I smell like. It *is* a girl, right? So why you wanna find her?"

Hiva answered just as simply: "I'm going to kill her."

PART ONE
Dark Specters

No brown specter pulls up a chair beside me when I sit down to eat. No dark ghost thrusts its leg against mine in bed.

The game of keeping what one has is never so exciting as the game of getting.

—ZORA NEALE HURSTON,
"HOW IT FEELS TO BE COLORED ME"

1

On the other side of the world . . .

TWO HOURS PAST MIDNIGHT, A WOMAN with too many names broke into the British Museum while the streets of London burned.

In her grip was the collar of the museum's director, still in his white nightshirt because she'd kidnapped him from his bed.

"You! You . . ." The director devolved into whimpers as he stumbled over his ankle-length shirt and struggled to keep his nightcap on.

The woman grimaced. She had become used to calling herself "Iris," but she'd collected too many aliases during her immortal life to be satisfied with "you."

This hidden hall below the basement of the museum was one of the secrets she'd wrangled out of the eccentric Riccardo Benini. The hall existed solely to lead the Enlightenment Committee, of which Benini was a member, to a secluded room tucked away from the prying eyes of visitors.

The Library of Rule. The secret room was home to a mysterious collection of artifacts curated out of the remains of the civilization she'd annihilated millennia ago.

It was why she needed the director and his key. It was why there were guards standing by in their silver-buttoned black jackets and pants, ready to bash in the heads of intruders. And here the intruders were. The guards' custodian helmets lifted a little as they began attacking with batons.

Iris didn't need to lift a finger.

"Wha's 'at?" cried one guard, pointing in terror. *"Wha's 'at?"*

He was referring to the white crystal sword emerging out of the chest of the young warrior trailing her. A girl with brown skin not quite as dark as Iris's and a damaged right eye. Olarinde. The frills of her yellow dress billowed behind her as she leaped out from behind Iris.

"Hold fast, boys, she's one of those freaks we've been told about. Bloody—"

The guard could not even finish his sentence before Rin sliced his lifted baton in half. There had to have been more than a dozen guards in this darkly lit hallway. Rin took them down one by one, clearing a path for Iris.

"L-let me go, you beast!" the director demanded to Iris in terror.

Beast. That was not one of her names.

Sweat dripped down his snow-white beard as she dragged him along behind her.

Men like him had given her names before. Isoke: She Who Does Not Fall. Given by the king of Dahomey, who'd forced her to fight as one of his warriors fifty years ago.

Iris Marlow. Given by the slave trader who'd kidnapped her and taken her to England. The name that the people she loved knew. If not for that, she would have thrown it away.

The Nubian Princess. Given by her old circus boss, George Coolie, before he'd tried to auction her off on the black market.

The cataclysm known as the Hiva. It was the first name she'd ever been given, long ago when the One who'd created her first molded her inside the earth. She didn't remember those days. Not clearly. They were too far away.

She knew that she was Hiva. She knew that every few millennia, the One would call her into existence to cause the fall of a wicked civilization. Only after she fulfilled her purpose would the One allow her to return to the earth.

But each life cycle she'd lived since her first was a blank page—no, a red page. Because pools of blood in ash were all that was left from those memories. Maybe something inside her wouldn't let her remember anything else.

"Don't engage!" said the director as Rin slammed another guard against the wall. "Go to Club Uriel! Check on the patrons—"

Iris yanked his collar to silence him, but then, as her shoulder grazed the purple ribbon by her ear that tied her braids in a beautiful bow, she thought of Jinn with a pang of guilt. She, Rin, and Jinn had escaped Club Uriel by the skin of their teeth only because Iris had knocked out her old circus partner. His fire was already spreading across Pall Mall Street. If she hadn't tied him up and kept him in a safe house, he'd still be fighting that ghoul Gram now. They didn't have time for that. They were to escape London tonight. But there was something Iris needed to do first.

One man smashed into another, hats and clubs flying into the air. Another crashed against the ground with a quick, feeble gasp. Blood from the tallest guard's mouth spurted across the lamps fixed to the mahogany walls. Iris expected nothing less from Rin, the sixteen-year-old warrior once prized as the youngest talent among the Dahomey military's Reaper Regiment.

"Rin, don't kill them," Iris reminded her, even though she had far more blood on her hands—lifetimes' worth. Iris spoke in the newfound authoritative voice she hadn't had back when she was just an amnesiac tightrope dancer searching for the truth behind why she couldn't die. Back in those simpler days, before she realized she wasn't an eighteen-year-old West African girl, despite how she appeared to the world—despite her youthful round face, full red lips, big brown eyes, and skin dark and shining as coal.

Iris had lived for eons. And this room, the Library of Rule, opened by the terrified director's little silver key, confirmed it.

A ghostly chill touched Iris so subtly that she almost lost her grip on the director's collar. Rin closed the door behind them and guarded it with her sword as Iris threw the museum director onto the floor, taking away his key. There were no windows in this room. The only source of light was from the candelabras affixed to the wall. Still she could see the magnificent displays of tablets and stones, tools and artifacts placed delicately behind reflective glass cases, symbols etched into their surfaces.

Ruins of a civilization she'd once destroyed.

She shivered as one by one, the static marks broke through the haze of jumbled memories clouding her mind, the signs becoming more familiar to her.

Each mark engraved in stone drew out images of green lands and quiet seas . . . and of a murderous people. . . .

"The Naacal." Her breath hitched, the word a treacherous spider crawling up her spine. Iris's gaze fell upon a stone tomb propped up vertically against the wall in the rightmost corner of the room. It smelled of death. The ruinous bones inside called to her. . . .

"How did you know about this place?" The director's question broke the spell. As she walked to the front wall, she glared at the man cowering in his nightwear. "Only the Committee knows," he said.

"The Enlightenment Committee?" Her temper rose at the sound of that vile organization's name. "And where's the Committee now to save you?"

He withdrew with a squeak, covering his mouth to muffle his breaths.

After a while, he lowered his hands and muttered, "Just what do you know, girl?" The director clearly didn't want to speak to her again, but he chanced it anyway. If he knew about this place, he must have been a member of Club Uriel, the death cult that had worshipped the apocalypse. Like everyone else in the club, he was obviously loyal to the Committee, the top seven members within the club. He was their glorified pet.

"I know that the Enlightenment Committee believes the world is coming to an end, just like the rest of you disgusting, decadent fools. The grand cataclysm: the Hiva." Iris wasn't looking at him. She was looking at the few stones made of pure gold behind the front glass display. And at the carvings that depicted faces in anguish.

Anguish she'd caused. The red page had begun to tell a story. The longer she stood inside this mausoleum, the clearer that story became.

"I know you all thought it'd be fun to toy with people desperate for a way out of poverty," Iris continued. "People with abilities."

Rin held out her mystical crystal sword.

"The Enlightenment Committee gathered us together and made us fight like cocks to see which one of them would 'win' the right to guide the next phase of humanity after the apocalypse. And you all relished it like sick spectators placing your bets." Iris's eyes were blazing. "Anything to add?"

But what was worth adding wasn't anything he would know. Club Uriel certainly didn't.

The Hiva wasn't an apocalyptic event. It was the bringer of the apocalypse itself.

The Hiva was Iris.

The director remained silent, sweat beading across his forehead.

"The Tournament of Freaks." Iris squeezed her hands into a fist. "Tonight was to be the grand finale, only things didn't go quite as planned, did they?" She remembered the pile of bodies on the second floor of Club Uriel—the corpses meant to be the audience for their final fight to the death—and shivered. "Lucky you, director. You decided to skip the festivities."

His fingers twitched. "M-my wife and child were sick," he confessed.

Loved ones. She wanted to calm her anger, but what about *her* loved ones? The club hadn't cared when they'd gossiped and giggled over who died during the tournament. They hadn't cared what the cost was for their entertainment. They thought nothing of the players' pain. . . .

She closed her eyes, only to find the cheeky, lopsided smile of a Salvadoran boy mocking her. Maximo Morales. The thought of his curly brown hair and tanned skin nearly sent Iris into a whirl of despair. He'd joined the tournament just so he could one day find his sister, and died because of it. The golden pocket watch he'd stolen for her ticked silently in the pouch of her dress. . . .

"Max," she whispered. Her arms dropped to her side, but she could no longer feel them. A panicked tingling rushed from her face, down her neck, and to her now wildly beating heart. It took great effort to raise her hand to clutch her chest, and when she did, her palms felt like sand.

Max . . . She gritted her teeth to force the word back down her throat. She wouldn't show weakness. Not in front of a man like this. That was what she thought. That was what she demanded of herself. Then she tasted the wet saltiness that began pooling between her lips. She turned and hastily wiped the tears from her face, but an ugly sob gave her away.

Max was dead. The Tournament of Freaks had killed him.

Iris dried her tears and faced the director once more. "Thank your family,"

Iris told him hatefully. "Otherwise you would have been among the club members slaughtered tonight."

With a shaky hand, Iris opened the glass case and touched the stones. Perhaps memory was tactile. The electric buzz that prickled her fingers was like a direct transmission of knowledge. She didn't want to remember, but she began to, bit by bit. The stones. The symbols. Together they wove a tragic story, the story of a fallen civilization: the Naacal.

And as her fingers slid across the grooves, suddenly, in her mind's eye, she could see the lush greenery overlooking the Atlantic Ocean. The hills upon which glorious cities were built. Humans in green robes and gold sashes walking across paved paths, silver bangles around their necks and ankles. Ah, yes. The Naacal had used an especially strong substance to build the tall pillars of their shrines and the perfectly portioned white bricks of their homes: Naacalian orichalcum. An advanced, mechanical mix of quartzite, copper, ocher, and other substances.

The Naacalians had wondrous technologies humans now could only dream of. Among the most advanced of their tech were crowns known as meridians, powered by technology smaller than the eye could detect. With these special bands, the Naacal could teleport anywhere they wished as long as they could see it in their mind's eye—quite similar, Iris noted, to the supernatural abilities of a young man she used to know, Lawrence Hawkins.

A young man who just tried to kill me, she remembered bitterly, her hands squeezing into a fist. Tried, yes. But killed Max in her place.

The meridian had still been in its prototype stage at the time Iris murdered them all.

A shock of pain split through Iris's skull.

"Isoke!"

Iris could hear Rin by the door worryingly calling her by her Dahomean name as she crumpled to her knees, gripping her head. No, Isoke wasn't her name. Neither was Iris. But her *true* name—she didn't want it.

Hiva, the cataclysm. *She didn't want it.*

The name was written on the tablet in front of her, symbolized by the

Naacal through two overlapping circles, one bright, one dark: the sun and its shadow. The ancient pictographs told the story of their demise. Five simple lines that belied the true horror of those days:

> *And so Hiva laid waste to the world.*
> *With a mighty hand and unforgiving eye, everything that fell upon*
> *Hiva's sight became dust.*
> *And in the same way, Hiva will rise again.*
> *For it is Hiva's fate to destroy mankind forever and ever.*
> *Misery unto eternity . . .*

Even now, as her recollection slowly returned, Iris couldn't remember every detail of her time with the Naacal. Inside the Crystal Palace just hours earlier, she finally remembered who she was, but . . . that was *eons* of history pouring into her all at once. Eons. Whatever details hadn't been lost by now were still clumsily sorting themselves out.

The Naacalian civilization was her most recent memory. As that had been the previous life she'd lived before this one, it was easier to recall their cities crumbling, the civilians and soldiers burning from the inside out. She remembered the One calling her back to the earth once she'd fulfilled her mission. Darkness. The peace of nothingness.

Then she was summoned again fifty years ago to eradicate the new civilization that had sprung up in the Naacal's place. *This* civilization. And so she was reborn.

But that was *Hiva's* mission, not hers. Hiva was the name that had cost her everything: the trust of the newfound friends she'd met during the Tournament of Freaks. The life she'd carved out for herself in this world as an innocent circus performer . . .

"Granny . . . ," she whispered. She'd almost forgotten she was still wearing the clothes Granny had sewn for her: a peach blouse with a high collar. A long skirt the color of green moss. Her eyes filled with tears as she remembered the old woman who'd treated her as a daughter in Coolie's circus. It was just too dangerous to go near her now. Maybe ever.

"Ugh!" Iris yelled again, her head splitting. The memories were too much. Too many years, too many deaths. Every second of every scene stumbled over each other, playing out of order. She felt like a spectator to it, as if someone *else* had set all those worlds aflame. Not her.

I'd never. She shook her head. *I would never.*

Being here among the ruins, feeling Naacalian artifacts with her bare hands, made the pain worse. Her brain felt scrambled. Details slipped through the cracks of her psyche as she peered around the room . . . at the tomb calling her. . . .

"Director!" Breathing heavily, Iris stumbled to her feet. "Bring out every bit of information you have on the Naacal. *Now!*"

The museum's director didn't need telling twice. The tablets were too heavy, so he scrambled across the room, bringing out scrolls from inside cupboards. As he worked to pile everything across the long wooden table in the center of the room, Rin approached her.

"Isoke," she said in Fon, the language they'd both used in Dahomey. "We need to leave this place before the others catch up to us."

The others. She meant the other teams they'd competed against in the tournament. The street urchins Hawkins, Cherice, and Jacob—Max's friends, whom she'd come to trust. Mary, Lucille, and Henry, an odd but strangely functional team she'd just begun to work *with* instead of against. Where once there had been a tentative alliance, there was now nothing but blood and fear.

Iris bit her lip and realized she was shaking. Was it out of fear or anger?

They'd turned on her. They'd refused to even *listen* to her. . . .

But could she blame them? From their perspective, she was Hiva, killer of worlds. If they wanted to live, then they needed to kill her first. It was as simple as that. For *them* . . .

"And not just them." Rin gripped her shoulder. "The guards. The Committee."

Adam Temple. Iris's expression darkened. A devilish, handsome young man with limitless wealth to match his fanatical worship of "Hiva." The only Committee member to know that Hiva was not an event but a creature. Her. How fun it must have been for him to manipulate her into joining the tournament, stringing her along with promises of "the truth," knowing all along how horrific the truth really was. The last time they were together, she'd left him unconscious on the floor of his own mansion, but who knew when he'd awaken? Who knew what else he had planned for her in that chess-like mind of his?

She had to disappear.

"We'll gather up all the information we can carry and leave," Iris told Rin. "Anything from this place that can help me learn what I need to know."

Rin narrowed her eyes. "And what's that?"

Iris looked at her very seriously, each breath heavy. "How to stop myself from ending humanity."

2

THE MUSEUM DIRECTOR THOUGHT HE WAS clever.

He had a gun in one of the cupboards and wielded it only after Iris was preoccupied with the twelve scrolls he'd set on the table. He aimed for Rin next to her, but Iris was faster. She grabbed the younger girl and swiveled around, letting the bullet pierce through her elbow. As Iris's bones ejected the bullet, Rin rushed at him, knocking him out with one punch.

"Ugh." Iris winced, waiting for her elbow to heal before moving it. Not being able to die didn't mean getting shot didn't *hurt*. Not to mention, dying felt like hell. She avoided it whenever she could. To think she used to agonize over why she couldn't die. Now she knew: the One who'd created her wouldn't let her die and return to the earth until she'd completed her mission.

What had made her do it the last time? And the times before that?

Each time there'd been a breaking point, something that tipped her over the edge, something that had finally made her *understand* that humanity needed to die. After she'd reached that point, there was no stopping her until her mission was complete.

It always happened like that. Without fail.

Slowly, Iris's eyes slid to the tomb. "No." She bit her bottom lip. "There has to be a way. There *has* to be."

She couldn't die, but she didn't want to lock herself up in a cage for all eternity. There must be a method, whether through magic or science, to take away these impulses—no, these powers—altogether. That was what she needed. If there was a way to make humans supernatural, then there had to be a way to transform supernatural beings back into humans. Right?

To live as a normal human. To grow old and die in peace. That was her dream.

Granny. Iris smiled as she suddenly remembered the day she'd first brought her pet goose, Egg, to Granny's tent. The old woman had been incensed that Iris wouldn't let her cook it. The ensuing argument wasn't one that could be so easily broken up, though Jinn had tried after hearing their squabbles from outside. The whole ordeal had ended with Granny whacking Iris on the head with a wooden spoon for her smart mouth and Jinn trying very hard not to laugh.

Before their performance that night, Iris had pouted and whimpered in the corner of her tent, her skull still smarting, while Granny braided her hair. Even still, Granny had giggled whenever Egg's feathers brushed up against her legs. Granny's laughter had tasted like sweet medicine. Iris wanted to hear it again.

Granny and Jinn. *Their* "Iris" wasn't a cold-blooded murderer.

All Iris knew of the One was that it was a divine being. It alone allowed her to live and die. But no matter what or who had summoned her into existence, she would never again commit genocide on its behalf. Right there in the Library of Rule, Iris swore it to herself.

"Isoke." Rin grabbed her around the elbow—the one that hadn't just been shot. "We should return to Dahomey. To King Glele. There may be information there from back when you were a warrior."

Iris watched Rin carefully. Max had told all the Fanciful Freaks what she was. It was why they'd turned on her. But Rin seemed determined to stick by her side. Did she even believe that Iris was Hiva? Did she even care?

"Now that you're finally yourself—"

Iris's fingers twitched. "And who am I?" she asked Rin pointedly.

Rin was such a young girl. Her battle scars and bloodstained hands belied the fact that she was only sixteen years old. When Iris had turned to her so sharply, the warrior had jumped in fear, betraying her age. But it had lasted a second. In the very next, she didn't waver when she answered Iris.

"A warrior queen with the power of the gods. The most famous of the *mino* under King Ghezo. She Who Does Not Fall. Child of Gleti, the Moon Goddess."

More names. Gleti, the moon goddess, was worshipped in the Kingdom of Dahomey. Iris had learned this during her time there. Celestial mother of the stars, whose mere absence caused the lands to fall under an eclipse. There had been an eclipse, too, on the day of Iris's rebirth, the day she'd risen up from inside the earth to begin her death mission anew.

Was it Gleti who had called her? Rin seemed to think so.

"I don't think you understand," Iris said, her hand on one scroll as she leaned against the table. "I was summoned here to end everything. Not just whoever your king says I should."

"And who says I want you to listen to the damn king?"

Rin had said it so quickly that Iris thought she'd heard things. But by the time Iris whipped her head up to stare at the girl, Rin's eyes were already avoiding hers.

"And what do you mean by *that*?"

Rin hesitated, her gaze darting here and there. "I just meant to say that . . . your will is your own. But if I don't complete my mission and take you to the king . . ."

When Rin's jaw locked, Iris couldn't help but recall how fearsomely Dahomey's sacred warriors treated their enemies—and how merciless they were toward traitors.

Rin stretched her arms out pleadingly. "At the very least, let me complete my mission. Do what you please after you meet him. Neither the king nor his warriors are a match for you."

Rin had only come to England in the first place on the orders of her king, to bring Iris back to the Kingdom of Dahomey as the king's warrior. That was what the king wanted. As for what Rin wanted? The young girl turned away, her lips curled inward as Iris studied her. She probably just wanted to avoid reprimand . . . or a far worse punishment. King Ghezo's punishments had been particularly brutal decades ago. Iris expected no more or less from the new king.

And what about what I want? Why isn't that ever enough?

25

Iris almost let out a whimper as despair began to flood her. Her head was a mess. She needed to focus. Rin was right. The Committee, the other Fanciful Freaks. Adam. There were too many enemies looking for her. They had to leave London. She'd figure this out later.

"We need something to carry the scrolls," Iris said. She and Rin searched the Library of Rule until Iris settled on taking the director's nightgown, tearing it open and tying it into a makeshift sack. Good thing the fabric was nice and expensive. Made for sturdy stuff.

"Hurry," Rin said while Iris took the bag.

And yet still Iris's gaze turned to the tomb.

Anima: the essence of life stored within one's very bones. She could sense the life of others. Use it to track them down. And like a spark to gas, she could turn that essence against them and use it to burn their bodies to ash.

But that was *not* how she'd murdered the Naacalian priest whose bones she sensed in that tomb.

She dropped the sack of scrolls wordlessly and followed the traces of that man.

"Isoke?"

Rin's voice was in another time now. Her mind asunder, her memories swirling, her fingers aching, Iris pried upon the casket.

The cobwebbed skeleton came crashing down on her, gaping its teeth as if to swallow her whole. Nyeth, the high priest of the Naacal, would have wanted the revenge. Out of the chaos of memories, she plucked out a bloody scene. Light streaming through a glass window on a domed ceiling. The symbol of the Naacal etched across the blue orichalcum that could withstand even the unforgiving pressure of these oceanic depths. Rows of pillars upon a speckled white marble floor, and one sweeping spiral staircase leading to the majestic central platform.

The Coral Temple . . .

The high priest, Nyeth, was doubled over upon the platform under a perfect pillar of light. The knife Iris had jabbed into his chest without feeling or remorse was strange indeed, not made of silver or steel. The remains of Nyeth's heart bloodied it. But Nyeth still had life in him yet—just enough to twist the round, coral-colored plate affixed to the ring around his finger.

It was called the Coral Ring. Nyeth never let it out of his sight. Why . . . ? It was as if she were trapped in her old heartless, mechanical body, forced to rewatch the horrors she'd committed without being able to stop them.

His blond hair fluttered across his narrow shoulders; his red-and-gold robes—worn by the Naacalian clergy—swept the floor as he swayed on his unsteady feet. Iris couldn't see herself reflected in his fading blue eyes, but she couldn't see fear, either. He smiled with maniacal glee.

"That blade," he said between labored breaths. "We made it out of his . . ."

"I'm well aware of what it is. And what you were planning to do with it."

Iris's voice. It sounded . . . different. Emotionless.

Terrifying.

Silence. Nyeth's bloodied lips trembled. "I hear no remorse. Not even a hint of anger. I once followed you. I would have done anything for you. None of it means anything to you, does it?"

It didn't. Not a trace of humanity could be found in Iris's words.

Soon, Nyeth's bloody coughing devolved into laughter. "Imagine how joyful I was when I realized that one *can* win against a god. Your wings can be clipped. If only we'd had more time. Then there may have been hope for us. . . ."

He looked beyond Iris to something behind her, something Iris couldn't see, not in this memory. A structure veiled in darkness. "And it'd just been completed too. . . . Damn it all. . . ."

"S-sister . . ." Behind her, a feeble voice called out in desperation, in despair. Iris looked over her shoulder just long enough to see the speaker's mangled body on the twisted steps. A creature of untold beauty. His arm missing. His eyes golden. A meridian across his forehead. And misery etched across his perfect face. "Why . . . ?"

"But!" Nyeth grabbed Iris's Naacalian robes in fury with one hand and flashed his ring on the other. "I can still stop you. I have the Coral Ring. This isn't over! This isn't . . . over. . . ."

The ring . . .

The light in the priest's eyes died. Nyeth's corpse fell upon Iris inside the ancient temple and his skeleton burst apart against her inside the Library of Rule. His dust entered her lungs as she held out her arms as if to receive a friend who'd tripped. She received Nyeth's warm blood instead, the memory of it pouring over her body. Part of the dusty skeleton's broken jaw cut her cheek. And inside the temple, she could see Nyeth's murderous eyes finally close. Was it past or present? Was she Iris or Hiva? She could no longer tell.

Iris was screaming. It took her only a second to register that the pain in her knees had been caused by the ground, and the pain in her head from her nails, but then she was lost in the flood of memories, too many memories. Too much *death*.

To know her true identity. The curse of a wish granted.

"That's not me! That's not me! I don't want it—!"

"Isoke!"

Rin's slap across Iris's face brought her back to the present. Iris let go of her head and stood up quickly.

"What is it?" Rin asked. "What's wrong with you?"

Sweat dripped from Iris's brow. Despite the humidity in the room, her body shivered deep to her core. The memory of Nyeth's hatred iced her veins.

I can still stop you. I have the Coral Ring. This isn't over. . . .

His ring. Iris frantically searched the broken hands of the skeleton in pieces on the ground. "It's not here." She shook her head. "His ring isn't here!"

"What?" Rin sounded impatient behind her. And a little scared.

Iris rushed over to the director and slapped him awake. She gripped his throat with such ferocity that even Rin was shocked.

"Isoke—"

"Where's the ring? The priest's ring?" Iris squeezed his throat as the man whimpered in confusion.

"I don't know what you're—"

"Don't lie to me!" Iris bellowed, grabbing his collar and forcing him to stare at the shattered skeleton. "That man never let his ring out of his sight. It was important. Part of his sacred duty. And part of their plan to . . ."

To stop her. Iris might not have known how. But she remembered that much. It had been admirable, the amount of effort the Naacal—their rulers and their priests—had placed into keeping humanity safe from her. Iris placed a hand on her head. Blurry. The memories weren't sorted yet.

Your wings can be clipped.

What Nyeth had called the Coral Ring was key to the Naacal's efforts to "clip her wings." She knew that much. But how? What did the ring do? How did it factor into this never-ending puzzle?

Your wings can be clipped. . . .

She couldn't die. But her wings could be "clipped." What was a bird without its wings?

What was a god without her powers?

A sudden start made her pause, her body numb. But after a violent shudder, she turned back to the director. "You curated this collection, didn't you? The man in this tomb. What do you know about him?"

"M-man . . . ?" the director repeated dully. But Iris's scowl snapped him out of his daze. "The Crown excavated his bones in West Africa. We believe he was part of an ancient civilization. That's it. . . ." Sweat dripped down his neck.

"I'm sure you would have peeked inside the tomb when you had the chance. You would have seen what was on his finger. So where is it? Where is the ring?" She wrapped her hands around his neck again. *"Where?"*

"I sold it!" The director was shivering. "To the son of the vice president of a shipping company: the Compagnie Générale Transatlantique. André Leroux. He lives in Paris." He clasped his hands together. "Please—not even the Committee knows this. You can't tell them. I just wanted something for myself—"

"What, like your wealth and prestige aren't enough?" The memory of Nyeth's hate infected her like a virus. Iris felt her blood boiling out of control. "Your amusement at the expense of people's lives isn't enough? You're all the same. Greedy, vile. The Naacal had their sins too. Many of them."

One memory blazed clearly in Iris's thoughts. The burning ball of fire swirling in the middle of the sea near what was now South America, courtesy of an explosion from one of the Naacalians' many underwater nuclear experiments. The earth had cried out in pain and from a desire for vengeance. Entire species had died, along with the poor community of fishermen who lived near the coastline. It was one of the many tragedies wrought by the Naacal's never-ending obsession with *advancement*.

"They were just like you. Doesn't matter who dies in the process so long as you get what you want, right?" Iris yanked his collar. Nyeth's face turned into Adam's. Adam's face turned into Maximo's, begging her forgiveness before disappearing forever. Her words caught in her throat. "Tell me, why shouldn't you die? Why shouldn't you all just pay for your crimes?"

"There you are!"

A lone guard burst through the door. It all happened so quickly. As Iris's rage burned inside of her, as she glared at the man, she let her mind go blank and her instincts take over. She could almost feel the man boiling from the inside before his screams took over, until his body disintegrated, until he was nothing more than a pile of ash on the ground.

Euphoria. A whisper of it filled her lungs like a lover's breath, tantalizing, her eyes glazing, her lashes fluttering before Iris caught herself. As if shocked with an electrical jolt, her arms flew around her chest and squeezed hard.

What was that?

What was that . . . that evil, sinful feeling?

Her body numbed. Her feet felt leaden. The director was crying. Rin was just staring at her, frozen. Iris gripped her head and shook it furiously. No, this wasn't her. This couldn't be her. As the director passed out, she stood and stepped back, burying her face in her hands.

"I'm sorry," she whispered in one strangled breath, to the man she'd just killed, to Nyeth, to everyone. To herself, whoever she was. "I'm sorry."

Inside she was screaming. *I don't want this. I don't want any of it! Get away from me! Get away!*

With the weight of countless deaths upon her shoulders, she stared at the pile of ashes. *Never again,* she vowed. *Never again.* Once more, she swore it.

"Rin," she said in a steady voice. The young warrior jumped, staring at her wide-eyed. She'd already taken several steps away from her. Iris didn't blame her. "You say you want me to see your bloody king. But I have things to do. For one, I will never allow what just happened tonight to happen again. You're free to go wherever you please. But if you get in my way, I *will* treat you as my enemy." She looked back at the younger girl with a steely gaze. "What's it going to be, then?"

Taking a deep breath, Rin closed her eyes, swallowed, and stood up straight, returning Iris's gaze with that of a fighter.

"I want to follow you," the girl said. "I'll go wherever you go."

"Even if it means you fail your mission?"

Iris watched her carefully as she considered it.

"That's my decision," Rin said. "And I won't get in your way."

But the defiant lift of Rin's chin told her this girl hadn't given up quite yet. Iris wasn't sure what to think. Still, there were more pressing matters. She looked from Nyeth's skeleton to the director passed out on the ground. The ring was with André Leroux in Paris. So she had a target. Catching her breath and wiping the sweat from her forehead, Iris coughed and shook off the dust from her clothes. Then she nodded to Rin.

"Let's get the hell out of London."

3

THE COBBLED STREETS NEAR PALL MALL had been closed off by police. Iris could see the fires in the distance, smoke rising in wisps from countless chimneys. They'd been sprayed by Jinn's mouth in his fury, hitting not only Club Uriel but even neighboring buildings. They'd gotten way out of control. It felt like the entire city of London would be enveloped. Jinn had done all *this*?

Iris followed Rin to Barry Bately's hideout—a basement in the slum district of St Giles near Covent Garden. Rin had been forced to partner with Bately during the tournament, but that alliance had ended with Rin's sword through the con man's rib cage. Needless to say, there was no love lost there.

Covent Garden was a court with nearly twenty-two houses; though most of the inhabitants were inside at this time of night, Iris spied a few men sleeping on the ground, the smell of putrid waste soggy in the air. Rin remained as the lookout while Iris went inside.

The floors inside Barry's building were squeaking horrendously and in some places nearly falling apart. Some steps on the staircases leading downstairs were missing, others nearly caving in. The plaster on the walls had already fallen in places. The basement was where Iris had left Jinn, unconscious and hog-tied. It was the only way to pry him away from his battle to the death with that monster Gram, one of the contestants in the tournament. The worst among them all.

But where was Jinn?

Iris's pulse began to race. It was pitch dark except for some light trickling through the tiniest of windows. Iris strained her eyes to search the basement. There was the sooty kettle of water atop the gas stove. Some filthy shoes from the place's former inhabitants tucked underneath one of the railings, and more unlit candles planted across its length. In the middle of the room, the blanket Iris had gingerly placed Jinn on was empty. Where had he gone?

He couldn't have gone back to Club Uriel. . . .

Iris felt cold. Gram might still have been there. That cannibal who enjoyed the kill more than the riches promised to the tournament winners.

Jinn couldn't have gone back. He wouldn't have.

"He absolutely *would*," Iris whispered through gritted teeth before running to a smaller section of the basement separated by an open, arched brick wall.

A rough hand seized her forearm the moment she stalked past the brick. In a flash, her back had hit the brick, her shoulders buckling under Jinn's grip.

"Jinn, it's me!" Wide-eyed, she looked up at his dark, catlike eyes, now wide with surprise. "It's just me."

"I'm sorry." He let go of her immediately, dazed for a moment, combing a hand through his hair. He was still on alert. Gram was still on his mind. She could tell.

But it wasn't long before he was gripped by anger once more. His whole body tensed.

"Jinn," Iris whispered.

"You had the *nerve* to do that to me," he hissed. His sandy skin flushing in anger, he ran his hand down his face and shook his head in disbelief. Though he refused to meet her gaze, he looked mad enough to breathe fire. "Knocking me out. Leaving me tied here. The *nerve*—"

"I had to." Iris grabbed his forearm, but he brushed her off, moving away from her. His jawline seemed somehow sharper as he grimaced. "You were about to kill yourself fighting Gram. We had to escape. We had to—"

"He *killed my father*." He whirled around. "My *father*."

Refik Ibrahim. Jinn had shouted that name just before rushing Gram. The only clue as to who "Jinn" really was. He'd never told her his own name. Never trusted her with it.

"I know. . . ." Iris lowered her head. Who was she kidding? They'd only been partners at Coolie's circus for two years. It wasn't as if he owed her anything. But during those moments when they were waving in front of an audience on their tightrope, smiling at each other after having finished a particularly difficult routine, she'd always felt an indescribable connection between them that was real . . . an attraction that was palpable. . . .

"Do you?" Jinn approached her slowly, but Iris couldn't move, not after noting his quiet desperation. "That day at the South Kensington fair ten years ago changed my life."

"And so many others." The mysterious day that had haunted Iris for ten years. The day she'd reanimated, causing the phenomenon that gave people extraordinary abilities. Jinn with his breath of fire. Max . . .

"Max."

The name escaped from her lips so suddenly, it shocked Jinn to a stop. Stepping back, he looked down at the filthy floor.

A familiar pain wrung her throat. She crumpled over, stomach heaving as she shakily gulped in air and remembered him. Max. Her tears fell once more.

The pocket watch in Iris's dress broke the silence with a *tick, tick, tick.*

"He's . . . gone. Probably dead," Jinn said. And when she squeezed her eyes shut and shook her head, he added, "There's no point in thinking about him anymore."

"What?" Incensed, she glared at him. "You're right, he *is* gone. And your father's gone too," Iris snapped back, dismayed at his heartlessness, surprised by her own. "And there's no point in losing your life avenging him—"

"My father's *dead* because of that man-eating monster, Gram. He *killed* my father at that fair ten years ago. *He* did that."

Iris thought of Gram's jaundiced pallor, stringy gray hair, and black lips sated only by the taste of human blood. *I never remember the names of my meals,* he'd once said. Iris shivered.

"I could have had him. I could have—"

"You could have *died*." And as Jinn turned from her, throwing his hands up in exasperation, Iris added, "I'm not going to let that happen!" This time she grabbed his arm. This time he didn't push her away.

"Why?" Jinn searched her eyes, a hint of vulnerability unmistakable. "Why are you so worried about me? Why do you care whether I live or die?"

Iris's fingers twitched upon his muscular bicep as she pressed her lips against the answer that was by now obvious to them both.

"You already know why," she argued impatiently, her face flushing. What a stupid question. She didn't have time for it. "That doesn't matter right now."

"No? So when will it matter?"

Iris sucked in a breath. "There are other things—"

"What other things?"

Iris couldn't answer. Jinn didn't wait any longer. The back of his hand brushed her hair, the purple ribbon he'd given to her, and then her neck, down to her collar. An electrifying thrill.

"Right," he said. "Let's decide this once and for all, shall we?" Then, unable to hold himself back, gripping her head, he crushed his mouth against hers. His kiss was deep, sensual, ravenous. She could feel his wetness on her lips, slipping down her tongue.

And finally she let her defenses drop, wrapping her arms around the small of his back and squeezing tight. It was chaos. Longing. His body hardened against her, his forearm stiff against the small of her back, curving her spine as he drew her into him.

Yes, this was how it was supposed to be between "Iris" and "Jinn," between two performers whose pasts were irrelevant to what they both felt burning inside. The memories of distant worlds felt so very far away. The memory of cities burning—she didn't want to think of it. Her body warmed, ached. She could feel her heart pounding in her ears, her legs trembling like they'd give out underneath her. A disorienting kind of bliss.

They'd been hiding in a makeshift shaft a few feet underground. It was shoddily made—just big enough to fit the three of their tiny bodies. The children must have dug it themselves. Once she tore open the dirt-covered roof and revealed their shelter, their eyes widened in terror. They pleaded for their lives. But Hiva's mission was clear. Even the children had to die. . . .

Iris couldn't breathe. Quickly, she pushed Jinn away, guilt rotting her where pleasure should have sung.

"Iris . . ." Her name dropped from his lips. The disappointment in his voice was palpable. He moved to search her face, but she'd already turned away from him. "I see. So that's your answer?"

She was not a god but a monster. There wasn't any other word for something that could turn those scared little dears to ashes so heartlessly. No wonder Max had betrayed her. No wonder he'd chosen that fateful day not to trust her. She thought of him disappearing before her eyes in Club Uriel. He'd told the others her true identity out of his pure fear of it. He'd turned them against her. But he'd been right to fear her. Jinn was the foolish one.

Lost, she shifted on her feet. It took her some time before she could look up at Jinn. What could she possibly say to a man who'd only lived one life? But Jinn didn't understand. And so his disappointment had turned to anger.

Once upon a time, in Astley's Amphitheatre, the two of them had waited for their cue to go onstage. Back then, Jinn in his circus outfit had stared down at her with an unreadable expression and asked her a question that made her heart skip.

What do you think of me?

"Then that's your answer," he said with a sense of finality that sounded like a gavel on wood. "That's good to know."

Things were now more complicated than they had been months ago, when they were on tour playing in the snow in Moscow or bantering back and forth in Munich while waving to the audience below. Iris knew the truth now, and so did Jinn. She was millions of years old. A mass murderer. Max was dead because of her, and one day, she might just make everyone else follow him to the grave. What were she and Jinn supposed to do with that horrific knowledge?

The silent gulf that had opened between them spanned lifetimes. Cataclysms.

"Jinn, that's not it," she tried to explain as he turned from her. "Look, Rin is with me. She's waiting outside with a sack of every bit of information on Hiva we could steal. Forget this silly blood feud."

"Silly blood feud?"

Seeing Jinn's face screw up in disgust made Iris want to collapse. "I didn't mean it like that!" Of course she didn't want Jinn to die. She wouldn't be able to bear it. "I just mean there're more important things . . ." She stopped and shook her head. "Just come with me, okay? I'm going to figure out how to stop . . . *it* . . . from happening."

"It. You mean the end of the world that you're supposed to cause?"

Hearing him say it struck her heart. "I won't let that happen." Iris grabbed his shirt collar with both hands, tugging him. "I'm going to find a way to stop it. I swear! Come with me! Let's find the answers together! Together. Just like before."

Once upon a time, Iris could stare deep into Jinn's dark eyes and watch the precise moment when his will buckled and was crushed under the weight of her trust in him.

But not this time.

Jinn brushed her hands away from him. "That's your mission. *Mine* is revenge."

Iris's hands fell to her side. "What do you . . . what do you mean?"

"I mean this is the end of the road for us, Iris. I've finally found my father's killer. I'm going to kill Gram. Even if it kills *me*."

Iris lowered her head, her voice fragile. "You won't stay?"

She could see his fingers twitch before he balled his hands into fists. "You haven't given me any good reason to."

Jinn used a sack to hold his twin *shamshir*. Iris used to have a pair too. Coolie had procured the weapons for them for "The Bolero of Blades": what was to be the defining routine of their partner act, "The Nubian Princess and the Turkish Prince." The silly and tone-deaf names Coolie had come up with now felt somehow quaint. Nostalgic. Jinn walked over to the wall where his sack rested and tossed her one of his two blades.

"Don't get yourself killed," he said after she caught it. He didn't even break his stride. "Then again, you can't die."

"Jinn!" she called out desperately.

But Jinn had already disappeared up the rickety stairs.

Iris and Rin escaped the hideout. But even as they ran, Iris's mind couldn't focus.

Your wings can be clipped.

Had Nyeth lied to her with his last words?

What did it mean to clip the wings of a god? Had the Naacal truly figured out a way to take away her power? Well, if anyone could do it, they could have. But they were gone.

How exactly was Iris supposed to stop herself from killing everyone now?

The fact that she couldn't think of an answer brought a particularly painful thump in her chest, but it was no more painful than the frustration building up inside her. Her memories were still scrambled—her most recent kills the clearest, yet still mixed in with eons of genocide.

It was as if her mind was trying to protect her. As if it knew she couldn't withstand all that information at once. Hiva could. Iris couldn't.

As Hiva, she had killed without remorse or emotion. But the person she was now didn't have the resilience to carry the weight of all those deaths, all those civilizations burned down. The very thought of the guard inside the Library of Rule and Nyeth's wretched bones bursting open caused her to panic.

And what of that armless man in her memories? That beautiful creature with golden eyes who'd called her "sister." Whenever she saw his face in her mind's eye, it was as if her body rejected it with all its might. Her anxiety manifested into physical pain electrifying her from the inside, causing her body to tremble and her skin to crawl.

What an awful life she'd lived. *Lives.* What if she could see the faces of each person she'd killed? What would she say to them? How would she go on?

"Isoke?" Rin said, because Iris had momentarily dropped to her knees. She was utterly exasperated with herself. Disgusted. The one thing she'd wanted for ten years was the truth. Only to turn into a coward the moment she touched it. Jinn had probably seen it too. That was why he'd left her. She bet he couldn't stand the sight of her any—

A hard slap across one cheek, then the other. Rin never pulled her punches.

"Is this the great warrior I had to spend all my years as an *ahosi* hearing about?" Rin yanked her up by the collar, forcing her to her feet. Iris could just imagine that little girl hearing about She Who Does Not Fall in tales sung by the other warriors in the Reaper Regiment. But that was a different "she." A different person entirely . . .

"Get it together. We're heading to the train station," Rin said, peeking around the corner of an alleyway as they made their way through the dirty London streets.

Iris touched Jinn's blade, which she'd strapped to her side with rope. Rin was right. She had to pull herself together. It was the only way to make it through this ordeal.

While on their way to the train station, they came across smatterings of police officers dispatched to find the arsonist who'd set part of Trafalgar Square on fire.

"Tell the boys to be on the lookout for a Negro female in a green dress," Iris heard one say, and her throat closed. "Heard two of 'em were running about near the museum."

"Negro? From America?"

"From Africa. So said one of the members of the club that got burned down—Adam Temple."

Quick and silent as a cat, Iris slipped behind the brick wall of a bakery, flattening her back against the building, her chest heaving as she gritted her teeth. *Adam.*

"Look at that, then," said the other police officer. "This is *exactly* what happens when you let a bunch of pickaninnies come to England. Someone needs to tell the Queen to stop bringing 'em in from the colonies."

Hot anger shot through Iris as the two continued to babble about their hatred of immigrants. But soon Iris tuned them out. There was something more pressing to worry about.

Adam was awake, and the first thing he'd thought to do was to sic the *police* on her. She should have tied him up and put one of his expensive ties in his mouth after knocking him unconscious.

"Adam Temple," repeated Rin. After the police had left the vicinity, she and Iris had started running again. "Your former patron?" Rin couldn't understand English, but she could glean the situation from the few words she'd picked up. "That man is quite obsessed with you, isn't he?"

The young lord's family had long been part of Club Uriel's death cult, and successions of Temple men had always had a seat at the table of the Enlightenment Committee. The apocalypse was deep in his blood. And as the bringer of the apocalypse, so was she.

Iris thought of his black hair and cold blue eyes and shivered. "That would be an understatement."

Iris couldn't tell what street this was except that it was empty, narrow, and filthy underneath her worn shoes. Washing lines stretched between two solid walls of buildings. Each hollow window was either pitch black or closed off with an apron. The narrow path felt endless.

Strange hooting noises piercing the sky above reminded her of owls or some other strange kind of nocturnal bird. But they were familiar. Oddly familiar.

Shadows flashed above her. Instinctively, she looked up. Whatever it was disappeared behind the ridge of a flat roof. Were they being followed?

"Isoke!" Rin put her arm out to stop her.

They were more than halfway down the road. In the middle of the flat cobbled path was a box that could have reached up to her knees. Though made of dark wood, Iris could hear little brass gears inside whirring ominously.

Iris's hunter-like senses flashed as smoke began rising from it. Something that looked like a child's toy but would sooner chop off someone's face than bring a smile to it? She knew who was behind this.

Iris pulled up the sack of scrolls she had slung over her shoulder. "Come out, Henry!"

A fourteen-year-old boy with light brown hair and silver glasses stepped out from the darkened doorstep of one of the buildings, his bright green eyes flashing beneath his newsboy cap. Henry Whittle, grandson of a toymaker dynasty. Which meant his tournament teammates Mary and Lucille couldn't be far away. Then it clicked that the hooting before had reminded her of the birdcalls Max and his street friends used to communicate with each other. Hawkins, Cherice, and Jacob. Were they here too?

"I had a feeling you'd all escape Club Uriel somehow," Iris said as Henry took his place behind his gadget, and in a strange way, she was relieved. It wasn't as if she'd wanted them to die.

Clearly, the feeling wasn't mutual. Henry lifted his hand over the box, and, as if invisible strings were attached to his fingers, the gears began whirring faster than before.

"You're alone," Iris observed. "Did you and Mary have a lover's row?"

Henry's ears turned bright red at the mention of that mousy pigtailed girl always at his side, and he was clearly furious about it. It was a short-lived reaction, but Iris smiled with satisfaction nonetheless. He was still quite adorable, even though he wanted to kill her.

"How did you find us?" Iris asked, but Henry wasn't in the talking mood. Well, he never was. But he looked as deadly serious as when he'd learned about her true identity.

"Henry," she started, choosing her words carefully. "I willingly confessed to you all what I am. After learning the truth, I had no intention of hiding anything. You know why, don't you?"

Behind her, Rin began silently summoning her white sword from within her chest.

"It's because it doesn't matter *what* I am. I'm Iris. I'm *me*. And I'm not going to harm you or anyone you love. I'm not going to kill anyone . . . a-anymore," she added quietly.

Iris thought of the men she'd burned alive only in the past few days and bit her lip.

"Max is dead," Henry said. "Hawkins confirmed it."

"Hawkins?" Iris shook her head, confused. "No, he went into the void with Max. . . ."

"Hawkins is alive," Henry said. "Max is dead. See? You've already started, *murderer*."

Iris went cold as she remembered Max disappearing through the portal Hawkins had made. The portal meant to get rid of *her* forever. How had Hawkins survived? Why hadn't he taken Max back with him? Why hadn't—

Max is dead. Her dry lips trembled.

Henry was usually miserable and far too serious for his age, but now he had the look of a crusader. A desperate one. "There's been a slight change to the Tournament of Freaks. No audience. No Committee. We're not after riches anymore. It's your head we want."

The box began unfurling into something bigger—impossibly bigger. Each joint snapped into place, each limb shooting out with a *shiink*, until what stood before her was an ugly wooden nutcracker with a carefully carved beard and gaping white teeth. It stood three times Iris's size. Henry's craftsmanship was admirable. His ability to turn the toys he made into weapons was always a sight to behold.

So was the long wooden sword in the nutcracker's hand. It was taller than she was.

"Sorry. Not letting you kill my grandpa," Henry whispered. "Lawrence!"

And as Lawrence Hawkins sprang out from one of the rooftops, Henry's toy attacked.

4

"DON'T LET HIM TOUCH YOU!" IRIS told Rin.

Hawkins was back.

He was back from wherever he'd taken Max.

And he was after her next. Hawkins lunged for her the moment he touched the ground.

"Why didn't you bring him back?" Iris demanded as she and Rin leaped out of the way. "Why didn't you bring Max back with you? Why are *you* here and *he's not*?"

The wild hatred and guilt glimmering in Hawkins's twisted expression mirrored that unsavory feeling of bile rising in her throat. Readying her fists, Iris rushed at him just as the nutcracker brought down its sword, smashing the street.

So much for stealth. The blouses and aprons drying on the washing lines blew back. People began waking up from their beds, lighting their lamps, and looking out their windows.

Still holding fast to her sack of scrolls, Iris jumped onto one of the washing lines, landing perfectly on the toes of her left foot. But when she looked down . . . this wasn't the Lawrence Hawkins she'd expected. His usually perfectly combed blond hair was stringy, a thick clump stubbornly obscuring part of his left eye. He was watching her moving adeptly across the wire, his chest heaving as he gulped in air. Strange powder clung to his vest and pants.

"Hawkins, what—" she started, before the former street urchin's portal brought his lithe body up onto the same washing line. But unlike Iris, he wasn't a tightrope walker. Iris jumped to a higher line the moment he hurtled toward her. A gasp caught in her throat the moment Hawkins lost his footing. She needn't have worried. Another one of his portals brought him back to the rooftop.

A faint smell lingered in the air even after he'd disappeared, and she recognized it immediately: sugar. *Sugar?* Just where had Hawkins been?

"Where did you take him?" The words spilled out of her mouth. "Where did you take Max?" He didn't answer. The sound of his childhood friend's name made his body stiffen, but she'd long run out of patience. "Open your damn mouth and answer me!"

Below them, Rin ran up the arm of the nutcracker with her sword primed for attack. Screams burst through the windows as the supernatural fight waged on before disbelieving eyes. Some closed their drapes. Out of sight, out of mind. None ventured outside.

"This is insane!" Iris bellowed from her clothing line, though she wondered how long it would hold her. "You're going to get people killed! All to catch me?"

As if she didn't deserve to live. As if anything was fair game, as long as he could get rid of her. So callous. So selfish, the lot of them. So . . . so . . . She gritted her teeth as her body flushed with heat. All because she was Hiva. But they hadn't met Hiva.

Not yet.

"Where is Max?" she finally shrieked.

"He's dead." Iris could hear the pain in Hawkins's voice even from where she stood. "He's gone."

"Where did you take him?"

"My mother's grave. Her coffin." Hawkins doubled over at the mention of it.

"What?" Iris blinked. She couldn't believe what she was hearing. "You teleported into a—? You were actually just trying to put me inside a coffin?" Iris's laughter was spitefully frigid. "I *can't die.* Do you think a little pile of dirt on top of a wooden box would stop me?" And her laughter turned hateful. Arrogant. She wanted every bit of sound to hurt him.

"Yeah. You can't die, but you can be buried alive, you arrogant little bitch." Hawkins spat so viciously, Iris's mouth snapped shut. "Buried alive in a wooden box underneath the solid stone floor of an abbey. Everyone in my mother's family has their own spot marked out. Not me. With Mum dead, her husband didn't have to take care of the family bastard anymore, so they threw me out. At least they let me come to the funeral."

He flashed his sharp teeth for just a moment before his wicked grin lost its confidence. "You can't die. But I can trap you. Keep you imprisoned as long as I can. But . . ."

He grabbed his hair as if the memories were coming hard and fast. "I started to panic." He sounded as if he'd hyperventilate. "Down there. Down there where my mother . . ." He shook his head. "There wasn't enough room inside the tomb for both of us. No room to move a toe. The pressure of my body against his, against the wood, underneath the stone. It was like the entire weight of the ocean was bearing down on me. The pain was excruciating. I couldn't breathe. I felt like I was being crushed. One of us was going to break. So I got away. I had to. But I forgot to take him with me. It all happened so fast. I panicked. I couldn't move. . . . I couldn't think. . . ." He stopped for a breath, shaking his head.

"So go back!" Iris demanded, her whole body quaking. "Go back for him!"

"I can't go back. Aside from my mother's bones, there's only room inside that coffin for one body."

Iris's lips parted silently and stayed open. Her eyes searched for the answer. The red flush of her palms. The silence of her breath.

Buried alive. Max had been *buried alive*.

No. Iris wouldn't accept this. Her hand instinctively went to her dress. The pocket watch. Stolen from their auction. That stupid boy. "It hasn't been too long. Just a few hours." Hours. Hours without air, deep under the earth. "Go back. You can still save him!"

"I can't."

"You can!"

"Max is *gone*," Hawkins screamed, and tears began streaming from his eyes. "I can't save him. I don't know how."

45

"And yet you're here, attacking *me*. Blaming *me*." Iris was baffled as to why she was grinning, because in truth she wanted to collapse and cry. But it all seemed so funny to her. She was supposed to be the villain. It was why Hawkins was trying to destroy her, trying to hold her up as some kind of scapegoat for his own blunder, his own cowardice. The audacity.

"*You* killed him," she whispered, trembling. "*You* killed Max, not me."

Iris wasn't sure if the whimper she heard was her own or his. She nearly fell from her makeshift tightrope. Sugar. She smelled sugar on Hawkins. She was sure of it. Why would sugar be inside his mother's grave? Something wasn't right. But Hawkins wasn't here for a chat.

After looking at his hands, he lifted his head up again. "You're right. Max is dead," he repeated, this time with a tone of finality. "I killed him just like you said. Got nothing to lose now. I'm not letting you out of here alive, you monster."

A little sly and a little pompous, but never one to let a friend down. That was the Lawrence Hawkins that Iris had come to know during the tournament. But now he was just another enemy who wanted to use her or hurt her. As if that were all she was good for. As if she didn't matter . . .

Dreams of ashes sang to her like a lullaby. Her hatred was too sweet, too irresistible not to taste. Hatred that turned into a kind of sordid hunger that wouldn't be ignored. "Ah, that's right. You haven't actually met Hiva," she said. His anima tasted sweet too. A forbidden texture. "Would you like to see one, Lawrence? A *real* monster?"

Tilting her head lazily to the side, Iris lifted her hands.

"Stop! Stop right there!"

The hurried sound of frightened men snapped Iris out of her trance. Down the street, police were already gathering, though very few dared to venture into the battle, especially not after Rin had managed to chop off the left arm of Henry's nutcracker. It crashed to the ground.

And Iris had almost burned Hawkins alive.

The thick, sour lump she swallowed went down like sandpaper. *What did I just . . . ? What was I about to . . . ?*

Frantically, she shook herself out of her stupor. "Rin," Iris called, running to avoid the debris before flipping down to the first washing line. "We've got to get out of here!"

But Hawkins's own hands sparked with energy. Not in the least aware of how close he'd just come to death, he was gearing up for something big. Maybe there was another grave he could send her to. A grave like where he'd—

Her heart throbbed in pain. *Sent Max.*

Hawkins's blue eyes shook with emotion but glimmered murder nonetheless. Murder.

Your wings can be clipped. . . .

A mysterious pang of fear seized her. Hawkins moved to strike.

Iris heard the spark of a motor first, a combustive crack and then a long screeching noise as an invention she'd never seen before turned the corner onto their street.

"What the hell is that?" Rin said from atop the nutcracker's shoulder.

Even boy inventor Henry stood shocked, his jaw hanging open. However mad a genius he was, he would never top the woman in the vehicle speeding toward them.

It looked as if a carriage had been dismantled and someone had placed a bathtub on its four wheels—a bathtub made of dark gleaming metal. But this vehicle was much faster than a carriage. It seated four, but the woman in the front was controlling it, holding on to a horizontal steering wheel perched on a secure pedestal.

Her silver nose ring—a cluster of gears—shone beneath the moonlight, while the stars brought out the luster of the bronze and silver headpieces against her brown skin.

It *couldn't* be her. But somehow it was.

Iris jumped down to the street, dumbfounded, as Uma Malakar drove her vehicle right down the center of the road, a pair of goggles shielding her eyes. The sparking vehicle forced Henry to jump to the side, and it seemed like there was a connection between Henry's mind and the nutcracker's will, for in that moment, the toy began to fall to the ground in pieces.

Rin leaped onto a window ledge as Uma maneuvered around the falling toy limbs, her blue sari flapping behind her. Her superpowered tub-on-wheels barreled past the nutcracker's head and came to a halt with the screech of tires at Iris's feet.

"Get in," she commanded.

Iris gritted her teeth. "I'm not going back to the Basement."

"Not to the Basement but to your destination of choice." And, letting out a satisfied sigh, Uma brought out her golden pipe from within her black corset and took a puff. "Or you can stay here while your enemy's reinforcements arrive."

Iris looked up. Hawkins was hesitating because of Uma's sudden intrusion, but she knew he'd work out a plan soon enough.

"So what's it going to be? Will you escape here? Or will you continue Club Uriel's Tournament of Freaks?"

Iris wondered if Uma should have been a contestant. "We're leaving London. Try to take me anywhere else but the train station and you're dead."

"Fine by me."

After Rin dropped from the window ledge, the two climbed inside Uma's miniature locomotive.

"It's an electric car," Uma explained as she drove back down the way she'd come, leaving the terrified police in her dust. "Powered by electric motors."

"A *what*?" Iris held on to her billowing skirt as she stared at the fisherman's wheel Uma was spinning around to steer the craft.

Uma rolled her eyes. "Electric motors. A pair of them. Not that I shy away from oil, you know—it's helping the dampening system at the front—but I have a feeling it'll be a lot more efficient than fossil fuels. A strange car by any measure, but I like strange."

Rin and Iris exchanged incredulous looks as they sat face-to-face inside the car, their knees knocking against each other, the sack of scrolls underneath Iris's skirt. Next to them was some kind of an instrument that seemed to measure the temperature, or perhaps the rising pressure of the steam coming out of the pipes at the back. Light beams shot out from the front of the car through some kind of headlamp.

"But that's not what you really want to know." Uma adjusted her goggles as the car zipped down city streets in the dark of night. "You want to know why

Boris Bosch's left-hand woman, head of Weapons Development at Bosch Guns and Ammunitions Company, someone you tried to kill earlier today—no, I haven't forgotten—is helping you out now."

"Right-hand," Iris corrected under her breath, because she couldn't think of anything else to say. Of course she wanted to know. Boris Bosch, a member of Club Uriel's Enlightenment Committee like Adam, had brought together his own team to participate in the Tournament of Freaks: Max's friends, though they weren't exactly loyal to him. More loyal was Uma, who was conducting research on ancient technology with the British Crown on his behalf.

"Translate for me, Isoke." Rin placed her arm on the ledge of the vehicle, staring at Uma in interest. "From what I could glean, she's one of the Committee's puppets. I want to hear what story this woman is weaving. And whether or not I need to kill her—"

"*No* killing," Iris hissed before casting a dark glance Uma's way. "Yet."

"The Helios told you something, didn't it?" There was a slight hint of mischief in Uma's eyes that made Iris wonder for one wild second if she could understand Fon. "Something a little horrible, but true nonetheless." Uma seemed fine steering with one hand while using the other to flick around her pipe.

Iris's silence was all the confirmation she needed. "I figured as much," Uma continued. "Something about you changed when you made contact with it."

"The Helios started everything," Iris said, thinking of the explosion ten years ago at the South Kensington fair.

"Not exactly." Uma lifted a finger from her pipe. "The Helios was pulled out of Lake Victoria in pieces by the Crown, putting it in their possession. But like the Moon Skeleton key, it was built by another civilization. The Naacal."

Iris sat very still as Uma kept one eye on her, buildings whizzing past them.

"The Helios: a machine that can open the door to other dimensions. I started studying it while John Temple was still a member of the Committee keeping tabs on the Crown's research. Never did I see anything react to it the way you did. It responded to you that day too, didn't it? The day of the fair ten years ago. *You* caused the explosion."

Iris turned to her, surprised. "How did you know?"

"Well, I know now!" Uma laughed as Iris's anger simmered inside her. "A little trick I learned in college. You were there that day. You and that crystal heart of yours."

Iris placed a hand on her chest almost instinctively. Her indestructible heart made of white crystal was what kept her immortal. She'd left a pile of the crystal behind on the western coast of Africa inside the earth where she'd awakened. Some of it was now in the Crown's possession. But the white crystal had chemical properties even Iris didn't know about.

"That explosion at the fair warped people's internal matter, turning them into, well, freaks. The Helios responded to you. Perhaps it was built *because* of you. In that case, what *are* you?"

Uma's question reverberated painfully in her ancient body. How many years had Iris asked herself the very same one, only to come to a horrifying answer?

"John Temple wanted to know," Uma continued. "The experiments detailed in his journal were vivid enough."

Iris's throat closed, squeezing the air out from her lips. As her hands chilled, she pressed her lips together, unable to say a word.

"I'm referring, of course, to the experiments the Crown conducted on you fifty years ago. That Cambridge team led by Seymour—"

"*Enough.*"

Iris's tone dripped with the blood she'd spilled across eons. Uma gave a little *hmph* and concentrated as they continued through the city. It was the Hiva within her, the ancient murderous god kept hidden behind the wall of "Iris." If there was anyone she could kill without hesitation, it would be the doctor behind the torture she'd experienced half a century ago. Doctor Seymour Pratt. . . . But to let the Hiva within her take the reins of her psyche would mean to lose control completely. She couldn't allow it. She *wouldn't.*

Swallowing her anger, she looked at Uma, feeling the memories of pain slide back down into the abyss inside her.

"Why would I tell you anything about me?" she asked in a measured voice. "If I tell *you,* then Bosch knows. The Committee knows."

"Maybe I don't need you to tell me anything. Maybe I just need you to find out for yourself. With this."

Uma placed her pipe down next to her, reached inside the sari hugging her body, and pulled out a book. A journal.

The words flew out of Iris's mouth. "John Temple's journal!"

But it didn't carry the scent of John Temple. She knew it well. Adam had wanted her to find his father, after all. It was one of the reasons he'd recruited her for the tournament. He'd had her practice feeling his father's life essence, his anima, as if she were a bloodhound. She could track anyone so long as she could get a good enough grasp of it. But the journal Uma held in her hands didn't even have a hint of John Temple in it.

"It's just a copy I created," Uma confirmed. "Wasn't easy dealing with his ridiculous codes. The real item is somewhere safe, but I think you'll make do with this."

When they were far enough outside the city, Uma parked at the foot of a little hill. Without waiting, Iris plucked the journal out of her hands and began flipping through the pages.

"Lord Temple was indeed a very smart man, like the rest of his noble lineage." Uma lifted her goggles and brushed back her long black hair. "His gift for cryptography is unparalleled. I've translated what I could. Made some notes here and there. The rest?" She shrugged, picked up her pipe, and began smoking it. "Well, I'm sure you'll fill in the blanks."

As Rin leaned in to inspect the journal, Iris watched Uma from the corner of her eye. The one piece of information the Enlightenment Committee didn't know was that Iris was Hiva. It was a secret Adam had wanted to guard at all costs. But John Temple did know. It was why he'd fled the Committee, taking his secrets with him. So what did Uma know?

"I can see the gears turning in your head," said Uma, her nose ring catching the light. "Relax." She took a puff from her pipe. "I've already said I want to know more about you. Everything about you. And everything about this impossible world I live in. I'm woman enough to admit I don't have the means to do that myself. So I'm giving you the means. I'm letting you do the deciphering for me."

Iris frowned. "And what if I don't take your bait?"

"You just did!" Uma laughed, pointing at the journal in Iris's hands. "Besides, you want to know too. Secret things about yourself. It's what drove you to the Crystal Palace that day. What led your charge into the Basement. You're as curious as I am."

Secret things about herself. How to stop herself from becoming what she feared the most.

"We'll figure it out together. You from your end, me from mine. We'll coordinate our information via encrypted letters. Two brown heads are better than one. Or three . . ." She winked at Rin, who scowled impatiently.

Impatient for what, Iris didn't know. Rin said she would follow her, but Iris still didn't know why. What was in it for her?

Then there was Uma. Iris could use someone like Uma on her side, even if it was a tenuous alliance. But the results of her last alliance still lingered heavily enough on her mind. Somewhere in London was a street filled with toy rubble that perfectly symbolized just how well her alliances turned out.

Jinn had abandoned her. Rin was still a question mark in her mind, but the girl was willing to listen to her and fight alongside her so far. As for Uma—

"I think not." Iris hopped out of Uma's vehicle with the sack of scrolls in her hand. "But we'll take the journal anyway, thanks."

Uma was unfazed. "You want to go it alone, then?" She considered it with two puffs of her pipe. "Well, all right."

"'Well, *all right*'?" Iris repeated incredulously. After she told Rin what was happening, Rin let out a derisive laugh.

"She would have betrayed us anyway. She looks the type. She would have fed information to the Committee." With one smooth movement, Rin, with her hand over her chest, brought out her white sword, its blade shimmering. "Better to get rid of her now . . ."

"Wait—" Iris put up her hand to stop Rin, but Uma only laughed.

"You can kill me. But before I go to the great munitions factory in the sky, let me tell you one thing: I have no quarrel with you, Iris Marlow. No quarrel at all."

Hearing the name reminded her of Granny. Thinking of Granny Marlow made it feel like someone was squeezing her chest so tight she'd choke on her heart. Iris placed a hand on Rin's blade, and, with an annoyed sigh, the young warrior lowered it.

"*Auspicio Regis et Senatus Angliae!*" Uma whipped her arms out, turned her head toward Iris, and grinned. "'By command of the King and Parliament of England.' The motto of the East India Company. My dad worked for them for a bit, then left India. Ripped me right from my crying Indian mother's arms to take me to merry old England. He needed me as his heir for succession. But his brother didn't exactly acknowledge me as a blood relation. Neither did the law. My mother being a colonized mistress meant his brother's half-wit children became heirs to the estate instead of me."

Uma crossed her arms and looked up at the sky. "And you know, I always wondered if that was just the way the world worked. Even if I was always the smartest person in the room, it never mattered. There was a hierarchy. The powerful meandered their way through life at the top. It was just the way it was. But I went to school with them. *Worked* with them."

Uma pointed her pipe at Iris. "Do you know what it's like to have an entire research team of white men handpicked by the British Crown who can't figure out how to use coaxial motors, cooling fins, front suspension parts, and a pair of batteries to make something I put together out of *boredom*?" She slapped the metal side of the car. "I worked out a steam-powered tricycle when I was fourteen, while my cousins struggled to finish *Jane Eyre*. An absolute crock. The earth's greatest empire, whose laws didn't recognize me as being worthy of inheriting a white man's estate, still needs *me* to hold their hand through reconstructing and weaponizing ancient technology. All the while, they know nothing of what's *truly* out there."

Uma got out of the car. Rin lifted her sword, pointing its tip in Uma's direction, but as Bosch's weapons developer came nearer, Iris could tell she wasn't looking for a fight.

"There's more to this world than the fantasy some want us to believe. I want to uncover that. I want to uncover the truth none of them know." Uma stopped just short of Rin's sword and smiled. "Who's really on top? Let's the three of us find out."

This woman. A kind of useful rage simmered beneath her scientific hunger. It was genuine, this desire to plunge into the unknown, to make the impossible possible in a world that deigned to dictate only her limits. A world that took the expansive mystery of life, its endless possibilities, and squashed it into something so useless, so insignificant, but only for women like them. Only for women like *them*.

Iris thought of Coolie. The Enlightenment Committee. She thought of this name "Hiva" that had been given to her. And suddenly a similar kind of rage simmered within her.

"Uma," Iris began carefully. "The combination of Naacalian technology and my own biology created the so-called 'freaks' at the South Kensington fair ten years ago."

"You are correct," said Uma, clearly intrigued by this sudden turn in their conversation.

"If it's possible to produce abilities, it may be possible to take abilities away," Iris said.

Uma rubbed her chin. "That is to say, if we can transform humans into supernatural beings, then we can make the supernatural human. . . ." She thought about it. "Depending on the technology involved, perhaps it is."

Iris's heart rate picked up. "If I could bring to you more advanced technology from the Naacal—something you may never have even seen before—would you be able to build it?"

"You mean a power-sapping machine?" Uma laughed. "Well, it'd be a challenge. Could take years. But then again, I like challenges." She tilted her head with interest. "And when do you think you might be able to bestow upon me this special, never-before-seen gadgetry?"

The Coral Temple: the underwater temple where Nyeth had died. That was the key. The Naacal had built something to "clip Hiva's wings" inside it—Hiva, the unstoppable god, but unstoppable only because of the powers gifted to her. Nyeth's ring might have been involved in operating it. How, she didn't know. But if the Crown could excavate the Helios from within a lake, then surely this technology still existed too.

If the Coral Palace was still out there . . . If she could reach it . . .

With a little laugh, Uma winked and leaned back against her car. "Of course, I'm still working for Bosch. He's got unlimited resources, and I've got an unlimited intellect, so it works out. And I can't promise what I would do with the information I do discover. . . ."

Iris lowered her head. "But you want knowledge, don't you?"

"For the sake of knowledge."

"I want it for a much better reason than that."

"Regardless, we're after the same goal. So go." Uma flicked her head at journal in Iris's hand. "Take John Temple's legacy and learn all you can. Who knows—you might be able to find the man himself and that Moon Skeleton he stole. I'm sure he'll have a lot to tell you. We might finally be able to see the world that lies beyond the Helios."

Rin nudged her. Iris nodded.

"I'm off then." Uma hopped back inside her electric car. "And don't worry, I won't tell anyone about this little gathering of minds. Let's simply make a good go at things, shall we?"

The motor revved up; Uma slid her goggles down. "No matter where the search for knowledge takes us. Even if it's right into the bowels of hell."

The car spun and took off in a cloud of dust, speeding back to a London in chaos. Where Granny was waiting for her. Where Jinn was on the cusp of his crusade.

Thinking of Granny reminded Iris of the confession letter she'd almost written in Adam's mansion. The one meant to explain to Granny everything the old woman didn't remember: the fact that she'd first met Iris as a child when Iris, with the Dahomey's women warriors, raided her village. That Iris, who was meant to be her kidnapper, was instead kidnapped *with* her and taken to England. That Iris had witnessed the death of her sister. That despite their long, fraught history, they'd somehow become a family. Yes, Granny was her family. Just like Jinn. And what was family if not the dream of a lonely god?

"Rin," she whispered, her hands gripping John Temple's journal tightly. "Who am I to decide who lives and dies? I just want to live in peace. Or am I foolish?"

Rin could only touch her broken eye in response. Tenderly. Bitterly.

What would happen to Granny if Iris were locked away or if she died for good? Who would read to her? Who would keep track of her medicine and laugh with her?

Iris squeezed her hands into fists. "I will come back to you. I'll come back as the Iris you know," she promised Granny, imagining the old woman asleep by now underneath this clear night. As the Iris *she* knew. Not the one for whom the taste of anima had come to carry with it an illicit pleasure deep inside her. Not the one whose hands were stained with death. She would start her life over as a regular girl. She would never again be the kind of monster that would have seen Granny hurt without shedding a tear.

"Never again," she whispered—what was becoming her own private oath.

And so her search for knowledge would continue, just as Uma said.

No matter where that search would take her.

REWARD

$12,000

IN GOLD COIN

WILL BE PAID BY THE U.S. GOVERNMENT
FOR THE APPREHENSION

DEAD OR ALIVE

OF

BERTA MORALES
and COMPANY

WANTED FOR MASS MURDER, ROBBERY,
AND OTHER ACTS ACROSS OKLAHOMA

CONTACT: FREDERICTON'S DETECTIVE AGENCY AND UNION PACIFIC RAILROAD COMPANY

NOVEMBER 24, 1884

Intermission

FABLES STUMBLED DOWN THE STEPS OF the red-painted, gold-plated train car and tossed his lunch all over the tracks. Berta's gloved hands still had a bit of blood on them when she grabbed his shoulder and pushed him out of her way.

"Emptying your stomach over every little thing." Shoving her gun in its holster, she rolled her eyes as she mounted one of the two horses waiting dutifully behind the train tracks. That was the job Berta had given him: mind the horses, because the idea of robbing a steaming train full of rich folks made his knees wobble. It was as if she could smell his weakness.

"Hey! Wake up!" Berta screamed when his foot slipped on the horse's stirrup. "This is the getaway. A couple of folks in there might stop wetting themselves long enough to chase us."

"You left some alive?"

"Pull it together, Twig." Ah, such a colorful girl. The burlap bag she held over her back with one hand swelled with gold watches and pearls. With a "*yah!*" and a kick, she rode off. It was all Fables could do to follow behind. Always trailing behind this girl . . .

Under the glaring sun and the clear blue sky, they rode across the expansive field of yellow grass. The stretches of clouds and the hills in the distance were the only things still innocent about this messed-up country after the war.

"Another robbery in plain daylight." Fables sighed while his horse trotted along. His skinny body wasn't built for riding. He felt like his lower back was going to snap in half. "You've got guts, I'll say that."

"While you spew yours."

Fables felt the hot sting of humiliation as Berta laughed. "Keep it up and they'll come for us, and that's for damn sure," he retorted. "You're not exactly being discreet."

Underneath her black hat, Berta's dark curls floated upon the wind. She didn't even bother wearing that bandana anymore. Berta was never shy about slinging her name around as fast as she slung her gun. It was like she relished giving it. If she was going to be that reckless, she should have at least made sure that no one who saw her face was left to tell the tale.

"We don't have anything to worry about. We've got an attack dog, don't forget."

Fables clenched his crooked teeth. "Hiva is no one's *dog*. He's a god. An angel."

His protector. His savior. The answer to all his sick prayers.

"He's a big ole freak, and as long as he's with us, we can pick off whoever we want."

I truly hate you, Fables wanted to say but was too scared to say it. Instead, he turned his thoughts to Hiva, holed up in that ranch with all those bandits, and felt a fit of jealousy begin to rise within him. Those thieves and crooks and murderers in Younger's Bend were the worst of the worst of humanity. They were Berta's sort, not his. Smelly, dirty bullies. He saw his father in every one of them. He hoped Hiva would dust them soon. But then Hiva had been dusting quite a few people along the way to the ranch Berta told them about. They'd left towns in despair all across the Canadian River. Now Hiva was tired. Like a stopped clock that needed retuning.

"He said himself he's here to punish the wicked," Berta said. "We're on the same page. I'm just helping him out."

"And stuffing your pockets at the same time."

"We'll need the travel money if we're going to find whoever *she* is."

The way Berta said "she" conspiratorially jolted Fables. It reminded him that there was someone out there in the world important to Hiva. That didn't sit right with him. Another Hiva . . .

"You know, I had a brother once."

She'd blurted it out so suddenly, it caught Fables off guard. "What?"

"I had a brother once. What didn't you understand?"

He stared at her, eyebrow raised and all. This girl couldn't be serious. There was someone else out there as annoying as she was?

"I haven't seen him in years . . . since I was a kid. Oh man . . ." Berta looked up. "On long journeys like this, he'd wrap me up in a blanket at night when it got cold. Like when we traveled to Guatemala from home. Or when we went around England. I was a tiny little thing, so I don't remember much, but I remember that."

"And why're you tellin' me all that?" Fables scrunched up his nose. "We sharing and caring now?"

Berta was unfazed. "He was the dependable type and really cheerful. I'd cry all the time, but he'd pull a face and brighten up my day in no time. He was a great guy. . . ." Then she looked at the confused Fables. "All that's to say he was way better company than you, Twig."

Fables's throat closed up, but he managed to mutter quiet curses under his breath.

They drew closer to the ranch. Just as the sun began to disappear behind the hills, Fables finally decided to ask the question that had been on his mind since the last town Berta robbed.

"Why do you leave some of them alive?" He looked across the yellow fields of dead, stomped grass, his curly hair flickering over his eyes. "Those folks."

"They're not all bad." Berta jolted the bag over her back. "I just kill the bad ones."

"Which ones are the bad ones?"

"You know the type."

"You seem to have a type."

Berta looked up at the sky. "The rich wives who have everything they could ever want in this world and still feel like a fun Sunday afternoon is taking their well-dressed kids to come see you in a cage. The wealthy husbands who drop coins at your feet 'by accident' because they want to see you bend over in your special 'savage' clothes."

Nothing she said made any sense to him. When she shut her eyes, Fables wondered what kind of sick memories were playing behind those pretty lids of hers. But then she turned to him, tilting her head and giving him a cheeky lopsided grin.

"What, you don't know that type?"

Fables shifted uncomfortably atop his horse. "Haven't come across 'em, no." Or maybe he had. There were many different kinds of cages in the world.

"Gotta keep some of 'em alive. Ever heard of Madame Moustache?"

Now she was just being deliberately confusing. "Who?"

Berta laughed. "You never heard of her? Well, that's all right. Not like it was her real name. I used to go by a dozen different names too."

"Okay. And what about her?"

"Moustache? She killed folks. Especially the ones who had it coming; got her lover in the gut with a shotgun. But never just shot off bullets willy-nilly. Gotta make money off some of 'em. Robbing dead bodies is a necessity sometimes, sure, but believe me, it ain't *real* fun unless you can see the fear in their eyes *while* you're robbing them."

"What're you going to do if it turns out Hiva isn't as selective as you are?"

"And who does El Diablo think is worthy of his 'divine punishment'?"

Fables's lips cracked into his nervous, tweaky sort of grin. The kind he always got when he dreamed of a client's corpse being picked at by crows. "What if it's everyone?"

Berta scoffed. She wasn't a believer yet. "What the hell good is it if you kill *everyone*?" she asked with a little laugh as they entered the woods that shielded the ranch from prying eyes. "What does that even mean, kill everyone? Like, *everyone*, everyone? The whole world? What's supposed to come out of that?"

"Something new," Fables said, but he kept his dark fantasy to himself for now.

A global catastrophe was what Hiva had promised him the day they first met. And then again one night when they were resting in an empty shack somewhere, after they'd put enough distance between themselves and the massacre in Okemah. When only the two of them were awake.

"I will destroy humanity," Hiva had told him. "And I will take her life as well."

It was only when Hiva mentioned "her" that he seemed to have any sliver of emotion, barely tangible and gone in an instant. Even that sliver made Fables seethe. Before he could sink deeper into his jealousy, he heard a child's voice calling them.

Lulu had jumped off from a log that was mounted like a bench in front of a long wooden cabin. Steam rose from the pot she'd tied to a bunch of sticks, the dirty tin whistling while suspended over a campfire on the ground. She ran to the dirt road to meet Berta more so than Fables, since Fables had spent the past few days avoiding her. Once Berta hopped off her horse and tied its reins to the hitching rail, the two hugged. The black pinafore, which Berta had bought her in one of the towns that Hiva had leveled, fit the girl's little body well and covered the dirty white dress she refused to change. Maybe because it reminded her of her family.

"You're gettin' famous these days," Lulu said in her singsong voice. Her coal eyes glinted with a manic energy that always made her look on the verge of flying off into the clouds. Fables took no pleasure in noting it, but this girl was flitting through life like a daze, whistling and humming that bloody hymn under her breath each chance she got, even as Hiva was turning people around her to ash.

Lulu gave the taller girl a piece of parchment. "Don't worry. No one else has seen it, and I didn't tell nobody." Then she spun around with her hands behind her back and pranced back to the boiling pot. After tying his own horse to the rail, Fables peered over Berta's shoulder. A swear jumped off his lips.

"It's a damn wanted poster!" Fables grasped his head with both his hands. "'Berta Morales and company'? 'Wanted for mass murder . . . *dead or alive*'?"

"Ha!" Berta smacked the yellow parchment with excitement. "Twelve thousand dollars! That's two thousand more than the Starrs!" Berta threw the parchment behind her and let out a guttural laugh. "Oh, I know Belle and Sam're gonna be pissed."

That bandit friends of hers who'd told her about this place. Fables bristled. "This isn't a joke! The authorities are gonna be on our necks!"

He looked frantically toward the cabin. Inside was the kind of dirty chatter and beer-swilling laughter Fables was used to from all the saloons he'd ever worked in. Here at the ranch, folks had a "code of honor," so to speak. No one turned the others in. But what the hell kind of honor could survive out here in the West when that much money was on the table?

"Lulu!" Fables called her, because though she said she hadn't told no one, he wanted to be sure. But Lulu was preoccupied. She was crouched around the corner of the cabin, her black pinafore pooled on the dirty ground. And she was petting something on the head. A cat?

Berta saw the same thing. The two of them exchanged glances and walked up to her. And once they rounded the corner—

"What the hell?" they both cried.

As Fables cowered, Berta pulled her gun out of her holster and pointed it at the man sitting in front of Lulu.

A man in a black cape. And a harlequin mask.

This was insane. Fables knew this place tended to attract sickos, but this sicko took the cake. His mask was half-black, half-white, with golden lips. With his top hat, he was dressed like some British baron—one who had decided to play dress-up after escaping an asylum. This guy clearly wasn't right, responding to Lulu's head pats like a purring dog. Berta grabbed Lulu's hand as if touching him would wilt it and pulled Lulu behind her back.

"It's okay," Lulu said, and Fables wondered if she had a hint of the danger she was just in. She shrugged dreamily. "He said he just wanted a friend."

"I'm *desperate* for one," the man said, and fell onto his side.

Berta gritted her teeth. "Yeah, that's what they all say to little girls before jumping 'em." Fables had never seen this kind of anger flashing in Berta's eyes. She held her gun firm. "What's your name? Hurry up and spit it out!"

"You can call me anything," said the man, his high voice on the verge of laughter. "Anything you wish."

"How about a joke?" Fables cringed at the sight of the man rolling on the ground, pleased with himself like a kept animal.

"A Joke, then! It's settled!" He reached out for Lulu. Berta was having none of it. "You should tell your leader," the man continued, looking at Berta. *"You're not the one who smells like the 'her' he's looking for. I* do. And as I've been following you, it seems he's confused."

"You've been . . . what?" Berta looked quickly at Fables, who could only shrug.

"I've seen her once or twice or thrice. Perhaps that's why I've caught her scent? Impressive that he can sense even just that hint of her." Shifting onto his back, he looked up at Berta's cocked gun in his face. "Dark brown skin. Gorgeous eyes. Why are Hivas so very beautiful? Perhaps because they're devils." He laughed.

Fables grabbed Berta's arm. This *thing* knew about Hiva? About *both* Hivas?

"Lord Temple will be surprised to learn there's a Hiva following me about. Such a mess the monster has left behind on his way to Younger's Bend, though you don't seem to mind, do you, little Berta?"

A frowning, bewildered Berta lowered her gun as the masked man escaped into the woods behind the cabin, laughing.

THE MAN IN THE BASEMENT

I T'S NO USE. WE'VE LOST HER, Lord Temple," said the Commissioner in his office doorway an hour before daybreak. "The fire's been put out and the damage is being assessed, but as for the girl, she escaped some nights ago. We've been scouring London since then, but . . ."

Adam Temple did not drop his steel pen or get up from his seat. A quick look up at the dark circles underneath the Commissioner's fearful eyes confirmed it. The round man's gaze darted around the office, at the first-edition-filled bookshelves, the bronze bust in the corner, the paintings of Adam's dead family hanging on the walls—everywhere but Adam himself.

"But we *have* been able to capture at least one of the assailants behind the fire at Club Uriel," the Commissioner continued quickly. "From the list you and Madame Bellerose gave us: Henry Whittle."

Ah, little Henry, grandson of the toymaker. Adam's mother had once bought the most magnificent train set from that store after he'd successfully proven he could recite most of Exodus from memory. Bright, sparkling red and gold. What a wonderful fourth birthday that had been. The Baroness Temple had never been one for gift giving, and if it were not for her untimely murder, Adam suspected she'd still be just as particular as to when to bestow praise.

"What about the other assailants? There was more than just a schoolboy present at the club last night."

The Commissioner rubbed his face, his large hand sweeping down his drooping black mustache. "Well, the boys were able to rescue one man from the fire. He'd been stabbed in the rib cage. We've transferred him to St Thomas' Hospital to see if we can get him well enough to talk. As for the rest . . . seems they've all either escaped or burned up in the fire . . ."

The Enlightenment Committee hadn't chosen their freaks lightly. Most of them were capable of escaping the flames, especially if they were willing to work together. Iris was more than capable since she, of course, couldn't die.

Adam finally placed his pen down upon his stack of papers—black-bordered mourning stationery for the letters of condolence he'd have to write after Club Uriel's burning. A lot of corpses meant a lot of letters. Better to get started sooner rather than later.

"There's no need to be afraid, Commissioner." He leaned back into his leather chair. "I know that the assailants behind this tragedy won't be captured so easily."

"But we do have a lead on the African girl." The Commissioner's sagging mustache perked up as the life returned to it. "The boys received a complaint from the British Museum director's wife. Her husband was kidnapped the night Club Uriel burned down. We talked to him yesterday morning. Didn't say much— still in shock. But the description he gave of his kidnapper fits your girl."

"Indeed." Iris was daring. She could do it. She *would* do it if there were something she needed to discover at all costs. But what? Iris's own bones were on display in the British Museum, but she already knew that. Adam had showed her himself. She knew she was Hiva. She'd confirmed it before knocking him out in his own home. His body was still throbbing in pain from the sheer violence she'd inflicted upon him that night.

Adam's lips curved into a tiny, approving smile.

William Flint, the museum's director, was a member of the club and one of the few alive who knew the identities of the seven members of the Committee. For him to keep his own kidnapping a secret from them meant he was hiding something, but what?

He didn't know what to think. At any rate, he made a note to check the

Library of Rule. It was the only other area of the museum that would have anything she'd want.

"You know I've done a lot of work because of all this nonsense." The Commissioner adjusted his black bowler hat. "What with those freaks fighting in the street, the club burning down, and all the damage control we've had to do with the public . . ."

Adam rolled his eyes. A former colonel, yet still so eager for a compliment. "You did well, Commissioner. The Committee will be well pleased, at least, to know you're working hard for them. Club Uriel will never die so long as even a few of its members still live."

The Commissioner himself was a member, though on the lowest rung of the hierarchy. The destruction of the club—and its perks—must have been excruciating for him. Of course he'd want them restored. A wide smile flashing his yellow teeth told Adam the man was indeed satisfied. "Don't worry, sir. We'll capture the Negro witch. That I know for certain."

After a salute, the man left, closing the heavy wooden door behind him.

Negro witch. Adam had half a mind to throw his pen at the door after him. Lesser men had no right to speak so carelessly about a creature such as Iris. No, *Hiva*: the great and terrible god of death. Stronger than Kali. More frightening than Nephthys. If they knew what she was, they'd have the appropriate reverence and fear.

Although Iris clearly didn't want to think of herself that way. Yet.

"What could you want from the museum?" he whispered to his goddess, resting his head upon his right hand, his messy black hair seeping through his fingers.

He'd told her the truth, and she'd rejected it. Rejected *him*. But Adam had faith. Soon, she'd come to understand what he'd known from the day he saw his brother's and sister's carcasses on the filthy streets while his father toured the African continent: that there was no hope for humanity.

Club Uriel was wrong. It wasn't just that the world was going to end. It *needed* to end. And Iris would make that dream come true. Even if she required his push to do so.

A rapping on the window behind him. Adam leaned back into his chair once again. "Come, Fool."

The double window opened and then shut. Adam could see his reflection in the glass case by the door, the one that held all the trophies he'd won at Eton—sports, mathematics, science competitions. Back when John Temple expected proof of his son's ability to take his place at the Enlightenment Committee's table, only for the man to flee from them all on his own years later. Ironic.

Fool always looked a little like a highwayman to him. Or a vampire from a penny blood with his top hat and long black cloak closed to obscure most of his body. He placed a white-gloved hand over half his face—or rather, the harlequin mask fused to it. Even without the mask's gold-rimmed grin, he could tell Fool was smiling. He always was.

A raven sat perched on Fool's other arm. At Fool's nudging, it flew onto the desk and dropped the folded note in its beak.

"From General Major Gerolt Van der Ven of Belgium," explained Fool. "He asks for your signature."

"Another letter." Sighing, Adam unfolded it. Van der Ven's writing was as strict and disciplined as he was. He'd already demanded an immediate cessation of the Tournament of Freaks and an emergency meeting to discuss further steps to be taken. Adam had agreed but delayed the meeting. They needed to wait until after the damage had been fully assessed so they could recover their assets. That was what he told them. In reality, he wanted to see if he could recover Iris first.

Van der Ven was at least smart enough to subtly question his motives, because in this new letter, he suggested Adam's home as their meeting place. The date: the first of December.

"'And there,'" Adam read aloud, "'we shall vote on another method through which to ascertain who will become the leader of the New World.'"

He scoffed, but what he read next in the letter was shocking indeed.

"'The boars are in my custody at a location of my knowing. They have confessed to killing the Club Uriel members, though have spoken of nothing else. At the meeting, I will propose further measures for dealing with them—and making use of their talents.'"

His boars. He meant the champions who'd fought under his banner during the tournament: Jacques, a former priest, and Gram, the man-eater. Both were trained assassins. It was obvious why Van der Ven wanted to keep them, but why would they murder the members of Club Uriel in the first place? What was in it for them?

A fight between the champions must have caused the mayhem that night. Jinn, one of Adam's own players, could have easily sparked the fire that had burned the club down with his dragon breath. But what had caused everything to spiral so out of control?

The Enlightenment Committee was in disarray. Adam had assassinated Luís Cordiero, unbeknownst to the other members. Boris Bosch had already left Europe for his munitions factory in Western Africa to check their progress on the Ark. Van der Ven had had to delay his trip to the European conference in Berlin in order to deal with the mess his champions had left behind. Benini, that coward, had fled for his life. He must have known it was only a matter of time before someone discovered his betrayal: he was the leak that had brought Iris to the Crystal Palace, where she'd learned of the experiments being conducted in the Basement. Albert Cortez wanted his head, though he and Madame Bellerose were still in shock from the massacre they'd witnessed at Club Uriel that night.

A shameful mess. And yet they still believed the New World was theirs. That the Helios would save them. A machine that opened a gateway to a new land ripe for conquer. All they needed was the Moon Skeleton in his father's possession to operate it.

It was all so they could continue their decadent lives after the end.

"There's nowhere to run," Adam whispered, thinking of Van der Ven's black beard and beady eyes brimming with pride he didn't deserve. "I'll make sure of that."

Adam scribbled his signature and handed it back to Fool. "Make sure you find Iris. And when you do, tell no one where she's run to except me."

"Of course, my lord." And the masked man bowed.

"You've done well." Just like the Commissioner, some men needed to hear it from time to time. *This* Fool was one such man. Adam could almost imagine his eyes shining.

"There's no other Fool so loyal as me," he said eagerly, bowing more deeply. Then he tilted his head as the sound of banging and wailing began to seep through the floorboards. "Though perhaps that isn't quite true."

Fool disappeared without needing to be told. And so Adam followed the noise, descending to his home's darkest depths. No one was allowed in the basement. It was a rule all the servants had been given. They wouldn't be able to understand the presence of the man Adam had kept chained to the concrete wall there for the past several months.

The man sat on the ground, his legs splayed out before him. Adam had sadly neglected his duties during the tournament, so the man's red blazer and pants were starting to smell, his yellow vest darkened.

"Dr. Heidegger." Adam knelt down next to him, propping up the man's flopping head. The room's few lamps were enough to help Adam scrutinize his face. The doctor's beak-like nose and thin brows squeezed in response, though his dark eyes were wandering everywhere. He wrinkled his forehead at the sound of his name but didn't seem too responsive. Adam had not yet fed him today, but that wasn't the reason for this. Both his mind and body had been in this state for the past ten years, ever since the explosion at the South Kensington fair had forced his complex emotions from his flesh in the most painfully physical sense. After he'd lost his soul, Dr. Heidegger, aka the Harlequin Slasher, had transformed into a decayed living corpse.

Even a murderer can have conflicting feelings about his own crimes. This murderer was easily taken into custody after the escape of those feelings—feelings given bodily form—had left his body an empty husk. He was meant to be hung for his crimes. But Adam had devised another use for him . . . one that not even the Committee knew about.

"What's that, Arthur?" Adam listened carefully, because the good doctor was mumbling something in a delirious state.

In the corner of the room speckled with dust and cobwebs was a portrait of Adam himself when he'd just graduated from Eton, his back straight, his blazer and pants perfectly folded and pristine, the rings on his fingers and his charming prince-like beauty the pride of the upper class. And yet, though painted by a world-class artist, something about it always bothered him. It was his shadow in the painting, mangled and deformed. It reminded him of some kind of aged, disfigured beast. And so he'd hidden it away in his basement with another beast.

"Speak louder so I can hear you." Which of his personas was the doctor channeling? The Spiteful Fool, perhaps? He, along with the Impulsive Fool, had driven much of Heidegger's crimes. But Adam could always tell which Fool it was from his expression. Right then, his drooping blue eyes carried no malice in them. No arrogance, either; thus it wasn't the Pompous Fool. Those three belonged to the Enlightenment Committee. And though the man's hollow mind still carried a connection to all the Fools, that connection did not go both ways. Using Heidegger's husk, Adam could glean information that all the Fools had, information they might have been keeping as spies for one Committee member or the other. He could keep tabs on them all, so long as the doctor was in a state to cooperate.

The pathetic look on Heidegger's face meant that he was channeling one of Adam's Fools, the ones he'd coaxed into being *his* spies, unbeknownst to the other Committee members. It didn't take too much doing. The Committee never paid attention to the little details the way he did. They'd found agents they could bribe to work for them in exchange for protection and immunity. But they didn't see Heidegger's insecurity. His wretchedness. The feeble cowardice that drove the man to secretly *want* to be caught and punished for everything he'd done. There was a part of Heidegger that needed someone to scold him. To forgive him. To understand him.

And that part of him would do anything just to please the man who could do so.

The wild, hopeful smile that suddenly stretched across the doctor's face told Adam that this was the Desperate Fool. The one he'd dispatched to America for a very special task.

"What is it, Arthur?" He cupped the man's face, feeling his greasy, stringy brown hair beneath his palms. "Speak more clearly."

"H-Hiva . . . Hiva has come to the woods . . . to Younger's Bend. . . ."

For some reason, Dr. Heidegger found the words "Younger's Bend" very funny, but Adam's face darkened.

Adam's two Fools knew about their primary body's whereabouts. The Desperate Fool knew his words, however many were received, would fly to Adam's ears faster than letters. Heidegger's lips snapped shut against his laughter. Adam waited.

"Lord Temple will be surprised to learn there's a Hiva following me about. Such a mess the monster has left behind on his way to Younger's Bend, though you don't seem to mind, do you, little Berta?"

Adam's arms dropped to his sides. Silently, and in complete shock, he watched the mad doctor laughing hysterically at his feet.

A . . . another . . . Hiva?

"Lord Temple? Lord Temple!"

One of his maids, Danielle, called him from upstairs. And when Adam went to meet her, he found her trembling form waiting for him by the front door, a note in hand.

"A messenger handed me this note. He was cloaked—he didn't show his face. . . ."

He took the folded note from her. The Pompous Fool had written it. As the Fools were all in charge of writing up the exploits of the tournament for the pleasure of Club Uriel, Adam had made it a point to recognize each of their handwriting, memorizing the little differences in their penmanship in case it became necessary. Adam's mind was already in disarray from what he'd just heard in the basement. He didn't need any more surprises. Unfortunately, the sun would not rise without one more. This Fool's note was simple. It was only one line.

The director of the British Museum has been murdered.

5

"THE HELIOS. THE MACHINE THAT OPENS the gate to other dimensions."

Iris had fallen asleep. The strange words of a long-forgotten memory began her dream.

Standing at the edge of a cliff, Hiva's black cloak disguised her in the dead of night. Ra was the old name of this central continent. After conquering it centuries ago, the Naacal had bestowed upon it a new one: Mu. As sea waves crashed upon the rocky shore thousands of feet below, Hiva spied an elaborate temple, white as bone, made of marble and orichalcum, stretching up to the sky.

Why was it that the imperial cities were kept so beautifully? This was where the supreme classes of the Naacal lived. And yet elsewhere, the Naacal had transformed communities into mechanical monstrosities weighed with endless fog. Hiva had seen them. She had seen the concrete enclaves of slaves trudging through dirt and waste, carrying the resources that would be shipped to the cosmopolitan colonies and the facilities that would transform them into technological wonders. She saw the unbreathable clusters of metal workshops and slums, the waste in the seas. The Naacalians had only managed to keep the oceans west of the central continent clean. Even still, underneath the seas, they were building scientific horrors that jeopardized the life of the planet itself.

Now they had built one more: the Helios. The tiny, podlike machine belied its power. A gateway to other dimensions. Other earths to conquer. Other earths to destroy with their hubris.

Their greed knew no limits. And her judgment was final.

"It seems the folly of men endures through space and time," said the man behind her.

"And even through other dimensions," Hiva answered. "You're proof of that."

Hiva's robes fluttered at her uncovered feet, her hood obscuring her face, her features. So different from her companion, the man from another world who'd come to observe. His long, bright curly hair, his pale robes. Even his serene voice full of emotion. Emotion. For that reason alone, Hiva knew: she was in every way his shadow.

He stood beside her. "So you've made your choice." The man smiled sadly. "Won't Nyeth be crushed? His love for you seems the most obsessive out of all those who worship you."

"They only worship me because of what they saw I could do for them," Hiva answered, and it was true. The One had summoned her ten years ago. On that day she'd been reborn and had appeared before the Naacalian leaders. The civilization to be judged. She'd shown them her power only to see how they would react. And like moths to a flame, they'd swarmed her.

The man lowered his head. "They used you to inflict so much pain and destruction upon their enemies. Upon cities and rebellious colonies."

"I let them use me," Hiva corrected him. "To witness with my own eyes the extent of their wickedness."

He nodded. "And that's what I find so different about you, sister. You live among them. You form relationships. You try to understand them before casting judgment." The admiration in his voice was not fanatical like Nyeth's. It was more curious. Searching. "Of all the worlds and all the Hivas I've seen, none take the approach you do."

He looked down and fell silent for a time.

"I once thought there was only one way to respond to such evil. I annihilated societies immediately upon my awakening. But after so many millions of years, I began to wonder if I was wrong. And I've been searching for answers across space and time."

"So you've told me," she replied. This Hiva was too chatty for her liking. His constant shadowing at times felt more like an annoyance. She allowed it only out of courtesy.

"Hiva," he continued, "this is not my earth. I am but a visitor here. An observer. Thus I leave the choice to destroy the humans here to you. I'm sure it is as you would do for me if our roles were reversed. Still, I—"

"That flower in your hand."

He jumped a little at her words and looked down. The scarlet daisy shook with the hand that gripped it. He must have now realized he was trembling. A small patch of the daisies grew behind a nearby orphanage. One of the children must have given it to him. He loved playing with them.

"Forming relationships, then?"

Shriveling under her pointed gaze, he instinctively hid the flower behind his back and stared at his feet, sheepish. He was too attached to this world. Too blind to its faults. To their destruction and generational evil.

His golden eyes brimmed sadly nonetheless. "Is there no other way . . . ?"

Shocking pain nearly split Iris's skull. Letting out a yell atop her cold, hard bed, she grabbed her forehead and let her body shake until the pain dissipated. In her little tavern room, she pulled up her legs and buried her head in her knees.

Every time she saw memories involving that man, it was if her mind would shove her back out again, and so *violently*, as if it were personal. Morning sunlight streamed through the small window just beneath the ceiling. The scrolls she'd stolen from the museum were strewn about the blackened floor, the yellow paper smelling of decay, hiding untold secrets.

The Helios: the machine to open the gate to the *Side Worlds*. That was the name the Naacal had given the other earths beyond this one, earths no eye could see and no hand could reach. Not just one New World like the Committee believed, but many. Maybe countless worlds. Iris had also seen the Moon Skeleton, the sought-after key that operated the Helios, mentioned in the scrolls. But there were other terms Iris had never heard:

The Solar Titan. The Shadow Titan. Strange symbols Iris had read on the third scroll. The writings said nothing about them except that the Naacal had planned for them to be the blessing of humankind.

Titans . . . like the monsters of Greek mythology. The first children of Heaven and Earth. How many did she remember from the books she'd read in the past? Hyperion. Phoebe, Titan of the moon. Cronus, Titan of time. How much time did Iris have? Oh, and Oceanus . . .

"Oceanus . . . The Coral Palace . . . ," Iris whispered, because she suddenly remembered it. Iris placed her head in her right hand, and when she closed her eyes, she could see that temple once again, the light streaming in from the ceiling onto the platform where she'd murdered the Naacalian high priest, Nyeth.

The Coral Ring. Iris searched her memories, but while she remembered its form and design clearly, its actual significance was another matter entirely. What *was* the Coral Ring? Why did Nyeth have it in his possession? Why did it call to her so powerfully even now?

"Try to remember," she whispered to herself. The ring on Nyeth's finger. The way its gleam caught her immortal eyes. The way his blood dripped from his lips and splashed upon its surface while he died. . . .

I can still stop you. I have the Coral Ring. This isn't over. . . .

That was right. Nyeth had been planning to use the Coral Ring somehow inside the temple. Use it to do what, she didn't know. But the fact that it could be "used" at all meant it wasn't just a ring; it was some kind of device. The Coral Ring was an important piece to the Naacal's scheme to "fell" a god. But she'd killed Nyeth too quickly; she never got to witness the ring's use. So how did the Coral Ring come into play? Could it really clip her wings?

As she let herself sink into her memories, she could see the shimmering streams of water beyond the temple windows. Shadows of fish swimming by. Sounds of the ocean.

The Naacal had somehow created many underwater structures. In most of them, they conducted countless experiments, polluting the water with leakages and runoff from their endless machine-making. But not all such factories were underneath the seas.

"'Heaven's Shrine,'" Iris read next, tracing her finger over the two symbols. She shivered. "'And so the sacred room to speak with God was changed into a room to clip his wings.'"

As she saw the symbols, shapes of memories came back to her one by one, forcing themselves through the indecipherable rabble to the forefront of her mind. Heaven's Shrine. Iris remembered the labyrinthine temple the color of beach clay. The feeling of relief as she entered the room of stained-glass windows to look up at the terrifying statue of a sun god looming over her. The slump of her shoulders before she died and stayed dead, having finally completed the gruesome task she'd been given.

But what was this?

Iris squinted her eyes, looking at the fourth scroll. It detailed the mayhem brought about by the Naacal's futile attempts to destroy Hiva. A weapon with the firepower of a thousand suns dropped on Hiva from the skies without warning to the people below, destroying countless lives. Iris still lived. Out of hundreds of thousands, Iris had survived the attack. It was the saddest day of Naacalian history.

But when Iris concentrated, she could see the faded outlines of a scratched symbol written on the parchment. The circle with four points referred to the sun, she knew that. But the circle with the black cross drawn upon it? Iris had never seen it before. It looked as if the sun were in chains. Could it stand for an eclipse? No, there was another symbol for that. Iris had seen it a few times in the scrolls when the Naacal spoke of her rebirth. But what was this crossed sun? It was as if the sun's very existence was being negated.

Suddenly the image of a pile of ashes staining the remnants of a building caused the food in her stomach to lurch up to her throat. Iris blocked her mouth with a hand, doubling over.

Recalling all this was an out-of-body experience, like watching and feeling a play starring another actress. The back of her neck ached and burned. How much more could she do this?

The terms she'd read in the scrolls were intriguing, to be sure, but she couldn't find much more context in them as to what they were and how to use them to her advantage. The Titans. The temple. The Pantheon.

Maybe this won't end until I'm really dead for good.

The thought flashed through her mind quick enough to send a shock through her spine.

Iris straightened her back, hearing the little cracks in her spine and neck. The thought of Granny made her want to slap herself. *I'm not going anywhere except where I want to.*

Sucking in a deep breath, she looked around the room. Rin's bed was empty on the other side of the room. Not that the bed was even needed—the girl barely slept. They were staying in a smelly tavern on the outskirts of the city, avoiding the lecherous and curious eyes of French drunkards while trying to clumsily sift through countless mysteries. This was how they'd spent their first few days in Paris.

Well, not entirely.

"Rin!"

After kicking a drooling man in the shins and knocking him unconscious in the hallway, Rin walked inside their room and closed the door behind her. They'd snuck onto a ferry that had taken them to Paris, but the fact remained that they stood out too much, and there weren't many ways to find André Leroux without any leads beyond his name. Iris had already decided she'd scour the city for him. She had few options beyond that.

But there were times when one could use standing out to one's advantage.

"Rin—" Iris said again before smothering a laugh with her hand. "Wherever did you steal those clothes from?"

Rin looked ridiculously uncomfortable in her new maid's outfit and positively murderous at the sight of Iris's teasing expression. Her wide Holland apron was crumpled over her black twill dress. Modestly impractical for a mystical warrior. At least with her beaded blouse, if she summoned her sword, the blade and handle would come out of her chest cleanly.

"It was a tactical decision. No one will question my presence this way," she reasoned, flustered. Her waterfall of braids swerved underneath her white crochet cap as she placed a hand over her hip.

Iris gathered up the scrolls. "Well, there's a small number like us living in the city," she explained, "from the Americas, the Caribbean, even Africa. A rather dashing porter who came to see one of our shows in Paris one day even asked me for an evening out."

Rin gave her a sidelong look. "And did you reject him?"

She hadn't. But it was a one-night affair, mostly attended to see how Jinn would react. When she came back to their tent, Jinn hadn't had a single reaction, but the morning after, when a botched juggling attempt ended with a bump on Iris's head, she couldn't help but wonder if it was on purpose. Good thing the balls were rubber.

Thinking of Jinn made her want to punch something. Iris steadfastly pushed the memories of that prat out of her head. "I am Isoke: She Who Breaks Hearts." And after a bow, she clasped her hands. "Did you get what I asked for?"

Apparently she had. Rin carried a heavy sack. When she dumped it onto the floor, the *clack* of wood sounded promising. But before Iris could paw through the contents, Rin stepped on the parcel with a boot.

"What about the scrolls? What did you discover?"

After a pause, Iris told Rin the terms she'd read from the scrolls. But they were useless without more context.

Rin sighed impatiently. "And John Temple's journal?"

Iris was well aware that Rin was watching her closely, well aware that the girl was now following her presumably because of the respect given by a fellow Dahomey Amazon, an *ahosi* like Iris had been all those decades ago. Perhaps the power and authority she'd displayed during the battle at Club Uriel had convinced the girl. Iris wondered how long that loyalty would last.

"There *is* something," Iris assured her. Just as with the book he published of his adventures, he'd mentioned the Kingdom of Dahomey. It was John Temple's research on the Helios, the Moon Skeleton, and Hiva—Iris—that had sent him to speak to the king directly. To learn more about the legend of She Who Does Not Fall.

Seymour's experiments on the girl who cannot die are too reminiscent of the African old wives' tale I heard during my last exploits in the West African region, about the warrior princess who never fell in battle regardless of how grave her injury was. This woman was taken to England from the same region. It can't be a coincidence.

Pratt. Iris stared at her left palm, imagined a scalpel slicing into it, before closing it shut and squeezing tight. Through his research and exploits, John Temple had figured out she was Hiva, the cataclysm. Adam had told her so the night that Club Uriel burned down. Father and son were the only Committee members who knew, and Adam much preferred to keep it that way.

But according to John's journal, the king of Dahomey had done some experiments on his own with the white crystal, the substance that made up Iris's alien, immortal heart. The catalyst for the explosion at the South Kensington fair. The source of the Fanciful Freaks' abilities. The king's experiments were not entirely unsuccessful. Rin's power was proof enough.

"I already know that old man came looking for the king," Rin said, unimpressed when Iris told her.

But Iris thought of something else. "Rin," she said. "The Forge. That workhouse where your people conducted experiments. Is it still in use?"

"*My* people?"

Rin's sudden aggression took Iris and, it seemed, Rin herself by surprise—though Rin brushed it off, awkwardly shifting on her feet but keeping her head proudly high and unreadable.

"Yes," Rin answered, this time a hint more quietly. "I would assume it's still in use. Their aim is to create warriors as strong as you. No matter the cost . . ."

Her voice trailed off.

Many cultures of ancient times knew all too well

that the unforgiving power of a wrathful god was absolute. To drag a god back down to earth required nothing short of divine intervention of a different sort. If what the king told me is indeed true, I'll find my divine intervention in the place where heaven dwells. I pray to whatever god that exists that my passage to the celestial realm will not come at the cost of my life.

The last page of John Temple's journal. Iris bit her lip. When she translated it for Rin, the warrior straightened up quickly. A kind of liveliness returned to the girl. Iris could tell the gears in her brain were turning and turning.

"That's it then," Rin said. "You must return to Dahomey with me. The journal makes that clear."

"I don't have to do anything I don't want to," Iris answered flatly.

"I want you to return," Rin insisted, her face hardening.

"I don't want to return."

"I *need* you to return." Her voice felt heavier, deeper, too deep for her young years. And desperate. A quiet warning flashed behind her good eye. Was Rin threatening her?

Iris watched Rin carefully. "You don't have to worry," she said. "I won't let them punish you for failing your mission."

Gritting her teeth, Rin turned from Iris in silence. She'd given up. For now.

The king of Dahomey might have more information on John Temple than Iris could glean from this journal. But she had a bad feeling about going. For starters, as Rin sat down on the hard bed by the opposite wall, Iris could tell the girl wasn't in a good headspace. She wanted badly to bring Iris back to the Dahomey, but why? Just to avoid punishment? Was that really all?

But for Iris, to go and relive everything she'd done as a warrior was a nightmare waiting to happen. Everyone she'd killed under a dead king's orders . . .

Perhaps it'd be no worse than the memories of past lifetimes already jumbled in her brain. But it wasn't something she wanted to go searching for.

And there was another problem. All the information she'd read so far about John Temple and the Dahomey was in English—translated by Uma. Which meant Uma was already well aware that a trip to the kingdom was worth taking in their never-ending search for knowledge.

It made for an excellent opportunity to ambush Iris.

Iris had never met Boris Bosch, and from what she'd heard of him, she never wanted to.

But if it came down to it . . . I can't turn away from that fight.

Shaking her head, Iris decided to look through the sack Rin had brought. Her eyes lit up immediately. "You got them!"

"Of course I did. Though some French brat will be missing his toy thanks to you." Rin kicked her feet up onto the bed and, lying back, cushioned her head with her arms. "You're going out again today?"

"Remember why we're here," Iris replied. "André Leroux. Searching the entire city with just his name is gonna take some time. Days. Maybe weeks. Like it or not, we'll have to be holed up in this dump of an inn for as long as we can. Which means we'll need money to stay here."

Rin scoffed. "To be honest, I'm disgusted that you would debase yourself for these people's enjoyment. As a fellow military woman, my professional opinion is that you should be ashamed of yourself." She said all that without emotion, then turned on her side toward the wall. "But good luck today anyway."

"Thanks," Iris muttered darkly, and began to change her clothes.

The Coral Ring was the key. Iris could picture it on Nyeth's finger in her mind's eye: a round plate affixed to a band the color of peachy orange. The day Nyeth died inside the Coral Temple, the plate had caught the light from the ceiling, its gemlike surface sparkling before it was stained with the priest's blood. What was it for? The first step to finding that out was to pry it off Monsieur Leroux's finger.

But for now? It was time to make some money. She was going back to the circus.

6

OR RATHER, SHE WAS BRINGING THE circus to the people. "The Devil's Game." It was meant to be Iris and Jinn's penultimate set on the tightrope, but Coolie had replaced it with "The Bolero of Blades" because Jinn couldn't master the diabolo. Not like she could.

And boy, had she mastered it.

"Look, Mama, the clown—she's returned!"

Or at least, that was what Iris thought the child had said from what bits of French she could piece together. The bystanders occupying the courtyard of the Musée d'Orsay were delighted that the mysterious clown had returned for another impromptu show. As she'd anticipated, the museum didn't shoo her away—she helped attract business.

It was not for free, of course, as the empty bowler hat in front of her suggested. Hopefully the audience would throw in enough coins to fund not only her stay in France but wherever Iris's search took her next. For now, the cool morning breeze brushed her arms as she pulled the handles of her rope and popped the diabolo up as far as it could go.

The diabolo was a particularly dangerous toy. Two hollow wooden cups were joined at the bottoms to form a bobbin, and the bobbin was placed on a string that had a wand tied to each end. The wands let Iris control the movement of the string, and by controlling the string she could spin the

SARAH RAUGHLEY-

bobbin in whatever manner she liked: tossing it, turning it around her body. This time, after throwing the toy up in the air, Iris jumped as high as she could, flipping thrice and landing upon one of the six statues lining the court-yard's esplanade before catching it perfectly on the taut string. The crowd went wild.

Rin had already spent some time seeking information in her own way, beat-ing up thugs in Parisian alleys and throttling them for information. Much more violent than Iris's approach of simply asking. *Whatever works*, Iris thought, but a tired voice inside her whispered, *Just how long are we going to be here anyway?*

Nonetheless, Iris continued to please her audience. She maintained her grasp on the diabolo even while cartwheeling from statue to statue, throwing it to the side and catching it again. The diabolo had caused many a death—so much so that its use as a leisure toy was banned in some countries.

But Iris could see the question in their eyes. Could this exotic Negro con-tinue to thrill them without getting herself killed? She could see the hint of bloodlust there too. She was used to it. And it still annoyed her, but these past few days, her usual tinge of disdain for ravenous European audiences had held a hint of nostalgia. And the unmistakable thrill and freedom of fleeing into the air made her feel somehow grounded again.

What would the audience do, she wondered, if they knew she was looking for a way to escape having to kill them all? To save her own soul?

"Are you Miss La La?" one woman in a fancy feathered bonnet asked. "Cirque Fernando? Olga the Negress?"

No, she wasn't. But Iris grinned devilishly and gave the woman a knowing wink. Miss La La, the German aerialist, had recently performed in Paris's night-club district with the Cirque Fernando. The two women looked entirely differ-ent, and yet, since the French audience didn't care, Iris decided to use this to her advantage if word ever got out about an African acrobat delighting crowds in the city streets. She didn't need anyone tailing her.

The costume she wore was part of the act: a short, white one-piece she'd adapted from a frilly pair of undergarments Rin had swiped. She didn't have the craftsmanship of Granny, but she'd managed to achieve what she needed:

84

enticing gawkers to her "wild" and wholly inappropriate daredevil performance. She gave the people what they wanted.

"*Maman, Maman, la négresse est drôle!*" said a boy in a sailor suit with shorts cut just above his knees. The boy's amused grin was sparkling when he picked up a rock to throw at her.

Iris dodged it with a flick of her head, but her sudden fury scared the boy's mother more than his attempt to harm her did. The mother hadn't even bothered to stop him. As the crowd's mirth disappeared, the audience's cheers turned to suspicion—of *her*, not the boy who had casually tried to *bludgeon* her. Iris tried to steady her breath before wondering why she had to. Why stay her anger? On whose behalf? Theirs? The audience that was more concerned for a scared white child's feelings than her safety?

Sometimes it didn't make any sense to her. This world and her place in it. But then again, it never made sense in the beginning. After being reborn, she traveled the world as she'd always done during previous cycles to learn about humanity, to understand why they were to be killed. Along her travels, she'd found herself in the Kingdom of Dahomey, fighting a king's gruesome wars. She'd been kidnapped by a slave trader who brought her to a Manchester zoo, inside which she and two other children were made to perform for the sick amusement of the "civilized" English. Slavery, death, kidnapping, and blood. She'd observed it all with a mechanical objectivity to discern whether humanity needed to suffer the same fate as the civilizations that had come before it.

Until—

"Anne! *Anne!*" When Iris closed her eyes, she could hear her own voice in her memories. She could see the little African girl being murdered senselessly in front of her by a callous rock to the head, thrown by a bored schoolboy.

What was it about that death that had set Iris over the edge? What was it about that little girl's demise, after all the injustices she'd witnessed, that had enraged her enough to slaughter the visitors at the zoo that day?

It was as if something within her had snapped upon seeing the life disappear from that girl's eyes, upon seeing the girl's sister, Agnus—now Granny Marlow—crying over her dead body. In that moment, her mission had made perfect sense, the conclusion clear.

But within moments of Iris's slaughter, she'd been subdued by British scientists. Experimented on and tortured. And when she was revived decades later, she had no memories—only a powerful feeling that there was a mission she needed to fulfill no matter the cost.

Did this boy know that once upon a time, a rock callously thrown had almost caused the annihilation of his civilization half a century ago?

Remembering Anne made her stomach turn. Performing for these people made her stomach turn too, no matter how much she enjoyed the art.

Still, you know what the right thing to do is, a nagging voice inside her head reminded her. To stop herself from teetering over the edge. That was why she was here. Because it was the right thing to do, and she was Iris. And Iris was a better person than Hiva. For starters, she *was* a person.

Before she lost too much of her audience, she playfully wagged her finger at the little boy and continued her set, wondering what kind of monster he'd grow up to be as an adult. She performed until dusk. Though she'd drawn the attention of some police officers, they were only intrigued by her panhandling. A colonial curiosity indeed. Eventually the crowd began to disperse.

Just then, her cap rattled with what appeared to be three gold coins—forty francs each. Iris lowered her arms, amazed, her diabolo clattering to the ground. The last few stragglers, annoyed by her decision to stop entertaining them, left in dismay, but the man who'd just given her the coins stayed.

Indeed, he had a very expensive-looking double-breasted frock coat and sparkling rubies on almost every finger. But none of them were the Coral Ring. His white linen shirt was unbuttoned, and his buckskin breeches were as flashy as his top boots. Because he kept his head low, Iris couldn't see his face, only his black top hat and golden hair, which flowed down his back like a river.

A wild thought seized her. André Leroux was a shipping mogul. He was rich. He must have connections with other rich Parisians, and the man before her was *clearly* rich.

"Do you know André Leroux?" Iris chanced, but something about this wealthy man filled her with foreboding. With each step he took toward her, she backed away until she could feel the marble ledge that carried each statue. She glanced behind her. The naked breast and jutting bare knee of the statue woman, *L'Afrique,* made Iris feel suddenly aware of herself. Quickly she wrapped her arms around her body and glared at the man who encroached too deeply into her space. Just as she readied herself to knock this man in the jaw, he leaned in and whispered.

"André Leroux, did you say? Hmm . . . I see you're looking for someone. This may be a fortunate encounter for both of us."

An electric pulse ran down Iris's spine. It was impossible. As she tried and failed to find the words, the man slipped a card in her hand.

"I can help—that is, if you're willing to help me, too. We have a history of helping each other, don't we? Come to this address after midnight and tell no one."

With one sweeping movement, he walked off. Iris buckled, leaning against the marble wall, her diabolo discarded on the ground.

"Benini?"

The last she'd seen of Riccardo Benini, he was a terrified mess spilling the Committee's secrets on the bed of a London brothel. Now he was in France?

She couldn't imagine the Committee would willingly let him go sightseeing after he'd betrayed them. And they had to know about his betrayal—the Committee seemed to always have their ways of keeping tabs on each other. Perhaps he'd run before they had a chance to find out. Perhaps they had found out and he was running from them.

Or perhaps they'd sent him here.

Still, this was an opportunity Iris couldn't let slip through her fingers.

"I'm coming with you," Rin said when Iris told her. "He's a Committee member. He doesn't deserve our trust. We'll kill him if we have to."

No killing, Iris reminded her impatiently as she walked back and forth inside the tavern. Then again, depending on what Benini wanted from her, she might have to revise that rule. "We'll hear him out. He may really know where this André fellow is. If he pulls anything—"

Rin looked as if she could see Iris through her damaged eye. *"Then we kill him."*

Hopefully it wouldn't come to that.

As stars began to fill the sky above the City of Lights, as she and Rin passed by the cabstands and avoided the splashes of dirty water from the wheels of carriages, Iris felt keenly present. But as she trudged down the narrow, cobbled streets, she refused to turn away even as ruddy-faced men in uniform gawked and whispered about the two of them like schoolyard children. She held her head high. Not because she was Hiva. She didn't want to rely on her ancient blood and terrifying power. But because she was Iris.

At the very least, she needed to match the energy of the girl beside her. The reaper who'd taken the heads of many men and was not easily shaken by their judging stares. It was easy to forget one's power under the prying, clinical gaze of others. But not for Rin. Iris smiled in admiration but kept her thoughts to herself.

It took some time, but eventually she and Rin arrived at Rue Chauchat on the right bank of the Seine to find Benini's building—gorgeous and modern where the gaslight illuminated the double doors. But Iris wasn't satisfied. With a glance to Rin, the two nodded and walked around to the side of the building. Together they scaled the brick and broke the window with a blow from Iris's elbow to enter the second floor. The plan was to spy on the Committee member to ensure he hadn't planned an ambush, or at the very least to catch him in some kind of shady act that would further justify their distrust.

But this was *Benini*. Iris should have known when she heard the fool screeching about "getting my good side" that stealth wasn't exactly necessary. Iris and Rin quietly descended the winding staircase to see flashes of light in the living room.

It was an expensive apartment. Even the receiving room was filled with flowers and expensive furniture. Iris walked into the living room with an incredulous expression as Benini tried out various poses in front of a photographer, who was hidden behind a mahogany glass plate camera on a tripod.

Benini himself looked rather ridiculous in his blue coat and starched frilly shirt complete with a white neckcloth. He plunked his leather boot on top of the love seat behind him and posed as if he were Napoleon.

The Pompadour furnishings fit. The Persian carpet and shining chandelier. Iris spotted a Rembrandt among the portraits lining the walls. If he were in hiding, then this was hiding in style. As expected of Riccardo Benini.

"Ah, Iris! And Bonus Friend, Bellerose's girl. That will be all, Alfred." He waved his hand to shoo out the photographer once he caught them gawking in the entryway. The photographer scurried past them with his camera and tripod each under an arm.

Iris smirked at the open bottles of champagne, the crystal decanter, and the wineglass on the small walnut table. "Wherever you go, you seem to bring the party with you, don't you, Riccardo?"

"Still such an opulent display of contempt." Benini ran his hands through his golden locks and grinned. "That feistiness of yours is the very reason for my exile, you know—the cause of my immeasurable pain and distress. But I'm glad to see it on full display."

"*Exile?*" Iris spat, and Rin seemed to understand the word, because she gawked and looked around her.

"Exile in *luxury*," Rin muttered, unamused. "Does he take us for fools?"

"After your escapades in the Basement, did you not think the Committee would figure out what had happened?"

Adam had covered for her in the moment, telling the researchers that it was he who'd sent his team down to the Crystal Palace. But of course he and the others would want to know what had really happened.

"And now, thanks to you, I'm on the run. My life is *asunder*!" With dramatic flair, he collapsed onto the velvet couch. "I've commissioned one last set of photographs in case the others find me and I die here, beautiful and alone. There must be records of my face."

"Wouldn't it be rather easy to find you in a place like this?" Iris gestured toward the bronze busts in the corner. "You didn't exactly disappear into the night."

"Why hide where they'd try to find me? No one in their right mind would think I'd hide myself in one of my own apartments, which makes this place the safest to be. For now."

Iris was sure the Committee was well aware of his quirks. There was nothing stopping them from giving it a go, but she wasn't about to poke holes in his logic.

Crossing her arms, Iris asked him, "How do you know of André Leroux?"

"Straight to the point!" Benini sat back and crossed his legs. "The son of the vice president of the Compagnie Générale Transatlantique. As a man whose family dynasty is based in the textile trade, it would be strange if I didn't know a few shipping magnates across the continent. I could set up a meeting. He's here in Paris, after all."

Iris straightened up and glanced at Rin, translating for her. "You can do that?"

"But only if you do something for me afterward." Benini swiped his half-empty wineglass and brought it to his lips. "Be my champion."

Iris narrowed her eyes. "Excuse me?"

"My plan is to eventually escape this continent. To Africa, in fact—you must be incredibly pleased, I know, a chance to return home, but for me this isn't a pleasure trip. It's business." Benini bobbed his dangling foot as he tilted his head up. "Ah, the Tournament of Freaks. It was a good idea in theory, but in practice, it ended up with far too many corpses. But the tournament is still on, as far as I'm concerned. The others surely must feel the same."

He sipped his drink. "Who will rule in the next life? Who will become leader of the New World? Clearly the one who has control of the Ark will have control of humanity's fate."

"The Ark . . . ," Iris whispered.

"Oh, it must have been part of the information you throttled out of me just a few nights ago. Have you forgotten already?" Benini's eyes glinted mischievously. "The Muvian Expedition in which the Crown discovered parts of the Helios two decades ago. The Helios, which opens the door to the other worlds. The Moon Skeleton key that can operate it. It can also be used to operate the Ark, its creation commissioned by the Committee over a decade ago. Just as with Noah's own, it will hold only those the Committee deems worthy."

Noah's Ark. The calm, calculated cruelty with which Benini spoke of the fate of humanity as he swirled his wine made Iris's blood boil. "And why do you Enlighteners think you have the right to decide who lives and who dies?"

"Haven't you read Darwin, my dear?" And he gave her a sleazy wink. "At any rate, my plan is to seize the Ark myself from the secret munitions factory overseeing its construction. I've secured a ship ready to take me to the western part of Africa. What I don't have is a guard who can't die."

Iris shook her head. "You must be mad."

"You owe me after you put me in this situation."

"I owe you nothing."

"Then think of it as a trade. My information and connections for your physical labor. Unless you've decided the Coral Ring isn't anything you need after all."

Iris froze to the spot. "How do you know of the ring?" And then she paused. "You didn't find me by chance, did you?"

Benini seemed braver than the last time he'd been threatened by a champion. Perhaps because this time he wasn't tied up on a bed—that, and he knew he had the upper hand.

"You were quite soft with the director of the British Museum," he said. "You should know that tying up loose ends is key to moving in secret. For me, it's a must."

A chilling silence interrupted their banter. Iris's fingers closed into a fist.

"I'm not a monster like you." Iris didn't want to ask what he'd done to the director after pumping him for information. If she did, she'd have to face the reality that her actions had caused yet another man's death. The very thought leached the strength from her bones until she was standing there in the entryway guiltily remembering the pile of ashes in the Library of Rule. She wasn't Hiva. She didn't want to be. But even as Iris, she'd already ended so many lives.

"You have your mission, and I have mine. Let's help each other, yes?"

Death followed Iris wherever she went. Ironic for someone who couldn't herself die.

Rin stared at Iris, waiting like a soldier for a command from her superior.

And when she saw Iris's will buckle, the disappointment was clear on her face. "Isoke, you can't be serious. You're taking the word of this man."

I'm not Isoke, either. Iris's lips trembled as she avoided the young warrior's eyes. "Benini," she said, before meeting his smarmy expression with a glare of her own. "I'll be your champion—but only after I have Leroux's ring in my hands."

And as she said it, she felt as if she were making a deal with the devil.

Benini looked quite satisfied. "I wouldn't have taken you as the type to be so greedy for luxurious jewels and trinkets. The ring . . . whatever could you want it for?"

Iris kept her mouth sealed tight as Benini laughed to himself.

A Gathering of Accomplices

THE DIRECTOR OF THE BRITISH MUSEUM was dead. Hanged in his parlor.

Right. Adam knew the handiwork of the Committee when he saw it. The morning after he'd received Fool's note, with a magnifying monocle tucked in his vest, he'd visited the director's inconsolable widow to inspect the farewell note the man had left. It held all the hallmarks of a forgery. But who among them would want him dead?

It wasn't Iris. She wouldn't murder someone so helpless in such a cold-blooded manner—at least not yet, which was something Adam planned on fixing. But for it to happen not long after her visit to the Library of Rule wasn't a coincidence.

As for Iris, there were more pressing matters.

Beneath the Crystal Palace was a foul den where Adam Temple would not have sent even the worst of his enemies. Inside a cold, dingy labyrinth, a gaggle of chemists, surgeons, and all manner of scientists paid for by the Crown conducted experiments on London's "Fanciful Freaks," as Iris and her friends called them. Those who'd gained powers never before seen in this world, thanks to Iris's reawakening at the South Kensington fair ten years ago. Adam was just a boy then when he'd watched Iris's body re-form before his very eyes. It was the moment that had confirmed everything for him. Gods of death were real. And this god of death was his.

Bodies being dissected inside the Graveyard. Wails of men inside the Testing Chamber, kept in rooms built to test everything from ability-reaction time to pain tolerance. Among the living subjects, he saw familiar faces. The little girls who were to be on Cortez's team during the tournament—that is, until failing Cortez's test by losing their battle against Iris, Jinn, and Max. What were their names again? Ah, yes, the black-haired Sparrow Twins. They lay doll-like and frozen atop separate tables, close enough for them to still be able to hold each other's little hands.

And in another room, a one-armed man—Barry Bately, hated foe of Maximo and his street urchin friends—was screaming from the electrical shocks emanating out of the helmet attached to his head. The helmet was attached to a power source; the live wires leached tears from his eyes. Adam peeked inside his room but for a moment. It all sickened him, but he was here for a reason.

He found Uma Malakar melting down a piece of white crystal inside her office in the Research Chamber. At the far end of the room, she stood in front of her workbench, her sari discarded on a wooden chair in the corner. With a pair of goggles shielding her eyes, she held a boiling flask over a Bunsen burner using a pair of metal tongs; the shard floated in an unknown blue liquid inside the flask. She only deigned to acknowledge his presence after the crystal had begun to melt inside the liquid.

"So interesting, isn't it?" She straightened up, placing the flask on a rack. "The white crystal we've mined is quite malleable—enough to create new and wonderful creations. And yet, Iris's own heart from which the white crystal comes is unbreakable. Well, that's not true—" She turned to Adam, brushing her black hair over shoulder as she thought. "It did break once, but only after years of horrific experiments at the hands of that awful man, Seymour Pratt. It took years more of dormancy for the heart to heal itself. At least this is what I've discovered so far."

As expected, she already knew too much. Adam narrowed his eyes but maintained a friendly demeanor. "Your research is going well, I see."

"Thanks to your father." She leaned against her workbench. "He's detailed so much of those experiments in that sacred journal of his. His father being friends with Pratt seemed to have helped him gain access to those old files. And who doesn't love access to secret things?"

Unceremoniously, and quite unexpectedly, Uma pulled his father's journal from a drawer of her workbench and tossed it to Adam. He stared at it, barely able to hide his shock.

Uma crossed her brown arms over her corset. "It's what you want, isn't it?" She arched a playful eyebrow.

"It is." And Adam added, with a challenging smile, "So where are the other copies?"

"You are a smart one." Uma tapped her chin. "Bosch was right about you."

"Where did he find my father's journal?"

"In the vanity chest of one of your father's many former lovers—the ones he had even before your mother died." And when Adam stiffened, she added, "Oh, did you not know? Well, I'm sure that as you were his son, there were plenty of indiscretions he wanted to keep from you—indiscretions he was far more comfortable sharing with his own peers. Fathers, you know. A terrible sort."

Adam checked the handwriting. The narrow cursive was his father's indeed, complete with every obnoxious flourish of the pen. Adam had touched the journal once one night when his father had left it out in his study. Every indent, every frayed edge, was just as he'd memorized. He'd felt like a fool trying to find it, enlisting Iris's help when it was in the possession of one of his father's whores all along. Far more insulting than his father cheating on his mother and betraying his family was the fact that John Temple had managed to outsmart Adam in the crudest way possible: playing on his own son's misplaced naïveté.

"You don't need to tell me where the other copies are," Adam said, tucking his father's journal into his inside jacket pocket. "I'll find them soon enough."

"Why? Is there something about Iris you don't want me to know?" Uma laughed as Adam tilted his head, expressionless. "What a scary face. You won't try to kill me, will you?"

"There're too many guards outside," Adam said with a smile, and indeed, Uma's devoted goons were so many in number that if he so much as touched the woman, he would never make it out of the Basement alive.

Uma laughed. "Don't worry, there's still plenty about that girl I'm not aware of, although it rather kills me to admit it. But I will, in time. I'll be traveling soon, in fact, to follow a few leads I've collected."

Adam's eyebrow arched. "Traveling?"

"Yes, isn't it a shame? And I *just* got to London. A genius's work is never done, I suppose. Well, you know how it is."

"I do." It bothered Adam to no end that Uma didn't so much as shiver at his deadly gaze. Then again, it didn't surprise him in the least.

"You know, Lord Temple," Uma began with a sly smile, "I'm not the one you should be worried about. Iris, she's a curious one, you know. Determined to make her own fate. Whatever plans you might have for her, she'll find a way to defy you, and she'll do it with a smile." Uma's admiration was clear.

"We'll see about that." Adam turned and left her office.

"It's only a matter of time before I learn the whole truth, you know," she called after him.

"I expect nothing less."

The "whole truth" was something not even he knew. Learning it took priority over sparring with Malakar.

Two Hivas . . .

On his way out of the Basement, Adam found Doctor Seymour Pratt in the Graveyard, blood coating his hands and arms up to his elbows. His large white beard had somehow escaped the mess from the organs he'd removed from a man's chest. Behind his brass spectacles, the doctor watched him, nodding only slightly when Adam greeted him as amicably as he could.

"Look after your ward, Lord Temple," he said. "But do not get too attached, for science is marching forward. Civilization is marching forward." Blood dripped from his fingertips onto the floor. "Don't look so pale, boy," he added. "This is all for our evolution as a society. By the time that evolution is complete, an endless number will have been eliminated by us, the higher civilized races of the world."

So a "great" scientist had recently written in *The Descent of Man*. With a scowl, Adam bid the old man goodbye for now.

—◦◦◦◦◦—

Dr. Heidegger's ramblings were worrying. Mysterious disappearances and mass murders in Oklahoma. Bodies burned from the inside out. Reduced to ashes. It was indeed the power of Hiva. Even if it were possible, what were the odds that the power of Hiva would appear so close to that girl? Maximo's little sister, Berta Morales . . .

A second Hiva existing in this world. Nothing in his father's research had prepared Adam for the possibility. Or was Iris not who Adam thought she was?

No. That Iris was Hiva was confirmed by her memories, her abilities. Adam couldn't glean much more from Heidegger's delirious mumbling. If it was true that another Hiva existed in America and was burning down towns as he traveled, news should be spreading by now. It hadn't reached England quickly enough to confirm. Adam had to find another way. And fast.

He would need two teams: one for the immediate threat, and the other on standby in case his best-laid plans fell to ruin. The latter wasn't a possibility Adam particularly wanted to consider, but he would have to if he was to achieve his goal.

Global annihilation.

The next few days were crucial to building his new teams. He chose his new champions carefully. Gram and Jacques were Van der Ven's boars through and through. Too bloody and wild to control. Others were easier to handle.

He gathered information and went to find them one by one.

It didn't take too much effort to pay the bail for Henry Whittle. The presence of supernatural freakery was fast becoming more real than a rumor. Based on the reports Adam received from the Commissioner, Henry's attack on Iris the night of Club Uriel's burning wasn't exactly a stealth endeavor. The Committee had already planned for this eventuality, first ensuring the silence of witnesses, then paying certain officers in certain departments to keep those with abilities in special custody. Henry's fate would then be decided not by some juvenile court unable to handle him, but by the Committee.

The pressing question on Adam's mind was why Henry would attack

Iris—and so conspicuously. According to the reports, there was another that night who'd managed to escape. Were the champions continuing the third round, their battle to the death, in hopes of still getting the payout the Committee had promised? Or was there another reason . . . ?

He let Henry go home first.

David Whittle, the Whittles' family patriarch, was drowning in debt despite running a successful family toy store for decades. Adam could only assume that was why his young grandson Henry had agreed to take part in such a bloody tournament in the first place. Henry had seen Adam once in Club Uriel. Now, a day after his bail was paid, Henry entered the toy shop to see Adam again, this time laughing with his grandfather behind the front counter. The store was closed. That was why David Whittle didn't mind having a bottle of champagne in his hand. Adam lifted his glass to a terrified Henry in the doorway.

"Granddad?" Henry shut the door behind him quickly and looked over at the Whittles' family servant in the corner: Mary, the mousy girl with the ability to heal others. She shook her head stiffly, but kept her gaze lowered, too afraid to say a word. If this new Hiva was truly *Hiva*, her skills could come in handy— that is, if this team survived.

"Wondrous news, Henry! The Temples have decided to sponsor us! Young Lord Adam Temple, he bailed you out of police custody, and now he's paid off my debts. He truly is an angel. If it weren't for his intervention, we . . . I . . ."

Adam could hear a sniffle caught in the old man's throat. It warmed his heart. Such a nice way to spend his day, doing a good thing for a kind, elderly man.

"Why would you do that for us?" Henry barked like a cornered dog, his eyes flashing as he backed into the door he'd just closed.

Mr. Whittle placed the bottle down in frustration. "Henry! A boy in your position shouldn't have anything to say to this man except 'Thank you, sir.' Imagine—today, without this young man's kindness, you'd still be in that jail cell for physical assault!"

Physical assault. That was the official story anyway. So the whispers hadn't reached the old man yet. Well, rumors were difficult to control, but the Committee was efficient when it came to these things.

"He's even paid for more workers at the shop. You know we've been short-staffed here!" Mr. Whittle then turned to Adam. "Please forgive him. He's always been a bit surly, but you know he's at that age." Mr. Whittle took off his cap and was squeezing it nervously as he explained. "The lad got into so many fights at Harlow, I had to take him home from school to start his apprenticeship. You've practically saved him from being shipped off to reformatory school."

"Granddad!" Henry squeezed his hands into fists, his ears flushing red, but his pincer gaze was on Adam and Adam alone. It was as if he knew that Adam had already found out the truth. Henry had been taken out of Harlow School not just because of his proclivity toward picking fights with boys twice his size, but because of his family's increasing inability to pay the tuition.

"He's young and moody, that boy, but he has a good heart."

Adam grinned. "Oh, I know. I've been there myself. He seems like a smart boy. I'm sure he'd do anything for you. That's admirable."

Setting his glass down, Adam left the beaming old man and approached Henry with his arms outstretched. A strong pat on the back gave him the excuse to draw the boy close.

"I have a task for you. Tomorrow, you and your maid will be brought to my Yorkshire estate. And you will tell no one."

Henry made a move, but Adam quickly linked his fingers around Henry's wrist.

"The staff I hired will be watching your grandfather closely. Of course, they'll murder him if you don't do what I say. Consider that before you try anything."

Another pat on Henry's back and a smile to the old man before the toast. "Oh, and by the way," he said quietly, his grin pasted on. "Your friend Lucille. Where is she these days?"

The shape-shifter named Lucille. It was typically quite difficult to find a woman who could change faces. But as per Henry's generous information, Adam found her in a brothel the next night—one of the many Benini frequented, as it turned out. Inside the stuffy, velvet-laden room, she sat atop a master bed passionately embracing the madam's daughter and top worker, "Lily," with, apparently, the longest list of clients.

He didn't know which was which, but he could guess. One was only half-dressed, her long reddish-brown locks dropping over her alabaster skin. The other was unmistakably the spitting image of a Manet painting Adam had seen two years ago in a gallery: *Jeanne*, it was called. Rosy cheeks, brown hair underneath a flower-covered frilly bonnet, long yellow gloves, pursed lips, and a nose pointed in the air with all the pompousness of the upper class. Though both women looked shocked, only "Jeanne's" eyes darkened with terror at the sight of him.

She and her team had crossed paths with Adam in Club Uriel; like Henry and Mary, she knew he was a member. Perhaps she had even been told by her patron that he had a seat on the mysterious and elite Committee. Either way, she must have known his appearance here was a bad omen.

Once Lily had dressed and left the room, Adam threw the file he'd readied onto the bed.

"What's this?" Lucille demanded quickly in a hoarse voice, sweat beginning to line her brow. Indeed it was her. No matter what face she wore, she couldn't fake her voice.

"I see you're fond of role play," Adam said. "Perhaps that's why Nevada's authorities haven't found you yet. But my connections in the city are still interested in finding you."

Lucille's entire body seized as she opened the file. There she found her real name and real face—and the crime she was on the run for: the murder of young Mr. McKnight, a gambler and con artist. The police photos were old and had been difficult to find, but Adam was sure she could remember the blood on the doorway of her Carson City ranch clear as the day she shot him.

"In terms of a motive, authorities guessed that it was a love story gone wrong. But I suppose business and love can never coexist, can they?"

Lucille began shaking. Adam glanced away as if to give her some privacy, but his lips spread into a cold smile when he heard her shaky voice, devoid of all pretention and theatrics.

"What do you want?"

Adam slid a photograph from underneath the papers in the file. "This is Gerolt Van der Ven, one of Belgium's premier military men."

Her eyes squinted in confusion. She didn't recognize him. Not surprising: Van der Ven hadn't frequented Club Uriel during the tournament, and it was doubtful Cortez would have shared information on the Committee members with his champions like Adam did for Iris.

"There is currently a geopolitical conference being held in Berlin," Adam continued. "Van der Ven was to join King Leopold II's party as a representative of Belgium, but he was delayed." Van der Ven's protruding chest, displaying every one of his military medallions, made Adam sick. "Soon you and your old teammates will be escorted by my men to my Yorkshire estate. Study this picture. When the time comes, you'll need to know every contour of his face."

Lucille furrowed her brows, one of the many sets she'd had in her lifetime. "Why?"

Because the only cure for a ruined plan is a reckless one. "That's for me to know. You'll be taken to Yorkshire, kept out of sight, and you'll stay there until I call for you."

Lucille sat taut on the bed as if ready to run.

"Oh, and don't try to escape," he added with a smirk. "I have eyes where I need them. You wouldn't get far."

Lucille's shoulders slumped, her hands rigid against her legs. "Is that so?"

"Did you really think the Committee would just let you champions gallivant around the city without keeping tabs on you? They won't let you go that easily. They have plans for you, I'm sure of it. Just think of me as being ahead of the curve."

He gathered up his file. "Ah, and, if you will, I have one question. About Iris."

Lucille froze up.

"I had the chance to ask Henry, but he was in a rather bad mood, and we had company, you see, so I'm asking you. I figured you'd be more forthcoming." He turned, watching the woman squirm on the bed.

"The night Club Uriel burned down, Henry was the only one taken into custody. But I know he wasn't the only one who'd been there. So why?" Adam's eyes darkened. "Why did you attack that girl?"

Lucille seemed to have a problem unsealing her lips. As she fiddled with her hands, Adam took a menacing step forward—as a gentleman, of course.

"I don't have much time, and I'm not very patient. Answer quickly."

She looked incredibly guilty as she began to speak. "Your champion, Max Morales. He told us—"

Maximo? Adam's frown deepened. "Told you what?"

"When we broke into the Crystal Palace, he saw something. He and Jinn. They found out something terrible about Iris. That's why we . . ."

"And what did you find out about Iris?"

He'd had enough practice not to let others see signs of worry in his expression, but he nevertheless held his breath while he correctly assumed the worst.

"That she was born to kill us all."

That was the reason behind Club Uriel's burning. The champions had indeed battled, but for another reason. Discovering Iris's identity, they'd banded together to try to save their own miserable lives. Gram and Jacques knew too. It was only a matter of time before the Committee found out as well. But if there was truly another Hiva . . . could Adam use that to his favor?

Lucille's, Henry's, and Mary's tasks were different from the rest. They were part of a contingency plan Adam hoped he would never have to use. But those orphans. Maximo's friends. They were key to what he needed *now*. He'd considered having all the champions killed to protect Iris's secrets, but their powers were simply too useful to waste. So he laid them out on his chessboard and began to move each piece.

Skeletons lay beneath Adam's feet, literally, caged under Bath Abbey's stone floor. The right wing had been closed off for "construction." But nothing was closed off to Adam Temple. He knelt down to inspect the broken floor. Grave robbers had come four weeks ago and stolen some bodies and coffins. But why would Lawrence Hawkins care?

"Yes, I believe the young man you described was here last night," said the graying rector. "Blond hair, correct? We tried to catch him, but he disappeared in . . . some kind of—"

"Flash?" Adam gave him a quick, blunt smile before continuing to inspect the ground.

The rector cleared his throat. "Well, such a thing isn't possible," he said with a hint of nervousness. "Probably a trick of the light."

"Yes," Adam answered, standing. "A trick."

It was Fool's intelligence that had brought him to the abbey. He'd need more to find where Lawrence Hawkins and his friends were now.

The dark of night helped Fool hide his harlequin mask from the carriage driver. He kept his top hat low and his black cloak high as he sat next to Adam on their ride out of the city limits.

"Don't worry, my lord. I can tell you exactly where he is," Fool said.

Adam nodded. "And what about Iris? Have you found her?" he asked without looking. He kept his steady gaze on the cobbled streets and passing buildings instead.

"No, my lord. But I've discovered something just as interesting." He covered his mask with a white-gloved hand as if it would dull his quiet laughter. "Benini."

What? Adam turned. "Where is he?"

"It seems he's run to Paris. What's more: some witnesses caught your old friend near the museum director's abode not long before the old man expired. A coincidence, perhaps?"

Adam lowered his head and clasped his hands together. "Well, we were never friends."

Paris. Inside the Library of Rule, the ancient casket had been opened, and Naacalian scrolls had been stolen. Iris was trying to discover more about herself. Did Benini know?

Schemes assembled and crumbled in his mind as he frantically tried to adapt to each new morsel of earth-shattering information he received. For any one of them to work, Adam needed Maximo's friends on board. His plan to flush out this new Hiva couldn't work without Lawrence Hawkins. But the Hawkins in front of him inside this dirty warehouse clearly wished he could kill Adam with a look.

Fool had told him about this old place on the outskirts of the city. It was nothing but brick with small black holes for "windows." A shadowy arch was the front door. It had been a shipping warehouse once upon a time before a cholera outbreak. Then the place shut down and became abandoned, with most too scared to step inside to try their luck except the desperate and destitute.

"So this is where you're hiding now." Adam looked at a few dirty mattresses on the ground, but taking his eyes off Max's friends was a mistake. From the iron gates of the carriage passenger lift, several playing cards flew at him along with the furious cry of a heartbroken girl. He barely had time to dodge them before he heard someone cry, "Cherice, stop!"

The boy from Labrador across the pond: Jacob. He held the girl back by linking his arms with hers from behind. The little thing kicked her feet in the air, tears streaming from her blue eyes, her short red hair whipping every which way as she demanded he let her go.

"You heard her. Let her go, Jacob." Over by the south wall, Hawkins stood up from the staircase and began descending the steps. Shakily. He almost slipped down a few. He'd been drinking. Adam could tell by the glaze in his eyes. A few candles lit up the dark, abandoned space through the small windows high up by the ceiling. "This is the bloke who used us to get to Max . . . and then used Max up like a washrag." Though Hawkins slurred his words, Adam could understand each one. "That's right. Max told us everything."

Hawkins was taller than he was, but as he lifted his chin, Adam could tell he was somehow trying to appear bigger as if to compensate for the huge gulf between their statuses. This was someone who lived resenting and envying while emulating the rich. Adam could always tell the type. But this was far more personal.

"Everything," Hawkins repeated, and then grabbed Adam's collar. "About how he had to kill for you."

"Lawrence—" Jacob started, because Hawkins had drawn Adam so close to his face, baring his teeth like an animal, that Adam wondered if the boy might just bite him.

"It was to protect her," Adam said.

"Iris? Your *obsession*?"

Hawkins laughed while Adam grimaced in annoyance. Obsession was such an obscene way of thinking about something so sacred. As expected from some low-class street urchin.

Jacob ran up to them and grabbed Hawkins's arm, giving him a soft, worried look Adam immediately recognized as love. Hawkins must have recognized it too, because he loosened his grip immediately. Jacob's tender touch, however, did nothing to sway his anger. Hawkins pushed Adam to the ground.

"Just wondering, though." Hawkins wiped his mouth and continued. "Did you know that the girl you're so desperate for is planning to kill us all one day?"

"She's already killed once." Jacob shook his head, running his hands through his long dark hair. "She killed someone at the Crystal Palace. She's killed throughout the centuries. And she's the reason why Max is . . ."

"Dead." Without Jacob to hold her, Cherice collapsed onto the floor. "He's dead. . . ."

As she burst into tears, Adam raised his eyebrow with interest, though given the situation, he imagined it'd be better to let more concern slip into his voice.

"Dead? What happened to him?"

"As if you give a damn." Hawkins spat on the ground next to Adam's feet. If he were sober, he wouldn't have missed his mark.

Adam stood. "He was my champion. Believe it or not—"

"Save it!" Hawkins lunged at him again. Jacob wrapped his arms around Hawkins's waist to hold him back, and as the two fought, some very light yellow crystals, small as pebbles, fell out of Hawkins's hair and onto his sleeve. A curious Adam swept the dust off the boy's arm and tasted it.

"Sugar." He stared at his wet finger as Hawkins froze in surprise. "Where have you been, Lawrence?" Adam asked calmly, a question that made Hawkins pause. "I went to the abbey."

Hawkins stumbled back, his eyes widening with shock before he turned and hid his face. Interesting. Adam stroked his chin.

"Weeks ago, they'd been paid a visit by grave robbers. But you were there just last night. Why were you there, Lawrence? What interest do you have in desecrated tombs?"

Hawkins tried to lunge at him again, but it was a feeble attempt. Jacob needn't have gripped his shoulder. The boy fell to his knees.

The three of them held a secret. A secret they weren't about to tell a stranger, an intruder like him. But one thing was for sure: they truly believed that their friend was dead. Max was no longer a card for him to play.

But he had another.

Adam sucked in a deep breath. Everything hinged on this performance. "When I recruited him," he started with just a hint of sorrow, "I never intended any harm to come to him."

"Fat lot your *intentions* mean," said Hawkins with an incredulous laugh.

"Why should we believe you?" Jacob said at the same time, while Cherice pounded the ground in frustration.

"I only wanted him to watch Iris. To make sure she wouldn't—" Adam shut his eyes. "To make sure she wouldn't awaken. It's why I chose her for the tournament. To *watch* her."

Jacob studied him closely. "You knew what she was all along, didn't you?"

"Yes," Adam said sadly. "You think I'm . . . obsessed. In love. Far from it. Iris can't die. Not until she fulfills her purpose. But I thought if I could keep her close, convince her, train her—"

"*Train* her? Was she your *dog*?" Jacob said, frowning. The word "train" clearly didn't go over well with him, but Adam continued anyway.

"Iris lost her memories in the explosion ten years ago. I thought it was an opportunity to turn her against her directive. To teach her how to stop herself from becoming Hiva. I needed someone neutral to help me keep an eye on her, at least until I was sure she would never inadvertently become Hiva again. All our lives are at stake. Even though I couldn't tell Maximo all the details about her identity, he took on this dangerous job because he cares so much about his family. And it's precisely because of his family that I now need you to help me."

Hawkins jumped to his feet and spat in his face, yanking his collar. "You must be out of your damn mind. I won't let you get to them like you got to Max."

He jerked his head in Jacob and Cherice's direction and gripped Adam's collar tighter. "I'll never let you—"

"Because Max's family is still alive: Berta." Adam let the saliva drip down his cheek without moving an inch as Hawkins let him go, stepping back in shock. "Maximo's little sister, Berta Morales, is in the United States. And she's in danger."

A beat of silence passed. That was when Adam realized Cherice was no longer crying, no longer screaming. At the sound of Berta's name, she simply stared at the floorboards, her hands trembling. He was almost there.

"Max knew I was keeping tabs on Berta with one of my spies," he said. "He did everything hoping that one day I'd reunite them. It's awful, I know," he added quickly, seeing all three glare at him furiously. "Blackmail. Well, it's not my finest moment. But I truly did aim to have them meet one day. All Max wanted to do was to find and protect his sister. Now that he's gone, that duty falls to you."

Hawkins shook his head in disgust. "Blackmailing *us* now, then?" He stepped in front of Jacob protectively, almost as if by instinct.

"I'm giving you an ultimatum. Stay here and waste your life mourning a lost friend, or carry on his legacy by finding his sister. She has the right to know what happened to her brother. But I need something from *you*. If you won't help me, you'll have to find Berta on your own."

"How are we supposed to believe you?" Cherice said, slowly stumbling to her feet. "That Berta's alive and in America."

"Hawkins." Adam's blue eyes glinted with a devilish flash he couldn't hide. "Your power holds the key to it all." And he reached inside his pocket. The reason why Adam had gone to Hawkins and his team last. It took a while to find something he could use, but this postcard of Haskell County Courthouse in southeastern Oklahoma was rather specific and thus difficult to secure.

"There's a community of bandits in southern Oklahoma. This courthouse is just a few hours away on foot. Photos of that area aren't so easy to find. This is the closest place I could get on short notice," Adam explained. He was sure Hawkins could see the flat grass and barren trees around the courthouse captured in black and white. "The bandits are hiding in the woods north of the

Canadian River. Your power of teleportation will take you here." Adam tapped the photo. "From there, you'll follow the river northeast until you find a ranch called Younger's Bend. Berta will be there. But she's not alone."

"Bandits . . . Berta?" A line of sweat began to form at the edge of Hawkins's blond hair. The look he suddenly gave Adam was one of a boy who'd had his secrets found out, even though Cherice insisted, "He can't teleport anywhere he hasn't seen with his own eyes, you moron!"

"You don't need to hide it," said Adam. "I talked to Bosch once during the tournament. He said there was something more to your power that you weren't telling anyone."

Silence. Hawkins placed a hand on his head, shaking it in utter disbelief. "That's not . . ."

"It's because he's scared of getting stuck in the photo," Jacob finally admitted, only to be met with Hawkins's fury and Cherice's shock.

"W-what?" She tilted her head, leaning toward Jacob enough to make the quiet boy uncomfortable. "Hawkins can do what? What are you talking about? Eh? Speak up!"

"Cherice—" Hawkins started.

"He did it once," Jacob told Cherice quietly. "When we were kids. He took Chadwick to Paris," he added shyly with a little hint of jealousy, shifting his feet. Hawkins looked between Jacob, Cherice, and Adam, then sighed, lowering his head as Jacob continued. "It's stupid, really. It was one night after they went to Paris. Cherice, you were asleep, but we were all playing cards. Chadwick was talking about our abilities, and after he told us what Lawrence did, he wondered out loud if he was ever afraid of getting stuck."

"Terrified the life out of me." Hawkins smiled. "But Chadwick and Max thought it was all very funny. They started talking about it incessantly. Max had Chadwick draw it into one of his stupid little comics—a kid getting stuck in a painting."

Chadwick Winterbottom, the author of those Fanciful Freaks penny dreadfuls. Yes, Adam had had them collected in his office. He remembered that issue. The boy who'd tried to travel into a painting and ended up being cut in half by the wall.

"That's why Lawrence is scared to do it that way. But he's done it before."

"Jacob . . ." Hawkins laughed, flashing the other man an annoyed but impish grin. "Of all the memories to bring up . . ."

"Lawrence, if there's a chance we can find Berta . . ." Jacob's kind brown eyes were wide and wet with desperation.

Adam seized on it. "That's right. *You* have the power. All you have to do is check my information. And if I'm wrong, you can come back to England on your own and flay me alive. But what if I'm right? And I *am* right. What would Max have wanted you to do—"

"Just shut up," Cherice ordered him as she put her hand up to stop the men in their tracks. "Just . . . *quiet*. We need to think about it. *I* need to . . ." She went silent, her expression softening as it drifted off to endless possibilities and promises not kept. "Maxey . . . Maximo . . ."

"Take your time and think about what I'm proposing. But not too much time. Tomorrow night, I'd like you to come to my estate at 19 Melbury Road. Lawrence, you especially should familiarize yourself with it once inside."

Hawkins narrowed his eyes.

"Then," Adam continued, "after I explain everything, you'll have your chance to find Berta and to protect her from the danger she's in before it's too late."

"What . . . what danger?" Jacob asked timidly. "You mean the bandits?"

He was willing to believe. Good. Adam needed believers. He needed to confirm this new Hiva with his own eyes—or at least, with eyes he could borrow. After determining who this Hiva was and what he was capable of, Adam would decide for himself whether to recruit him for Iris's mission or keep him out of her way—by whatever means necessary. These three would serve their purpose and then be discarded. Such was simply the fate of some men.

"Worse than bandits." Adam let his voice drip with concern to sell Jacob his lie—a lie tucked away inside the truth. "The danger I'm talking about is the same danger Iris poses. The danger Max tried to protect you all from, even at the cost of his own life. Since the day I was born, I've been given everything I need: wealth, power. Everything. I have no reason to die. So if I can use what

I've been given to stop the world from burning, I will. I'll stake my honor on that."

He thought of his dead family, rotted and eaten in the ground.

His honor.

The mission would soon begin.

THE MASSACRE AT YOUNGER'S BEND

HIVA NEEDED A FEW DAYS MORE to rest. The bandits still didn't ask any questions, just watched the "freak" from afar. Better for them. In the meantime, Fables kept a lookout for the masked man who'd escaped into the woods. Lulu wasn't permitted to stray from the ranch or go off by herself, but every once in a while, she'd stand by the edge of the woods in her black pinafore and whistle as if it'd draw her new friend out. Worked for hound dogs, didn't it?

Berta kept her wanted poster to herself—but wanted posters had a funny way of appearing in the oddest places. That must have been the reason why, just as darkness descended on the third day, while Fables cut an apple with an army knife, guns started shooting in the air.

Berta had been playing cards with a Cherokee man who had to lift up his eye patch to see his hand and a white man with a mustache long enough to brush his collarbone. All three were up in the hollow ranch, guns drawn. Lulu, who'd taken to staying near Hiva for safety, dropped her porridge and jumped to her feet.

"What's going on?" She clasped her hands together in distress. "Why are y'all fighting?"

A whooshing sound. A blue light. Someone screamed.

That dark-blue light. Looked like a whirlpool. Fables searched for the source, but he couldn't find anything. He did notice, however, that the old man at the far end of the cabin was missing. The one who liked to pick his teeth with a small cat bone he'd found outside.

"Who's that?" cried one woman, perched on the window ledge by the candle lights. Her green eyes darted around beneath some rather thick dark red bangs. The candle lights flickered and went out, plunging them into darkness.

"What the hell's going on?" cried Berta.

Fables couldn't find her, but he wanted to strangle her. "I bet someone's after you!"

"I didn't do nothing!"

Another scream. This time, Fables could see flashes from the blue light behind him. He could feel the blond woman next to him being pulled away into nothingness. The light disappeared before he could turn around to catch it.

"This is bedlam!" Fables screamed, ducking for cover as folks started running out of the cabin and shooting at nothing but ghosts.

"It's God's justice," Lulu whispered, eerily calm, kneeling down next to him. "It's what happens to bad people."

"What? *We're* not bad!"

Fables balked at Lulu's unmoving, pretty face, her deep, soulless stare as she quietly sang, "'He hath loosed the fateful lightning of His terrible swift sword.'"

"We're *not* bad!" Fables insisted, and looked over to Hiva. It was thanks to the moonlight he could even see him, but despite the chaos surrounding him, Hiva still hadn't moved. He stayed as he had for the past few days, sitting on his chair in the corner with his head back against the wooden log walls. Uninterested.

Or maybe a little interested. His eyes were open. He was watching.

Sniffing.

"Hiva?" Fables cried as another bandit disappeared. Fables was sure he'd be next. Hiva had to help. He had to save him. That's what Hiva was here for.

And like a tin man that had been fed sufficient oil, Hiva sat up straight in his chair and turned to face the mayhem, the dandelions growing in his hair breathing as if they'd come to life. There was a glint of blue light, then suddenly several playing cards shot out of the darkness, out of nowhere, cutting a man's hand so his gun clattered to the ground. Fables peered through the shadows at the attackers. He spied a short girl moving quickly, but when the starlight caught her just right, he could see her piggish face and reddish-orange bowl cut.

Berta appeared before him in a flash, using her gun to push up her hat. "We're getting out of here," she said, kneeling next to him. "Tell your precious pile of cans in the corner—that is, unless he'd actually like to help us out for once."

But Hiva wasn't as disinterested as she'd assumed.

"Hey!" Berta yelled once she caught him watching. "I said we're leaving."

"No, you're not." Bowl Cut. Fables guessed the cards were coming out of her sleeve, as if she were a magician's assistant. A moment passed, and another card was in her hand. Berta's gun was ready.

"Berta," Bowl Cut said in a thick English accent. "It is Berta, right? Max's little sister?"

Berta's gun dropped from her hand and clattered to the ground. It was the first time Fables had ever seen her spooked. Her face fell, her doe eyes lost. Maybe he liked this piggish-looking girl after all.

All the bandits had been cleared out of the cabin save for them. Another whirlpool of blue light, and two more strangers waltzed through.

"What is this?" Fables ran his hands through his hair. "This ain't bloody *Gulliver's Travels*." He looked at Hiva watching them in the corner.

Lulu tugged his sleeve. "I like that book too," she whispered very seriously, her eyes still on their visitors.

Two guys: a blond one as lanky as he was—the oldest, clearly. A shorter one. Fables couldn't see him fully in the dark. Like Bowl Cut, they were dressed like Dickensian orphans.

Berta picked a knife up off the cabin floor and threw it at the shorter boy's head. The lanky blond boy practically jumped in to protect him without even a thought. For half a second, the blond froze. The knife was going to land, Fables was sure of it. Berta's aim was a *killer* in every sense. It was going to gut him good.

"Lawrence!" the boy next to him screamed.

Snapping out of his stupor, the blond quickly created one of those blue swirling whirlpools with a sweep of his hand. Berta's knife disappeared into the vortex. Where it went after the dust cleared, Fables had no idea.

"Lawrence! What were you thinking?" Dickensian wasn't far off. He had the same thick accent as the girl. Grabbing the blond's arm, he pulled him around. "Since when do you cut it close like that, huh?"

"Jacob . . . ," the blond replied absently, and paused. "Are you . . . okay . . . ?"

This Lawrence guy looked lost. There was no other way to put it. He looked like he wanted to die.

Jacob gripped both of Lawrence's cheeks, his fingers curling, probably scratching his skin. "What were you thinking? Is this . . ." He paused. "Is this because of Max?"

Jacob then gripped the taller boy's wrist so delicately, Fables wondered if there was something going on between them and felt a strong pang of jealousy. That was when the girl with the bowl cut spoke again.

"Berta," she said. "You are . . . you are Berta, aren't you? Oh my God, you look like him. . . ."

The way Berta backed away, you would have thought this tiny thing was a rottweiler. But the British tyke approached Gunslinger Girl with the utmost of care, her eyes swelling as if on the verge of tears.

"We're not here to hurt you," she explained quickly. "I swear we're not. Hawkins, pull yourself together, goddamn it!"

Because the tall blond was in tears. He didn't sob, no. His face wasn't scrunched up ugly. He just . . . cried. In perfect serenity, he stared at Berta and wept.

"We're just here to—" The girl struggled to find the words before looking behind her. "Ugh, Jacob, Hawkins! Will you help me out, you wankers?"

But they were at a loss for words too.

"Berta," the girl said again. "Berta Morales. Maxey's little sister." She shook her head, her lips trembling in a little smile. "You really do look just like him. It's really something. . . ."

"How do you know Maximo?" Berta's voice was so hollow, Fables wasn't sure she was really even there. Her hands were shaking. Her whole body. "Where is he? Is he okay?"

The tall blond bit his lip, shut his eyes, and looked away. Guilt. Self-loathing. Fables was acquainted enough with the expressions; he saw them every time he had the courage to glance in a mirror.

"He's okay, isn't he?" Berta asked again. "You're friends of his, aren't you?"

But when they didn't respond, when the redhead began sobbing, Berta understood. She nodded, sucking in a little breath. "Who did it?" she asked quietly, her hand squeezing the handle of her gun. "At least tell me that."

"Wait. Who's that?" asked Jacob, because Fables's savior had finally begun to move. Immediately Fables, Berta, and Lulu backed away, clearing a path.

"He is Hiva," said the masked man—the same one who'd run off into the woods the other day and who had suddenly appeared at the window. Holding a lamp, he climbed onto the sill after clearing away the candles.

"Fool!" Bowl Cut shouted, annoyed. "Why the hell did you just disappear after taking us here from the courthouse? Could have told us how many bandits we'd have to deal with. What if one of us had got killed? Huh?"

"I've been renamed 'A Joke,'" the masked man replied, nodding his head eagerly. "Do you like it? Oh, how I wish you'd say you like it. . . ."

"If this is Hiva," said Jacob, "then Adam was right. There was one in Oklahoma all along. But that means Iris . . ."

"Wait." Fables shook his head in frustration. "Fool? What's that? Who the hell is Adam? And Iris? What's—"

"Iris. You mean *her*." Hiva was on his feet. Closing his eyes, he soaked in the atmosphere with a deep breath. "Her essence hovers over you all. Her anima. I can smell her. . . ."

"Iris . . . ," Lulu repeated, touching her lip as she pondered the name.

"That's who did it." It was the blond, Lawrence, who spoke. After wiping the tears from his eyes, he said it, hatred dripping from his words. "A pretty African wench I wish he'd never met. Iris killed Max."

Berta said nothing. But her wide-open brown eyes whispered unspeakable things.

Hiva paused and searched the cabin. "But she is not here. Where is my sister?"

The flowers in Hiva's hair seemed to writhe on their own as Hiva approached them: first the two women, sniffing them as he passed. As they shuddered, Fables's face stretched with a wild smile. Whoever these freaks were, they were going to get it now. It didn't matter what strange powers they had. They were no match for a god.

The three intruders certainly seemed to get it. They stepped back quickly, their hands up. Lawrence stood in front of the other two, eager to protect them. But the question was clear in their eyes. Even if all three attacked together . . . could they take him? Could they survive the force of nature called Hiva? The name seemed to mean something to them. Why else would they be quivering?

Just then Fables heard murmurs and voices from outside the back window. That didn't bode well.

"Ah, that's right," said the masked man. "The reason I came. They'll be here soon, you see. Not from the road, but from the back woods—"

"The back woods?" Lawrence glared at this "Fool," who slipped off the windowsill onto the floor. His knees hit the floorboards with a painful bang.

"Yes, I heard them coming and saw them with their pitchforks, but I didn't know you wanted me to be a lookout. I only do what I'm *told* to do. I did well, didn't I?" He rubbed his hands together as the voices coming from the woods behind them grew louder. "There's no Fool as loyal as I!"

"Who's this 'them'?" Fables spat.

"Some sheriff's departments from a few neighboring towns, I suppose." The masked man tilted his head. "And a few concerned citizens. You're quite well-known, Berta, though I wonder if it's your handiwork or Hiva's that brought them here. Perhaps both?"

"Dang it!" Fables screamed, sending that joke of a man scrambling on the floor and begging for forgiveness again. Lulu went over to pat him on the head.

"Enough," the tallest boy said. "My name is Hawkins," he said, introducing himself to Berta, who was still as a stone. "And I was best friends with your brother. We've been sent here to take you back to London with us. And not just you."

Hawkins looked at Hiva, but the man who was not a man had already opened the front door and walked outside without anyone brave enough to stop him. No one moved until the voices were so loud, they could hear every curse. Fables followed Hiva outside and to the back of the cabin. Before him must have been fifty—no, one hundred angry sheriffs, deputies, mayors, and townspeople with torches and pitchforks, ready to skewer who they needed to. One sheriff held Berta's wanted poster, before crumpling it up in his hands. The aliens from England followed after Fables, frozen at the sight of the mob.

Good. They needed to see this trick with their own eyes.

"Does she go by 'Iris' now?" Hiva said, not to Fables or to the mob, but to the English invaders behind him. "I see you've all been touched by her presence. It's why you've each transformed. It's why you've evolved."

Fables furrowed his brows. Evolved? He looked around and realized: he was surrounded by monsters every which way.

"But your evolution isn't enough. It's just another tool in the hands of humans committed to evil. Tell me, why hasn't she killed you yet?" He turned his chiseled face to stare at them through his golden eyes. "My sister should have set this world on fire by now. She would have in the past, without hesitation. It's been on my mind for many days. . . ."

"What's he babbling about?" cried someone from the mob. "Someone get him!"

But nobody moved.

"No matter. The task will fall to me. I've already accepted that burden. But first you will take me to her. Take me to Iris."

And just as the mob descended upon him, a massacre occurred at Younger's Bend.

PANDORA'S BOX OPENS

J OHN TEMPLE'S PORTRAIT CAST A SHADOW upon the dining table in the grand hall. Adam had kept it there for appearances—that at least he was the type of son who respected the man his father was. That his "murdering" of his father wasn't at all personal but simply a show of his loyalty to the Enlightenment Committee.

But Adam couldn't say that killing the rest of the Committee members wouldn't be personal if it came down to it. Right now, he was still considering it. It all depended on what they knew about Iris. Adam had to assume Gram and Jacques, wherever they were now, had been willing to tell Van der Ven what they'd learned about Iris that night in Club Uriel. But would Van der Ven believe them? Would he hold his cards close to his chest and keep the information to himself? It seemed to be what he was doing.

Almost every member was gathered here at the long black oak table. Van der Ven, the violet boar. Cortez, the green stag. Violet Bellerose, the golden swan. And himself, the red ram. This was unlike the meetings they'd had during Club Uriel. None of their banners were hung from the cream-colored and gold-rimmed walls or from the dark oak ceiling. No candles were lit inside the skulls of their enemies. In the quiet hours of the night, their sources of light were the standard lamps and the chandelier above, all wrought iron and helped along by the trickles of moonlight slipping through the curtain covering the bay window.

Van der Ven didn't let on that he'd learned anything particularly profound. As per usual, he had, without asking, taken his seat at the head of the table closest to the roaring fireplace. He slammed his fist on the table and began berating Adam.

"It's unacceptable that we cannot find the other champions," he bellowed, his stained teeth adding a splash of yellow to that thick black beard colonizing the bottom half of his face. "Given the secrets they know about the Committee—"

"As I've said many times, I have my spies watching them," replied an exasperated Adam. "I told you then what would come of cornering a wild animal. I have things under control."

Adam didn't want anyone using his trump cards but him. It was from his mansion that he'd dispatched them all to Oklahoma to confirm whether Iris's shadow truly existed.

"Not to mention it was *your* champions, Van der Ven, who caused this mess in the first place." A twitching Cortez stood up from his leather seat. "Your *boars.*"

Ever since they had witnessed what Van der Ven's champions Jacques and Gram had wrought at Club Uriel, it seemed like Cortez's goatee had grayed even further. Adam could tell some wisps of hair atop his head had fallen out. Bellerose was not faring any better. Despite how beautifully her burgundy hair was twisted into an elaborate style, despite her expensive hat and gorgeous wine-red evening dress, the stress was clear on her face. The usually calm and confident madame rubbed her temples with her white-gloved hands as Van der Ven scoffed.

"And where are your assassins, Gerolt?" Cortez demanded. "I'm sure they offered their continued services in exchange for escaping the death penalty. Whereas, if you'd seen what I had seen, you would know those vipers deserve a good hanging. Did you even discipline them? Or are you letting them run loose as long as they stay loyal to you?"

Van der Ven's lips quirked into a malicious grin. "You're very curious, Cortez."

"I'm curious as well," Adam chimed in. "I'm curious as to why they went on their rampage in the first place. Why they massacred our club. Did they tell you?"

It was a test. By placing Van der Ven on the spot, he could read his expressions. And Van der Ven's expressions were always so easy to read. The man was a braggart whose insecurities required him to display his superiority at all times. That was why the tiny, satisfied smirk on his lips told Adam everything. The man knew Iris was Hiva. His boars had told him.

"It's not like you to keep secrets from the Committee," Adam said, touching the base of his empty wineglass with a finger.

"It's so very much like *you*, though, isn't it, Adam? I daresay among all the members, you're the one I have the most difficulty keeping track of."

"Benini's the one you seem unable to keep track of. Wasn't watching him your job, or were you too busy scheming with your assassins?"

Van der Ven bristled.

"Besides," Adam continued, "I have nothing to hide."

"Except the murder of Cordiero."

Maintaining his calm expression, Adam glanced at Madame Bellerose, who looked elsewhere, sipping her drink. "That's a blatant lie. I'd have no reason to kill a colleague."

"But you'd have reason to keep secrets. Especially about one of your own champions."

"What?" Cortez looked between the two of them. "What's this about secrets and champions?"

Adam wanted to roll his eyes at the military man's display of pomposity. Van der Ven thought he was clever. So what if he knew Iris's identity? It wasn't ideal, but plans could always be revised. And there was a card Adam still had yet to play.

"As for secrets and champions, the worst are your boars, Van der Ven!" Cortez screeched. "Tell me, how do you plan on using them? We should all have the opportunity to employ their skills if we're not going to hang them as they deserve. They should, at the very least, answer to us for what they've done!"

Van der Ven glared at him. "If you'd like, I can arrange a close and personal meeting. . . ."

"That's it—enough," Madame Bellerose finally said, slamming her dainty fists upon the table. "We need to get this meeting back on track. What is the status of the Helios?"

"Bosch's weapons guru, Uma Malakar, is currently working with the Crown to make it operational," Adam answered. The thought of that woman unnerved him.

"Good. That's good." Bellerose swept from her brow a stray strand of hair that had fallen out of place. "Until we find the Moon Skeleton, we may have to count on finding a way to make the machine itself operational. Though I don't know why so many of you trust that brown woman's so-called 'intelligence'."

While she laughed at the very thought, Adam squeezed his hands into fists. Malakar could do it. He'd asked Iris to find his father, who was still very alive, and destroy the Moon Skeleton. But there would be no point if the Committee could engineer another way for humankind to escape the coming apocalypse. Could he destroy the Helios if need be? He didn't have nearly enough agents inside the Basement, with all its security, to do so. And Malakar herself made sure she was untouchable.

"Boris is in Africa making sure the Ark is prepared," Bellerose continued. "What we need to know now is *when* the cataclysm will descend upon us. The Hiva."

Adam twitched at Van der Ven's chuckle disguised as a cough. "I have my best astrologers studying the phenomenon."

"Not quickly enough!" Cortez's eyes were bulging, his chest heaving. This intensified version of his usual irritability was unsightly, to say the least. "With the tournament unfinished, we need a revised plan for our escape from this dying world and our entrance into the new one. How can we do so without knowing the time or the place?"

Van der Ven sat back in his chair. "If what Gram and Jacques told me is true, a tournament may not have been needed after all. What if I told you I knew how to stop the apocalypse?"

All eyes were on him. And Adam knew he relished it.

"Stop the apocalypse?" Bellerose arched an eyebrow. "But the scriptures—"

"—were not fully translated. There may be more to the Hiva than we know."

"You seem proud of yourself," Adam said quietly, and this time it was difficult not letting his annoyance show. "Do tell how you aim to stop what is inevitable."

"Nothing is inevitable, my dear boy," Van der Ven answered. "What if I told you I had a way to save this world? That if we saved this world and continued our research, we could rule both this earth *and* the other earths opened to us by the Helios?"

I'd say you were still the same greedy bastard that you always were, Adam thought to himself while Cortez and Bellerose gawked at him in surprise.

Madame Bellerose scoffed. "Oh, Gerolt, you were never much of a tease. Get to the point. What exactly are you hiding?"

"He won't tell us," Adam guessed. "Because if his desperate bid at playing the hero of this story goes well, he's hoping we'll make him leader of the New World by default. The one who saved our world from its end. Who better to guide humanity's next imperial conquest?"

Adam must have guessed correctly, for Van der Ven's face screwed up in a volatile sort of discontent that would have terrified lesser men. But after calming himself, he patted the long dagger he kept at his side as decoration for his military uniform: the Carnwennan, which Adam had procured for the man himself.

Maybe not just a decoration. Van der Ven was as greedy for blood as he was for wealth and power. And when Adam saw the man's beady black eyes soak up the sight of the other Enlighteners, he knew exactly what he was thinking.

"Well, young Temple, there are other ways to decide who rules." Van der Ven's lips spread into a wicked smile as he unsheathed his dagger. "Darwin's way. Survival of the fittest."

He'd figured it might come to this.

Adam frowned, his hand calmly reaching for the pistol at his side. But as Cortez's curses pierced the air, a swirling blue light flashed above the dining table, blowing back their hair and clothes. Adam shielded his eyes from the brightness, only to start when he heard several thumps land upon the black oak.

Boris Bosch's former champions fell out of the portal and toppled onto the table one after another.

The Enlighteners jumped out of their seats in shock. Adam's guards ran into the room, Van der Ven held his blade at the ready, but none could move. Cherice and Jacob fell out of the portal first, holding two strangers: one a girl dressed like a highwaywoman from America's Wild West, her long, curly brown hair spilling over Cherice's vice grip; and the other a young girl in a black pinafore, her dark brown body curled up in Jacob's arms.

"He killed them all." Jacob gripped Madame Bellerose's sleeve as the little one he'd been carrying ran into the safety of the highwaywoman's arms. "Oh my God. *All* of them. With a *look*." Jacob swallowed as Bellerose brushed his hand off her as if he were dirty. "Iris isn't the only Hiva. The other Hiva was there, and he's coming. He's *coming*."

Adam's expression tensed as he glanced up at Hawkins's portal.

"Hiva? What is the meaning of this?" Cortez shrieked, his chair overturned on the floor. "Who dares—?"

A man who must have been built of iron landed atop the table in a crouch, his boots slamming the black oak before he dropped the other man he'd been carrying: Hawkins. The others jumped out of the way. Hawkins lay groaning on the table as the man straightened up—no, he wasn't a man. He was the statue of an Olympian god come to life, his long gold curls alight with spring flowers and his forehead adorned with a crown—a touch of the divine. It made his attempts to blend into humanity, by wearing the clothes of a regular man, all the more ludicrous. The moment his golden eyes crossed paths with Adam, the young Lord Temple knew. There was indeed a second Hiva, and this was he.

Hawkins . . . Adam gritted his teeth. He'd shown the orphan thief the inside of his estate. He was supposed to report back to Adam after seeing Hiva. Not bring Hiva with him. . . .

Just before Hawkins's portal closed, another young man happened to slip through—a curly-haired boy whose thin, gawky body landed unceremoniously on the table next to the god.

The god didn't seem to notice.

"Her anima saturates this place." And Hiva glared at Adam specifically. "Where is she?"

"You!" Cortez leaned over the table, gripping Hiva's ankle. A worthy feat of courage he'd soon regret. "Did you hear me, boy? I asked you—who are you? How dare you—"

"I am Hiva," the god said.

Then he burned Cortez alive from the inside out.

After a moment of horrified silence, Bellerose started screaming. Van der Ven twitched in surprise, blowing the ashes that had once been Cortez out of his face.

Hiva turned stiffly, an unstoppable automaton with gears that needed greasing. "Bring her to me: the one you call Iris."

"Iris?" Adam heard Bellerose hiss, and a pang of anxiety gripped him as he felt his carefully laid plans spinning out of control. "Why that blasted girl?"

No. You knew this was a possibility. Adam turned to Van der Ven. "That man identified himself as Hiva. Take him down!" he yelled.

Van der Ven didn't need telling twice. He'd already lunged forward, stabbing Hiva in the chest, then cutting off his arm while Hiva was distracted by his first wound.

Gasps. The arm hit the floor with a thump. Hiva only glanced blithely at his missing arm before looking back up at Van der Ven.

"The same arm she took," he said calmly, and closed his eyes. "Yes, I can sense her. Her anima . . ." He breathed in and out. "One hundred and forty-nine degrees southeast. Over a body of water. In a bustling city two hundred and thirty-seven miles from where I stand . . ." He turned to Adam. "You bear her scent the most among the men I've met. You will bring her to me—"

With a roar, Van der Ven swung his blade and severed Hiva's head from his body. The Carnwennan had had a particularly bloody night, though not the one Van der Ven had envisioned.

The imperial wreath that Hiva had worn upon his head flew off and smashed into pieces against the wall. Adam's breath hitched as he stared at the old general. As perplexed as Van der Ven was, a kill was a kill. And a swift one. The man couldn't contain his pride.

The gawky young man who'd come out of the portal last was screaming, shrieking in disbelief and despair as Hiva's body collapsed upon the table. "You took him from me!" he screamed, sobbing. "You've destroyed me! Just kill me!"

Inconsolable, he held on to Hiva's headless body in tears, squeezing it against his chest like a child would his favorite toy. He didn't know what Adam knew: Hivas couldn't die, not with the indestructible crystal hearts beating in their chests. Not until they'd finished their mission. He'd regenerate. Maybe soon.

"Men! Take them all to the Basement," ordered Adam.

"A bustling city two hundred and thirty-seven miles southeast over a body of water . . ." The brown-haired girl Adam didn't recognize nodded. "Got it loud and clear."

She reached for her gun and shot one of Adam's guards in the face.

"Lulu!" The gunslinger grabbed the little girl's hand and made a run for it.

"Berta!" Cherice sounded desperate as she knocked one of the guards down, just as he aimed at their fleeing backs. "Berta, wait!"

Berta. Yes, she and Maximo looked alike. Adam gritted his teeth. "Men!" He wanted Berta here. He wanted all his chess pieces under his control, not wild and on the run. But Cherice, Hawkins, and Jacob wouldn't let the guards pursue. It was all his men could do to keep them subdued. Berta and the little girl Lulu had escaped. What a mess.

With a heavy sigh, Adam lifted his hand. "The Basement," he repeated. "Quickly. And from now on, if any of them move or even so much as *talk*, shoot to kill." He couldn't afford any more loose ends or loose lips, not with the Committee members so close.

The freaks were surrounded, glaring as the guards' guns were trained on them.

"That monster . . ." Bellerose wrapped her arms around her body. "We understood Hiva to be an *event*, not a person. But was that thing really Hiva?"

"I have no reason to believe otherwise," Adam said. "He said as much. He demonstrated his power. He is Hiva. The cataclysm. Which means this is a wonderful turn of events."

"What?" Madame Bellerose spat in disbelief.

Adam thought quickly, trying to spin the situation to his favor. "We have Hiva. *Here.* Therefore, we can stop the cataclysm. We only need to keep him locked away in the most secure part of the Basement—along with his co-conspirators."

A furious Cherice opened her mouth, but several guns clicked before she could utter a word of complaint.

"Then what about that woman? Iris—your champion?"

Adam grunted as Madame Bellerose lifted her chin, watching him carefully through narrowed eyes. She flicked her head toward Jacob. "That one already said it. 'Iris isn't the only Hiva.' Tell me, what in God's name did the boy mean by that?"

When no one answered her, Madame Bellerose's cheeks flushed, incensed. "The Hiva is an *event*. The event that will cause the apocalypse. The event we've been preparing for all this time. That *girl*—" She shook her head in disbelief. "The bestial little—but that can't be. That—"

And then Madame Bellerose stood up straight, her eyes narrowing as a sudden realization came over her.

"My dear Adam . . ." She touched her bottom lip as she considered him with a suspicious glare. "The truth about Iris. Did you already . . . ?"

"Van der Ven—this is the news you wished to tell us, no?" As fast and sharp as a knife's edge, Adam pivoted the conversation to the older man. "The information you were dangling over our heads earlier. That Iris is Hiva. Gram and Jacques told you, didn't they?" He shook his head, baffled, enraged, whatever he needed to be to sell his sense of betrayal. "You knew and withheld such an important piece of information from us. Kept the secret to your own advantage. What else are you keeping from us? If you'd warned us, Cortez could still be alive—"

Van der Ven's beady eyes widened in shock. "That isn't—!"

"'There may be more to the Hiva.' Weren't those your words?" Madame Bellerose folded her arms. Adam could tell she was still struggling to grasp the situation, to accept the shocking truth. Beads of sweat that must have been out of pure shock and frustration began to mire her perfectly done bangs.

"And letting Gram and Jacques go, all for your own sake? Like Adam said—were you trying to gain the upper hand?"

It worked. Van der Ven was now the sole target of Madame Bellerose's suspicious gaze.

"Men," Bellerose said. "Escort Gerolt Van der Ven to his home. The Committee rules that he should be under house arrest until further notice. He *and* his assassins. Put extra men on them if need be. We'll decide what to do with him later. Are we in agreement, Adam?"

"Unfortunately, yes. We have no choice."

Van der Ven was a violent fool, but there were too many guards, and guns and bullets were faster than the swing of his blade. With an incredulous laugh, he sheathed his blade and stroked his black beard as a few guards showed him out of the room with the rest of the champions.

An extra nudge and Adam might be able to pin Cordiero's death on the gaudy man too, but that would have to come later. For now, witnessing Van der Ven's utter defeat was enough balm for the confusing events that had marred an already tense night. As for Iris's identity being known, it was something he could work with still.

Once they were alone, Bellerose turned to him. Or rather, *on* him.

"As for that African champion of yours . . ." Bellerose managed to squeeze an extra hint of disdain into her voice as she brushed back her hair. "We still need proof of her identity. I'm sorry, but I have trouble believing such an inconsequential *Negro girl* holds the fate to all mankind."

"We'll learn more after studying Hiva inside the Crystal Palace," Adam said. "As for my champion, it's something I can look into."

"Because you can certainly be trusted when it comes to her."

"I killed my own father for you. My own flesh and blood." Adam earnestly placed a hand on his chest where he supposed his heart should have been. "If that isn't enough to show my loyalty to the Committee, I'm not sure what is."

Madame Bellerose, ever suspicious, wasn't satisfied with his answer. Though she feigned apathy, he could see the beginnings of a plan hatching in that beautiful, sick head of hers, and the very idea infuriated him. Adam didn't like surprises unless he orchestrated them himself. But Pandora's box was now open. From now on, his role was to stay ahead of the tide. There was only so much he could do to keep the Committee and this new Hiva off Iris's trail.

Adam showed Madame Bellerose out of his home, following the procession of Van der Ven, the guards and champions, their new Oklahoma friends, and the corpse of Hiva. Then he went up to his room and readied himself for Paris.

7

THE HEM OF HIVA'S ROBES BRUSHED the dirty streets as she passed by rows of little houses built with cheap blue bricks.

"And so, my goddess, our latest inventions are almost complete." Nyeth kept a respectable distance from her, though his sandals seemed to scuffle inches closer when he thought she wasn't looking. "With them, and with your blessing, the Naacal will become a civilization greater than any other in history."

"Any other," Hiva repeated. "Are you sure, Nyeth? The earth's history is long. Atlantis was once a great civilization too. Greater and more terrible than this."

"Atlantis?" Nyeth cocked his head to the side. It was a foreign word to him. He'd never heard of such a people before. Of course he hadn't. They were long dead. "I'm sorry?"

"Never mind."

The town of Zoar was a poor one, and poverty looked the same everywhere in the land Naacalians had built. Women holding their filthy children close on their doorsteps. Destitute men begging for alms. Nyeth ignored them all, enraptured instead by Hiva's presence. His tax collectors dealt with them, hassling them for tithes to the church. Pain and suffering. She'd seen it all before.

"So tell me," she'd once said to the One who'd created her. The One who'd called her once more from the depths of the earth. "Why did you awaken me? Every civilization is the same. Why judge this one when the next will be just as wicked?"

But the One only spoke to her when necessary. Now was apparently not that time.

"Teach me about these latest inventions, Nyeth," Hiva said as a group of children played a game of who could outrun the tax collectors.

At this, Nyeth brimmed with pride. "Ah, yes. Well, we have one invention I believe to be our greatest invention. It'll be completed in just a few years: the generation of artificial life."

"The creation of new life?" asked Hiva, eyebrows raised.

"To replace those deemed useless, whom we can quickly cull by your hand, of course. The Naacal thrive on productivity." Nyeth placed his hands behind his back, his blond hair flowing. "We can advance much further than where we are now. It's the detritus of society that keeps us from reaching the greatest heights as quickly as we can. We need to rid ourselves of those who cannot work and produce."

And someone caught Nyeth's eye. A withered old man lying on the ground, famished. Boils infested his skin. Though he lay in the middle of the road, no one would go near him.

Nyeth shuddered in disgust at the sight of this man, his hips covered in sack-cloth and wisps of hair clinging to his skin under the sweltering sun. "Move," he ordered. "You're in the presence of a goddess and the clergy of Naacal."

Of course, he wouldn't. He couldn't. The man was awake, but his legs were too thin to stand on. Hiva stared at the frail man—this human who'd captured her attention with a frightful suddenness.

What is the purpose of humanity? she'd once asked the One in those rare moments it would appear before her. And once it had answered:

I leave the answer to you. Though it seems, after all these eons, there's still much for you to understand.

"I said, move!" Nyeth spat on the ground and gestured arrogantly in the air. "This, my goddess—this is who I mean by detritus. Waste." With an impatient sigh, he took a sharp knife he kept at his side and walked up to the sick man.

"Nyeth...," Hiva said, her mouth hanging open as blood splashed onto the ruby handle of Nyeth's small blade. After he'd cut the man's neck, he ordered the tax collectors to dispose of the body.

"Keep it out of Hiva's sight so as not to offend the goddess," he ordered, giving the knife to one of his men to clean. He dusted himself off and approached Hiva, annoyed as if his time had been greatly wasted, though he did not seem to want to show it. In front of Hiva, he bowed and gestured toward the road. "The road is free. Please continue," he said.

But Hiva was paralyzed. The men and women who'd watched the murder cowered on their doorsteps or else, once they'd paid their tithes to the church, ran back inside their tiny houses. Nothing had changed in this town. The earth too had continued to spin without ceasing. Nothing had changed at all except that the man in front of her had been murdered on a whim. Gone in an instant for a reason Hiva couldn't fathom.

A strange emotion murmured inside her. What was it? This hot whisper stirring within her?

Ah. Was this... rage?

Hiva gazed up at the sky. White birds soared in clusters toward faint clouds. The sun blazed. And that man, alive mere minutes before, was now gone.

What was the purpose of humanity? Since her rebirth, she'd spent many years among the Naacal, learning their ways. She'd witnessed deaths. She'd caused deaths on their behalf. But this death. This cruelty. This grain of wheat upon a balance grasped by unfeeling hands... a scale tipping...

What was the purpose of humanity? Why did such brokenness seem to follow them wherever they went? Was suffering and anguish endemic to them? Or was there another way?

But Nyeth was confused. He couldn't understand. He refused to see. "My goddess?"

That was the moment Hiva decided. Perhaps the next civilization would do better.

"You're wrong, Nyeth," she said quietly. "You all must die."

"Isoke?"

Iris awoke with a start inside her tavern room, sweating and heaving, Rin gripping her shoulders. Iris pushed her out of the way and threw up all over the floor.

Iris's hands felt as cold as the December snow on the Parisian streets. As the bartender brought plates of food to her table, she hit her left leg with her fist to keep herself from remembering the dream—and that man. Disposed of like a morsel of dust stuck in one's eye. Just a poor, sick man. An unsuspecting innocent. Like Anne. What had either of them done to deserve—

No. She couldn't let herself think of it, because the more she thought of it, the harder that similar, unspeakable rage began to scratch at the surface. She held it at bay. It was just a dream. A dream of a long-ago memory. She wasn't Hiva anymore. And never would be again.

It was already such a dreary morning. There was no need to add any more gray to it.

"Sailing out to sea?"

"Yep."

That was what Iris could glean from the conversation of the two bearded men drinking in the tavern behind her, but the rest was a jumble. She caught their reflections in the mirror: sunken red cheeks, navy-blue jackets, and loose-fitting pants. Berets that didn't fit on their cone-shaped heads. A lot of slurping, belching, and drunken giggling. It didn't exactly make her miserable potatoes appetizing.

Max loved potatoes, an annoying voice in her mind reminded her—a voice she shushed immediately, but not before catching her lips in a sweet, nostalgic smile. In the short time they'd known each other, they'd barely had enough time to learn about each other. She'd barely had enough time to learn about *any* of the tournament participants, but then perhaps that was owed to the nature of a two-week battle to the death. Still, Max had loved potatoes. Such a little detail. She clung to it as if it were her lifeline.

She looked at Rin in front of her, who'd eaten quickly and mechanically so as to keep her body functioning. Leaning back in her chair, Rin focused her one good eye out into the tavern while she sat with her arms crossed.

"Benini's informant should be here soon, no?" Rin said, looking impatient. "With information on your scheduled meeting with Leroux. You've waited long enough."

Iris nodded. "Where and when. That's what I need to know. I have to know how to prepare myself. . . ."

"There are some things I need to do in the meantime myself."

Iris raised an eyebrow. "Such as?"

Rin had remained by her side all this while. Woken her out of strange dreams. Iris was happy she wasn't alone, but she still couldn't be entirely comfortable around the young warrior.

Rin stiffened a bit, but eventually relented. "I'm meeting an old friend."

"Old friend?" Iris had responded so incredulously, Rin bristled with indignation. "I mean . . . I didn't know—"

"That I have friends?"

The heat rushed to her cheeks. "No, well . . ."

Rin sighed. "He's from the city Ajashe in the Oyo Kingdom. Yoruba," she added, and Iris nodded as if it made things clearer. "He goes to school here at the École Cambodgienne, training as an interpreter. One of the few students *not* from Cambodia. He taught me a lot of my French in the time I've been here. He helped secure my connection to Madame Bellerose."

"Bellerose? He's rather well connected, then."

"Quite connected, yes."

Iris had heard of such secondary schools, the ones that trained children of prominent families in Asia and Africa—though in some cases, the children were kept more as hostages than anything else. Jinn had said his father had come to Paris while exiled from the Ottoman Empire. Had he gone to a school like this?

"Why are you meeting him now?" Iris leaned over with interest, propping her chin up with her hands. "Rekindling a secret love affair I don't know about?"

Rin's stone-cold expression said no.

Despite her slight disappointment that Rin wouldn't humor her, Iris was still intrigued. How much did Iris really know about this girl, aside from the more fantastical details of her life? She was still in many ways a mystery. Nevertheless, by now they were at the very least accomplices.

"Um." Iris squirmed in her seat. "I'm sorry about your mission. Messing it up, I mean." She wanted to stop, but a pang of guilt kept her talking. "But I want to make sure you know that I won't let anyone hurt you. Not the king, not the *ahosi*. You have nothing to fear."

"There's very little I fear," Rin responded flatly, folding her arms.

Iris scratched her head, because the ensuing awkward silence stretching between them was almost too much to bear. In a way, wasn't Rin doing her a favor by sticking with her? Helping her? It couldn't kill Iris to try to bridge the gap between them. Get to know her better, maybe. But what should she ask? *What's your favorite color? What are your deepest, darkest fears?* Did she even have a right to know?

"So you're meeting a friend," Iris said. And when Rin didn't respond, Iris sighed and gave up. Rin was meeting a friend. How nice. Iris lowered her head and thought of Jinn, sucking in a long, silent breath and blinking her eyes to keep them dry. Being in Paris made her think of him—how she'd once wondered if they could visit here together again, this time by themselves, to find the home in which he'd grown up with his father.

Please be okay, she thought to herself as the chatter of the tavern continued.

"What nonsense," Rin said suddenly after a while. She took a sip of water. "Then again, perhaps there's some truth to it. . . ."

Iris cocked her head to the side. "Truth to what? What are you talking about?"

"The men behind you are talking," Rin told her, "about a ship that was taken over several days ago near the Gulf of Guinea."

Iris tilted her head. "A takeover?"

"By *ghosts*. Apparently, whispers are spreading among the sailors to stay clear of the cursed ship where spirits disappear and appear with the shadows of the moon." Grimly amused, Rin laughed, her voice quiet and low. "Ghosts lost at sea, perhaps. I'm sure all the bodies killed and thrown into that blood-soaked ocean over the years would have unfinished business with certain ships and sailors."

"Do you believe in ghosts?" Iris blurted it out and immediately felt stupid. And when Rin raised an eyebrow, she added, "Just curious."

"Hmm? What do you mean by that? Do you not see your ancestors in your dreams?" Rin started, truly surprised and confused, but then she nodded as if she understood. "Ah, that's right. You're an otherworldly being. You *have* no ancestors. No family."

Rin had a way of speaking that kept Iris never entirely sure if the under-lying sharp edge of judgment was just part of the girl's blunt personality or a planned, subtle attack. It struck nonetheless. Iris thought of Granny and immediately wanted to fight back, only to remember that she'd met the old woman fifty years ago in an attempt to kidnap her and did not even know her real name. Rin had a culture. A heritage. Family members that had given birth to her and her ancestors. Iris's blood flowed through no one. She wasn't human. She was *of* the earth, yes . . . and yet somehow not a part of it all.

Iris touched her glass of water sheepishly. "Is that one of the reasons you want to go back to Dahomey? To see your family? The *ahosi*?"

"The . . . ?"

Iris sensed Rin's body twitch then and there. And when she looked up, Rin's good eye was trained on hers.

"What exactly is your definition of family?" Rin asked darkly, her shoulders slightly lifted around her ears.

An irregular thump of her heart stopped Iris from answering. She thought of Jinn, Granny, and even little Egg, but dared not speak. The anger simmering beneath Rin's skin frightened her.

Rin scoffed, shaking her head in disbelief. "How idiotic. But what can I expect from someone who only *observes* humanity—"

"But can never be one of them, right?" Iris swallowed, her lips trembling a little, but did find the courage to look at the younger girl. "An oddity such as myself..."

"An oddity indeed." It took a while for Rin to speak again. "You want to save humanity. But then what? What do you think your responsibility is here on this planet if not what you were created for?"

Responsibility? Iris had never thought of it that way. Her reasons for defying her mission were rather simple.

"What is your *goal*, Isoke?"

"To live."

"Among thieves and murderers? Is it okay to just live with the power you have without ever using it to help others and cut down the merciless?"

Iris shifted uncomfortably. "I just want to live in peace. I don't want or *need* to judge anyone. Not anymore."

Rin looked away. "Some of us *should* be judged."

Just then, a man in dirty clothes with his cap lowered over his eyes walked past the matronly waitress, who was picking mugs out of a drunkards' hands for refills. After dropping a parcel onto their wooden table, he turned the corner, disappearing around the grandfather clock to another section of the tavern. Rin watched Iris, confused, as Iris pulled the white string apart and opened the paper package.

"From Benini. *Finally*," Iris whispered after she pulled out a card. "I'm to meet him at seven o'clock tonight. He'll escort me to a party that André Leroux's wife is hosting in their home—some grand apartment in the Boulevard des Capucines."

Rin raised an eyebrow. "The woman just happens to be holding a party tonight?"

Peeking out from the package was a bit of red lace. Iris checked around her to make sure no one was watching, then pulled out the rest of it. The blood rushed from her face.

A gift for this evening's special guest and anticipated entertainer.

"What is this nonsense?" she almost screamed, before shrinking back down again when men started to look her way. The tiny, sparkling crimson bra and underwear were not nearly big enough to cover what they were meant to. She shoved them back into the package.

"A sight to behold," Rin said sarcastically with a little smile as she sipped her water.

At least now she had a game plan. A chance to meet that man and get Nyeth's ring. But there was no way in hell she was wearing the hand towels that pervert Benini had gotten for her.

She stood up quickly, tossing Rin the package. "I'm going shopping. Man the room."

Rin shook her head, amused, while Iris scurried out the tavern door.

Of course, being a performer, Iris was used to appropriately skimpy outfits for the time and occasion, but this time, Benini was just being deliberately *heinous.*

And so that night, after using a bit of the money she'd gained from days of panhandling, she appeared in Benini's living room dressed as a proper mime with her tuxedo, white gloves, and dress shirt. Her charcoal-painted lips spread wide when she saw the man's disappointment, her yellow sun hat sliding askew on her head. The violet bow Jinn had given her was still tied resolutely around her braids.

"This is . . ." Benini looked her up and down with a wineglass in his hands. "Quite the disappointment." He took a sip. "What I'd prepared for you would have suited you and your clientele so much better."

"Really?" Iris checked herself. "I feel I'm quite lovely, if I do say so myself. *You,* on the other hand . . ."

And now it was Iris's turn to look him up and down. His ensemble looked like a cross between a Victorian dressing gown and Joseph's many-colored coat. "Aren't you in hiding?"

"One must never hide his splendor." And, tossing his drink behind him, he grabbed Iris around the elbow. Iris yanked her arm out of his grasp and strode out the door.

Rin was still out meeting her friend, preparing something on her own about which Iris knew nothing. She propped up her head with a hand, her elbow on the window ledge, watching Parisians stroll by as Benini's extravagant carriage whisked them down the foggy streets. She'd left her usual outfit back in their tavern room, but she'd remembered, at least, to take Max's pocket watch with her. Checking it, it seemed they'd be right on time.

Leroux's apartment was in a white five-story complex with freestone facades, wide rectangular windows, and balconies. A Haussmann delight, Benini called it, though Iris had no idea what he'd meant. They arrived to the party at the same time as many of his guests. By the entrance, an usher announced their arrival: "Riccardo Benini," she heard the gray-mustached man say, though her name was conveniently skipped. What a surprise.

Guests exchanged greetings underneath the chandelier inside the expansive drawing room, some single, some paired up as couples. A woman in a peach-colored dress trimmed with exquisite lace welcomed Benini with open arms as soon as they arrived, while other women stood by the porcelain lamps, hiding their faces with white fans as they stared at Iris, gossiping.

"Ah, Madame Leroux—" Benini started after kissing the woman on her pink cheek, and as they babbled in French, Iris's heart jumped up into her throat.

Leroux. Then where was André? Was he among the monotonous horde of Frenchmen who stood with their top hats properly upright on their heads or held in their hands? With the exception of perhaps Benini, European gentlemen all seemed to favor the same dull style. The stiff backs and brass buttons reminded her of the elites in Club Uriel, now corpses. Was Leroux in one of the easy chairs lined up by the gilded arched windows? Was he discussing politics with the men by the fireplace? Or was his heeled shoe among the many on the wooden floor?

"I'm so very happy I was able to convince Madame Leroux to hold this party on such short notice," Benini said to Iris. "Who knew an esteemed entertainer who'd worked under the famous proprietor Pablo Fanque himself would be here in Paris? Of course, after I told her, she just *had* to show off in front of her friends."

Iris snorted. If only she'd been so lucky as to work under Fanque instead of Coolie, but as far as employment opportunities went, she'd missed that one by a couple of decades. Madame Caroline's famous near miss on the tightrope in Bolton was already fifteen years ago. What a thrill that must have been. Iris wished she could have seen it.

Madame Leroux babbled and tittered behind a white-gloved hand. Benini expertly followed along. "How charming," he said, and clapped Iris on the shoulder. "It seems you're only a warm-up to the main event."

"Of course."

"They're to have a séance soon. The medium is on her way. The women insisted. Such a common parlor delight; I've had quite a few in my time. Why, I know Daniel Dunglas Home personally, that pithy Scot. Could never stay in his chair, always levitating, that man."

Iris didn't care. "Where is Leroux?" she hissed.

"Not here. In his study on the second floor, conducting some business. I just asked." Benini maintained his smile even as some of the gentlemen sneered at his ridiculous attire. "But you've got to a job to do first, my dear. The one I booked you for."

Madame Leroux's blond ringlets of hair bobbled as she bent her head a little to stare at Iris. Benini seemed to be introducing her, given his outstretched hand and her responsive giggle. Turning to the crowd, she clapped her hands together, drawing their attention. Iris imagined, by the excited red flush of the woman's round cheeks, that she was being introduced to her audience.

"*Chocolat!*" the woman and Benini announced together. Wait, was that supposed to be *her*? When Benini winked, Iris rolled her eyes. The thunderous applause and pleased laughter pretty much confirmed that "Chocolat" was being called on to perform.

Benini bent down and whispered in her ear, "I hope you have your routine ready to go," before pushing her out into the center of the cheering crowd.

She did. Being in the circus for ten years made a simple mime routine pretty easy. Making crowds laugh by playing the fool, twirling about, and stumbling over her own feet wasn't all that difficult for a consummate professional. Hearing the mocking laughter from women and jeers from young men while trying not to notice the lewd faces from "gentlemen" old enough to be the father of a bride—now that took discipline and mental fortitude. As she pulled flowers out of a vase for magic tricks and juggled wine bottles, she suddenly remembered Jinn and felt an ache in her chest. Performing with him always made the indignity of being stared at by white faces so much easier. Was he still chasing his ghost? Had that sickening cannibal Gram fallen to Jinn's flames, or had he made Jinn his supper instead?

Loud gasps sucked the air out of the room as she almost dropped an expensive Château de Goulaine wine bottle on the rug but caught it in the crook of her right leg in the nick of time. Applause, applause. Yes, yes. The usual thrill just wasn't there as she impatiently handed the bottles over to some rather excited young gentlemen.

Benini reminded her of Coolie as he roused the audience to even greater applause. She gave one final bow and then was led out of the room like she knew she would be.

The entertainment isn't exactly allowed to mingle with the guests, Benini had told her on the way there. *You should know that. But then there are benefits to being excluded, aren't there?*

Four servants passed by her, carrying a round table and a candelabra inside the drawing room. The usher cried, "Mademoiselle Pascal!" and in walked an older woman with brown ringlets down to her bare shoulders. Her long, thick black dress exposed her neck and chest as well, just below her collarbone. Iris had seen other mediums, and this one fit the bill. Her thick dress, a long skirt of layered frills sweeping the floor, seemed so heavy that Iris wondered how she could move in it. Her lace sleeves billowed behind her as she walked.

The crowd was so riled up and excited to start their silly séance that nobody noticed when Iris knocked out the usher and stuffed him in the closet under the stairs. Then she climbed up to the second floor. It wasn't hard to figure out where André might be hiding. The voices behind the sturdy third door on the right of the narrow hall were not exactly subtle.

"How many more ships do we have in that area?" Iris heard the furious bellow. She was surprised to hear English, though a Parisian accent very clearly weighted down each syllable.

"Just one." An English accent answered this time. "But she's staying clear of the British fleet, sir. Every ship in the area knows to stay clear of that mess. There's nothing to worry about, Mr. Leroux."

So the man who sounded like his neck was about to pop was indeed Leroux. But what was this about a "mess"?

Making sure the hallway was still empty, Iris leaned in close to the door.

"Once they've successfully cornered and captured the *Ataegina*, your vessels should be clear for the Gold Coast, sir."

Footsteps. Heavy boots clicked toward the door. Iris straightened up, readying herself. "Well, you'll excuse me if I refuse to relax. I have a lot of money on the line. Continue to find out what you can about the standoff. I have to attend my wife's nonsense—"

Max had taught her a few tricks during their short stay together, namely how to spirit objects away without anyone noticing. When combined with a circus performance that encouraged audience participation, it was all the more useful. For example, if one were to slip a pocketknife out of the jacket of a pompous young gentleman too busy laughing at your strange clothes and exotic face to notice he'd been looted, one could then use said blade to threaten information out of a not-so-young, but no doubt equally pompous aristocrat.

The moment the door opened, the blade was at Leroux's throat.

"I'm here for the ring," Iris said, and forced André Leroux to stumble back until she could close the door behind her.

8

THE MANET PAINTINGS HUNG ON EACH side of the filing cabinets. A man in a beige suit cowered near the paneled walls near the window. He'd tried his luck and gotten away with a nasty bump on the head thanks to Iris. Leroux sat in the chair on the other side of his wooden desk, staring down the blade of the deadly mime threatening him.

"The ring," Iris said again once they were all settled. "I know you know which ring I'm talking about."

Leroux twitched. Account books, filled no doubt with many business transactions, were stacked behind him. Iris had told him to keep his hands on his lap.

"Gutsy that a filthy *négresse* would steal from me," said Leroux.

"Spare me the superiority complex." Iris kicked the arm of his chair. He grunted as his side slammed against his desk. Three leatherbound books shuddered and tumbled down. "The director of the British Museum sold it to you for quite the sum. You have it. I want it."

"Why?"

Iris answered him with a wicked smile. "Turns out the one with the knife doesn't have to answer that question."

Iris could see his legs twitching. He didn't look all that intimidating, not with his gelled black hair split in the center like a schoolboy's. Still, he didn't flinch as he peered at Iris through his glasses. "The chest."

There was one of great size and with exquisite carvings in the right-most corner of the room. Iris ordered his colleague to unlock it. As his knees knocked, the man opened his mouth to yell, but when Iris put a finger to her lips and flashed her knife, he shut his own quite quickly and scurried to the corner, then twisted open the iron plate.

If it were Iris, she would have kept something so precious inside something unassuming, like a box—not this: a red leather ring case, which saw Nyeth's ring snuggled inside a marshmallow of satin. Whether they were in black britches or flowing robes the color of the sunset, European gentlemen certainly had an insatiable need to sate their own inflated egos.

The Coral Ring. It'd been cleaned, because its surface was glimmering bright beneath the globes affixed to the walls, lighting the room. Something within it cried out to her. Or someone. Nyeth? No, there were more voices growing louder, pressing against her heartbeat. As if in a trance, she passed by Leroux and held out her hand. He gave her the case, which she threw to the floor after plucking out the ring.

Its quiet cold seeped through her white glove, causing a shiver to run deep into her core. She sucked in a long breath, her heart beginning to pound as ancient fear and hatred poisoned her immortal blood.

"Can you hear them?" Iris whispered, because she could. The howls of the Naacal begging for mercy. The apocalyptic end of a corrupt civilization to make way for a better future. "This ring carries so much sadness. So much pain. But you wouldn't know. How could you? Even if you did, you wouldn't care. Someone like you . . ."

Leroux's man must have received some kind of signal from his boss, because suddenly a clammy hand wrapped around her neck. Still, the hold was hesitant at best. Iris was able to twist out of the trembling coward's grip. Pulling him down by his bow tie, she kneed him in the forehead, knocking him out, just as Leroux made a run for it behind her.

"Help!" he cried in French as he stumbled down the hall, but Iris was too fast. The lights had been dimmed down there for the sake of their parlor game. With the ring in one hand, Iris threw her elbow around his neck and forced him to his knees.

"You must be a member of Club Uriel too. Your family knows Riccardo Benini, after all. Am I right?"

The quick, nervous flinch of Leroux's eyes told Iris she was right. The Club Uriel members weren't supposed to know anything the Committee wouldn't want them to—like details on the civilizations they'd studied, or the machinery and artifacts they'd procured. But with his connection to the museum director and the director's connection to the Enlightenment Committee, it was more than possible for Leroux to know what he shouldn't.

"What did the museum's director tell you about this ring?" Iris whispered, on the chance her hunch was right and both knew more than they were letting on. "There are countless rings you could've bought. I saw a few pretty ones around your wife's fingers. This one's special."

But a normal ring wasn't enough for men like the Club Uriel patrons. They needed something exotic. Unique. Something that spoke to ancient histories untold, known to man only by the devil-may-care, death-courting tendencies of explorers willing to go to the farthest regions of the world and face any danger to search for treasure. That was why he kept Nyeth's ring in his own office instead of giving it to his wife, like many a gentleman would. A special object to make a lesser man feel special himself.

Iris thought of the elite who had sat self-importantly in their chairs at the auction meant to sell her. The storeroom filled with sarcophaguses and half-crumbled skulls. The way they stared at Max, too, as if he were a piece of meat.

When Leroux cursed in French, Iris yanked his collar. "I'll ask again: What did the museum's director tell you?"

Leroux let out a grunt and spat. "Only that it is an ancient ring believed to belong to the people of Mu."

Mu—the continent where the Naacalian aristocracy had resided. The richest and most decadent.

"He had his colleague, Churchward, examine some old ruins and tablets. The ring. I-it . . . it's connected to a place where gods once spoke and made all the earth shudder—the place where heaven dwells. . . ."

The place where heaven dwells ... Iris frowned. Where had she heard that before?

"But I'm not interested in all that nonsense," Leroux continued quickly, sweat dripping off his chin. "I heard what happened to the club. Please. I was only hoping to auction it off to pay for some shipping losses—if you want it, just take it! Take it and spare my life!"

And just as he began to scream for help again, she knocked him unconscious. She sighed. She really hated doing this. The last thing she wanted was to let her anger get the best of her, knowing what she was capable of. The memory of that man in the Library of Rule still hadn't left her no matter how hard she tried to push it out of her mind. Nor the one in the Crystal Palace. She wasn't Hiva any longer or Isoke, but Iris had blood on her hands as well.

The crowd below was cooing and gasping. Iris snuck downstairs and peeked around the corner of the drawing room entrance. She couldn't believe how many white-tied gentlemen, generals with military sashes, and women draped in expensive jewels sat enraptured around the table, lights off but for the candles in the center, holding hands with each other. All led by Mademoiselle Whatever-Her-Name-Was, whose eyes were closed as she lifted her head up and mumbled deliriously. Having a chat with Napoleon, was she?

These people had no idea what it felt like to truly be haunted. To have spirits cross time and space just to howl things at you. Iris saw them in her dreams. She looked at her hands, at the ring that seemed to weigh more than it should in the center of her palm.

The Coral Ring. This tiny, unassuming ring had once adorned the finger of a man who hated her. A man who wanted to save his people from her. She could feel his hatred.

It arrested her, this ring. She should have escaped by now, especially now while the gentle breeze from the windowless room fluttered the hair of the guests, while they closed their eyes and felt the presence of their dead loved ones. But Iris couldn't move.

Your wings can be clipped. One can win against a god....

She could still see Nyeth's blood spurting from his mouth inside the Coral

Temple, the underground refuge that would become his tomb. She couldn't get that image out of her head.

"Imaginez que vos esprits sont suspendus," the medium said. It was already so dark inside the room that for a moment, as she stood underneath the staircase, Iris forgot her senses. *"Ils flottent dans les étendues de temps. . . ."*

The medium's voice was far away, as far as the ashes of the Naacal in civilizations past. Back during the time when gods were real. When gods walked.

The place where heaven dwells. Right. It was from John Temple's journal. The place where heaven dwells . . .

The ring was now ice cold. It bore into her palm.

"Retournez avec moi. Entendez les voix des Titans qui faisaient la guerre et des démons qui saignaient avant l'ère de l'homme. . . ."

The Solar Titan. The Shadow Titan. Iris closed her eyes and saw a mechanical contraption big enough to blot out the sun, climbing spiderlike down the Atlas Mountains, its great pincers penetrating stone. She felt as if she were floating, carried by the wind.

Carried to the place of her rebirth.

The dark cavern that would become a mining site owned by the Crown through their National African Company. In the fertile Oil Rivers region in West Africa, where the white shards of her crystal heart still lay. Where she'd climbed out of the earth, ready to do her work again. But there was something deeper inside the earth. Deeper than even the Crown knew . . .

"Retournez avec moi . . . et entendez des voix depuis longtemps oubliées. . . ."

Sister, why? Iris closed her eyes. Out of the pool of darkness, golden eyes mesmerized her with the despair of betrayal.

"Les voix des morts . . ."

Sister . . .

Iris walked forward, but to where? All she could see was night.

"Voices . . . of the dead . . ."

Iris turned and saw him. Not just his gold, pupil-less eyes, but a newfound emptiness in them Iris had never known before. The last she'd seem them, they'd been so filled with emotion, with empathy, with a love for life and pity for the people she'd come to annihilate. His body was a statue, a bronze-plated god; his crown, his meridian, just as she'd remembered it—made for him by the Naacal. His curling chestnut hair fell over his eyes as he bent his head low, but it couldn't cover them, couldn't blanket the inhuman resolution in them as they stared at her without blinking. This man. This brother.

The other Hiva.

He stepped out of the shadows without the Naacalian robes she'd remembered him being so fond of. She could see every muscle outlined against his skin.

His left arm was no longer gone. He'd grown it back. Of course he had. He was immortal. First the bone, then the flesh and skin. He was capable of it, just as she was. And that was when Iris remembered.

The blade she'd murdered Nyeth with was made out of Hiva's left arm.

Back then, Iris had threatened a priestess inside one of their land shrines. The fear in the woman's eyes was not unlike what she'd just seen from Leroux and his underling. It was that fear that had compelled the priestess to tell her what Nyeth and Hiva were up to.

"They're working together, then." Iris could hear her own emotionless voice. Her passionless, bloodless whispers in those ancient days truly frightened her now. "That the other Hiva has grown *this* attached to humanity . . . a pity."

Nyeth had become her enemy the moment she'd declared her intent to wipe out humanity in a manner indiscriminate of Naacalian hierarchy. Everyone must die. Nyeth had finally gone insane after she'd turned their capital city to dust.

"Hiva! *Hiva!*" Iris could hear his mad, frantic voice crying in the ruins. "My goddess! My being! Why have you betrayed us? You've destroyed me. You've destroyed me!"

"No." Iris tried to shut her ears to his desperate, inhuman howls, but they pierced through anyway. "No! That's not me anymore. That's not me!"

"A pity," said the Hiva in front of her, with none of the life he'd had in those days. It was if she were looking into the ruthless eyes of her former self. "Sister . . . you've forgotten yourself."

Iris wrapped her arms around herself, only to look down and find that her clothes had vanished. Without any artifice to hide them, they stood in the abyss, both beautiful and horrible. The two Hivas.

"It took me some time to reach this earth again," Hiva said. *Was* it him? Or was it his spirit? His consciousness reaching through the expanses of space and time to find her?

No. Here, she could feel his life force. In the quiet of her mind, in the silence of his hatred, his overwhelming presence overpowered her. His anima was unmistakable, coursing through her, beating as if it were her own pulse.

"Oh God," she whispered. "You're really here. You've come back."

"Do you remember the last thing you said to me?"

Many memories of civilizations past still waited to be unfurled, but this memory Iris did recall: of her dragging Hiva up to the platform in the Coral Temple underneath that pure pillar of light. Even with Nyeth's blood pooling around her bare feet, she didn't flinch, nor did she listen to Hiva's pleas as she clicked the coordinates of Hiva's meridian and sent him traveling back through time and space. Away from her earth. Away from the Naacal he'd tried to save.

Now, there in that in-between space, Hiva touched his emerald crown. "You know, don't you? This technology came from my earth many eons ago from a civilization I'd once destroyed. I brought it to the Naacal."

"It was the basis of the Helios." Iris bit her lip. "The contraption they would have used to conquer other earths after they were finished destroying theirs."

"You couldn't have known that."

"Don't be so *naïve!*" When Iris shouted, she could hear the ageless authority of an ancient god that felt wholly separate from her and yet so familiar. It made her shiver.

Hiva's smile was beautiful and delicate and yet struck a pang of panic in her so strong she could feel her heart contract and her throat squeeze.

"Yes, that's it. That's what you said. 'You were always too naïve.' That's what you told me before you sent me adrift through dimensions. How many hundreds of thousands of years did I spend lost in that great expanse, my feet unable to find soil of any earth, let alone my own? By the time I'd landed, I fully understood your words. By the time I'd settled onto an earth, I'd already put away my naïveté."

Iris frowned. No. She'd meant to send him back to his own earth. Something must have happened . . . something must have happened to the meridian.

The sound of his crown cracking along with his head pierced through Iris's skull as she remembered their desperate fight in the Coral Temple: Hiva lunging for her with only one of his arms, trying to stop her from reaching Nyeth, who was fiddling with his ring. Her merciless onslaught, which caused his bloody fall on the steps to the dais . . .

"And in putting away my naïveté, I became like you, the sister I adored and admired."

Iris couldn't believe she was having this conversation with this man, this creature, a creature like herself, here in this realm of nothingness where seconds ceased. "What . . . what have you been doing all this time?"

"As I said, becoming more like you." Hiva lifted up his hands. The way he tilted his head reminded her of a wooden toy. Lifeless. Emotionless. "Traveling through dimensions. To different earths. Judging humanity. Destroying worlds. World after world after world . . ."

But was he so emotionless? It was quiet, but Iris could see a spark of insanity inside those golden eyes. She imagined herself stranded in time and space for hundreds of thousands of years with only the memories of death and loss, of pain and betrayal, to accompany her. Taunting her . . .

"I had always hoped I'd come back here again. That I'd see you, sister."

"To kill me?"

"To *destroy* you." Hiva's judgment was resolute.

"For revenge?" Though Iris's fists were shaking, she still gave him a lop-sided smile. "Not so emotionless then. You're not like how I was in those days at all."

"Neither are you. But it won't stop me."

It was then that Iris noticed the humming in the background. It grew louder, forming sounds, vowels, consonants. Words.

Accusations.

"Can you hear them? The fruit of our labor. The work of our hands. The spirits of the murdered. Countless of them."

One accusation rolled over another until she could barely differentiate them, but she could hear their venom nonetheless.

"Can you hear them calling us?"

Hiva . . . Hiva . . . Hiva . . . Hiva . . .

Spirits rose out of the ground, shimmering. Iris covered her ears. "Stop."

The Hiva. The Hiva! The Hiva begins anew!

"I said stop! Stop!" The spirits of the countless people she'd killed swirled around her, lifting her off her feet, flinging her here and there. "Stop! Stop!"

Off in the distance she could hear screams. Were they hers? Theirs? She'd heard enough screaming for a lifetime, and yet they wouldn't leave. They wouldn't leave her be! The men she'd killed in the Library of Rule and the Crystal Palace. The people she'd murdered as Isoke, part of the Dahomean army. Death. Death. Death. Death. It filled her. Strangled her.

"Stop!"

"They'll never stop," Hiva told her, though she could no longer see him, not through the whirlwind of spirits. "Not until you're dead."

It was a promise.

"I'll come to find you soon. . . ."

The spirits dispersed, dropping her to the hard ground.

Iris pried her unsteady hands from her head just in time to hear one more familiar voice calling her. *You have forgotten. But now do you remember?*

One last specter appeared, a haze of light buzzing around her brown body softly as a firefly.

Thick, bristly black hair; a moon around her head. A single hair clip shaped like a monarch butterfly, pinned close to her right brow. A slender figure in a white sundress.

Anne Marlow: the girl who'd been kidnapped from Africa along with Iris and Granny and taken to the Manchester Zoo half a century ago. The girl who died there. Granny's sister . . .

No. This wasn't her. It was not even her ghost. This *thing* with round white eyes, plump but death-cracked lips, and graying skin only posed as her. She'd appeared before Iris throughout the tournament, goading her, prying into her mind, trying to force her to remember. But each time she'd appeared, Iris could never understand.

Ah. Because she hadn't yet awakened.

"You're the one who summons me," Iris whispered because she knew. She just *knew*. "The one who summons me from the depths. Each time. Every time..."

"Anne" nodded. *It is time once again,* she said.

"To what?" Iris yelled. "To kill more people? More blood on my hands?" Iris could still feel Nyeth's blood dripping from her fingers.

It is time once again....

"How many Hivas are there? One for each earth? For each dimension? Do you call them all, or do they each have their own masters?" Iris clasped her hands over her ears. "Well, even if you're mine, I won't listen to you. I refuse. I'm not Hiva. Not anymore!"

A cosmos of memories, of lives, and of eons of cataclysms enveloped her.

The One just stared at her, saying nothing.

"What about what *I* want?" Tears dripped from her eyes, slipping down her cheeks.

You've misunderstood everything, said the One. *You misunderstand me still.*

And she held out a coin. Day on one side. Night on the other.

Which side? The One turned the coin over in her hand. *Which?*

"What..." Iris swallowed, staring as the One flipped the coin again. "What is this?"

You misunderstand me still.

"I don't *want* to understand!" Iris could still hear those hollow-eyed ghosts screaming at her, demanding justice. "Get away from me! Get away!"

The ground quaked, broke, and tumbled into the dark depths below until a gulf stretched out, separating her from the creature who would be her "master."

The One stood on the other side of the chasm, shaking her head.

As you wish.

She seemed disappointed.

But the truth shall always be, she said. *Though at times you may seek to block it, and at times it may become difficult for you to reach, it will still be there as sure as the dawn. Waiting for you,* the One continued ominously, her voice softer, distant, but still clear.

On the other side of the great chasm, a shadow passed over the One's face.

And one day, you will be ready.

"Qu'est-ce qui se passe?"

"La clown s'est effondrée!"

"Get up, you fascinating wench, get up!"

The last voice was Benini's, furious and panicked enough to snap her out of her trance. Iris felt a grip around her forearm, yanking her up. She looked around, exhausted, her body heavy.

Why in the world was she in the drawing room?

Iris lay against the wall. A plant stand was knocked over, a vase smashed into pieces. Madame Leroux's guests were on their feet staring at her, terrified. The medium's table had toppled over.

"When dear Mademoiselle Pascal told us to soar through the expanses of time, I didn't think anyone would, *literally,*" said Benini. "How did you do that? Flying around like a stage actress strung up by a wire? I thought immortality was your specific brand of freakery."

Flying? Iris remembered the spirits picking her up and tossing her about, but . . .

"Although séances do seem to have a terrible effect on people with certain sensitive constitutions," Benini continued absently. "Indeed, there was that time Anna Eva Fay started speaking in tongues, and it was actually quite genuine *that* time. . . ."

Iris looked around the room, her head spinning. The paintings hanging askew . . . the overturned table . . . the drawn curtains . . . the open window.

The masked figure standing in the trees, his cape fluttering in the wind, his top hat illuminated by the moon and stars above.

"Fool," Iris breathed. Somewhere inside her exhausted body there was the spark of an all-too-familiar fear. She sat up, boosting herself off the wall with a huff, her body struggling. "Fool . . . ?"

Suddenly a man's voice cried out over the terrified chatter. *"Qui sont-ils?"*
As Benini lifted Iris to her feet, two women grabbed his arms.

"Mais qu'est-ce qui se passe? Qui sont-ils?" they cried.

"Who . . . are . . . they . . . ?" Iris's mind had just begun to translate when the grand doors to Leroux's apartment slammed open.

And Gram and Jacques walked in.

9

THEY SHOULDN'T BE HERE. NO. THEY should be in London, falling victim to Jinn's thirst for revenge. They shouldn't be *here*. But they were. They were, and Jinn wasn't.

A terrible thought sent Iris's pulse racing. Where was Jinn? Where *was* he?

Jacques's footsteps were heavy. The crowd parted. The poor fools might have thought him a true priest, with his black Catholic robes and the white collar of a cleric around his light brown neck. He *had* been once upon a time, before he turned assassin. No gun was necessary. He pointed his deadly finger up to the sky, waiting.

If Jacques was the priest, then his partner, Gram, was his chained devil. A ghoul with only a few strings of gray hair left on his scalp, long enough to sweep across his collarbone. He licked his black lips as he walked toward Iris, his eyes on her. Only her.

Jinn, where are you? Iris thought, paralyzed. *What happened to you?*

Benini flattened himself against the wall in his kaleidoscopic robes. "What are those devils doing here?" he nearly screeched. "How did they know I was here?"

"Why wouldn't they know? You're not exactly an expert in stealth," Iris snarled back, shoving Nyeth's ring into her pants pocket, though as she glared back at the tournament's deadliest pair, she wondered the same. What—or *who*—had taken them out of London? Had Jinn found them first?

No. Maybe he missed them. Maybe he's still in London. . . .

She glanced at the window again, but Fool was gone. A shiver shook the last bits of fatigue from her body. Fool, Gram, Jacques. The Enlightenment Committee's catastrophes had followed her across the English Channel. She smiled grimly and maybe a little recklessly, her fists ready.

Jinn's okay, she thought to herself. *Jinn must be okay. . . .*

"We only want the young clown—and that *gentleman,*" Jacques said, pointing at Benini. He was polite and straightforward as usual, but with a deadly edge that warned others not to challenge him. "The rest of you can leave." He said it in French for good measure.

Gram grunted, staring at Madame Leroux's terrified guests with a kind of sick hunger Iris had seen before. He started toward her, but Jacques quickly lifted his hand to stop him.

"It seems you've forgotten the Basement," Jacques told him. "That tiny electrical contraption Uma Malakar placed inside your chest in case your hunger becomes wild. Radio-controlled—or so she said."

"I haven't forgotten." Gram tore open his black coat, revealing a sickly chest with a red, pulsating scar stretching down his torso. There was a bit of blood on Gram's yellow teeth as he flashed them angrily.

Jacques pulled a smooth wooden device from inside his jacket pocket—like a chainless pocket watch, except in place of time, the gears shifted wires around a button switch. "You were ordered to do as I said. Go wild and I will set it off."

Gram's body twitched. He was ready to feast. When Jacques shook his head, he bent over, furious, but kept his bloodshot gaze on Iris and the cowering Benini behind her.

"Go!" Jacques ordered the crowd, and, lifting up his right hand, shot one bullet into the air. The tip of his index finger smoked. "Now!"

He didn't need to translate. The crowd dispersed in terror, nearly knocking one another down to flee out the door. Bowler hats, necklaces, and wineglasses were left strewn about the floor. Benini tried to inch toward the window, but Jacques fired a shot near his head. It pierced the frame of a painting, which dropped to the floor.

"I've come for you, girl," said Jacques.

Iris's eyes shifted back to Gram, who straightened his back and began stretching his emaciated neck. A man who'd eaten the corpses of his brothers to stay alive in the mines would have no problem feasting off strangers. A man who'd become accustomed to flesh.

Flesh.

"Jinn!" That terrible thought once again seized her. "Jinn!" The worst couldn't have happened. It *couldn't have*. Her heart pounded in her chest as the most horrible scenes played out in front of her in her mind's eye. "No." She shook her head. "What did you do to him?"

"We're under orders of the Enlightenment Committee," said Jacques, ignoring her. They had been Van der Ven's champions during the tournament. So they were still working for him. "We've been hired to take the two of you into custody: Riccardo Benini, traitor to the Committee—and you, Iris Marlow. Former champion of Lord Adam Temple. Also known as Hiva."

"I said, what did you do to Jinn?" Iris screamed, because all she could think about was his mangled body lying somewhere alone in a London alleyway. Tears of rage filled her eyes. *"What did you do to him?!"*

She thought of how helplessly he'd trembled that night outside Club Uriel, facing his father's murderer. "Is he even alive?" Iris whispered.

Gram only opened his black lips and breathed in a low grumble. "The hunted need not speak in front of the hunter."

With the bolero blade Jinn had given her still in her tavern room, Iris dashed to the fireplace and grabbed the poker. Jinn's anguish as he cried out his father's name set fire to the rage inside her. "I've had enough!" She gripped it tight. "It's time for you to go back to hell."

She ran at Gram, swinging down her weapon.

"Yes! Go, my champion, go!" Benini cried behind her. "Fight! Protect me! Please?"

Jacques leaped out of the way, while Gram dodged each of her strikes with small but swift movements. Bending his neck here, shifting to the side there. A wisp of his hair floated in front of her eyes for just a moment. That was when

Gram avoided her latest thrust by catching her arm. Iris let out a gasp as he squeezed—hard.

"The surgery was not an easy one by any measure," he said as Iris tried to wring herself out of his grip. "I need flesh to heal. Give me yours."

He began to pull. Iris screamed. She could feel her skin tearing. A shot rang out. Gram screeched and stumbled back, a new bullet hole burned through his shoulder. "Jacques!"

Iris turned to see Jacques place his arms at his sides. "She's not someone to be consumed."

"Well, aren't you pious?"

Another bang stole the breath from her lips. Benini squealed like a mule. With a nervous grin, he froze, one leg already through the open window. Smoke rose from the curtain.

And to Iris's surprise, Jacques stretched out his hand to her. "Come with me. Quietly."

Iris stepped back. "And what will you do with me?"

"The Committee has not told me every detail—"

"And you're okay with that?"

Jacques stiffened, his lips giving a slight twitch. He didn't need some kind of device to control him. This was a man who did everything for his family. Or so he'd once told her.

"As is my understanding," he continued, "you'll join the other Hiva, who is currently dead and under their control. What happens afterward is none of my concern."

Iris's throat closed. "The other Hiva . . ." She lifted her chin, trying to catch her breath, but her heart was beating too fast. The other Hiva . . . so she was right. He *was* here. Then their earlier meeting hadn't just been a vision at all. She'd really connected with him. With Hiva. With his spirit as he lay deceased under the Committee's control . . .

I'll come to find you soon. . . .

Hiva was no longer the kindhearted man in her memories. He'd escape the Committee's control eventually. Which meant that even if she got rid of her powers, there was another Hiva who was both willing and able to destroy humanity just fine.

Sweat began to bead at the edge of Iris's forehead. "Damn it." She shook her head. "Damn it!"

Jacques flicked his hand. "Come!"

Memories of being held by Doctor Pratt inside a secret, dingy lab at the esteemed University of Cambridge held her. Her arms and legs strapped to the table. The surgical instruments they'd used to cut into her. The vicious, vile experiments in the name of science.

Never again. Iris gritted her teeth, her eyes burning. *"Make me!"*

Jacques lifted his hand, but the shot never burst out of his finger. Before he could fire, he withdrew his hand to avoid the sword flying at him, threatening to cut off his arm. Iris dove out of the way as Rin's blade plunged into the wall and disappeared in an explosion of white crystal smoke.

"Rin!" Iris looked up from the floor just as Rin dodged Jacques's gunfire and downed Gram with a sweeping low kick. Iris jumped to her feet and ran to her.

The large sack tied to her back with rope didn't slow Rin down at all. She tried summoning her sword again, deep within the hollows of her chest. Her fingers had just found the hilt when Jacques's left hand found her face. He batted her hand away and lifted her off her feet, her sword half-exposed, half-buried in her chest.

"You've been designated as collateral," Jacques said. "I'm sorry, child."

Still gripping Rin's face tight, he placed the tip of his index finger on her forehead.

Iris plunged the poker into his left leg. Jacques let out a grunt and released Rin. Just as Gram lunged at Iris, Rin took her sword and sliced his wrist to the bone, nearly taking off his whole hand. Blood sprayed her face. Gram's hand dangled at an ugly angle as he screamed.

"Come on," Iris said. She grabbed Rin's hand, and they made for the door, but bullets hailed from Jacques, piercing the front entrance. Ducking around the corner, they changed their trajectory—upstairs.

"You should have gone for his neck and cut off his head," Rin hissed, wiping Gram's blood off her face as they ran up the stairs. Whatever Rin had shoved inside that sack clattered against her back with each step. "Do you remember nothing from your days in the army?"

She remembered too much. The gruesome battles with other tribes and colonial militaries she'd fought on behalf of King Ghezo. Those days when she only emotionlessly observed the world through the eyes of one trying to discern the workings of this current civilization. That wasn't who she was anymore. "Sorry, but my beheading days are over."

When she thought of murder, she thought of Gram, and when she thought of Gram, she thought of Jinn, somewhere out there, maybe dead. Her heart lurched and her eyes filled with tears. *Jinn . . . Jinn, where are you?* Emotions were a new development from her eons as Hiva. There were times she'd rather do away with them.

They came across Leroux, still knocked out. Rin was livid when Iris took the time to stash him inside one of his rooms, a guest room by the look of the lavish bed. She wasn't Isoke, and she wasn't Hiva. She wouldn't abandon him to be gobbled up by Gram. But where to next?

"Come," Iris said, and ended up charging into Leroux's bedroom. "The window!"

It was open behind Leroux's desk. And—what was that? Iris ran up the window for a closer inspection. A rope ladder with pegs was already tied to the ledge. They used these mock ladders as fire escapes to quickly get out of a burning building. She noticed Leroux's man was gone too. Was *she* the fire? Iris almost laughed. But the problem was obvious as she looked down the white brick. It was a flimsy rope. Some of the pegs had fallen to the ground. And it was a five-story drop. She could survive it. Even if she didn't, she'd revive just fine. What about Rin?

As if gleaning her worry, Rin nudged her and nodded. "Let's try it."

There was no more time to hesitate. The door burst open. Jacques limped inside, shooting. Iris and Rin ducked behind the desk.

"Go!" Iris ordered, and Rin made for the window. Iris hurled one of Leroux's leather-bound books at Jacques, throwing his aim off course as she dodged.

Jacques lowered his hand and lifted his chin, sizing Iris up. "Just let me know this," he said, and though his wounded leg wobbled beneath him, he stood firm nonetheless. "Are you truly the bringer of the apocalypse? Will you ultimately sound the horn that will end this world? Is that your destiny—and the reason you cannot die, child?"

Iris stumbled back. "I won't kill. I swear."

"Is it inevitable? Do you have a way to stop it?"

Another two steps back. "I'm looking for one!"

Jacques lifted his hand. "But you haven't found it. And yet you deny the obvious choice."

"Obvious choice . . ." Iris lowered her hands.

"When King Sisyphus ensnared Thanatos, the winged god of death, in his own chains, there ceased to be death among mortals for a time."

Iris lips quivered into a nervous smirk. "Thought you were a Catholic . . ."

"I left the priesthood."

"Isoke!" Rin called from the window behind her. "Hurry!"

"Forget it, Jacques. I'm not going to let anyone chain me up in the Basement," Iris said, inching toward the window. "Damn it, I just want to live in peace. I just want to be free!"

Jacques shook his head. "I have a family."

"So did Jinn! And you're working with the man who killed him. How dare you speak to me about what's right and wrong?"

"We're assassins, girl. I work to feed my family, and Gram works to feed himself. Your friend's father was an enemy of the Ottoman Empire. His price was high."

Iris shuddered angrily, thinking of what it must have been like for Jinn, just a child at the time, seeing his father being dragged away at the South Kensington fair.

"As long as you are unwilling to do *everything* it takes to stop the inevitable, we are *all* in danger," Jacques said. "Innocents. My own children."

Iris wouldn't dare reveal it, but she was shaken. She *was* being selfish. Every experience she'd had as Hiva told her that her turning on humanity was inevitable. The world was safer during the years her heart had been damaged and locked away. Maybe submitting herself to the whims of the Basement *was* the only way. . . .

But then she thought of that man, Seymour. And she wanted more than what he had to offer. She wanted life. Even if that meant fighting for it. Even if her refusal to do anything less put the world in danger. Her eyes stung with tears. Even if people hated her for it . . .

"No." Jacques's eyes hardened. "No one else will be sacrificed to your selfishness."

The man she'd turned to dust in the Library of Rule flashed before her eyes, but Jacques's heaving breath brought her back to the present. Even while limping, Jacques had considerable speed. She picked up a book and threw it at him, hoping to distract him long enough to follow Rin.

A flash of a red-and-beige contraption outside the window passed by her sight. A familiar voice. An *impossible* voice.

"Iris! Jump!"

Confusion rippled through her. She paused, one leg already out the window, and then Jacques's shot burst through her chest. A snapping pain caused her body to shrivel, and with a gasp, she toppled out of the window. For a time, everything was dark.

But Jacques must have known that a bullet would never stop a god of death. Not for long.

She awoke on a hard surface made of layers of woven straw or maybe willow, an entire box of it, moving through the air. Rin was hovering above her, watching for any signs of life.

"She's up," Rin told someone. Iris rubbed her head, then her chest, still throbbing with pain. The sound of gas hissing and the heat warming her skin dragged her body upward until she was sitting. Her eyes caught the sight of one of the finest pairs of shoes she'd ever seen, black and pompously expensive. Britches and a vest hugged a slender male form. She wiped her eyes.

"You've been up to quite a lot, haven't you, little goddess?"

Iris was on her feet. "Adam."

10

ADAM TEMPLE WAS LEANING AGAINST THE wicker basket of what Iris just now realized was a hot-air balloon. The red-and-beige contraption she'd glimpsed just before Jacques's bullet found her back—it was the balloon that had taken them up into the air, far away from the Boulevard des Capucines. Iris couldn't believe it. Caught between feelings of repulsion and marvel, Iris ran to the opposite side of the wicker basket and stared down at the streets of Paris below. Some Parisians were staring up at them, pointing, but they were nothing more than tiny toys, their mouths open, their voices barely a murmur as the wind whistled around her ears. A small part of her wondered if Benini was among them, still alive. Not that she cared all that much, but something told her that man would have found a way to survive.

"Entertaining the rich again, I see?" Adam crossed his arms over his chest. His blue eyes were alight with dark mirth as he took in the sight of her outfit. "It's good to see your role in the apocalypse hasn't completely stolen your spirits."

"I should have known." Iris glared at him. "When I saw your dog, Fool, I should have known you'd be close by."

Adam shrugged. "Not all the Fools are my dogs, but yes, I do have one keeping track of you." And when Iris grimaced, he added, "It's rather important business, you know. The end of the world. I can't just let you wander around freely."

"*Let* me?" Iris curled her right hand into a fist. She was suddenly feeling remarkably better, healthy enough, at the very least, to punch him out of the balloon. "I told you, I'm not going to do as you please. I thought I got the message across when I knocked you unconscious."

"I appreciated the pain, at least." Adam's smile was wicked. "I always appreciate violent women."

His eyes slid from Iris to Rin, who, despite not understanding his words, caught his expression and turned her back with a roll of her eyes. At least Adam was smart enough to keep his distance from the two of them.

"Your circus partner isn't here," Adam observed. "Your *Jinn.*"

Caught off guard, Iris turned away with a short huff. She saw that tiny grin on Adam's smug face and felt like slapping him. But her hands were suddenly too numb and weak to make a fist. Gram and Jacques wouldn't be slowed down for long. And as for Jinn . . . She shook her head. She didn't want to consider it.

She changed the topic. "Where did you even get a hot-air balloon?" Iris demanded.

"Bosch's weapons developer, Uma Malakar, lent it to me before I went to London. She thought it might come in handy. I can appreciate the gesture as a fellow fan of Jules Verne."

Iris frowned. "Uma? She helped you?"

"It seems she doesn't want to see you captured by the Committee any more than I do."

"I came close, that's for sure." Iris looked back at Leroux's building, drifting away from them. "Jacques and Gram crashed the party. Seems they're working for the Committee now."

"Just Bellerose," Adam clarified, and a dark shadow passed over his face. "Bosch is in Africa. Van der Ven is on house arrest. Benini is wanted. Cordiero and now Cortez are dead. Violet pretended as if she was willing to lock up Vander Ven's assassins, only to sic them on you herself." He laughed. "I should have known."

"Wait. Cortez?" Iris frowned. "Cortez is dead?"

"A lot has happened since you escaped London, Iris." Leaning against the box, Adam looked over the edge to the city below. "There's another Hiva."

"So you know, then."

"So *you* know?" Adam gave her a sidelong look. "Hm. But of course you do. He could sense you. Why wouldn't you be able to sense him, too?"

Iris pursed her lips. Truthfully, she could only sense him while in that dark trance, but if she tried hard enough, she was sure she'd be able to sniff out his anima. It was just a matter of which Hiva found the other first.

"Another Hiva." Adam shook his head. "I never would have guessed. My father couldn't have known either. None of his research pointed toward the existence of two destroyers."

"Well, I guess the Temples don't know everything after all." Iris smirked. "What a twist."

Adam returned her biting hatred with a smile that felt almost warm. She hated that most about him. "Some of your friends are locked up in the Crystal Palace with him as we speak. The Basement, I mean. With all the other freaks being experimented on. Hawkins. Jacob. Cherice."

Iris gasped, but then quickly caught herself. "They're not my friends," she said, but somehow she couldn't stop herself from worrying. Despite everything that had happened, the thought of them being violated in that dingy hellhole horrified her. "They . . ." She swallowed. "They haven't been harmed, have they?"

"Not yet. But I can't tell you what will happen to them in the future. Doctor Seymour Pratt has been given control over researching this new Hiva. He has these new champions in his sights as well."

At the sound of that man's name, a cold rage chilled Iris from the inside out.

"Besides . . ." Adam paused. When Iris saw his eyes dart from her shiftily, she knew he was hiding something. As usual.

"Besides, what?" Iris demanded. "What is it? What aren't you telling me?"

He was usually a lot more subtle than this, moving in silence without even a hint that anything sinister could possibly lie behind that gentlemanly smile.

"How did you find Hiva? What else happened before you came here?"

It was then that Adam looked her dead in the eyes, the hesitation gone from them. "Danger is headed your way, Iris. Your secret is out. Some are not quite sold, but it's only a matter of time before they realize it's true. And then the Committee won't stop until they have both Hivas under their control. Imagine the power they could accrue with two gods in their employ. Their greed knows no bounds."

Some fates were worse than death. To be trapped in a cage for eternity. Kept in that sliver of existence that lay between life and death. Undead and suffering in perpetuity.

"No." Iris pounded the basket ledge with her fist. "I won't let that happen. I won't be captured and observed under a microscope by the likes of you people. Never again."

"Nor would I have anyone do that to you." As Adam began to cross the bas-ket, Rin stood in his way. He bowed his head slightly in deference, then raised his hands in surrender. But he didn't need to be near Iris for his words to reach her. "You know who you are now, Iris. You can never be ruled. You are the ruler. So do what you were born to do."

"What I was born to do . . ."

Was that why its taste was so tempting? The anima of the guard she'd mur-dered in the museum. Hawkins's anima that she'd touched just before bringing herself back from the brink. It had been like that during her former life as well, and probably in the lives before that. Even as emotionless Hiva, she could tell the act of purging came with a kind of catharsis she neither indulged in nor took for granted. Adam waited, a silent prayer on his lips.

Iris quietly lowered her arms to her sides. It was in moments like these that she remembered that what Adam desired was not her, but her power. This mad boy was in love with a death goddess for reasons she couldn't fathom. In the past, she would have thought nothing of it. It was the same with Nyeth. Like him, there were fools among the Naacal who had worshipped her as the bringer of death before she'd decided to bring death to them. And it was all the same to her. Her prerogative was only to judge and murder.

But the Iris of today resented Adam's outstretched hand, flipped so she could see his flushed palm welcoming her. So many in her current lifetime had wanted to give her names that didn't belong to her. Names of their choosing. Adam was just another one of them.

"No."

"What will it take, I wonder?" Adam asked with an impatient huff, lowering his arm. "What will it take for you to see that human civilization is a blight? Will it be the death of someone you care about? Or perhaps something bigger. Perhaps a war? It's in war, after all, that the greatest atrocities are committed. Shall I make for you a war, then, Iris, so that you can finally see how evil men are?"

"I'll say it again," Iris whispered, the warning in her voice loud and clear. "I won't do as you please. I won't do as *any* of you please. Never."

"Then you'd better find a way to stop a death god soon," said Adam. "Because if *you* don't bring about the destruction of all humankind, the other Hiva surely will."

"Won't that be good for you, then?" Iris spat back. "You don't need me. You have a backup."

"No." Adam shook his head. "It has to be you, Iris. It always had to be you. I *want* it to be you."

Iris took in the sight of this man's fervent hope, innocent, like children's dreams. Eerie. She gripped her hands tight to stay the tremors. "Why?"

"Because I believe," Adam told her simply.

Iris didn't understand. She didn't want to understand. She didn't want to see what he did. The reflection of herself in his eyes frightened her. Silence stretched between the three of them.

Just as it reflected the moon in the night sky, the Seine had held the fortunes of many men in this city. This city's artery, its all-important lifeblood. The Eiffel Tower was in sight, once a place she'd wanted to take Granny again, this time not as part of Coolie's circus but as visitors. *Oh Granny, I miss you,* she thought wistfully, pained as she remembered the two of them inside her tent, with Egg squawking about and Jinn helping Granny with her sewing.

As Iris looked over the edge of the basket to the flowing river below, Jacques's accusation echoed like rippling waves.

As long as you are unwilling to do everything it takes to stop the inevitable, we are all in danger. Innocents. My own children. No one else will be sacrificed to your selfishness.

From Jacques's perspective, *she* was the villain of this story. From everyone's perspective. Max's friends. Humanity. The tournament was over, but this new game was a dangerous one. If she failed, what would happen to Granny? *I just want to live in peace.* Was that a selfish wish? Shouldn't she be able to sacrifice herself if need be for the sake of everyone else?

"There." Rin pointed at the harbor. "Isoke, tell him to drop us off."

Following the direction of her hand, Adam looked over his shoulder. "That harbor?"

"Harbor?" Iris repeated in shock. Sure enough, there was a small steamer being prepared for voyage. The motor was already running. "Rin?"

"We're leaving the country," Rin told her. "It's too dangerous here."

"And going where?"

"Dahomey."

Iris's back stiffened. "Excuse me? I told you I wasn't going. What are you playing at?"

Rin flicked her head toward the young man walking up a wooden plank to the first level of the steamer, carrying a barrel—at least from what Iris could see.

It clicked. "Your well-connected school friend. Is this what you were setting up while I was entertaining Benini's social circle?" But after seeing Rin's noncommittal shrug, Iris frowned. "You couldn't have known things would turn out the way they did at Leroux's party. Were you always planning on taking me here?"

"It's the obvious next step in our journey. Temple's father came to King Glele to seek you. And by your own admission, he knew more about your powers than anyone else. The more clues we find as to the true depths of your power, the closer we get to learning how to control them and rein in your destructive impulses."

"Destructive impulses," Iris whispered. She wanted to argue, but Rin had seen firsthand what she was capable of when she'd impulsively murdered a man inside the Library of Rule. She looked over at Adam, who was watching the two of them with interest, an eyebrow raised and a small smile on his lips, leaning against the basket with his arms folded. He couldn't understand them, could he? Iris shook her head. "Well, your king should be happy."

At "your king," Rin grimaced, her young face suddenly revealing the many lives she'd taken in her short years. Iris's breath caught in her throat, but Rin only closed her eyes. "The Committee now knows who and what you are. Do you have a better place to run to?"

If she went back to the circus, Granny could end up in danger. They probably had spies watching the tents in case she returned. No one in London could harbor her.

But it wasn't only that. Iris placed her hand in her pocket. The moment she touched the Coral Ring, she felt her mind lifting, traveling again, carried upon the breeze across time and space until she could see the earthen cavern she'd arisen from in the Oil Rivers region. Something was there. Yes . . . she'd left something behind, and not just the white crystal shards. She'd felt that back at Leroux's home during the séance. She'd felt it as strongly as Nyeth's sorrow.

To drag a god back down to earth required nothing short of divine intervention of a different sort. If what the king told me is indeed true, I'll find my divine intervention in the place where heaven dwells.

The place where heaven dwells. John Temple's words. Leroux had mentioned those words too.

The place where heaven dwelled was the Coral Temple. Yes . . . the place where a god could be dragged down to earth. Where Nyeth had meant to clip her wings. Where Iris would find her divine intervention. This only confirmed it.

"If you're going to see the king of Dahomey, perhaps I can come with you?" Adam said casually, examining his nails. "I'd like to know what secrets my father might have kept out of his journal."

Rin and Iris whipped around at precisely the same time. "Did you understand what we were saying?" Iris asked in alarm, her eyebrows raised.

"I understood the word 'Dahomey,' and I know the king's name," Adam said. "That's all I needed. And no, you're not getting rid of me, Iris. Not again."

"You want to wager on that?" Iris showed him her closed fist, ready for a fight.

Two loud cracks from below, then the hiss of escaping air. The wicker basket shook underneath her feet. Iris looked up to see holes in the balloon.

"What's going on?" Iris yelled before several more gunshots tore through the fabric. They were going down.

"We're under attack." Rin ran to the edge of the wicker basket. "Who is she? Another of the Committee's assassins?"

She? So it wasn't Jacques? As Adam strode up beside Rin, Iris wobbled on her unsteady feet. "Who is it? Who—"

"Damn it," Adam cursed. "She's good, I'll give her that."

"But who—?"

Another bullet ripped apart one of the wires tying the balloon to the basket. Iris screamed as she, Rin, and Adam stumbled and fell, gripping the ledge as the basket started to swing dangerously in the air. The men loading the steamer stared up in terror at the hot-air balloon approaching on a collision course.

"Hold on!" Adam yelled.

The wicker narrowly missed the main mast, brushing one of the flickering white sails before crashing into the Seine.

For a moment, Iris saw only blackness as she was thrown into the river. The crash had knocked the air out of her lungs. Below the water was the chaos of bubbles and debris and kicking limbs, and then Iris broke the surface, gulping in a huge breath.

Iris took in the scene around her. Adam seemed fine, almost unruffled, even while soaking wet. But Rin was thrashing about, struggling to keep her head above water. The sack the girl held steadfastly might have been weighing her down. Iris swam over to her and grabbed one of Rin's arms, wrapping it around her neck to keep her afloat. Rin flung the other around Iris as well, squeezing her collarbone as Iris and Adam swam to the wooden plank leading up to the steamer. Iris hadn't swum in a long time, especially not such a long distance. Rin didn't exactly help by wagging her feet helplessly. The girl was a warrior on land alone. Iris wanted to laugh; she spat out river water instead.

"Olarinde!" A young Black man in a brown vest squeezed in between some gawkers to get to the plank as the trio pulled themselves up onto the wood.

"Abiade . . ." She coughed the name out along with a spurt of water.

Once on the plank, a soaked Iris doubled over on her knees, trying to catch her breath while Adam collapsed, his legs and feet still in the river. Not exactly the athletic type, was he?

Iris wrung out her braids, feeling Jinn's ribbon slop across her neck as she moved her head from side to side. Without thinking, she checked for Max's pocket watch. It was there, next to the Coral Ring, thank goodness. Neither had been lost to the waters. But how could the watch still be working? It was wet, but still somehow ticking nonetheless. Like it didn't know how to die.

This young man, Abiade, tiptoed past Iris and Adam and helped Rin to her feet. Rin pulled the sack over her shoulder. They chatted together in Yoruba. Thankfully, Iris could understand.

"What happened, Olarinde? Why were you in that balloon?"

When Rin shook her head, her long, tiny braids sprayed water everywhere. "Abiade, is the ship—is La Daphnée ready to go?"

"Yes, of course!" he answered, and Iris could feel the motor warming up through the plank. "We've just been waiting for you."

Rin grabbed his shirt collar. "Then hurry and let's get going before—"

Another gunshot sent them ducking for cover. Abiade and some other men preparing the ship began shouting in French to each other, and suddenly everything started moving in double time. Iris looked back toward the docks. The loaded rifle in the young woman's hands was still smoking. Light brown skin. Blue dress and a red corset, silver buttons down the front. Her curly brown hair tied up in a bun above her head, probably so it wouldn't get in the way of her aim. She was kneeling on the docks in front of a little girl in a dirty white dress and a long black pinafore, who was covering her ears from the noise with her dark brown hands. Iris's heart skipped another beat when she thought it might be Anne. Her shoulders rose and her neck tensed before she realized it was someone else entirely.

This shooter didn't strike Iris as an amateur. Every shot she made was deliberate.

She was the one who'd taken down their hot-air balloon. There was no doubt about it.

They were sitting ducks on the plank. She could have taken any one of their heads off, and the smirk on the girl's face proved to Iris that she knew it too. That was a warning shot.

Iris instinctively stood in front of Rin, shoving the young warrior behind her while this new young woman stood up and brushed back the few curls that had slipped out of her bun.

"Berta!" the little girl in the pinafore called to the shooter after lowering her hands. "Careful!"

Berta...

A wild thought crossed her mind. Such a ludicrous idea; it should have disappeared just as quickly. But she couldn't stop seeing him in her.

Berta...

No, it couldn't be. Iris felt her mouth go dry, the cold air bite her skin through her wet clothes. It couldn't be. But why did they look alike? Right down to their lopsided smiles...

The chilly wind carried the girl's voice to them with all its confidence, with all its charm, with all its bloodlust.

"My name is Berta Morales," she said, stopping Iris's heart dead. "Now which one of you is the 'pretty African wench' who killed my brother?"

11

WHAT?" IRIS COUGHED THE LAST BITS of Seine out of her mouth and gripped her aching chest. This girl sounded like a cowboy and looked like she ran a saloon. Berta. Maximo's sister. Maximo's reason for . . . for everything. For every sin he'd committed.

"What did you say?" Iris couldn't focus. "What did you—"

Her vision blurred. She looked down at the plank, and it looked so wet and muddy. Her shoes squished as she stumbled back and bumped into Rin.

Memories of Max came in dull shards of broken glass.

My mother sent my sister, Berta, and me to England. . . .

A merchant had promised that he'd give us an education. . . .

She could see him, see the light brown skin of his bare chest, the same tone as this girl. See him tied up in chains in the auction room, surrounded by frightening objects, yet still recounting his youth wistfully, sadly.

But we were to be displayed in an exhibit. . . .

"No, it can't be. . . ."

Somewhere along the way, my sister and I were separated. . . .

She was only five years old. . . .

Iris covered her face with a hand.

And out from the darkness, Max's sorrowful confession:

I don't even know whether she's still alive.

"You're Max's—" Iris's words caught in her throat as Berta searched her guilty face.

"Now, I didn't tell you his name. . . ." Berta lowered her chin. "I've been scouring this whole city. Interrogating folks. But this? This is the lucky break I've been waiting for. Thank you, El Diablo." Berta strode toward them, cocking her shotgun. "So. You killed my brother?"

"This can't be happening," Iris whispered. "This can't—"

"Isoke!"

Berta aimed and shot just as Rin grabbed Iris with one hand and Abiade with the other and pulled them down upon the plank, now creaking dangerously from their weight.

Someone yelled out in pain. The shot had gotten someone's shoulder, one of the men on the ship. Everyone else ducked for cover, hiding behind the masts or tripping over themselves to flee down into the lower decks.

It was only Adam who, with his wits about him, stood and drew out a gun. And Iris had seen it before—the roses and thorns etched down its barrel. Gripping the golden handle, he fired several shots. Berta's instinct was to fly to the little girl behind her, to push her to the ground while the bullets flew.

"Everyone onto the ship!" Iris ordered, waving her hands. The urgency on her face was one everybody could understand regardless of the language barriers.

Off the plank and onto *La Daphnée*, which rumbled on the docks. Berta chased them. Iris tried to push the wooden plank into the river, but an expertly aimed shot nearly took off her foot.

"Was it you?" Berta screamed, kneeling on the wood, a few steps away.

"I'm sorry," Iris whispered, because her mind was swirling and she didn't know what else to say. "I'm sorry!" she blurted out.

Berta cocked her gun.

"No, don't!"

The bullet soared into the air, missing its target by a mile. It was the little girl who'd screamed, throwing herself onto Berta at the last minute, ruining her kill shot.

Iris let out a sharp breath and stared at the little girl. Her skin was dark like

Iris's own. African, but with an accent that told her she was from the American South. A doll-like girl with a pretty, cherubic face now scrunched up, her eyes closed as she held Berta tight around the back. But when she opened her eyes . . . yes, Iris could see it. Pain. Utter, devastating pain, the kind that one could only see if one had experienced the same kind. Iris knew that kind of pain. She'd spent eons causing it. She could recognize it anywhere. What had happened to this little girl?

"Lulu, I told you not to keep clinging on to me!" Berta said this, but it seemed she'd done her fair share of clinging too. She looked at the girl not with annoyance, but concern. "You gotta get out of here. It's dangerous!"

"Don't kill her!" this girl, this Lulu in her pretty white dress, begged. "Please! Please!"

"She killed my brother!" Berta screamed.

"I know, I know!" Lulu clung to her gun-wielding arm like she wouldn't let go.

Adam pulled Iris around with a wet hand. "This is your chance."

"What?"

"Annihilate them. Burn them both."

Iris stared at him, horrified, but Adam's expression was dead serious. He gripped her cheeks, his palms sliding against her skin, stinging cold like a corpse. The man who wanted to see the world end. "Use your power. The more you do, the more you'll get a taste for it."

A *taste* for it. Iris's heart flickered like a lover's would, but just that flicker made her hands go numb. "Get away from me!" Iris shrugged him off, sickened, her stomach heaving while the girls continued to argue on the plank.

"Lulu, goddamn it—"

"Just don't do it! Don't—"

"*Kill* her."

Gram came stomping up the wooden plank. *Gram.* She hadn't the time to wonder how far behind Jacques was. Adam was yelling at the crew to get the ship out of there faster. But it was a big lumbering steamer, not a cannonball being launched into the sky. *La Daphnée* took its time while Iris's pursuers caught up to her one by one.

Berta's eyes darted in every direction. She hardly could have known she had anyone else to track. Iris gripped the ship's railing.

"Berta! Watch out!" she screamed, her knuckles bloodless.

Before Berta could react, Gram had tossed Lulu into the Seine. Iris gasped, her heart pounding. The hand Rin had nearly cut off had healed quickly. Like Iris, he could restore himself from grave injuries . . . but only under special circumstances.

"Oh God," Iris whispered. Who had he eaten?

Berta had already dived into the water to rescue Lulu, but Gram wasn't interested in them at all. He walked up the plank slowly, licking his lips, savoring every second. Iris froze. Gram jumped forward, his black cape flying, his jaundiced skin silhouetted by the moonlight. He launched himself at the ship, aiming for Iris.

A blade struck him through the stomach. Gram's mouth opened in a low, breathless gasp, and he dropped onto the plank. Iris looked toward the docks.

Jinn.

Her breath stopped. *Jinn.* His throwing hand was stretched out. His eyebrows furrowed. His dark eyes glimmering. He was unmistakably *him.*

"Jinn . . ." Iris's lips trembled as she tried to see him through her blurry vision. "Jinn . . ."

His chest heaved as if he'd run a marathon just to make it here. Iris's mind went blank. There was too much to sort out from the chaos. But he was alive. The only takeaway that mattered was that he was alive. He was alive, and he was here.

Jinn was alive.

And so was Gram. A few quick steps and Jinn was upon him, catching with both hands the hilt of the blade Gram had pulled out of his stomach and turned on his attacker.

"You killed my father, and you have no regrets." Jinn gritted his teeth as he struggled against Gram's swing. "You're sick. You're a monster. It's only right for you to disappear like he did—*screaming!*"

"It seems you are a man haunted by monsters." Gram shoved him back, but the blow had made him sluggish. Jinn caught his next swing, wrenching the blade from his grip. After Jinn kicked Gram's stomach, the man fell back down onto the plank, blood gushing from his mouth. Jinn raised the blade above his head, ready to deal the final blow. Gram couldn't move. He must have been in pain so intense it caused his body to twitch uncontrollably. He was about to die.

So why was he smiling?

"If *I* am a monster for killing your father, then how much more so is the woman who will destroy the world and everything else you hold dear?"

Jinn's blade remained frozen above his head. His wide eyes darted to Iris, and suddenly, as their gazes locked, they softened. But not out of love.

Out of fear. Confusion. He was *listening* to Gram.

"Monsters do not just appear, boy," Gram continued, jerking his head to the side. "They become. My first kill frightened me. My second made me curious. Slowly it became nature. It will be so for the girl if you let her go free. She's already killed, hasn't she?"

The feeling drained from Iris's face as she watched the gears in Jinn's mind turning, wondering perhaps if she had killed, or remembering her confession in Club Uriel. She wanted to cry out, to shut Gram up for good, but the memory of all the deaths she'd caused began to strangle her. She couldn't speak.

"You're a man haunted by monsters," Gram said again. "It's only a matter of time before this one consumes you. It's inevitable. . . ."

The plank plummeted into the water, taking Gram and Jinn with it. Shocked, Iris looked down and saw the steamer's propeller turning. *La Daphnée* finally began lumbering along. A plume of red stained the waters as Gram drifted in the Seine. Jinn swam for the docks, but Gram needed flesh to heal, and he'd found his next targets. Before long, he was swimming for Berta and Lulu, who were struggling to keep their heads above water.

"A rope! A rope!" Iris yelled, but nobody moved, not even Adam, who shook his head.

It was Abiade who ran for one even though Rin tried to hold him back.

"Isoke!"

"I won't let them die," Iris spat back, summoning just a little bit of that ancient fortitude that had carried her through the eons. Rin backed down. "Jinn!"

After lifting himself onto the docks, Jinn ran toward the moving ship. He made a powerful leap, so powerful that he nearly crossed the distance. Leaning over the railing, Iris caught Jinn's hand before he could land in the river and pulled him up just as Abiade came back with a rope and threw one end down into the Seine.

"Climb!" he ordered Berta as Rin helped pull Jinn aboard. "Climb up, fast!"

Jinn fell on top of Iris, and the two collapsed onto the ship's deck. For a moment, it was as if everything slowed to a halt. Jinn was on top of her, gripping her around the waist. His face inches away. Jinn. Jinn was alive. . . .

Lulu screamed. Snapping out of their trance, both Iris and Jinn stumbled to their feet. Berta swam desperately for the rope, carrying Lulu on her back, but Gram was coming for them.

Not her. Iris wouldn't let Max's sister die too.

"Rin!" Iris yelled.

Out came Rin's sword from her chest, but Iris wouldn't let her charge into the river. Iris looked at Jinn, who nodded back. They didn't need words—just muscle memory from many routines practiced together. Like one knife-throwing act they'd rehearsed for months to perform in this very city. Iris grabbed Rin's sword and threw it high into the sky. Jinn jumped onto the ledge and, with a swift kick, brought his foot down on the handle, launching the sword at Gram. The blade pierced Gram's shoulder instead of his head, which had no doubt been Jinn's target. She could see the rage in Jinn's eyes. But it was enough. The attack stopped Gram dead. As Rin's magic sword dematerialized, he began to sink.

"Grab the rope!" Iris told Berta, encouraging Max's sister until she finally caught it. It took Iris, Jinn, and Rin's strength combined to lift them up onto the deck. The two girls flopped soaking wet onto the floor, but in a matter of moments, Berta was on her feet, readying her fists in lieu of her shotgun, lost to the river.

Pulling Iris back, Rin caught Berta's punch, twisted her arm, and quickly forced her into a kneeling position.

"Stop it! Don't bully her!" Lulu hit Rin with her little fists. Iris swept the girl off her feet.

"It's okay," she said, trying to calm her down. Setting her gently onto the floor, she hugged her, feeling her heart beating in her chest through that white dress she had on. "It's okay. This is all just a misunderstanding, I promise."

"That's right," said Adam, staring at Berta and Lulu. "A misunderstanding. A strange one." He stepped forward, his eyes on Jinn, who glared at him with a quiet, simmering fury that honestly frightened Iris. "Jinn. You followed Gram and Jacques here, I suppose?"

Jinn said nothing. His expression darkened at the sight of Adam. The ship lurched away from the harbor down the river.

"What an interesting turn of events. And here I thought Gram had already eaten you." Adam laughed, sweeping his wet black hair off his forehead. "Well, now that you're here, there are some things you should know. A lot has happened since you abandoned your Iris. And I venture a guess that you're not ready to comprehend—"

With one swift movement, Jinn strode toward Adam, grabbed his arm, and flipped him over the railing of the ship. Iris gasped, but didn't stop him, couldn't stop him, before he threw Adam overboard. The young Temple plummeted into the ocean.

"J-Jinn?" Iris stuttered.

Now, suddenly more relaxed, Jinn breathed in deep, his shoulders slumped as he closed his eyes and lifted his head to the sky, taking in the fresh air. Then he turned to Iris.

"So. What are those *things* I should know?" he asked.

Iris buckled over in disbelief while Rin laughed and tied Berta up with rope, carting her off to the lower decks. Lulu grabbed Iris's sleeve.

"I'm glad you didn't die," she said. "You look a lot like my mom used to—in those old photos she showed me. I'm glad you didn't die."

The little girl, Lulu, smiled and followed Rin and Berta downstairs.

I'm glad you didn't die. The innocent words of that child burrowed deep inside her, cavalier and almost cruel. Max had died, but by some fearsome twist of fate, she'd been able to meet his sister. Eventually, she would have to tell that girl the truth of what had happened that night in Club Uriel: that her brother had died because of the choices he'd made for her out of his fear for what and who Iris was. What Berta did with that truth would be up to her. But at least she was alive. No one else should die. Not because of her.

Iris looked at her hands, checking her fingers. Five on each, nothing lost, except maybe the feeling in them. She took Jinn's hand in hers and squeezed again and again to force the blood flow. Warmth flooded in.

Hesitantly, she gazed up at him. Memories of the last time they'd stood this close teased her, flushing her face with heat. But just as she opened her mouth to speak, Jinn, suddenly skittish and rigid, pulled himself away from her and stepped aside. Whatever she had wanted to say in that moment simply vanished at the sight of his expression.

You're a man haunted by monsters. Gram's voice taunted her.

"Well, now that I'm here on a ship, I suppose I'll be going where you are," he said, gazing out over the waters. "Where are we headed, then?"

Iris wrapped her arms around her body. "Dahomey. I'm going to see the king of Dahomey. There's technology out there made to stop Hiva. I'm . . . I'm searching for it. The thing that'll take away this curse." She stared down at her body and bit her lip. "That'll keep me from hurting anyone else . . . and let me live in peace with Granny and—"

You. With Granny and you. She couldn't say it.

At first, Jinn didn't react. Iris squeezed herself tighter, partly for warmth, partly to steel herself for whatever Jinn was about to say next, because she knew it wouldn't be pleasant.

"And what if nothing like that exists?"

Iris gripped her flesh even tighter. "Then I'll find the technology and make it."

Jinn whipped around. "And what if it's impossible?"

"*Jinn.*" Iris stared at him, incredulous. "Do you *want* it to be impossible?"

"No!" Jinn said quickly. "No . . . but. Well. What I want, I can't have, can I?" Jinn stared off into the distance, lost in the stars.

"Y-you mean . . . revenge, right?" Iris stuttered, wondering if he could have meant something else.

Jinn frowned at the Seine, glinting eerily underneath them. "The life I once had is gone. My father. Everything I held dear."

If I am a monster for killing your father, then how much more so is the woman who will destroy the world and everything else you hold dear?

It was nonsense. Jinn couldn't have been foolish enough to believe in that ghoul's words.

Even though Iris had watched with her own eyes as he listened to each one so intently.

Iris ventured a step closer, but his shockingly dark eyes on her froze her. Neither spoke.

"It's not inevitable," Iris told him as Gram's bloody smile glinted in her memories. "It's true. I've killed scores more people than Gram has. Fathers, mothers, sisters, brothers. I've destroyed civilizations. But that isn't me anymore. I won't do it. Never again. I swear it."

"Iris." He said her name with tenderness, but the underlying hint of apprehension in his tone made her insecure.

"I swear it!" she said again, grabbing his wrist. "If it's impossible, then I'll make it possible! I'll find a way!"

Jinn was silent. He looked like there were a thousand things he wanted to say. And yet he settled on one word. "Okay." Two bloodless syllables that not even he believed. She could see it in his eyes. He wasn't sure. He wasn't sure if he could trust in her.

She wasn't sure either. And it was as she watched Jinn walk away from her that she fully realized just how painful that was.

A Young Man Thinking, III

ADAM DRAGGED GRAM'S DYING BODY ONSHORE. "Will it really take a war, Iris, before you see how desperately this world needs your judgment?" he whispered to himself.

As he renewed his purpose, quiet footsteps approached in the dark.

"Fool," he said, after he'd gasped in enough air to steady his breaths. Sitting on the ground, he planted his elbow onto his right knee and buried his head in his hand. "Which Fool are you?"

Adam only heard his voice, on the verge of laughter and yet so pathetic at the same time. "I am your Fool, my lord. And there is no Fool as loyal as I."

It wasn't the answer Adam wanted to hear. He'd glimpsed Iris's expression as he plunged into the river, shocked, but on the verge of laughter herself. And in the waters, as he'd struggled to stay afloat, he'd seen that brute of a man touch her hand. It was disgusting. A goddess among peons. The anger within him simmered to a boil.

"I asked, 'which Fool are you,' Heidegger. The name I gave you. Answer me truthfully."

Fool didn't answer for a time. He wasn't used to Adam calling him that name. But the weak part of Heidegger would have to respond, because as cruel and evil as the man was as a serial killer terrorizing London, there existed a small part of him that desperately wanted forgiveness. That whisper of a shattered soul crying out for forgiveness he could never deserve. That pathetic sliver of hope that desired a second chance he hadn't yet earned and never would, after the crimes he'd committed.

"The Broken Fool, my lord," he answered, his voice wavering only slightly.

More desperate than the Desperate Fool, ironically enough. Adam had offered him a second chance, and he'd taken it. A purpose, and he'd devoured it. Adam knew this Fool would never betray him because within this Fool, Adam saw himself.

What did it mean to be a "monster" in this world full of monsters? Ever since Adam was a child, with his father's callous absence, his uncle's drunken hand, his mother's and siblings' brutal deaths, he'd wondered himself what it would take to be called a beast in this world that created them so easily. And then after years of loneliness, pain, and torment ripping apart his mind day and night, Adam realized: such a world didn't need to exist. Not only death, but justice. That all-equalizing justice that would bring an end to all sins. That was their second chance.

And Iris was to be the one to give it to them. That he was sure of.

He didn't acknowledge the other Hiva. Wherever he'd come from, he wasn't needed. This wasn't about the ability to kill. It was about the realization that killing was necessary. It was about the process through which one lost faith in the world and saw the reason for its end. It was what he wanted Iris to come to see, just as he had.

Iris was the one. *She* had to be the one to bring about the end. He'd known that as a boy reading his father's research. He'd known that as he'd carried her heavy crystal heart in his hands and watched her glorious rebirth in the South Kensington fair exhibit. He'd known that as he saw her searching for her identity, lost like a lamb in a tournament of murder. There was an order to things. Iris's innocence and determination were but a prelude to her eventual understanding of what this world really was. Just like him, she was to realize the bitter, awful truth. Just like him, the truth would purify her. Then she would ascend to her rightful place as this world's judge and executioner. Only he would stand by her side in the end, he who had been denied a family, denied the bonds that tied hopeful men together. It would be the ultimate gift for him before death.

The Iris he saw sailing away from him wasn't ready. Why didn't she understand his pain? Why couldn't she see everything he had done to bring her to this point? Every carefully laid plan, every chess piece moved at exactly the right time. The powers he'd awakened her to. The truth behind her identity. Everything so callously pushed aside for such meaningless dreams.

But he would make her ready. Perhaps by killing everyone she loved until the only bond she had left was the one with him. Yes. Then he would make her ready for the end.

"Find Jacques and dispatch whatever medical care he might need," Adam ordered Fool. "I doubt he made it out of his battle with Iris unscathed. And make sure Bellerose knows that Iris has escaped and is voyaging to the Kingdom of Dahomey on the vessel *La Daphnée*."

Knowing Bellerose, she would make sure those British captains on the seas under the Committee's control would be on the lookout for Iris's ship.

"Oh," Adam added, "and tell her that her assassins will now be pursuing their target under my orders." There was no quicker way to bring Bellerose to Paris. What Adam wanted to do, he couldn't do by himself.

"What is your plan, my lord?"

Adam's fingers slid through his damp black hair as he gripped his forehead. "Iris is heading to the Kingdom of Dahomey. Then that is where we will head as well."

Bellerose still wished to capture Iris. It was as Van der Ven said: Why settle for one world when you could have two? If the Committee could get rid of the threat of an apocalypse dangling over their heads but still hoard the ancient Naacalian technology that would allow them untold power—well, what more could one ask for? As far as Bellerose was concerned, he was guiding Gram and Jacques to fulfill the Committee's purpose.

He slid a knife out of his pocket and pulled the dying Gram close to him until the man's head was upon his lap. Rolling up his sleeves, he pointed the tip of the knife at Gram's throat while placing his forearm upon his mouth. The knife was a precautionary measure. To make sure this ghoul didn't get carried away.

He was guiding Gram and Jacques. That was what he would tell what was left of the Committee. But the truth was that he needed his own help in pursuing Iris. He needed help in getting rid of the army of redundant bodies orbiting her. And that was why he would gather his own army.

Van der Ven's assassins were now his.

"Fly now, Fool," he said, before Gram bit his flesh and the bloodletting began.

PART TWO
Divine Wrath

Mine eyes have seen the glory of the coming of the Lord:

He is trampling out the vintage where the grapes

of wrath are stored;

He hath loosed the fateful lightning of His terrible swift sword:

His truth is marching on.

"THE BATTLE HYMN OF THE REPUBLIC"

HELL-RAISERS

THE BASEMENT SMELLED OF FECES, BUT Fables got used to it quick. This dark, dank pit was already putrid with the smell of dashed hopes. But Hiva was here too, somewhere. Why would those flunkies have spirited Hiva's headless carcass here?

To tinker with him? To bury him? Or . . .

Hiva was a god. Could he have survived?

Old bricks surrounded him, clumsily laid atop one another, cobbled together with cracking cement. How many days had he spent curled up on a pile of hay on a dust-ridden floor, listening to the pathetic weeping of his fellow cellmates? Cherice, he thought the girl's name was. He wished she'd shut the hell up. *Everyone* was messed up in here, not just her. He couldn't count how many times the creaky door of their jail cell had opened and those serious-looking Basement scientists had dragged out a new prisoner.

"Hawkins!"

It was usually him.

"Hawkins!" that Jacob guy yelled as Hawkins pushed him down and offered himself up to the scientists like a sacrificial lamb. Again.

"You lot have already taken him once. Take me next." Hawkins lifted his head and gave them a defiant, crooked smile. "Come on." Hawkins tapped his own shirtless chest, now cut up with the scars of experimentation. "You've poked around inside enough to know I'm a better specimen. And unlike him, I'm not a screamer."

"Hawkins, stop this!" Jacob reached out and grabbed his ragged pants to pull him back, but his grip was too weak. Hawkins shook him off with ease. "Stop!" he cried again as the scientists nodded to each other and led Hawkins away once more. "You're going too far! This won't bring Max back."

"Bring Max back?" Hawkins laughed as if he hated himself. "I don't even know where the hell he is anymore. I told you about the abbey."

Jacob squirmed. "This won't change anything," he whispered.

"It won't." Hawkins looked behind him at Jacob, at the crying Cherice. "But I'll never lose anyone again. I won't let you two die."

As the door shut, Cherice's incessant sobbing filled Fables with the irrational desire to punch her in the face. All these London freaks had powers. And they were all messed up because of it, but even still, none of them could possibly understand what Fables was going through.

Fables had seen the face of God and survived. He'd touched his salvation only to see his savior slaughtered mercilessly in front of him. He wasn't some disloyal dirtbag like Berta and Lulu. Even if he could run, he never would, but it was the not-knowing. For days he'd had no idea what they'd done with the body. He still had no idea. He was all alone here with these freaky English kids. All alone. His evil father would be laughing at him if he could see him now—if he'd even believe this story in the first place.

Place in the world? You ain't got no place in this world, boy. You don't deserve it.

Which was why Fables wanted the world gone. He was so close, too. . . .

Hours later, the door opened, and Hawkins was thrown in. As many times as he offered himself up, it was only a matter of time before they went back to the other two. The door slammed shut with a loud shuddering sound.

Lying against the dirty brick, Jacob pulled the boy up to him so Hawkins's head was on his lap. They were on the other side of the cell—far away from *him*, Fables noticed, not that he cared, though it annoyed him a little. Hawkins was barely breathing. There was a bloody wound where his spleen should be. Fables couldn't look, it was so gruesome. A doctor would be in soon to give him some drugs, but how long could these freaks possibly last?

Blood wetted Jacob's fingers as he tentatively touched the wound. Then his tears began to drop upon Hawkins's cheeks one by one until he was cradling Hawkins's face, pressing his forehead against his.

"You sweet on each other or something?" Fables asked, lying on his side, not bothering to hide his bitterness.

Jacob didn't answer. Cherice slid up next to him, and together they watched over Hawkins. The boy's breaths came ragged, but at least they came.

Scoffing, Fables flopped onto his back and cushioned his head with his arms upon the prickly hay. "I heard something funny last night," he started while Cherice's quiet sobs wafted through the jail cell. "They were talking about it in the other room. A tournament with you folks? A cash prize for whoever wins?" He let out an incredulous laugh. "I get being poor and looking for a way out, but this world isn't worth living in, let alone dying for. You're all loony as hell."

Jacob wiped his eyes, and for the first time, Fables saw a wry grin far too self-hating for his gentle features.

"I didn't want to do it. But I went along because I was too scared to speak up. That's how it always is with me. Too scared to make the hard calls. It's easier just to go along with things and keep the peace. That's how I watched Max disappear. Now we don't even know where he is. He was supposed to be underneath the floor of the abbey, but robbers dug it up weeks ago."

Now this was interesting. Fables balanced a leg over his knee.

"But the way Hawkins told it, they were both definitely buried in a box somewhere. Somewhere he couldn't move. He couldn't even breathe. That's why he had to get out."

Jacob shook his head. "The abbey floor was broken. A lot of caskets were stolen. The casket Hawkins's mother was buried in was gone. So where did he take Max? Where is he? Is he dead? Is he somewhere worse?"

Cherice bit her lip. "Hawkins told Berta he was dead."

Fables bristled at the sound of her name, but he listened on.

"To get her angry. But not even he knows the truth anymore. Max could be anywhere. He could be dead, and he could be anywhere. This is a mess, and it's all my fault."

"It isn't," Cherice warned him.

"Well, Hawkins thinks it's *his*," Jacob said. "Why else is he being so irrational, throwing himself into danger like he wants it all to end?"

Fables didn't see the point of being so dramatic about it. So his lover had a death wish. Who didn't?

"It's not your fault," Cherice said. "It's not his, either." And her voice turned deadly. "It's hers. Iris." Shadows danced across her face.

Iris. The girl Hiva had mentioned? Just as Fables began to feel his jealousy flaring up again, Jacob shook his head wildly.

"No, it is all my fault," he insisted. "It's all my fault!"

"No, it's *my* fault," Fables repeated in an exaggerated, whining voice. "It's my fault. Oh no, no, it's *my* fault! *God.*" Rolling his eyes, Fables glared at the three of them. Life was simple for Fables. Since meeting Hiva, it'd become simpler. Whoever did wrong should be punished. Whoever hurt you, cut them off like a diseased limb and keep moving. Even if that meant the whole world. Fables had no room and no care for shades of gray.

"Folks like you are the worst," Fables told Jacob especially, because the boy was gripping his head as if it'd explode. "Do-gooders like you feel torn about every little thing. The second you do a little wrong, you torture yourself with guilt. Torture and repress yourselves so bad that the second you let yourself slip, let all that crap go and embrace your bad side, you ride that horse naked straight down to hell."

"That's not who I am at all!" Jacob said. Fables could hear the weakness in his street-urchin English.

Fables scoffed. "I bet it's coming."

"Ugh, will you shut your dumb arse *up!*" Cherice screwed up her piggish face and balled her hand into a fist. "You'll forgive me, but I don't quite feel like having a little chat while we're down here stuck in this never-ending nightmare!"

"You think *I* need to shut up?" Fables could have spat on her. "If you have time to cry and whine, why don't you think of a plan to get out of here? Y'all are the ones with the magic tricks, not me. What about him?" He jerked his head toward Hawkins. "Isn't he the one who can make folks disappear?"

"They did something to him." Fables could barely hear Jacob. "Whatever they injected him with, his powers haven't been the same since."

"Yeah, because they know he's our ticket out of here," said Cherice.

"God, what are they going to do to us?" Jacob sounded on the verge of a breakdown. "This is like Chadwick all over again. First Chadwick, then Max. If Lawrence dies too, I swear, Cherice, I don't know what I'm going to do. I honestly don't—"

"Quiet. Stop your crying, for God's sake, you teary git." But Cherice wasn't so convincing while swallowing her own tears.

I don't know what I'm going to do. Fables didn't want to admit that he understood the boy, but he did. Get to Hiva. He just needed confirmation that his savior was alive. That *some* gods kept their promises.

The door opened. This time they called for Cherice. She didn't cry, even when they returned her with electric shock burns on her body.

It went on and on like that: scientists coming in and out of their cell, dragging folks out, throwing them back in. And not even a hint of Hiva.

Until one day, or night, Fables's cell door creaked open, jolting him awake. A shadow of a man's profile blocked the sliver of light leaking in from the outside. His lips moved. "The Enlightenment Committee shall live forever. Eight Grandage View. Quickly."

And the door closed—after a pair of skeleton keys on a ring were plunked onto the floor.

Keys. Keys? Confused, Fables swept the cobwebs from his eyes. On his left, Jacob slowly lifted his head from his knees.

"Eight Grandage View. I know where that is." Jacob looked at the keys for a moment before going for them, crawling on his hands, grabbing and feeling them as if to make sure they were real.

"No, wait!" Fables sat up, waving his hands. "We can't waltz out of here just because we got the keys! There are scientists and guards and stuff out there. C-come on!"

Fables felt his cowardice slipping in again and in that moment thought of Berta. How she'd be mocking him mercilessly if she could see his legs suddenly going weak after days of talking shit to these people.

"You sure you don't want to escape?" Cherice asked with a sly glint in her eyes. "After all that mumbling you do about 'Hiva' in your sleep night after night? I saw you crying like a baby when they took his head off. Don't you wanna see him again?"

Fables straightened up. "Hiva. You mean he's really . . . he's really . . . ?"

"Alive?" Cherice finished for him. "If he's anything like the other Hiva, my bet is on yes."

Fables's eyes swelled with tears. He knew it. Fables knew his god couldn't be taken down so easily, not by the British, not by anyone. Hiva *was* alive. His god hadn't abandoned him yet. . . .

"Like you said, there are scientists and guards and stuff," Jacob said, putting the keys in his pocket. "And, as it turns out, there are also freaks like us. Angry ones."

Cherice nodded. "I heard you loud and clear, Jacob." A wicked smile stretched her face like the Cheshire cat's. "Let's raise some hell."

12

MOVING AT FOURTEEN KNOTS, *La Daphnée*, carrying casks of alcohol and spices along with Iris's group of fugitives, would take eleven days to get to Freetown. Then, after a stay of two or three days, it was five more days until they reached a famous port in Dahomey. From there, Rin said, they would have to travel on foot. Rin had brought Iris's regular clothes from the tavern. The cotton Granny had sewed itched a little bit. It had gone through as much as she had. But she was thankful for anything that kept her close to the old woman.

Until Berta was willing to drop her deadly designs on Iris, they kept her tied up in the bottom decks, in a room where some of the alcohol barrels were stored. Her little friend Lulu, however, was harmless. After being assured of Berta's safety, she was left to play around on deck, talking to the passengers.

For the first two days, Iris was hesitant to approach her. She was a girl filled with innocence, so much so that Iris feared if she asked of the trauma hidden beneath her red-lipped smile, she would be given an answer as honest and straightforward as a comment on the weather. For now, she stayed away but close, watching to make sure no further harm would come to her.

There were various types on this voyage, after all. A multilingual merchant named Olivier who planned to sell some of his fabrics in the port city they were headed to: what he called Porto-Novo, and what Abiade called Ajashe, his home.

"I'm on break from school. I was already planning on going home to put my interpreter skills to good use," Abiade told her. "Rin just had me bring up the date a little bit."

"You seem to be very good friends then."

"Well, I want to help." And he became very quiet. "We're both friends from the same village, but our fortunes turned out so very differently. To think that at her age, she's a military woman for a foreign country . . ."

"Yeah," Iris said, her head low. "It's not something I would wish on anyone." The sounds of King Ghezo's battles raged in her memories. She tried not to remember those violent times.

Olivier walked around deck with the flimsiest boots she'd ever seen, telling everyone within reach about his lucrative business, how much he loved traveling on the high seas, and what an expert he was at smelling the change in weather before it occurred, then giving out lessons on how to sniff the air at exactly the right angle. He wasn't any worse, however, than Moyra, a Scottish missionary who came to bring the good word to Africa's "savages." She didn't seem to know what to do with Iris and Rin, who met her zeal with disdain and indifference, and so turned to Lulu, who seemed well versed with the inner workings of the Presbyterian Church.

"Mama was in the choir at our church," Iris overheard Lulu telling the missionary, who'd tied her red hair up modestly in a no-nonsense bun. "She taught me this song."

And she began singing of the coming glory of a wrathful god.

"What about you, Jinn?" Iris asked Jinn in private later that night as he watched the rolling waves of the ocean. "Do you believe in a higher power?"

"Father and I practiced Islam, but in those days, he and his political circle were more interested in creating a society that didn't depend so much on theocracy," Jinn answered simply. "Not exactly an idea welcomed by the Ottoman Empire."

"Do you still—"

"No." Jinn turned his head so she couldn't see his expression. "I believe in what I can see."

Granny had told her once that death often made people cling tighter to gods or reject them entirely. And yet still some traded in their deities for ones that would wield death as their weapon upon the heads of their enemies.

Lulu's little hymn eventually became stuck in Iris's head.

Jinn spent most of his time on the seas alone, shrugging off whoever came to him to preach or drink. Iris stayed close, but not too close, sometimes watching him out of the corner of her eye from afar like a common stalker; other times daring to venture close to him, casually pretending to be more interested in the fresh ocean air.

One morning, Iris noticed Rin watching him too.

"You two," Rin said while sitting on the ship's wooden forecastle, when both Jinn and Iris were near enough.

After exchanging awkward glances, Jinn and Iris approached her.

"Aren't you lovers?"

"W-what?" Iris stuttered, turning to face the ocean quickly while a startled Jinn scratched the back of his head. "Of course not. We're former circus partners. Nothing more."

Nothing more. Suddenly feeling the weight of Jinn's presence near her, Iris stiffened. She refused to look at him. If she had, what kind of expression would she have seen on that gorgeous face of his?

Rin stared at the two for too long. "What's this disagreeable air about you, then? You were close during the Tournament of Freaks. Are you no longer?"

Iris spun around. "That's . . . ," she started, but couldn't finish.

Rin had never shown much interest in them before. She'd barely spoken to Jinn during the tournament. Now her good eye studied him.

"You're mistaken," Jinn told the young warrior. "There's nothing wrong between us. Nothing disagreeable."

Iris wondered. His voice was as neutral as his face. She took him in. His long lashes, brown skin, and sharp jaw. The vein traveling up Jinn's right arm reminded her a little of a winding river, like the Seine that had carried them into the open seas. Iris hated noticing little things like that. She also noticed that Jinn wasn't that interested in looking at her much at all these days.

Rin was watching her watch Jinn but said nothing, even after Iris had been caught. But after the three had parted, sometime in the afternoon, Iris saw the two chatting. It wasn't a big deal. Still, she noticed, with a pang of bitterness, that whenever the quiet Jinn did speak to others, he spoke with a casual friendliness he hadn't bothered to show her, not here on this ship where he seemed more comfortable avoiding her.

It wasn't as if she had expected an emotional reunion. They hadn't been apart for long, but after days of wondering if he'd taken his revenge upon Gram or died trying, she had expected something more than his skittishness.

It was all Gram's fault. That bastard had managed to play with Jinn's mind before dying.

If I am a monster for killing your father, then how much more so is the woman who will destroy the world and everything else you hold dear?

"We are not alike," Iris whispered, before she realized that she was much worse—and still could be. Jinn must have realized that too.

Their second night on the ship, Iris had gathered the former tournament champions in a private room in the lower deck. There, under a rickety ceiling light, Rin had emptied out her sack and spread out John Temple's translated journal and the Naacalian scrolls she'd taken from the tavern—gingerly, of course. Rin had spent a day drying them under the sun, but after being waterlogged, they were brittle to the touch.

Iris had told them everything she could glean between the scrolls and her jumbled memories. She told them her plan: to use Nyeth's ring to find the Coral Temple and the anti-Hiva technology stored within. To bring it to Uma and, with the power of the white crystal, create something that would safely transform her into a human being, just like the Helios and the Forge had transformed them.

"How is the ring supposed to point the way?" asked Jinn.

"Anima." Iris thought of Adam's lessons in Club Uriel. "It's the life force that all living things have. And sometimes traces of it linger on certain items. Remember when Adam wanted me to find his father? He thought I could do it by getting a reading from his father's journal."

"You're talking about psychometry," Jinn said, caressing his chin. "You have the ring with you. Why don't you try it now?"

Iris wasn't sure why she hesitated. But the moment her fingers wrapped around the ring, she understood. It was still just as cold and unforgiving. A lump formed in her throat that was painful to swallow. She closed her eyes and searched for a path, but none was made open to her. It was as if it was refusing to bend to her will. All she could feel was Nyeth's bones in the Library of Rule and his hatred for her. Then she saw him die. The sputter of his blood from his lips. His despair at the loss of his world overwhelmed her.

Finally, she dropped the ring back into her pocket. "I guess I was naïve to think it'd be that easy," she said with a sheepish shrug.

"You still aim to meet the king, don't you?" asked Rin.

Iris frowned. Even with all she'd said, that was all Rin cared about? "Yeah," Iris answered slowly. "He oversaw the creation of the Forge, didn't he? He may have an idea of how to do this. Plus, John Temple went to him seeking remnants of the Naacal and information on . . . well, me. I just need clues, wherever I can find them, whoever can give them to me."

To drag a god back down to earth required nothing short of divine intervention of a different sort. If what the king told me is indeed true, I'll find my divine intervention in the place where heaven dwells. Had John Temple found the answer? Had he eventually figured out how to change the supernatural to human? Perhaps the king of Dahomey knew where John Temple himself could be hiding. And if John could also help her find the Coral Temple . . .

Finding John Temple was a must. Where better to find all this information than from the man who seemed to know "Hiva" the best?

Jinn, though he'd listened to everything with a kind of measured neutrality, still seemed skeptical. "Your plan isn't a bad one," he assured her, staring at the scrolls on the wooden floor. "But we're dealing with a serious situation. Serious enough to consider every option. If you fail, more people could die. Granny—"

"I would never lay a hand on Granny!" Iris snapped, staring at him wide-eyed.

"I'm not saying you would," Jinn clarified, frowning, his cheeks suddenly flushed. He looked defensive. Angry. With *her*. "I'm *not* saying you would."

"So—what, you think I'm evil like Gram?" Iris pushed on. "You think I'd hurt Granny?"

"No! Well—"

Jinn's frustrated pause was pure devastation. It shattered her in two. It was enough to make her ignore the emotional glimmer in his eyes and the quiet tremble of his lips.

Rin glanced between the two of them with a curious expression but didn't interfere.

"Damn it, Iris, that's not what I said." Jinn lifted himself off the floor and brushed off his dark, dusty pants. "I've lost everything before. I don't want to lose anything more. So we need to be cautious, that's all. We need to consider every angle. I don't care if that hurts your feelings. If you're too immature to see that, then that's on *you*."

"Immature." Iris let out a derisive laugh as he began to leave. "I'm millions of years older than you."

Jinn stopped. "You're right," he said quietly. "You are. You're not who I thought you were. We're not at all alike. Not even the same species. I guess we can't . . . I guess we shouldn't . . ." He didn't finish his sentence before leaving the room.

Iris was stunned into silence.

When Iris finally made time to sit with Berta and tell her everything, it was something the girl threw back in her face with the utmost glee.

"So you can't die—and what, you think you're all good and noble for trying to stop yourself from killing everyone even though you've done it before?" She laughed. "How am I supposed to believe you give a damn about us regular folk when you've already murdered so many of us?" Berta was not only tied with rope, but extra chains had been brought in to tie her to a wooden load-bearing pillar. They needed it. Berta's expression alone could kill. "You're the reason my brother's dead."

"I told you, that was all a mistake." Iris held her head in her hands, thinking of that day. Max confessing his misdeeds—his murder of Carl Anderson. His lies. Exposing her secret to the rest of the tournament champions. Hawkins's desperate attempt to get rid of her, only for Max to sacrifice himself in her stead, disappearing into that whirling vortex. Iris shook her head. "It all happened so fast," she whispered.

"Stop playing the victim, princess. By your own admission, everything went south because he was scared of *you*," Berta spat. Then, her shoulders slumping, she lowered her gaze. "And because he wouldn't stop looking for me . . . the way I stopped looking for him."

Iris recognized the guilt now plaguing the girl, because it was a curse she knew all too well. "How did you even get to America?" she asked. "What have you been doing all this time? I'd like to know—"

"Then you'll have to ask someone else, because I ain't telling you shit."

Berta's spit hit her square in the cheek. But Iris wasn't upset. This was someone who'd lost everything. Iris could only offer her the truth. As she wiped the saliva off her face, she hoped, at the very least, to give Berta some closure on her brother. It wasn't much, but she could tell by how much Berta's expression had softened, how quiet she was when Iris began speaking of her brother, that it meant something.

"There's lots I can tell you about him," Iris said. "I mean, I didn't know him for very long, but if you ever want to hear any stories—"

Berta let out an exasperated breath. "Please . . . just leave," she said, and turned away.

The hatred of others. It was during those quiet nights on the ocean that Iris had to contend with it. The out-of-body experience that was remembering her past lives and past deeds. The terror she felt when certain scenes of civilizations destroyed flashed in her mind's eye—like reading bloody tale after bloody tale with the knowledge that you were the villain in each one. The ghoul devouring innocent souls in a child's penny dreadful. The devil lurking in the shadows. Hiva could be seen as such a being. Isoke, for some. But she was Iris. She was *Iris*. . . .

No, someone *else* had given her that name without permission, and she'd accepted it.

She was . . .

She held Nyeth's ring in her hand, then stared at herself in a broken mirror that hung in the bare room she shared at night with Rin and Lulu. A reflection split into pieces.

"You're a murderer."

Shocked, Iris whipped around only to see Lulu on the small wooden bed. There was only one in this tiny room, and Iris had given it to Lulu. Iris slept sitting up against the rightmost wall. Rin stayed with Berta, watching the girl's every move.

"You're all murderers . . . but you're all gonna get it soon. God's coming for you. . . ."

It looked like she was having a bad dream. Iris went to wake up her up. In that split second, that first brush of wakefulness, Iris could see a fear so piercing it made her own body shake. But after a few seconds, those big eyes softened. Lulu remembered where she was.

"You were having a bad dream, that's all." Iris brushed the girl's thick hair back. She was surprised when Lulu had let her comb and braid it earlier that day. It was a little messy when she'd first boarded *La Daphnée*, and Iris didn't see Berta as the type to know what to do with it. Several long, straight rows of braided hair reaching up to the crown of her head. A string holding the ends in a little makeshift tail. Granny had done it for her all the time while she was at the circus. It felt good to do it for someone else. It had softened Lulu up toward her as well.

"Yeah." Lulu nodded. "I was dreaming of when they killed my family."

Iris's throat went dry. Her hand froze upon Lulu's cheek.

"Hung 'em up in a tree. They do that a lot where I'm from, but I didn't think it would happen to me. I really didn't think so."

Shaken and confused, Iris withdrew her hand.

"That's when I met them—Berta and that funny, twiggy boy. Oh, and Hiva, the angel."

"Hiva?" Iris breathed and sat up straight as Lulu's eyes grew rounder, as hope sprang into them. "You know . . . Hiva . . . ?"

"Sure I do." Lulu yawned and wiped a tear from her lashes. "Mama said angels exist. You know Michael? He's God's warrior angel. He leads the army in

Heaven to war. And on the last day, there's gonna be a big one. Fire and brimstone. Judgment Day."

Iris wrapped her arms around herself. "And you think," she asked carefully, "that Hiva is this angel?"

"From what I seen, yeah," Lulu answered matter-of-factly. She shifted from her side onto her back and pulled the white sheet over her. "That's why I'm not afraid of them anymore. No matter how big they think they are, they can't bully an angel."

Without needing to ask, Iris understood who "they" were. She nodded.

"Why?" Lulu continued. "What do you think he is?"

Hiva, an angel? For some reason she thought of Adam and shuddered.

"What if I told you that *I* was Hiva?"

For a moment, Lulu just stared at her. Then she reached out for Iris's cheek and smiled. "Yeah," she said quietly. "That makes more sense. Much more sense. Cuz you look like me. You look like us—Mama, Daddy, and Joey. It makes sense."

Iris wasn't sure what she meant. She wasn't sure what any of it meant. Upon her head was the hope and despair of too many lives. But what about Iris? Did what she wanted matter?

After shakily getting to her feet, she left the room and let the girl sleep.

13

THE FIFTH DAY AT SEA PUSHED *La Daphnée* to the limit. The waters near North Africa were treacherous. Every passenger received the warning to remain belowdecks. But one night, Iris heard their voices calling to her. The voices of the dead.

The storm raged in the dead of darkness, the wind howling murder, hollow and furious like the voices of the Naacal—no, the Atlanteans. Or the Lemurians. All of them. Names of civilizations past, destroyed by her hand. Turned to dust. As the cold sea and pelting rain battered her body, she slipped Nyeth's ring upon her finger and made her way to the front of the ship, holding on to the bulwark and shutting her eyes as the ship tossed back and forth.

There was a chance this wouldn't work. Nyeth's body was in the British Museum, after all. His anima inside the ring kept pointing her in that direction. But once she touched it, she could also see the moment Nyeth died inside the temple. Perhaps, if she really concentrated, she could see the way there.

She inhaled and gave it another try.

The Coral Temple. Deep in the ocean. Where? How did she get to it? The ring gave nothing away. It bled death into her. Mocking her: *I won't tell you.* And yet she saw it: the temple. The great inner dome, like a throne room. The long, winding steps upon which lay her brother's mangled body. The filtered underwater light shining down through the glass ceiling. Shining down upon Nyeth's ashes littering the platform.

"Iris!"

Iris heard Jinn's voice only barely through the raging winds.

"The key to rid the world of 'Hiva' is there," Iris whispered through gritted teeth, knuckles bloodless as she held the bulwark in a desperate grip.

"Iris! What the hell are you doing?" Jinn was fighting his way to her.

"The key to rid the world of 'Hiva' is there!" Iris yelled it this time. "It's inside the Coral Temple. I know it is. I know it is! I know—"

She screamed. One violent toss of the ship sent her hurtling back. Then she was gliding across the deck toward the opposite end of the ship's forward.

"Iris! Get ahold of yourself!"

Iris blinked away the drops of water and saw, through narrowed eyes, Jinn sliding toward her, reaching out for her. The slippery wood took her away from him, but she stretched out her arm, a splinter of wood catching her wrist as, just barely, she grabbed his hand. He pulled her in, wrapping his arms around her as they hurtled together. It was his back that slammed into the railings. Iris panicked as he heard him cry out upon impact.

"Jinn? Jinn!" His pained grunt snapped her out of her delusions. "Jinn! Are you okay?"

Part of his left leg was dangling over the deck underneath the railing. If he didn't pull it in gently, he'd lose his shoe to the violent waters below. But he didn't move. Because neither of them would be able to find their footing until the ship settled, he continued to hold her while the ship teetered and thrashed.

"It's not fair," Iris whined, and she didn't know anymore whether her wet face was due to the rain, the sea, or her own tears. "Every day you've been here, you've done everything to avoid me. Is it because of what Gram said? You think I'm a monster too, don't you? Don't you?"

Because she *was* Hiva: a threat to everyone. An angel. A devil. An entity she could never accept. That was why she wanted something, *anything* to take this burden from her. Whatever friend, whatever enemy could perform this exorcism, she would accept them with open arms. Then maybe she could begin to peer through the heavy veils and find her true self. A self she could live with. A self who others could love without losing their own lives as recompense.

"It's not fair," she whimpered as Jinn silently held her.

He held her until the seas had calmed and the ship had leveled. But he never answered her question. Not once.

With the morning came serene seas, but the danger had not yet passed. The ship's mercenary captain, LeBlanc, told them that sailors often tried to avoid coming too close to Morocco because of the ever-changing sandbars along its Atlantic coastline and the high-breaking seas. That had been his original plan, until a four-masted, iron-hulled British ship almost twice their size had cornered them.

It didn't take long for the naval officers to line them up at the orders of this Captain Slessor of the HMS *Diana*. After boarding their ship, he set loose his large and vicious crew to scour their cargo.

"Whatever you're looking for, you're sure not going to find it here," said LeBlanc, though his voice was not quite as commanding as he'd meant it to be. "Why are you all here?"

"Apparently you haven't gotten the memo." The taller and brawnier Slessor had no trouble intimidating the other captain. "Several days ago, the British Crown sent vessels to this area to contend with the illegal trading of sugarcane in these parts—in particular the *Ataegina*. Its stash was stolen from Mozambique. You wouldn't know anything about that unseemly vessel, would you?"

LeBlanc shook his head. "We have no connection to that ship whatsoever, I swear!"

Captain Slessor didn't look convinced. "Oh? Well, it's strange that you're here in the first place. Most ships have stayed clear of this area since. And they'll remain out of our way until we've arrested those devils, rescued our men, and avenged the ones they've already murdered."

"Murdered?" Iris repeated, incredulous, while beside her Jinn nudged her in the ribs to stay silent.

"Two of our ships are at a standoff with them," said Slessor, his combed blond goatee in stark contrast to LeBlanc's shaggy mane. "The captain—or whoever's in charge of that bloody ship—already killed twelve officials from both crews and took five of them hostage. Negotiations are ongoing. That's why we can't take any chances."

"But we're not with them at all," said Abiade. "We're a legal vessel sanctioned to travel to Ajashe—Porto-Novo," he clarified, but when Slessor looked at him with disgust, he furrowed his eyebrows in frustration and lapsed into silence.

"Uh . . ." LeBlanc stepped in, though Iris wasn't sure that was helpful. The man smelled of cigarettes and flatulence—not that it was an issue on their ship. He'd never done anything Iris would have to smite him for. But she wasn't surprised the uptight, squeaky-clean Captain Slessor would suspect him as some sort of nefarious agent. The number of gunports *Diana* had was a bit intimidating as well. "We are, of course, on the level," he said, using the English he knew with a firm nod and a wag of his finger for good measure.

"Whether or not that's true, we'll see after we're done with our inspection."

Sweat dripped down Iris's cheek, and Jinn must have known why. When Slessor was out of earshot, Jinn leaned in conspiratorially. "Berta?"

"Under the floor panel." Rin had stashed her there quickly while *Diana*'s crew was preparing to board. "She's a fugitive in America. Has a bounty on her head. Lulu told me some of what she's gotten up to. She'll want this all to go smoothly too."

Yes, smoothly. A thorough inspection of Olivier's colorful fabrics and the casks of wine, and then off they would go. Iris wouldn't abide any useless interruptions on her way to Dahomey.

Perhaps that was why Berta was so eager to screw her over.

"Captain, we got someone here! A hostage!"

Iris whipped around, her blood freezing when she saw a dirty Berta tied up with rope, tripping over her feet and gasping for air while two of Slessor's men dragged her up from the lower decks, one on each arm.

"What the hell is this?" Captain Slessor strode forward.

What the hell indeed. Iris looked at Rin, who shook her head, as confused as the rest of them. Her hand hovered dangerously close to her chest, but Jinn stayed her arm.

"Don't escalate this," he warned in a low voice. Iris could tell he was racking his brain to come up with an excuse. She would have been too if her mind hadn't gone blank.

Lulu, happy to see her friend, waved. "Berta! Come look at the sailors!"

"Berta, is it?" Captain Slessor grabbed Berta's chin and lifted it up, inspecting her. A flash of anger crossed Berta's face before she went back to acting helpless, breathing heavily and whimpering. Ridiculous. *Dangerous.*

"What happened to you?" Slessor demanded. "Why are you tied up like this, and who did it to you? Was it this ship's captain?"

LeBlanc might not have understood English all that well, but when Slessor aimed an accusatory finger his way, he knew he was in trouble. He shook his head furiously, holding his hand up with a "No, no, no, no, no!"

Berta gazed woefully into Slessor's eyes. "I was in Paris visiting family . . . but then . . ." She paused for dramatic effect. "I was . . . kidnapped."

Iris was shocked by how effortlessly the girl could cry on command. She held her breath, letting the icy wind batter her braids about as she squeezed her fists into numbness.

"I said, who did this to you, young woman?" Slessor gestured for his men to untie her. Iris gritted her teeth. "Speak!"

As the ropes fell to the ground, Berta's lips flinched upward for a split second. Iris wasn't surprised by what she heard next.

"That Black woman over there. Iris. She kidnapped me. She's the ringleader."

All eyes were on her.

"That's not true," Jinn said, even though it *was* a little bit true. "This girl is lying."

"Then why is she tied up? Can you tell me that?"

Berta's eyes met Iris's with a faint but unmistakable malicious glint that was nothing less than a challenge. But what could Iris say in response? There was no way in hell he'd believe the true story. She could bring up Berta's bounty, but with what evidence? As far as the captain could see, she was a pretty girl in a blue dress and red corset.

And even if Iris could send Berta to prison on an accusation alone, she wouldn't dare. Whether Max was in heaven or hell, she knew his spirit would never forgive her.

"Iris is the one who kidnapped me!" Berta, her "frail" body now suddenly filled with life, pointed straight at her. "Please, she's a menace to society. You have to arrest her!"

"Now hold on a minute!" Iris yelled, turning around and stepping forward, but when the men aimed their guns her way, she didn't dare move an inch forward.

"Yeah, Berta, don't pick on Iris; she didn't kidnap you," Lulu said. "And besides," she added with a shrug, "you *did* try to shoot her."

Berta pursed her lips angrily, but luckily for her, Slessor wasn't listening to Lulu's innocent confession. He had repeated the word "Iris" a few times now. It made Iris nervous.

"What did you say her name was?" Slessor asked Berta again.

"Iris."

"Iris Marlow?"

Jinn's rough hand flew to her wrist. Without wasting a second, he pulled her behind him. He had the right idea being nervous, as the captain and a couple of other men began speaking to each other in low voices. What would a naval captain know about her?

Captain Slessor flicked his head toward her. "Come with me," he said.

Jinn's mouth sparked with flame, and before Iris could stop him, a stream of it escaped his lips. Shrieks. Lulu stared in awe. Olivier and Abiade fell onto their backs. Moyra the Scottish missionary dropped to her knees, crossed herself, and began praying. One of Slessor's men had to stomp out the little flame that had landed on the wooden mast, but Jinn had controlled himself; his flames dissipated after slashing the air—a warning shot, Iris supposed. A show of his power. But instead of scaring them off, it only seemed to confirm the captain's suspicions.

"A messenger bird's been sent out about you, girl, and I reckon it's true," said Slessor with a smile. "Tell me you've heard the name 'Uriel.'"

Iris gripped Jinn's arm. Rin stood ready, hand on chest.

"I have a proposition for you," Slessor said, wiping the sweat from his forehead, trying very hard not to look as if Jinn's fire hadn't made him nearly jump out of his skin. "Come with me to the lower decks. You too," he added, gesturing at Jinn.

Jinn narrowed his eyes. "And if we don't?"

Diana's officers clicked their guns.

Slessor laughed. "Will you set this place on fire, boy? Where will you escape? Or do you prefer seeing your friends die by *our* fire instead? Nobody would know. Nobody would care."

"Jinn." Iris tugged his sleeve. "Let's do what he says for now."

He wasn't happy about that. But then who could be happy in this situation? Was Bellerose tracking her? How did that nasty woman even know where she was?

"Hey!" Berta yelled, as Jinn and Iris followed Captain Slessor. "What about me? You heard me, right? She kidnapped me! What the hell is *Uriel*?"

"That's the angel who guards the gate to the Garden of Eden . . . ," Lulu tried to answer, but Berta wasn't listening. She'd dropped her act entirely, and her attitude was back in full force.

"Hey, did I stutter? *I'm* the victim here!"

"Quiet," said one of Slessor's men, nudging her into line with the rest of them.

Iris saw her angry sneer before she descended to the lower decks.

This Captain Slessor had a head shaped like a long raisin, with precisely the same texture. The squeaking ceiling lamp swiveled back and forth on a wire as he sat on the opposite side of the wooden table. Jinn sat next to Iris, unimpressed by the sight of the four men standing upright behind him.

Iris looked at the captain's pristine blue suit and saber attached to his golden belt and scoffed. "I thought you worked for Her Majesty," she said, folding her arms as Slessor stroked his ruddy beard and looked the two of them up and down.

Slessor smirked. "Many of us diligent employees of the Crown are also members of the club. Thus we have loyalties to the Committee as well. They know where you are and where you're heading. You were champions in the Tournament of Freaks, weren't you? So you have powers. Powers that can be useful to me."

Jinn slouched in his seat, but he looked ready to tear out the man's throat at a moment's notice. "Useful to you or to them?"

Slessor leaned over and propped his elbows up on the table. Intertwining his fingers, he placed his chin upon his hands. "I need a way into the *Ataegina*. I need to rescue the men on board. Loyalty to my men, that takes precedence here."

Iris was surprised. So there were a few Club Uriel stooges who cared about something more than prestige and power. Though . . . there was something very off about the way this Captain Slessor looked at her. Like he wasn't really looking at a *person*. Iris caught it once or twice. It chilled her.

She shifted uncomfortably. "You have a lot of men at your disposal already."

"And he's killed many others, this . . . this ringleader." He squeezed his fingers together in frustration, his thin pink lips curled into a snarl. "I don't know what kind of witch or warrior he is, but his skills surpass the imagination. He's holding members of the British navy hostage."

"What does he want?" Jinn asked.

"Immunity for his murders and safe passage to England. It's absurd. He killed members of his own crew. Took the ship by force. Who knows how many other people he's killed."

Iris glanced at Jinn. Each of them had the power to take on a fleet, but one simple fact remained: "I don't want to hurt anyone." The fabric of her skirt dragged beneath her fingers. Jinn watched her carefully.

"You rescue my men and kill that tyrant, I let you off to whichever jungle you're headed."

Iris narrowed her eyes, wanting to kick this man in the shins, but she remained still.

"The Committee won't ever know we crossed paths. Or I can capture you here." He lifted his head and sat back in his chair. "Not without a fight, I imagine, but a fight won't be without casualties. What are you willing to sacrifice, then, girl?"

What am I willing to sacrifice? Jacques's stern face appeared in her memories. The answer was obvious: no one. And yet she felt as if she were expected to go one step further: herself.

That was the right thing to do. But it felt unfair.

Still, Iris nodded stiffly. Slessor and his men smiled.

"It's an assassination mission, Iris Marlow," Slessor said. "I hope you're prepared."

14

IANA AND *LA DAPHNÉE* TRAVELED TOGETHER to the Morocco coastline. It took several more hours to reach the two ships at a standoff with the fearsome *Ataegina*, a tiny but formidable merchant ship perched defiantly on the other side of a long sandbar. Whoever controlled the ship now sent up emissaries to let them aboard for the "negotiations."

"Jinn," Iris told him quietly as they marched aboard the *Ataegina*, prodded along by the points of rifles in the hands of Slessor's men. "You don't have to come with me."

Boots clomped along the wooden plank. "Don't be stupid. He wanted both of us."

Iris squirmed uncomfortably, looking up at the black sails flapping ominously in the evening sky. "Oh, that's why you're coming, then. Of course, your hands are tied. Not like you'd come for me when you want me gone."

Jinn gave her an incredulous look. "What?"

"Well, you already abandoned me before, so who knows if I can count on you now?"

"And what do you mean by that?"

"Shut *up*," an officer hissed behind them, jabbing Iris and Jinn with his gun.

Iris wasn't sure what she was expecting aboard the ship. No one was on deck except a pile of dead bodies obscured by several sailors who guarded the corpses. Iris shivered. The men were armed with guns and knives. Slessor's men didn't dare try them. They didn't want to be added to the pile.

The sounds of drinking and shouting grew louder as they descended belowdecks. After she climbed down the ladder, chickens scurried past Iris's feet, causing her to start. They went through the main hatch. Then they were let into large, dark quarters below by two dirty, angry-looking men with broken teeth.

Shouting. Cheers. Dice thrown on the rickety wooden floor. Chickens pecking at each other as drunken men leered, laughed, and circled them. An unseemly sight.

Over in the corner of the room by the broomstick were five navy men tied together with socks in their mouths. Their bloodshot eyes rounded at the sight of the newcomers, but they didn't dare make a move. This ship's sailors spoke Portuguese and English mostly. Some French. Many wore the recognizable sailor suits, with white hats and long blue handkerchiefs tied around their necks. Iris spotted a few dark newsboy caps and gray turtlenecks. And yet, however they were dressed, quite a large number of them had the same emptied-out expression, like they'd been through hell and back. Iris wondered whether they'd rather escape.

"Welcome!" said a sailor tall enough that his newsboy cap hit the low ceiling lamp when he took it off to bow. "Ah, I see you've come with some guests! But what about what our captain here has ordered?"

"Safe passage to England!"

"Yeah, tell those ships to get out of our captain's goddamn way!"

Diana's men pushed Jinn and Iris forward and immediately backed away. What exactly were these buffoons expecting? That they would incinerate these men right here, grab their fellow officers, and run? For navy men they had very poor planning skills. But their pale faces told Iris that fear had done all the planning for them.

The rowdy cabin momentarily stopped drinking and playing with their toys to stare at them. A crowd of men at the very end of the vast room dispersed, revealing a man covered in a dirty blanket. It looked heavy. It weighed him down. Or maybe something else had caused this man to hunch over while sitting on the hard floor, his arm on his knee. His murders, perhaps. Iris knew the feeling.

The blanket veiled his face in shadow. He lowered his head anyway, so Iris couldn't see him. All she could see were his dusty brown britches.

He didn't speak to them directly. He spoke through an intermediary—a big man with a bald head and a scar down the left side of his cheek. Given to him, he explained, by his captain. He seemed half-proud, half-resigned. Well, Club Uriel had been a lesson that many men followed power blindly, even if it led them into the abyss. Slessor had warned them that this man had taken the ship by force. They had to move with the utmost care.

The man whispered to his intermediary.

"Yer names!" the intermediary said with a Cockney accent. "What're the names of our lovely and handsome negotiators, he wants to know?"

Iris sucked in a breath, ready. Perhaps instinctively, Jinn put out a protective hand to stop her, but she shook her head and, lowering Jinn's hand gently, took a step forward.

"I'm Iris Marlow," she said, loudly, clearly. "And this is my . . . my tightrope partner, Jinn. We're here to talk to your leader."

The man, covered in his blanket, moved his head up ever so slightly, shadows still obscuring his face. A moment of silence passed, filled with a few rumblings of low laughter. *Ataegina's* captain tapped his knee with a long finger. Then he gestured for his intermediary to bend down low.

"He wants to know what you're doing here," the larger man said, *"Iris."*

"How annoying." Iris folded her arms impatiently. Was this captain really so fearsome and important that he couldn't speak to her with his own bloody mouth? She felt like berating this childish, silly man, but Jinn tapped her wrist from behind to remind her this was a delicate situation. She cleared her throat. "What am I doing here?"

At that moment she was suddenly aware of just how many people were here, just how many people she could burn with a thought should she concentrate hard enough. It was how she had felled civilizations before. But the very thought made the hairs on her arms stand on end. That nameless man in the Library of Rule. The man in the Crystal Palace. How many more?

She clasped her hands together in front of her chest, in the dank, musty air, and lowered her chin. Then, raising her head, she said truthfully, "I'm not here to fight. I just . . . would like for these men to be returned to their ships without a fuss," she explained. "You want to return to England, don't you? I'm sure there's a better way that can be arranged."

"A way without bloodshed?" said the intermediary, and this time it seemed he was repeating his master's words exactly instead of paraphrasing. His style of speaking had suddenly become more refined. "Is such a way possible, Iris?"

This captain seemed to use her name whenever he could. It unnerved her.

"Yes," she said. "I want to believe that."

The jeers and laughter from the crowd were immediately silenced when the captain put his hand up. He waved for his intermediary to bow down and hear his directives one more time. It was longer this time. The man looked confused; Iris wondered if he'd remember it all. But after a while, he straightened up and puffed out his chest rather confidently.

"He says he appreciates the earnest appeals of a beautiful woman."

Jinn stepped closer to her as the mocking laughter erupted again, and as uncomfortable as they made her, Iris was more curious as to how he could even tell what she looked like with his head perpetually covered in that stupid blanket.

"He's more than willing to do what you say, so long as you do something for him first."

"And what's that?" said Jinn, stepping forward again until he was half shielding her.

The man under the blanket smirked. Iris could tell by the way his head bobbed up and down and his shoulders rose a little. He was having *fun*.

"Perform for him," said the intermediary.

"What?" Iris and Jinn said at the same time, glancing at each other.

"You're circus performers, aren't you? So perform."

Iris opened her mouth but then closed it again, confused. What was this man thinking? Jinn must have been thinking it too: a circus performance in the middle of a deadly standoff?

They turned to face each other.

"This prat annoys me." Jinn's eyes shot daggers at the man under the blanket.

"Nothing for it," she whispered. "We just have to do it. It's better than fighting our way through these lugs."

Besides, whoever this man was, she wasn't sure she wanted to face him in a fight either way. She'd already noticed he wasn't armed. He'd taken his captainship by his own hands. This man wasn't someone to mess with, especially now that Nyeth's warnings reminded her: she could be killed. Somehow, she could be killed.

"What about 'The Sand Sonata'?" Jinn suggested.

One of their most well-received acts. Iris nodded. Anything would do so long as this captain was entertained. She asked for a rope. The murderous crew seemed excited. They grabbed some and began affixing it to chairs that they placed on opposite sides of the room.

It was different than an amphitheater, but the stakes were just as high. Iris tapped her shoes upon the wooden floor and then jumped on the rope. Jinn followed.

"Ladies and gentlemen," she proclaimed, dredging up that entertainer persona from deep within her, though it was not without effort. "Don't you dare sleep. Don't you dare miss a beat. We now present to you our best and *deadliest* routine: 'The Sand Sonata'!"

It was neither their best nor their deadliest, but the crowd bellowed anyway. As Iris and Jinn stood upon the rope held taut by the chairs some men had plunked themselves in, Iris watched Slessor's men out of the corner of her eye. It seemed they were using the distraction to inch closer to their fellow navy men tied in the corner. Whatever worked.

Jinn flipped only as high as the ceiling would allow. Iris cartwheeled and jumped into his arms, letting him raise her into the air. He stood firm on the rope. Their crowd was a nasty one. She could smell filth and dried blood, but Iris kept her eyes on Jinn, only on him, as he spun her around. It was how she'd performed for the past two years together with him. How she'd survived the Tournament of Freaks. How she'd survive this. Yes, she kept her eyes on him.

One cabin boy was a little too excited to see the ruckus and tripped over a barrel, which exploded, spilling sugar onto the ground. The cheers ended in a hush. Everyone turned to look at the scene.

"What the hell is this?" a man said, equal parts furious and scared. He was one of the crew who'd taken over the ship. "I thought I told you to get rid of the sugar! You bloody idiots."

Nervous glances toward the captain, who had started twitching where he sat. Sugar. But why was everyone so agitated over a little accident?

Jinn set Iris back down upon the rope. As his men rushed to clean the mess and clear out the barrel, the captain began trembling. It reminded Iris of the opium addicts she'd seen before, in the alleyways of some of the British cities she'd visited while on tour with Coolie. With a shake of his head and a deep breath, he calmed and gestured for his intermediary to speak.

"The captain ain't pleased with your performance," the man said.

"What? Why?" Iris demanded.

"You said that this was your best, but he knows for a fact it ain't."

Iris scoffed, and before Jinn could stop her, she jumped off the rope. Who did this jerk think he was, toying with them?

"He wants your best."

She squeezed her hands into fists, but before he could speak, the captain's head lifted.

"I want your best, Iris," he said, and his voice stopped her heart.

She stood up straight, and all feeling in her body flushed away. Ridiculous. She was hearing things. There was probably opium being smoked here, and it was messing with her mind. She looked back at Jinn, but her partner's face was contorted in shock as well.

"Come on now. Show me the *best*." The blanket shifted away and fell onto the floor. "Show me the 'Nubian Princess and the Turkish Prince.' 'The Bolero of Blades.' Pretty please? For old times' sake?"

Crash. Slessor's men had freed the hostages, but one whose body was likely weak and unsteady had tripped over a casket of alcohol. Slessor's men raised their guns. *Ataegina*'s men put their knives in their mouths and readied their pistols. Chaos erupted.

And then Iris blinked.

Several daggers stuck out of the throats of the captain's own men, who fell dead upon the floor. Slessor's men were disarmed. *Ataegina*'s ruthless captain stood in the midst of the crowd, which quickly dispersed. Rifles lay upon the ground at his feet, but he'd kept one in his hand. He turned. Iris saw his lopsided grin first.

"Show me, Iris," he said.

Iris fell to her knees. "Max."

15

H IS LARGE HANDS PUSHING HER ASIDE.

Max falling into Hawkins's black hole, tearing a hole in the air.

A sad smile on his lips.

One final goodbye: *Iris, you'll forgive me, won't you?*

Iris went through the memory again and again, as if this time she'd discover a hidden one she'd missed all these days. As if Max's "death," which had repeated itself unforgivingly in her dreams, was merely a magician's illusion. She just had to figure out the trick.

This wasn't a trick. This wasn't an illusion.

In the loosest of filthy white shirts, ripped, with the drawstrings dangling, Max stretched out his arms. The sleeves were torn. She could see every bulging vein sliding up his skin.

"There he goes again doing that . . . that thing he does!" said a sailor, staring in terror with the rest of them. "He's unbeatable." He said it with a hint of defeat. Regardless of who their "captain" chose to kill, there was nothing they could do to challenge him.

Power often inspired obedience. Iris knew all too well.

They looked like worshippers at a church. Iris stumbled to her feet with a shiver.

"Go on, Iris, perform!" Max said, and began clapping. As he egged the two on, the crowd's terror slowly morphed into rowdy excitement. The cabin boy helped drag away the dead bodies. No one was fazed for long. This was a common occurrence.

Iris's dry, trembling lips cracked open, only for Jinn to step in front of her quickly, pulling her behind him.

"Maximo." He was much more direct, much more composed than her quivering self, though the alarm in his voice was unmistakable. "What's going on? How . . . ? Why . . . ?"

He stopped, because where did one start picking apart this nightmare? Maximo had taken a life before, but it was after being manipulated by Adam. That had been a few short weeks ago. A few short *weeks* ago. And now he was killing with a smile on his face?

"Come on, you two. You're not gonna show me up here in front of my boys, are you?" He gave an affable grin that was all too familiar to Iris. "All I want is one little performance. I mean, why not? We performed it together once—at the auction, remember?"

She did. She did remember, but she couldn't speak.

"But now I want to see the real deal: the real Nubian Princess and Turkish Prince. Why not? You know I've always been your biggest fan, Iris."

"What the hell are you doing here?" Jinn demanded.

Max cocked his head to the side. "And here I thought we were having an emotional reunion." He smirked. "You haven't changed at all, mate."

Hawkins had buried Max alive in his mother's casket. Underneath the floor of some abbey. That was what Hawkins had told her. So what was this? *What was this?*

"How many people have you killed, then?" Jinn stepped over the rope separating them and took a menacing step forward. Max wasn't fazed at all. "You just *kill people* now?"

Max rolled his eyes. "For once take the stick out of your arse. All I've ever done is what I *had* to. Sometimes you've got to get your hands messy."

"What you had to? Like betraying Iris's secret?"

"That she's some kind of million-year-old death god?" Max rubbed the back of his head. Another all-too-familiar trait. Iris couldn't believe what she was seeing. A ghost. "Was that supposed to be a secret?" He laughed.

"Maximo!" Jinn was quick with his fist, but Max was behind him in a blink. That was right. Like his old fighting name. He'd caught Jinn in a headlock, but it wasn't enough to subdue Jinn. A knee to the stomach made Max recoil back. The crowd screamed, watching the two men fight like the rabble in the Pit where Max used to make his bread and butter. Jinn's mouth began to spark with threatening flames.

"Stop!"

Iris's scream split through the pandemonium. She shut her eyes against it, secretly praying for a new scene to emerge when she opened them again. To no avail.

How had he survived Hawkins's attack? How had he ended up on this ship?

But the question that found its way to her lips: "What do you want, Max?"

Max's eyes seemed to soften at the sight of her. His gaze reminded her of Adam's, but it made her skin crawl in a different way. It was just so . . . friendly. Adam could never manage that. He could manage neutrality and arrogance at best. Not friendliness. That was Max's forte.

"I want you, love." And just as a lecherous grin began to spread across his face, Max waved away her shock with a little chuckle. "I'm kidding, I'm kidding. What, it's been a few weeks, and you can't take a joke anymore?"

"Max . . . ," Iris said, her voice hollow.

"I want to see a performance for old times' sake," Max answered. "Or," he added with a mischievous lilt to his voice, "if you're too shy in front of this lot, you can always entertain me privately. Maybe I wasn't kidding after all."

Jinn's hand found Max's shirt. Even with the other boy's knuckles against his neck, Max didn't take his eyes off her.

Iris's mind blanked. A sharp pain cut into her chest from the inside. *Courage,* she told herself. *Courage. There's an explanation for everything. There's a solution to everything.*

A solution.

"Fine," she said, swallowing, ignoring Jinn's surprised expression. "Let's go somewhere private."

Max looked taken aback himself for a moment, but then he gave her a gentle smile. When Jinn's grip loosened, Max pushed him off and straightened his shirt. Then, bowing, he stretched his arm out to the entrance.

"Right this way," he said. "Men? Watch the hostages."

"Yes, sir!" a few of them cried, some in Portuguese. They fell in line so quickly. Jumped at his every word. Feared the twitch of his hand.

Iris stepped over the rope and followed Max. She felt the touch of Jinn's fingers against her hip, a worried exhalation of breath against her ear, but she couldn't look at him now, not without losing her nerve.

Just before leaving the room, there was a loud crunching noise. Max stopped. He'd stepped on something. Iris could see a light green stalk—like celery or artichoke—underneath his boot. His face stiffened. His smile disappeared as he looked slowly to the side.

It was as if the air had been sucked out of the room. The men, cheering a few moments ago, were terrified into silence.

"What is this beneath my shoe?"

"I'll get rid of it! I'll get rid of it, sir!" said one sailor in a high voice, his words tumbling off his lips in a clumsy stupor.

It was sugarcane.

"I told you I don't want to see it," Max whispered. "Smell it. Feel it . . ."

Two other men followed the sailor, and, as they removed the sugarcane from underneath Max's shoe, they brushed the old, dilapidated leather as if it had been corrupted by its mere proximity to the sugarcane. Once it had been cleared, Max gave his men an order: "Retie the hostages and these new naval blokes. Tie up Jinn, too, while you're at it."

Then, as Jinn struggled, Max looked at Iris over his shoulder.

"This way!" he said with one of his bright smiles, and left the quarters.

A dark room without even a bed. The lamp affixed to the walls flickered. His *shadow* flickered on the walls behind him. He plunked down onto a bunch of rags. Iris could only look at him, numb, as he patted the ground next to him and pulled half a deck of cards out of his pants pocket.

"Wanna play?" He squeezed a card between his fingers and winked at her. "It's been a while. You're not opposed to a bit of blackjack, are you?"

When Iris didn't move, he spread the cards against the ground and picked one up. "Queen of spades. How about it? If I win, we continue where we left off in that brothel."

The memory of the heat between their bodies made Iris flush. But it also brought the Max before her into sharper contrast—and she didn't like what she saw.

She shook her head. "You've changed," she said. It made Max laugh.

Long boxes filled half the room, piled on top of each other all the way to the ceiling. Illegal merchandise, likely, the kind they'd been stopped and checked for before this hostage situation began. The other half of the room was a pile of rags and empty bottles of wine.

He smiled genuinely. Leaning against the wall, he pulled up his knees and balanced his arms upon them, gazing at her. "You haven't. You're still a beauty. A softhearted beauty."

"I thought you died."

"There were plenty of times I wanted to. Believe me." He gathered up the cards and set them aside.

"How did you get here? Hawkins attacked me in the street. He told me he put you in his mother's coffin. They're all after me, you know!" she added, not even realizing she was yelling now. The panic bubbling in her gut had swelled so abruptly, it surprised her, but the words were pouring out of her mouth nonetheless. "You told them I was Hiva. Now everyone's after me. Hawkins. Jacob. Cherice!"

"Cherice." He said the name with a hint of whimsy and nostalgia. "How is she doing?"

"She's beside herself because she thinks I'm the reason you're dead! Are you listening?" Her voice was a high shriek now. She wouldn't be surprised if the entire ship could hear her. "How did you get here?"

Max let his head roll to the side. He stared at the boxes for a while before looking at Iris again. "You know this ship is constructed out of parts imported from Britain?"

Iris frowned. "What does that have to do with anything?"

"What does anything have to do with anything? You'd be surprised. The strangest things connect in the oddest ways."

"But—"

"They sometimes take used coffins, you know. Throw out the bones and use them for wood." Max laughed. "I bet Hawkins never knew. All those times I offered to visit his mother's grave with him, but he never went. He said her bones could be in the Thames for all he cared. She let her husband abuse him, see. I guess not all mothers are worth reuniting with." The sadness in Max's sigh was unmistakable. "Hawkins. I hope he's okay. . . ." He trailed off.

Iris slowly started to understand. This ship. The box that Hawkins's mother would have been placed in . . . but that couldn't be right. Hawkins said that he'd buried Max alive. He was so sure of it. The space had been so tight he'd had no choice but to retreat and leave Max there. . . .

"Iris," Max said before she could take her speculations too far. "I'm trying to find my way to Europe."

Iris noticed her shoulders had risen to her ears. Forcing herself to breathe, she relaxed them. Yes, Slessor had said getting to Europe was his main demand. The navy ships were in his way, hence the hostages. "To see Hawkins and the others?"

"This is about more than that." Max opened his mouth and then shut it again. He hesitated, staring at the floor as if fighting something within himself.

Iris bit her lip, the heat rushing to her cheeks before she realized: "It's your sister. You're still looking for Berta."

The Berta currently held captured on her boat, dreaming of revenge against the one who had "killed" her brother. As Max nodded, Iris sucked in a breath. She had to play this right.

"Adam Temple roped me into his game by promising to reunite us, you know. That bastard. He said he knew the location of the man who had brought us to London. I want to go to London, Iris." Max looked deathly serious. "And when I do, I'll beat the information out of Adam."

He said everything with such candor that it frightened her.

"You wouldn't have a problem with that, would you?" Max must have misread her fear. He looked at her sideways. "He did have a thing for you. Don't tell me—" He balked. "Don't tell me you two are—"

"No!" Iris snapped. The thought sickened her. "Of course not! Give me more credit than that. But don't give him any: what he loves is a flaming sword. The kind wielded in judgment."

"And aren't you that? What was that word?" He looked up, trying to remember. "Hi- . . . va. Hiva. Isn't that you?"

She wanted to shrivel up every time she heard the name from anyone else's lips, let alone her own. "Not anymore. That's why I'm here. I'm looking for a way to get rid of my powers. To transform me into a regular human."

Max narrowed his eyes. "Are you sure that's possible, Iris?"

Iris squeezed her forearm to keep her own skeptical thoughts at bay. "It is if I try."

"'It is if I try,' she said." Max shut his eyes and smiled. "I had that kind of optimism too. It goes away after you've been tortured a few times."

Iris's hand slipped off her arm. The dusty, humid air lingered in her throat. "What?"

"And all I asked was for them to take me to England. But from their perspective, I was some random bloke suddenly on their ship. They thought I was a stowaway. A thief. Maybe even a spy. They tortured the answer out of me. For days. I managed to escape, barely, but there was nowhere to go. Nowhere but ocean for miles around. I was scared. Rageful. So I killed them."

"You killed them. . . ." Repeating his words didn't make Iris understand them any better. He was in a coffin. How had he escaped? How did he end up on a ship, murdering the crew? There was so much Max wouldn't tell her. But the shadows beneath his eyes made her too scared to ask.

"I had to." Max slid his fingers through the curls of his fluffy brown hair. "Sometimes you have to do what you have to do to live. That's all I've ever done."

Like working for Adam and lying to her. Iris had no right to judge. She had killed so many for so much less. And yet a pit settled in her stomach as she looked at Max, this boy whose eyes had once glimmered inside a toy shop. Who had promised himself he'd take his sister there one day. A cheerful boy ruined by men far lesser than him.

Pain, torture, and grief. She knew them all too well, but she was standing here. Nobody could be ruined forever. She wouldn't give up, and neither would he. She'd make sure of it.

"You did this all for Berta. Well, she's on my ship." Iris didn't know how to tell him, so she told him in the simplest terms possible. Perhaps that was why Max's only response was to raise a skeptical eyebrow.

"My little sister's on your ship?"

"Yes!"

"Oh, she is now, is she?"

Though Iris wasn't surprised, she still didn't appreciate his skeptical tone. "Long, brown, curly hair. Dark eyes, round nose. She looks just like you," Iris added, and when she thought of the girl, she realized how true it was. "I met her in Paris. She barged onto my ship trying to kill me, because she thought I'd killed you. We had to tie her up."

Max was silent for a time. She couldn't read his expression one way or another.

"It's true!" she pleaded. "I swear it's true."

Max stood, brushed off his slacks, and walked up to her so quickly, Iris didn't have a chance to ready herself. He grabbed her cheeks in his hands and laid his forehead upon hers. He breathed in, taking in the smell of her. It must not have been very pleasant—she hadn't bathed for days—but he remained like that for a long time.

For one wild second, she thought he might kiss her. She remembered how his kisses felt. They used to fill her with a guilty, warm kind of honey feeling, but now his hands felt cold enough to stop her heart.

"All right then, let's go." He patted her on the shoulder.

"What?"

"Let's go. To my sister. Come on, then."

Iris couldn't keep track of Max's erratic behavior. His moods swung like trees in the wind. But when he took her hand in his, it almost felt like old times. Though there were fresh scars she'd never seen before that bit deep into his hands, he held her fingers gently. Hands he'd just used to kill. Mixed messages. Mixed signals. She couldn't wrap her mind around it all.

Inside the busy, crowded quarters, Jinn was tied with rope, a sock in his mouth that must have tasted of sweat and sickness. He looked comforted at the sight of her, but frightened for her nonetheless. Iris wished there was something she could do to give him solace, but with her own hairs on end, all she could do was give a curt nod and hope Max didn't notice.

"Hello there." Max walked up to one man with an eye patch over his left eye. "Mind if I take that?"

He was referring to the rifle in his hands. The man had nicked it from the officers. Shaking at the sight of Max, the man didn't argue. He handed the rifle over without hesitation.

Max surveyed the room and began choosing men. "You. You. You. You. Oh, and you blokes." Ten of the fittest among them, including his bulky intermediary. "Come with me, will you? We're going aboard Iris's ship."

A wave of relief rose and fell within Iris's chest. "You don't need them," she said.

Max shrugged. "I may not, but I figured I might, you know? By the way . . ."

He grabbed Jinn's ropes and tugged until Iris's circus partner was in front of him. Then Max cocked the rifle and pointed it at the back of Jinn's head.

"Men. Take those uptight naval officers with you," Max ordered. "All of them. The hostages too."

"What are you doing?" Iris screamed, as she watched his men grab and threaten the officers with weapons.

Max swung his gaze toward her, the dark circles heavy beneath his eyes. "Just so you know: if my sister isn't there as you said she is, I will blow out Jinn's brains. Then my men and I will kill everyone we do find. That's fair, isn't it?"

Iris teetered on her feet as she stepped back, her lips parted, unable to reconcile what she'd heard with the amicable face of the boy who'd fought alongside her mere weeks ago.

She shook her head. "What are you talking about? You wouldn't do that. . . ."

"I would if I find out you've lured me out with such a sick, horrific lie. But you wouldn't do that to me. Not you." He looked at her. "You wouldn't. Would you, Iris?"

Above all, Max looked tired. Too tired to believe, to dare to hope. It broke Iris's heart.

Her fingers twitched. "She's there."

"If she's there, we can trade for our safe passage. Simple," Max said. "But if you're lying to me, Iris . . . if *you* are lying to me, I promise I won't hesitate to respond in kind."

Jinn yelled against the sock in his mouth, but his muffled voice fell to silence once Max nudged his head violently with the rifle.

Iris gazed sadly at the two boys who had once stood side by side. The blooming camaraderie first cut short, now crushed. "Why would you do that?"

Max looked at her strangely. It was as if he wasn't seeing Iris anymore but an inhuman creature wearing her clothes. He looked at her like one would a vampire or a ghoul dashing across the streets. With wonder, fear, and curiosity.

"It's just the way it is, Iris," he explained very seriously. "Sometimes you have to do what you have to do. That's all I've ever done."

16

BEING HURT BY THE WORLD MADE one want to hurt others in return.

How different from the Naacal, this society of humans. She thought this as Max and his men marched their hostages across the wooden plank that connected their ship to *La Daphnée*. Naacalian society was one of strictly controlled hierarchies, entrenched so deeply that despair had long crushed the very hope of resisting them to dust. That despair produced compliance. But here, despair had the awful side effect of sometimes producing monsters.

Under the moon, two of Max's men led the procession. Then Max, with his gun to the back of Jinn's head. Iris followed, flanked by the hostages, nudged along the wood at gunpoint by more goons. Max had lost a little bit of his hair. She could see that the back of his head was not as cushioned with curly chestnut as before. The scars down his neck were fresh. This was her fault. The very act of meeting her had set him on this path. What should she do?

She didn't want to be judge, jury, and executioner. She wanted to be a normal human, but what did that mean in a situation like this? What was her responsibility?

She touched Max's arm tentatively, compelled by a sense of duty—or a sense of guilt, maybe. "Max," she said, summoning her courage from deep within. "Think about this. What you're doing is dangerous. You'll be on the run with your sister, probably for the rest of your lives. Is that what you want for the two of you?"

Max answered by knocking the back of Jinn's head with the mouth of the gun. As impatient as she was terrified, Iris tried again. "Do you really think these officers will just let you go? Are you going to get rid of everyone? How do you think that's going to work?"

"Why, missy?" challenged one goon from behind her. "You think he can't get rid of everyone if he sets his mind to it?"

They would know. They seemed very used to Max's terrorizing and had subsequently fallen in line like cowards would. As they crossed the treacherous waters and grew closer to *La Daphnée*, the row of prisoners from their ship slid into sight. The backs of Abiade's and Rin's heads told her that Slessor had forced them to face away from the men pointing guns at them. Slessor himself faced the western side from where they approached, watching them carefully with his own flank of guards to make sure Max didn't try anything as they boarded.

This situation could get messy very quickly. With an exasperated grunt, Iris grabbed Max's dangling left arm. One last appeal to his senses. One last appeal.

"Look at what you're doing," she said, hoping to be the conscience he seemed to have lost. "Do you want to meet your sister this way? Do you want her to see you like this? Weren't you going to take her to Whittles? Can you still do that with blood-soaked hands—?"

It took only a second for Max to wring his arm out of her grip and even less for his hand to find her collar. His knuckles dug into her throat. At the sound of her pained gasp, Jinn turned, maybe hoping to catch Max unawares, but in a blink, Max positioned the gun between his eyes while swiveling Iris around, dragging her feet off the plank until she was dangling over the edge.

When Iris swallowed, the skin of her neck rubbed against Max's fingers, which smelled like an awful mix of dirt, alcohol, and dried innards. The sea sloshed beneath her. It was a long drop.

"I am going to get what I want," Max told her, his voice shaking as viciously as the seas. "I've suffered enough. It's *owed* to me."

"Nothing is owed to us." Even with the barrel of a gun pointed at his face, Jinn looked at Max with disgust. "And you're not the only one here who's suffered. You sound like a child, blaming the world."

"You're right. So I'll be an adult and take what I want with my own hands from right under your nose." He grinned at Jinn. "It's not like I've never done that before."

Max let go of her. As gravity pulled her down, she felt like the wind had been knocked out of her. But just as Jinn cried out in shock, she managed to grab the board with both hands.

"Keep moving!" Max ordered.

Iris could see nothing but boots shuffling ahead, some maliciously stepping on her fingers as she tried desperately to hold on. The cold air from the waters lifted her skirt from below, chilling her bare, dangling legs. After everyone had passed, Iris summoned her strength and lifted herself up with a groan, but she had no strength to stand. She flopped onto the wooden plank, alone, while Captain Slessor met his guests and ushered them to the other side of the hull. Not one of the officers seemed to care that she'd been left behind.

She could still hear seagulls at this time of night. See the reflection of the moon and stars in the black waters. "Oh, Max," she whispered, and cried.

How did she get here? Was her existence as Hiva enough to cause this utter degradation of a young man she'd once admired?

Iris lifted her arm off the plank and stared at it, though her cheek stayed flat on the wet, splintered wood. What was the purpose of humanity? She'd asked that question before, but she'd never found the answer. Was pain and suffering inevitable?

In her immortal bones, Iris felt the answer was all too clear: total destruction was much easier. It was hope fulfilled, the hope that something new and better would rise from the ashes of death. The earth could wash its hands clean and begin again.

But that's not who I am. Not anymore. She gritted her teeth. *Not anymore!*

Iris dragged herself off the plank and boarded *La Daphnée*, flying to the other side of the hull, where Max's voice carried through the air.

"That isn't her." His left hand squeezed Jinn's neck, holding him off to the side with his gun still pointed at the back of her partner's head. His men held the naval officers hostage. Slessor's men guarded *La Daphnée's* raggedy crew with their own rifles. Slessor stood to the side, flanked by his men, with his hands behind his back.

The HMS *Diana* had already lowered its bridge onto the other side of *La Daphnée*. Its guns were ready and aimed, but none of Slessor's men would be escaping until Max had what he wanted. But as Berta stood in line, staring at her brother for the first time in over a decade, her mouth open, her brown eyes wide with emotion, with confusion, Max shook his head wildly.

"This isn't her. That's not my sister."

"It is," Jinn told him, his voice measured. "That's Berta."

"It isn't. That is not her."

From where Iris stood behind the crowd, Max looked . . . terrified. Yes, terrified. He tightened his grip around the back of Jinn's neck, but he wasn't looking at him—or his sister at all. He was staring down at the floor with wild, bulging eyes; it didn't seem like he saw anything at all.

"That's not her," he said stiffly. "Berta was little. She was innocent."

"She's got a bounty of twelve thousand dollars in gold on her head." Jinn seemed to relish telling him. "Her friend told me."

"She's *wanted* in America?" Max could hardly believe it. "Jinn, you're lying to me."

"You said this guy's my brother?" Berta wrapped her arms around her red corset. "*This* guy? The one who killed those folks?"

Different accents. Different histories, perhaps, but both siblings seemed to speak the same language of denial.

But Lulu, next to Berta, wasn't listening. Kneeling down, she shoved her hands against her ears and shut her eyes. It was what Iris wanted to do too.

"You're a bloody liar," yelled Max. "My sister was an angel."

"And who the hell are you to judge me? Surrounded by filthy idiots who barely have a row of teeth between them? Who the hell are *you*?" Berta's chest swelled with anger. Iris noted that kind of indignation—like it didn't matter who was insulting her, only that she was being insulted in the first place. Siblings stolen from their homeland and separated in England. Longing to see each other. Fearing the other was dead. Now facing each other after many years . . .

Which one of them was more disappointed?

"This is the reality, Max," Jinn told him. "We can't always get what we want. Face it!"

"No!" Max struck Jinn with his gun and knocked him to the ground with his fist. His foot was on Jinn's head, crushing it against the floor before Jinn could make a move against him. "I was on the streets. In the Pit. In the tournament. I killed for my *sister*, not an American murderer." Iris gasped, panicking as he started stomping on Jinn's back. "This is my life now because of my sister. Because of my sweet baby sister."

So it had to be worth it. That was what he was trying to say.

Iris had had enough. She lunged for him, too fast for his men to catch her. She tackled him, both of them flying away from Jinn and hitting the ground. He struggled against her, but she kept her arms tight around him in a vice grip.

"You don't know what I've been through!" Max cried desperately. "You don't know what they did to me."

Out of the corner of her eye, she could see Berta watching her brother's descent into madness, her shoulders slumped, her face drained of its rosiness.

"I know," Iris said, keeping Slessor in her sights. He watched, disgusted, but he wasn't about to make a foolish move with his men still hostage. "I know; you endured so much—"

"I was in that box for days, breathing through a bloody hole. I couldn't move, didn't know where I was; I couldn't see anything. Just darkness. Everything smelled of sugar. Still, I had to get back to her."

The nonsensical stream of words made no sense to her. But as he continued to thrash her about in their struggle, something heavy dropped out of Iris's pocket and slid onto the floor.

And it played music.

Max's pocket watch: the one he'd stolen for her from Coolie's auction. He recognized it immediately. His resistance fell away. His muscles tensed and then slowly relaxed into a stupor as melodic twinkling sounds filled the silence.

No one spoke for what felt like eons. Max looked at the watch but did not dare touch it.

Then, without lifting his head, he said, "Your name. Tell me your name. Your full name. Mine is Maximo Alejandro Morales. My middle name is after my father."

A sob escaped Berta's lips. Burying her face in her hands, she dropped to her knees. "Berta Carina Morales. After my—"

"After our mother." Max nodded. But he was shaking, shaking from deep inside his core. He turned over his hands. His palms used to have a healthy flush.

"I killed Carl Anderson and lied to you about it," he told Iris. "I sold you out. . . ."

"For her," Iris finished. He'd already confessed that night the members of Club Uriel were massacred.

Tears began slipping down his cheeks. Under the crescent moon, the Morales siblings cried. Max's men didn't know what to do, watching the man who had so viciously commandeered their ship weeping before them. Shock peeled back their defenses, and that was when Captain Slessor struck.

"Fire!"

17

THE SHOTS WERE SO LOUD, SO abrupt, that Iris let go of Max and covered her own ears against the bangs. One of Max's men crumpled dead to the ground near her. Everyone but Max's goons and Slessor's men ducked for cover, holding their heads. A hand gripped her foot from behind. She jumped, but when she looked behind her, it was Jinn, still on the floor, blood dripping from his mouth because of Max's boot on his head.

"Stay down," he hissed as another one of Max's men crumpled behind him.

One of Slessor's men fell too, shot by one of Max's men before return fire blew him back. Bullets cut down the hostages who couldn't dodge fast enough. As gunfire reigned, Slessor reached into his pocket, pulled out a whistle, and blew. The screeching noise pierced the air and echoed upon the ocean waves.

Moments later the wood beneath her shuddered. *Diana* began to shoot. Iris watched in complete horror, fingers grasping her head, as cannonballs soared over their heads and collided with Max's rebel ship, blowing half the *Ataegina* to pieces.

The waters groaned underneath a mushroom of fire stretching to the moon. Jinn and Iris ducked for cover from debris that crashed onto their ship.

"Get rid of the rebels!" ordered Slessor. "Kill their leader. Take Iris Marlow aboard the *Diana*. Then we salvage what cargo we can from the *Ataegina*. Make sure you kill anyone on this ship who interferes."

Iris frowned. "Wait. What?"

She didn't have enough time to figure out what was happening before she felt Slessor grab her arm and begin dragging her away. "The Committee still wants you in their custody, after all, and they are willing to pay handsomely for it. I've got my men back. Who says I can't have it all?"

"You *rat*," Iris hissed, fighting his grip just as she heard Rin's battle cry and a man's wail. She whipped around. Rin's sword had cut two rifles in half and maimed the naval officers who'd held them.

"Isoke!" Rin called out to her before ducking. Her attack had started a bloody battle. The naval officers had been given an order, and they didn't care who stood in the way of their bullets.

Iris kneed Slessor in the stomach, knocked the gun out of his grasp, and escaped him. Berta wasn't going down without a fight either. She slammed into one officer's body, wrested his gun from his grip and shot him in the stomach, then shot one of Max's men, who in his confusion knew neither friend nor foe.

Jinn's eyes darted from person to person, but if he opened his mouth now, he couldn't be sure he'd keep *La Daphnée*'s bystanders out of it. Olivier the merchant and LeBlanc huddled together. Abiade shielded Lulu with his body.

And Iris shielded Max with hers. One of Slessor's men fired, his bullet grazing her arm. Max let out a gasp as Iris crushed him to the ground. Rin kicked the man back before he could fire again, but it was only a matter of time. *Ataegina's* leader was one good shot away from his execution.

Iris jumped to her feet and charged Slessor. He saw her approaching and, with a stiff smirk, bent down to pick up his gun. He aimed it at her. Better to shoot her dead before kidnapping her. But the gun—

The gun jammed. *Click.* His lips parted in shock.

This was the hesitation Iris needed to grab his rifle, knee him in the groin, and catch his neck in the crook of her arm.

"Drop your weapons!" she demanded to Slessor's men, holding the rifle to their captain's head with one hand. "I said drop them!"

"Don't you dare!" Captain Slessor responded, and to his men, his word was law.

"What the bloody hell are you doing?" she cried. "What about your men?"

But Iris knew as well as he did: his men outnumbered Max's.

As for Max, he was still huddled on the floor, his eyes on the pocket watch.

"I—I mean it!" Iris threatened the men, her eyes wild. "Drop your weapons!"

"And who has more to lose here?" Slessor smirked. "Even if you had the guts to shoot me, my men would have no reason not to massacre your entire crew."

Iris glanced at Rin, who looked quickly from left to right, likely trying to calculate how many she could take down on her own. But she couldn't guarantee everyone's safety. No one could. No one but Iris. And Rin knew that too.

Iris tensed under her silent gaze. Then out from underneath Abiade's arm peeked Lulu, whose innocent, hopeful eyes fixed on hers. Berta glared, her lips pursed. Waiting.

Waiting for her.

It wasn't fair. None of this was. Iris felt bound by rope, bound by their stares.

"Leave quietly with your men," Iris warned in a hoarse voice. "If you all don't leave right now, I promise you—I'll . . . I'll kill you!"

Slessor snickered. "You don't sound too sure of yourself."

She wasn't. Which was why Slessor was able to elbow the rifle out of her hand. The military man grabbed Iris's neck while she was distracted and forced her head onto the floor.

"The Committee's going to lock you up for a very long time," Slessor whispered in a deadly promise. "How very fitting for an animal like you."

An animal like you. Such hatred. Such inhumanity Iris heard in his voice.

In that moment, he sounded so much like Doctor Pratt.

Slessor turned to his men. "Get rid of them! Take out the leader!"

"Max!"

Iris looked up to see Berta running toward Max desperately, forgetting everything and everyone around her. She was an easy target for a sniper to pick her off midstride. The mouth of an officer's gun sparked and fired. Berta barely had the time to react to the shot. She turned her head to where the shot was coming. She gasped, confused, when the bullet lodged in her brother's back instead.

She cried out in her brother's arms. She fell to her knees with him. And throughout it all, Iris watched as if it were happening in slow motion. Watched Berta scrambling to stop the blood from gushing out. Watched the officers aim their guns at the siblings again.

"Just a couple of pickaninnies," Slessor said behind her. "No one will miss them."

And then there was Anne falling to the ground dead, dressed in an outfit for the exotic tastes of the very audience that murdered her.

"Who knows, Marlow? Maybe once they've locked you up, they'll let us have a go at you for our good work." Slessor's hot whisper against Iris's ear sent a rough, sickening shiver sliding up her thighs, her stomach, her chest. Unwanted touches, the kind women like her were all too familiar with from the likes of beasts like him.

"Th-this is what you wanted all along," Iris spat, frozen beneath him, disgusted by his hands on her, but no less disgusted by her own naïveté. How could she have thought that a man from Club Uriel was capable of better? "People like you are all the same."

"People like me have power," Slessor hissed. "And when you have power, you don't ask permission for what you want. You take."

Iris felt alone. Dismembered. Like the flesh had been stripped from her body and her bones had been cracked and laid to rest in separate parts. And then she remembered, with anguish, with fury, that such a fate was an evil she was all too familiar with. A fate dealt to her by the hands of men like Slessor, who felt they ruled the world.

In a way, she understood Max. One had to do what one had to do. It was a law of survival. Some would argue that only the fit could survive. Then what happened to the weak? What were the powerless supposed to do? Forfeit their lives?

When she'd first come into this present life, she observed the world objectively and saw hatred and bitterness. Power struggles and ignorance.

She was never haunted by it then, but Iris was different now. She observed the world with a bleeding heart that wrung tears of frustration from her eyes. It hurt so much, she couldn't stand it. It made her sick. It shriveled her soul. She didn't want to care anymore. She just didn't want to have to care. . . .

Hiva never had to care. Never had to cry. Hiva judged indiscriminately. Hiva was justice.

Hiva was power.

And when you have power, you don't ask permission for what you want. You take.

Iris smashed the back of her head against Slessor's skull, and while he was writhing, gripped his throat and forced him onto the deck. He was not a god. He was a human. A fly.

She was a god.

And when you have power . . .

You don't ask permission for what you want.

You take.

"You're exactly right," Iris said in a hollow tone.

She felt Slessor's anima and burned him from the inside out.

It was as if she'd been holding her breath for centuries. She exhaled, a tear dropping from her lashes. Then she stood up and reduced the rest of his crew to ash. Their life force had a metallic taste and a fresh smell that filled her whole body with electricity. So this was what it felt like when she didn't fight it. When she let the energy of death flow through her body undeterred.

Her head tilted to the side, languid. The faint sound of rifles clattering to the ground mixed with the pocket watch's music. Straightening up and lifting her head, she followed the sounds as they stretched up into the dark sky, her arms limp by her side. She felt all eyes on her. She felt their fear and terror, but also their relief.

When she closed her eyes, she could feel his arms wrapped around her from behind. Her brother, the other Hiva. Or maybe it was her imagination.

She could hear the priest Nyeth laughing at her too. *This is what you are, you monster,* he was telling her. Maybe that was her imagination too.

"Tell your ship to depart and give us safe passage." She'd left one of Slessor's officers alive so that he could carry her message. He scurried away as Iris dropped to her knees.

Van der Ven's Proposal

FABLES DREAMED A DREAM OF HELL on earth.

Cages mysteriously unlocked. Doors left open. Every manner of beast, torn to shreds and stitched back again, conscious or mute or screaming like mad. They lumbered out of their prison cells hungry for revenge. Terrified scientists cried in their very British accents for a savior to rescue them as the beasts they'd kept under cruel control unleashed the full wrath of their supernatural power upon them—power Fables could never have imagined. Some scientists were turned to ice and broke apart into pieces. Others were eviscerated from the inside out with claws as long and sharp as a wild animal's.

Yes. Fables dreamed a dream that hell on earth had descended upon a filthy hole called the Basement.

The scientists died begging for a savior that never came. They cried but never had their prayers answered, because the fools had locked up the only savior this earth had ever known. And Fables's savior was unforgiving.

Jacob carried Hawkins on his back, promising revenge. He had the power to mess with folks' language, and it wasn't too long before Fables was given a demonstration. The fear of suddenly losing one's tongue. The confusion it brought about. It gave his redheaded friend enough time to slash up their faces with a knife she'd found lying around.

Fables separated from the group, searching and avoiding mayhem until he found *his* savior in a dungeon infested with cobwebs. His god lay inside a coffin suspended in the air, chained to every stone wall. And suddenly an ax was in Fables's hand, one already stained with blood, left lying idly in the hallway. As he chopped wildly with tears in his eyes, each warded lock sealing his god inside shattered.

Hiva was beautiful, lying there naked with his arms folded across his chest and his eyes shut, like a vampire awaiting an ample neck to drink from. Fables would have offered him his, but it wasn't necessary. His head had regrown. His luscious brown locks of hair wound down to his hips once again, flowers springing from them like the Adonis he was.

But Adonis wouldn't wake. Fables frantically tried to shake him conscious, but to no avail. Hiva too was caught in a dream, placed under an evil spell like Sleeping Beauty.

The scientists must have done something to him. Fables was glad they were dead. He slung Hiva's arm around his shoulders and ran as fast as he could. Fables wasn't a strong man like his father. But even if his body broke, he wouldn't let his king down. Even if his flimsy bones shattered, he'd carry his god to the ends of the earth.

The directions strangers gave him were confusing and their accents were hard to understand. But eventually Fables found it. Eight Grandage View: a brown-bricked London town house with too many windows. A blue Persian rug led him into the drawing room, where an angry-looking brute of a man awaited them. He was built like a titan, with black eyes and black brows almost as thick as that black beard he kept military clean. Yes, he was a military man. Fables could tell by how he stubbornly wore a uniform decked out in gold medals and silver pins, though there were no troops to command.

Or maybe there were: Cherice next to the roaring fireplace. Jacob by the grand arched windows. Hawkins sitting in front of an imported vase, weary but awake. On one wall were rows of swords and knives behind a glass case. Each one, pristine and sharp, could have been plucked from a book of fairy tales. On another wall were animal heads—bears, boars, and Siberian tigers—mounted and framed on the finest wood, their mouths agape, frozen in the final moments of their deaths.

This man too looked like a wild boar, prepared to attack and kill. And then Fables remembered. This was the man who'd taken Hiva's head.

Hiva remembered too. He began to stir.

"Hiva?" Fables bit his lip as the god awakened.

Hiva stood up straight, his spine cracking into place, his shoulders squaring. The trio were ready to fight, but the military man lifted a hand to stay them.

The man and Hiva glared at each other. This man was strong, but there was something sick about his strength Fables didn't like. He reminded him of his father, all bluster and no elegance. A man who wanted to be bigger than he was and took it out on everyone around him when he fell short. He would never stack up to a man like Hiva, whose serenity stemmed from his beautiful lack of filthy human emotions, emotions that always led lesser men to chase after glory and ruin themselves.

"I am Gerolt Van der Ven. And you—you are Hiva." It was a question posed in a way that didn't sound like one. Men who had questions but didn't want to appear weak did this all the time. Fables truly did not like this man.

"Indeed, I am Hiva."

This man, Van der Ven, stroked his bottom lip. "And the other Hiva?"

"I aim to kill her."

Van der Ven smiled. "Then we all agree on at least one thing. I can help you with that. The world doesn't need two Hivas."

"Well, I certainly never agreed to that."

A brown woman casually traipsed out of the dining room with a steaming teacup in her hands. Now this was new—Fables had never seen anyone like her before, with the brass nose ring shaped like gears attached to a long chain, the chestnut-brown corset atop the long, flowing yellow dress that didn't seem to be European at all. She looked at Hiva, cocked her head to the side, and waved her fingers.

"So this is the other one. Hello there." She spoke with a kind of confidence that made Fables feel one inch tall. "I didn't think he'd make it out of there, what with the massacre you sanctioned in my current workspace. I'm leaving the Continent first thing in the morning. What a terrible sight to be stuck in my head as I sail the high seas." She shuddered.

"I ordered him to be released and brought here with the rest," Van der Ven said. Really? Fables hadn't seen anyone near Hiva's dungeon—but in the chaos that he'd just managed to escape, who was to say who had been among the corpses left in the Basement and what their specific allegiances had been? "In any case, Malakar," he continued, "Hiva's come as I intended."

"Not without depleting the scientists needed to learn how to work the Helios properly."

Van der Ven dismissed this "Malakar" with a wave. "And they'll be replaced by a bevy of smarter ones. The loss here is in time. Fool!"

The red curtains fluttered open. Fables jumped. He could see his top hat first, then his pointed shoes and his cape—and that mask. It was the same madman they'd caught sniffing around Lulu at Younger's Bend. The others tensed at the sight of him—maybe they were even more familiar with this lunatic than he was.

But as the Harlequin Masked Man unfurled a long piece of paper, Fables noticed he seemed different from before. The "man" he'd met in Oklahoma rolled around like a dog wanting his stomach rubbed. This one held his back pin straight, his head high like a town crier. He seemed almost like an automaton, a nutcracker soldier who took his job—and himself—very seriously.

"I hold in my hands a message from the esteemed Lady Madame Bellerose, written for one Uma Malakar." He spoke as if through a megaphone and rolled his r's in such a ridiculous way, it made Fables cringe. "She will soon reach the Dark Continent safely, and though she has not yet reached the facility, she has been told that the Ark is nearing the end of its construction."

"Is it now?" Malakar took out a pipe and began to smoke it. "Well, I guess I'll see for myself soon enough."

"All that is needed is the completion of the power source," the Harlequin Man continued, "which the Gentleman Bosch believes cannot be done without the extraction of Hiva's heart."

"Yes." Malakar seemed to understand this incoherent message, because she rubbed her chin and nodded. "John Temple's journal seems to indicate the same. And I've been thinking about it for a while." She took a brown booklet from within one of the gold cloths wrapped around her dress. "I'd hoped by sending Iris off on her own journey, she'd find a different answer . . . but it looks like we may need her heart after all."

Harlequin Man cleared his throat as if in competition with any other voice that wasn't his. He was a pompous ass. "And please do remember," he continued to read with the utmost self-importance, "do not in any way speak of this to Van der Ven or Benini. Benini is a nonfactor. But Van der Ven aims to team with Bosch and control the Ark himself, and that role belongs to me."

Van der Ven gave a deep, full-throated laugh that frightened Fables. "Well, she's right about that," the man said. "Fool, did Madame Bellerose speak to you about becoming her secret informant, answering to her alone?"

"Why yes, General Major Van der Ven, and indeed I found it the most presumptuous display of obvious cunning. I was *aghast*. I am, as always, a loyal servant of the Enlightenment Committee, not a whore to be bought and sold."

"Yes. A loyal servant of *every* member of the Committee, I see," said Malakar, glancing from him to Van der Ven. "Even the ones under house arrest. He takes his job very seriously. How very lucky for you, Gerolt. Though it may end up being a problem one day."

The military man sneered. He didn't seem to quite like being called by his first name, not by someone of her gender or hue. As "Fool" clicked his heels together, Fables and his fellow jail escapees exchanged confused and baffled glances. Malakar, on the other hand, began snickering.

"One man, multiple personalities. Multiple errand boys. This information network you Enlighteners have built is quite remarkable," she said before sipping some tea.

"*I* want the Ark and the Helios," Van der Ven said. "I want Bosch's weapons. In light of losing the Moon Skeleton, I want you to create exactly what is necessary to power both. It's the only reason I had you spirited out of the Crystal Palace before the massacre began."

"And I want to create what's never been created before. But I'd rather not take that girl's heart." Uma frowned as Fool nodded and disappeared out the window. "She's got guts, that girl. I like her. Plus, we've got another Hiva here."

The way Uma took a step toward Hiva made Fables furious. But before he could begin to muster up the courage to berate her for her disrespect, she backed down.

"Well, at any rate, he's someone who, as I'm told, can burn a man alive with a thought, so I suppose I don't have any say in this matter." She sipped her tea again, though Fables noted the hint of bitterness in her expression.

"Kill the girl and let me have her heart," Van der Ven ordered. "If she stays dead, we won't need to worry about her regenerating and causing trouble. Oh, and your partnership. Give me that too."

Hiva's golden eyes shimmered. "What reason do I have to partner with you?"

"Because you don't know this world. I do. I've been around the world and back. I know where the other Hiva is headed, and I have the means to take you there. After you kill her, you can do as you please—I wouldn't be able to stop you." It seemed to pain him to admit that. "But allow me, at least, to prove to you all that I can give you. All that this world has to offer." He gestured to the blades and the heads on his wall. "It would be such a waste to destroy *everything*."

Fables scowled in disgust. Here he had been making fun of this Madame Bellerose earlier for trying to poach one of his employees, and now here he was, like a snake-oil salesman, trying to seduce a divine being to his side. Hiva wouldn't fall for it. He was made of higher stuff than that.

But he wasn't saying no, either.

Fables looked at him.

Malakar sidled up to Hiva, staring sideways at his forehead. "That contraption you're wearing." She was getting too close. Fables didn't like it. "Is that the white stone I spy?"

Hiva touched his emerald crown, the sign of his royal divinity. "The meridian," Hiva answered. "Based on pieces of technology from a dead civilization many dimensions from here."

Malakar's eyes glinted with a dangerous kind of excitement. "You don't say?"

"A people called the Naacal were able to use the technological pieces I brought them and fashion them into this new device . . . and many others."

"I can learn a lot from you." Malakar stroked her chin. "I've got some time before I set sail. I wouldn't mind a quick chat in the meantime."

As Fables bristled, Hiva turned, uninterested. "My meridian no longer works as it's supposed to. I managed to make it back to this world, and yet I cannot teleport where I please at will."

"Which means you can't teleport to Iris whenever you want to kill her." Everyone stared at Lawrence Hawkins. The street urchin, sitting on a small chair with his arms balanced upon his knees, shifted and shriveled beneath their gazes.

"It doesn't matter anyway," Hawkins insisted. "Iris—Hiva—whoever she is, she can't die. She can't be killed. She just gets back up again. We've all seen it. She's unstoppable, like this bloke." He gestured to Hiva with a flick of his head.

"She gets to live on, no matter many times she kicks it, while everyone else dies. Chadwick. Maxey—" Cherice bit her lip. "I can't forgive her. No matter what, I just can't—" Her little chipmunk face turned red. "And I considered her a friend, too. . . ."

"But she *can* die," said Hiva. "The method through which to murder her exists. The One who created me told me the day I was born for the first time. It should be the same for her. Hmm . . ." He paused. "Perhaps she's forgotten that, too. One of her many changes."

"What . . . what do you mean?" Jacob asked as he and his orphan friends exchanged baffled glances.

"A very simple weapon can do it. Effective. It's near here. I can sense it." And when Hiva shifted his head toward Fables, he could almost hear the gears turning in the god's neck. "You will come with me as I follow the scent of her anima."

Being spoken to, being needed, made Fables's heart race. He nodded enthusiastically.

"I'll do whatever you tell me to," Fables said, blinking a tear away when Hiva tore his golden gaze away from him.

Uma Malakar, that heathen, frowned suspiciously at him. "I've read nothing of this. What exactly is this weapon that can kill Hiva?" she asked.

"Of course he won't tell you," spat Fables, finding his voice from the boost of courage Hiva had given him. "In case you use it on him."

Malakar shrugged with a little laugh that made Fables blush with embarrassment. "Fair enough. Then tell me, how do you know it'll work? I'd like a little proof."

Hiva's eyes seemed to smile. "The proof will be Iris's dead body."

18

A STRIP OF WOOD BROKEN OFF A plantain tree stifled Max's desperate screams until it fell from his mouth. He gulped in each sloppy breath he could.

"Oh, you're enjoying this, aren't you," he said between gasps. "You can admit it. *Ugh.*"

And he gritted his teeth against the pain.

The humid air and bright sun of the port town Ajashe drew sweat from all over Iris's body as she watched the boy struggle on his stomach atop a wooden table. The doctor Abiade had found was using some kind of metal tool, now wet with blood, to take the bullet out of his back. Little bottles of various drugs lined the shelves. Rin seemed particularly captivated by them, though Iris couldn't be bothered to ask why. There were more pressing matters.

Max let out something between a growl and a moan. "I'll trade you that nice, shiny medical instrument you're poking me with for a sparkling British shilling. Stolen by yours truly. Believe me, that raises the value—"

"Quiet!" Berta snapped, and shoved the wood back into his mouth to stop his cries.

Inside this one-room hospital, next to the curtained window where the sounds of the market seeped in, Berta crumpled the white cloth she'd been using to dab the blood.

Biting her lip, Iris glanced discreetly at Berta before turning her gaze on Max. With her body stiff with trepidation, she watched the doctor work. All they had been able to do aboard *La Daphnée* was keep Max conscious and change his bandage. Iris had honestly thought that he was done for. It was divine intervention that had kept him alive. Which god was looking out for him, she didn't know. It wasn't her.

As Max screamed and screamed, Lulu peeked through the window curtains. Holding a half-eaten plantain in one hand, she pulled them back. A group of children were watching through it, trying to figure out what sorry bloke was getting what sounded like his arm sawed off at the local doctor's office. Iris was sure Lulu was as fascinated with them as they were with her. All of them children, with skin dark as coal. On the other side of the window, the children wore fabric wrapped around their whole body, their arms and shoulders bare. Lulu waved in her pinafore, shyly and with a cautious but excited smile. Max's screams didn't seem to faze her as much as the invisible, palpable, but porous barrier of culture and chance that separated them.

Abiade watched, next to a bed where another patient was resting, his missing leg wrapped with white bandages. Rin was picking up bottle after bottle off the shelves, inspecting the drugs she found inside.

Jinn, on the other hand, stayed by the door, watching Iris. She could feel his meddlesome eyes on her, the same inspecting glances he'd given her during the rest of their voyage. Always staring, never speaking. Keeping his distance, but staying close. Feeling her out. That stern Jinn look, always with a hint of judgment. Iris had refused to care then, and she refused to care now.

And it felt good.

A strange thing had happened to her the night of the standoff with Slessor's men.

Horizon. She'd touched the horizon.

Respite from guilt. Respite that her mind accepted with open arms. What a nice feeling. The texture slid down, warm and smooth like fruit. She didn't drink much, but the buzz was quite similar.

It felt good not to care.

Perhaps this was true power. She understood now, a little, why those men in Club Uriel had always had the smirk of gods as they clinked their wineglasses and passed down their judgments upon those they deemed lesser men.

The doctor took out the bullet, put some herbs and other medicines Iris didn't recognize on Max's wound, and wrapped him up with clean bandages. Once he was done wiping the sweat from his dark forehead, he turned to them.

"I've done all I can with him," he told Abiade, in Yoruba, Iris noticed. There were too many languages in Ajashe, layering and interweaving like the humid wind with the various smells of spices and foods in the market outside. But she could understand this one. "Whether he lives or not will depend on if he can survive the night."

Berta's wet eyes grew large with worry when Abiade translated for her. "Max . . ."

Jinn helped the doctor and Abiade carry Max to the empty bed next to the amputee, gingerly placing him down on his stomach. He'd long since gone unconscious. Probably better for him. Berta bent down low next to him, watching the sweat dripping down his body, down his bare back, wetting the white bandages already soaking up his blood. She reached out to touch him but withdrew her hand at the last second. Iris wondered what she could be thinking. Maybe that he'd break with a touch.

"You'll take care of him, won't you?" Iris asked, speaking perfect Yoruba to the doctor.

"Of course," he said. "We'll keep an eye on him."

Iris nodded. The thought of Max dying here made her throat dry up. He couldn't die, not after finally finding his sister. Not after everything he'd lost trying to reach her again. After the death of Slessor's men, Iris had made a mental list of consequences she no longer cared about. Max's death was not on it.

"I need some air," she said.

"Iris . . . ," Jinn started, but once again, she refused to care. She walked out the door. Jinn, annoyingly, followed behind.

Ajashe to some, Porto-Novo to others. It buzzed vibrantly. The reddish-brown sand underneath her shoes, the women wrapped in fabric of all colors carrying baskets on their heads. The smells of spices, fruit, raw meat. Goats and chickens scurrying across the roads, in front of tents selling everything from cooking ware to weapons. It buzzed with a kind of life that breathed differently than the cold mechanical shuffle of dull London life. She was finally here, after all Granny's stories and all the years reading about West Africa.

And yet she was still out of place. She still drew eyes from locals, merchants, and missionaries. With all the shades of people in all manner of dress, she could not find one Black girl in a stitched-up London skirt, blouse, and shawl. She couldn't very well stay in it while the sun was glaring. Plus, for some reason, the staring here hurt more than it did in London or France. But she didn't want to let Granny's outfit go very far from her sight. It was as much a comfort as a child's blanket, especially now.

Granny always told her she worried too much about things. *Well, I won't worry anymore,* Iris thought, just as Jinn nearly tripped over a child carrying a basket of palm leaves on her head.

"You're ridiculous, you know," she said, spinning around to catch him and keep him upright. "Why exactly are you following me? I find it a bit eerie."

Jinn stiffened, and a red blush bloomed uncharacteristically in his tan cheeks. "What's eerie is how you're acting."

Unlike her, he had no allegiance to his clothes. He took off his vest and opened the top buttons of his white shirt, showing off a strong chest earned by years of hard training. It wasn't an unpleasant sight.

"Did you so quickly forget what happened with Slessor's men?" Jinn asked her.

Iris kept her face neutral. "I made a choice. What's the use in worrying? It's not like I can change things."

Her bluntness clearly took Jinn by surprise, and she relished it, relished the little shake of his head like he wasn't sure what he'd just heard.

"Don't you feel anything?"

"You mean, why aren't I crying and throwing up and all that, right?" Iris folded her arms. "You're so used to seeing me suffering and tortured that it almost feels off to you when I decide *not* to apologize, right?"

Jinn was stunned silent, but she refused to care. She was *tired* of caring. Of crying. She couldn't change her past, nor the truth of her identity, which she'd fought so desperately to discover. She couldn't change it. Why feel guilty?

Jinn grabbed her by her shoulders. "I just don't want you to lie to yourself. Denial is one of your go-to coping mechanisms when there's something bothering you. Like when Granny was sick and you had to make three new outfits for your solos in Lyon in seven days, and for five of them you acted like you weren't even in the company."

Oh right, Iris remembered that.

"I'm not in denial." She brushed off his hands. "And I'm not going to apologize. I killed a group of monsters who had it coming to them. I don't feel guilty for what I did."

You are the ruler. So do what you were born to do.

She couldn't feel it: the resistance and disgust that usually filled her whenever thinking of Adam's words. Instead, those words made her wonder dangerous things. . . .

"And what is a monster?"

Jinn asked her as if he didn't quite know himself. His eyes softened to show the kind of vulnerability Iris wasn't used to seeing from him.

"What is a monster?" he repeated. "What do you think it is? Tell me, Iris."

Iris shifted on her feet, counting the wicker baskets women carried on their heads as they passed by. "The Enlightenment Committee. Those Club Uriel fiends and their friends. The scientists. The administrators. The bloody royal family."

"Because they never ask permission," Jinn replied, touching her wrist. "Because they do as they please to whomever they please. Because they don't recognize the humanity in others. . . ."

Jinn's touch was tentative. Trembling. Almost fearful.

And then she remembered what Gram had said about her, and that Jinn had listened.

"Enough," Iris said, and left.

Jinn called after her as she slipped between two merchant stands selling fabric and toward the edge of an off-path dirt road lined with palm trees.

The trunks were thick and wide at the bottom. Iris remembered those. She'd rest under the giant fanning leaves back when she'd just awakened as Hiva, exploring this new world she'd found herself in. In many ways, she'd always been more innocent than any one of the human beings she'd come into contact with—else she wouldn't have let herself be drafted into the Dahomey military to fight on behalf of someone else's king, the way she'd once fought on behalf of Naacal's leaders.

Iris sat down, leaned against a tree, and when she shut her eyes, she saw Slessor and his men burning. That unique sensation of her panic swelling before dissipating just as quickly was euphoric. Lulu's expectant gaze turning into utter relief. Rin's acknowledgment and respect from one warrior to another. Berta hugging Max and crying. She'd accomplished everything through her own power.

"I'm tired of people telling me what to do," said Iris. She felt Jinn bearing down on her as he stood in front of her, blocking the sun. "And who I am."

"And who are you?"

Iris refused to look up at him. "According to you: another species. And maybe we should just keep it that way."

Jinn fell silent.

She stood and touched Jinn's cheek, tracing a line down his sharp jaw. She could taste his anima too. She could taste his confusion and fear. "There's nothing to be afraid of, Jinn," she told him. "I haven't gone wrong. I'm just fine. I'm going to live in peace. I'm going to be free. I'm not sacrificing myself for anyone. But you see, I thought I had to get rid of my powers to have all that. What if I don't? What if I can just . . . *be*?"

Once she suppressed her guilt and terror, all she felt was the reckless desire to be true only unto herself. It was like layers of clothes falling off, heaven's wind brushing against her back and hell's fire warming her front.

But Jinn didn't understand. She could tell when he cupped her face and asked her, in a voice so tender it made her shiver, "Gram was wrong, wasn't he? Tell me he was wrong."

At the sound of that ghoul's name, Iris bit her lip, frustration burning beneath already-hot skin. "Believe what you want."

She walked away.

Max survived the night. Iris didn't feel comfortable leaving him there wounded with a distraught sister in a foreign land. So she decided to stay with them for a few days.

"It's only until Max can get back onto his feet," Iris told an impatient Rin behind the doctor's office one morning after it rained. The ground was still damp, though the dry heat would surely do its work soon.

"And what about King Glele?" Rin folded her arms. "That was to be the next step of this journey, was it not? Discovering more of what John Temple knows about you. Learning how to rein in your impulses. Have you forgotten?"

"What if I've decided my impulses don't need to be reined in?" And Iris looked at her very seriously, so much so that it made the younger girl visibly shiver.

Never taking her eyes off her, Rin hesitated before speaking again. "I thought that was what you wanted," she said. "To fix yourself."

Iris stared at her reflection in the puddle at her feet. The water was clear, but the ripples distorted her face into something she couldn't recognize. "I don't need fixing."

Rin stepped back from her, squeezing her hands into fists. "We *have* to go. You told me you'd come with me. . . ."

"What were you talking about with the doctor the other day?"

Rin jumped, startled by the sudden question. "W-what?"

"I saw the two of you talking alone. Something about the efficacy of certain drugs—"

"I was just curious," Rin spat out, and immediately wilted like a child being scolded by her mother. She paused. "Curious about . . . what he'd been giving to Maximo."

Rin couldn't meet her eyes, and Iris couldn't figure out why.

Iris sighed. "Let's stay here until Max recovers." She gripped Rin's shoulder tightly and felt it tense even more. "Then we can decide on where to go next."

And she left the girl where she was.

Fix herself. The very thought brought a grimace and then an impish smile to her face.

"I'm fine the way I am," she whispered.

A few days turned into a fortnight. One night, when the moon was full, Iris came to check on Max. Only Berta was with him, scrunched up and asleep in a wooden chair next to him underneath the white plaster ceiling. He was still on his stomach, but once she'd shut the door behind her, despite how softly she'd done so, Max's eyes fluttered open. He hadn't been sleeping.

"I ended up in a casket, you know," he said quietly, maybe so that his sister wouldn't hear him. He didn't apologize. He only explained himself. "At least, it felt like one. But really, it was one of those wooden cases they use to transport goods on ships. Fabrics. Jewels. Spices. Sugar." He shivered. "I'll be using honey in my tea from now on, I think."

Iris trembled a bit, still not understanding.

"I told you they built these ships from imported wood often reused from old caskets. Sometimes they took old caskets and refurbished them as containers."

Max stopped talking and sat up, swinging his legs over the bed before slumping over. He ran his fingers through his shaggy hair.

"I don't think Lawrence knew," he continued. "Like I said, he never visited his mother. Lawrence always said his mother's bones could be dumped in the Thames and he wouldn't lose a wink of sleep. Well, her bones *are* probably at the bottom of the Thames by now, tossed in by grave robbers, but how would he know that? He'd meant to bury you alive inside his mother's grave. He ended up burying *me* alive instead."

It was then that Iris began to understand. By the time Hawkins had teleported Max into his mother's coffin, it was no longer underneath the abbey. It was on a ship, its wood repurposed to hold sugarcane. That was how Max had ended up a stowaway.

Iris shook her head, trying to imagine it, but there were still too many questions. "You couldn't escape a box?"

Max laughed. "Not one buried under dozens of other boxes," he said, and she remembered the room he'd taken her to inside the *Ataegina*, the one with half the room filled to the ceiling with crates. Bile began rising like poison from her stomach. "Sugarcane. The box I was in was filled with it. But there were other boxes above me and to my side, filled with other things. I would have suffocated if I hadn't found a hole in the wood to breathe through. I couldn't move for days. I almost lost my voice. Eventually someone heard me, but after I was free . . ." Max smirked. "Well, that's when all the trouble started."

The ship's crew had thought he was a thief and tortured him. That was when Max had turned deadly. She thought of how callous he'd been, dropping her into the ocean. Being hurt by the world made one want to hurt others in return. She knew that by now. It softened the bitterness.

Iris buried her face in her hands until she felt Max's rough fingers curling around them. He drew them away from her. And tenderly, he kissed them.

"Don't cry, Iris. It is what it is. Can't change anything now. No point in regretting . . ."

"Even if people died?"

"Even if people died."

The chirping of crickets outside the window was like a chorus filling the silence. Iris stayed seated at the foot of his bed.

"You know, I thought about you quite a bit," Max whispered, his lips still hovering close to her hands. "Once or twice I wondered if you'd escaped Club Uriel. If Jinn was still with you, protecting you. If I'd ever see you again." He kissed them again.

She remembered Max's lips that night in the brothel. His body on hers, soaking in the lewd sensuality of lustful portraits hanging on the wall. His mischievous smile. As if she'd been transported to that hot room, Iris's body tingled in delight. But then she remembered. This wasn't the best room at one of London's top establishments. Where she and Max sat now, as the moonlight streamed through the window, was a liminal space unknown to them both.

So much had happened between them.

"I did manage to escape the club," Iris told him quietly, biting her lip. "But you . . ." She paused. "You were the one who told everyone about me."

Max twitched. She wondered if he could hear the hurt in her words.

"They didn't stop trying to kill me after you disappeared through the portal. They tried even *harder*. They blamed me. They're probably still in London, waiting to spring another attack the second they see me again. They think I'm going to destroy the world."

Max drew himself away from her and stared darkly at the floor.

It had been a betrayal. Nothing short of it. So why did it still hurt to remember the pain in his voice when he apologized to her?

"Do you hate me?" Max finally asked. He rested his hands upon his lap.

Iris swallowed, considering it before shaking her head. "You did everything for her," she said, and looked at Berta, still asleep in the wooden chair next to him. "That's all you ever wanted. To find her again. I . . . I get it."

Even when they were tied up and about to be auctioned off, Max had thought of his sister. She could still see it in his eyes as he turned to gaze upon her. Berta meant the world to him.

"Time slowed down the moment I saw her being taken away from me," Max whispered. "When I realized I was alone in the world. Even though it all had happened in the blink of an eye, it didn't feel that way to me."

He hesitated before touching her face, letting his hand rest upon her cheek. The warmth and moisture felt heavy upon her skin. Felt familiar. She leaned into it.

"Iris. You won't destroy the world, will you?"

His sudden question sent a shock wave down her spine. She straightened up, slipping out from underneath his touch, staring at him. But he was serious.

"You killed Slessor's men," Max continued, his face neutral. "And you seemed to enjoy it. I saw it in you."

For a moment, Iris squirmed. Then she remembered. *I won't apologize. I shouldn't have to anymore.* "They deserved it," she said. "Just like the men you killed, wouldn't you say?"

Max let out an amused huff. "I guess we're all murderers here." He glanced at his sister before shutting his eyes. "Berta and I have blood on our hands. But Iris, the damage you're capable of doing is far worse. So much worse."

"I don't need fixing," Iris said again, almost as if it'd become her mantra. "I am who I am. So what if I have power?"

More power than them. She looked at her hands and remembered the vile words Slessor had whispered to her before she showed him what *true* power was.

"I am who I am," Iris repeated, "and I bow to no one. But that doesn't mean I'll commit *genocide*." The very words sounded so ridiculous that they almost made her crack a smile. Max, on the other hand, wasn't laughing.

"Can you be sure of that?" Max gripped her hand in both of his a little too tightly. A frantic plea had suddenly slipped into his tone. "Can you be sure you won't end up doing what I *saw* you do down in the Basement to that other civilization? That contraption. Those memories . . ."

The memories of Hiva awoken by the Helios. Max and Jinn had seen them too. Civilizations crumbling. They knew what Hiva was. They knew what Iris was capable of.

And what is a monster? Jinn's question sank, stone hard, through her throat down into her stomach. Maybe that was why she couldn't speak. And when she hesitated, Max's eyes widened in alarm.

"You don't know, do you?" he whispered, straightening up. "You don't know what you're going to end up doing—"

"That's not true," Iris said, and gripped the sheets of his bed. He'd fallen silent as a ghost. The gears in his head were turning. And when he looked at his sister, Iris knew exactly what he was thinking. "I won't hurt Berta," she said.

It was frustrating to think Max didn't trust her. Then again, he hadn't trusted her in Club Uriel, either.

"I won't," she said again with more finality. "I don't need to be fixed. I control my fate. I control these powers. If I don't want to become Hiva, I won't. Simple as that."

Simple as that. Iris glared at him in defiance, her lips pressed together. It was really as simple as that. She could do whatever she wanted, and if that meant picking off a few prats like Slessor, then so be it. But it didn't mean world annihilation. It wouldn't come to that. There was nothing for either of them to fear—not Max, not Berta. And not herself.

Silence stretched between them. For some time, Iris couldn't see Max's expression as he turned his head, his face covered in shadows.

And then, with a little laugh, Max turned back toward her with that charming, lopsided grin. "No looking back, then? I guess it's the same for both of us. I've got my sister, and I'll do whatever it takes to protect her. She's my priority. *She's* what I care about now, Iris."

The way he said "Iris" almost felt like a lover's goodbye. That hint of sadness as he squeezed her hand. Iris lowered her head.

"Now that I finally have Berta, I'm moving forward without apologizing. Whatever happens next happens."

Moonlight from the window to her left danced upon the sinews of his muscles, highlighting his meticulously trim figure. When he withdrew his touch, she lamented it in a little corner of her heart.

"Forward." Iris considered it, considered Max's grin, his touch, her release. "Max. You know what? I think I'm going back to London," she said. "I'm going back home."

She shoved her hand into her dress pocket, only to touch Nyeth's ring. She didn't need it anymore. This was a mission brought on by panic and dread of the future. Whether it was right or wrong; whether she was being noble or selfish; whether any of it was even possible—she was tired of worrying about it. Tired of torturing herself with questions that had no answers.

She wanted to live in peace, so she would. She would move forward without apologizing.

And whatever happened next happened.

19

THE NEXT MORNING, RIN GRABBED IRIS and pushed her against the wall of Max's hospital room. "We came all this way, and now suddenly you want to go back to London?" she growled. "I won't accept it."

"Rin," Iris tried wearily, but Rin pushed her again, this time stamping her foot like a bloody child. And then Iris remembered—she was.

"Girls, girls. I'm trying to sleep here," Max said wearily. "Usually I would be game to watch, but take it outside, will you?"

Iris let Rin drag her out the door because she understood all too well why the young warrior was angry. To be so close yet so far from completing her mission.

But Rin had been nothing but loyal to her since she'd fled Club Uriel. Iris owed her something in return. The girl's one good eye shimmered with tears of frustration Iris wasn't used to seeing.

Iris sighed. "Okay. Okay, look, I don't want to fight. I'll tell you what." She rubbed her temples wearily. "I'll go talk to your king. I'll see what he has to say and decide for myself. Then, when I go home after that, at least you completed your mission like you said you would. It won't be your neck on the line. Okay? Deal?"

Relaxing, Rin shifted on her feet. "Deal," she said, her chin raised high as if she hadn't just thrown a temper tantrum. It was a little cute. Iris grinned.

Rin was agitated and pensive the morning they set out to Abomey, the seat of power where her king and fellow military members awaited her. The young warrior washed at the public well and bought new cloth to wrap herself in. Checkered red and white, the fabric wrapped around her from chest to legs like a towel, coming up just underneath her arms and tied in a knot for extra fortification. She wrapped parts of the same cloth around her head.

"Ah, so you're coming too, eh?" Iris said, as Jinn came back to the hospital with provisions for the road ahead.

"Just to make sure you don't go off the rails."

Iris scowled. "Oh, I won't. Not for you."

Rin had brought some provisions herself, including a strange little bottle Iris had spied for just a moment before it quickly disappeared underneath Rin's wrap.

"You'll be given what you need once we enter Abomey," Rin said, and then paused. "You are ready for this, aren't you, Isoke? To meet the king?"

Iris shooed away the nervous flutter of her heart. "I'm as ready as I'll ever be. What's there to be afraid of anyway? He's just a man."

A smile twisted its way across Rin's face, wider than she'd ever seen on the scarred girl's skin, but it disappeared in a flash. "That's exactly what I wanted to hear."

Iris wasn't sure what she'd meant by this, but it was of no matter. It was time to go.

"It'd be nice if you could come with us," Iris told Max inside his room. She made sure Jinn was in earshot when she spoke, and just as planned, her circus partner stiffened.

Max leaned over on his bed. "Oh, you would enjoy that, would you? Can't get enough of me. Like old times?"

As Iris's cheeks flushed, Jinn gave him a withering look. "Talking like that. You think this is old times after what you pulled earlier playing pirate?"

Max shrugged. "From what I've seen, times have *definitely* changed, old friend. I've never seen you so careful around Iris. So cold. I guess her turning Slessor to dust has you a bit spooked, eh? Look at that. True love is dead."

Iris gave Jinn a sidelong look. For a time, he only pursed his lips and said nothing.

"True love," she muttered, rolling her eyes, ignoring the pangs of anger and hurt deep within her.

"At any rate, I'll be staying here. I've come a long way, but I still need to heal. And I don't know about this 'king' you're going to see. My sister's been through enough, so I'd rather not bring her into any more surprising situations."

Surprising situations. To be honest, Iris wasn't sure what to expect when she faced the king, but Max was right to want to keep his sister out of it.

"She's your top priority, after all," Iris said with a little shrug, understanding, though Max's returning nod made her acutely aware of her sadness. "As she should be. You've finally found her. You need to do whatever it takes to keep her safe."

"Whatever it takes is all I've ever done."

Max's serious gaze bore straight through her. He looked as if he had more to say, but he thought better of it, just gave her an amicable smile and a wave goodbye.

Abiade had his business. Berta stayed behind with Max, though not before she grabbed Iris's skirt with a shaky hand.

"Hey," she said, and hesitated. She pursed her lips together, searching for the words. "You know, you're a lot like a lady I knew once."

"A lady?"

"A lady named Moustache. Madame Moustache." Berta laughed. "Don't ask. She was from France originally. Or California. Or maybe New Orleans? She was never clear on that. Fled to Europe after she shot the cheating bastard who stole her money. Stole me from a show when I was a kid and took me back to Nevada. Carson City."

"Why?"

"Who knows?" Berta laughed and shook her head. "Guess she took a liking to me. She owned a brothel. Probably thought I'd make a good worker. She taught me how to shoot instead." Placing her elbow on her right knee, she looked up at the ceiling, reminiscing. "We did a lot of crap together. Bought a lot of shotguns. Held a lot of folks up. Then she went and killed someone and took off. The idiot."

"And you've been alone ever since."

"Here and there and back again. Not the best life, all things considered. Not in the slightest." She paused. "I . . . I hate being alone."

It was then that Iris noticed that in Berta's other hand was Max's pocket watch. Rusted and nicked, perhaps, but when she opened it, its music twinkled brightly nonetheless.

And then Berta looked at her, her brown eyes wide and brimming. "Thank you," she whispered in her chair next to her sleeping brother's bedside. "Thanks for getting us here."

Iris met Lulu sitting on the ground outside the little hospital. She was eating some cooled-down bean cake fried in palm oil. Iris was sure Granny had told her about it at some point during their ten years together. She'd always talked about the food she missed, and it had made Iris miss it for her. The bean cake had that crispy orange surface that looked unlike anything you could get in London. After swallowing, Lulu looked up at her.

"A lot's happened in the past few weeks, but I'm glad I made it here," she said, wiping her oily lips. "You know my brother Joey always wanted to come to Africa one day. It's different, but it still feels kinda right here, you know? It's better than there anyway."

"Here," "there," "they," "them." Even with her unconsciously ambiguous way of speaking, it was always somehow understandable. Iris nodded through the pit in her stomach. "I'm sure he's watching you and smiling right now," she told her.

"Hmm . . . hey, Ms. Iris?" Lulu hesitated before asking her next question. "You gonna keep killing 'em, right?"

Iris was taken aback. She didn't know how to answer.

"You should," Lulu remarked, and she looked off at a young mother passing by, who was carrying a basket of laundry on her head and a baby strapped to her back with thick cloth. "It's a long time coming. A long time coming."

Some forms of anger expressed themselves so innocently, they rolled upon the ear like a child's rhyme. She waved goodbye to Iris, and as Iris walked away, she could hear that little hymn, the one Lulu tended to sing every now and again. Iris had it memorized by now.

Mine eyes have seen the glory . . .

Abomey was a day's trip on foot. They walked along dusty roads, near forests, through sparse villages. Iris had seen many caricatures of African women, drawn sloppily in European magazines and newspapers that had cost a penny or two. She dug deep into her memory of when she was Isoke, and a sense of familiarity began to bloom. Many houses were circular huts made of clay with thatched roofs—one room, but that one room was wide enough to fit large families.

"*Ahosi* means the king's wives, doesn't it?" Iris asked Rin. "I remember back then we were called mothers, too."

"It fits," Rin replied with a dark scowl. "The king takes wives and mothers from families. Or sometimes families send off their daughters because they won't listen."

"And other times they're taken in raids."

Dahomey was a rich kingdom with often fraught relationships not only with neighboring tribes and kingdoms, but also the British and French. The protection of their wealth and power fell upon the shoulders of those four thousand military women, regardless of where they came from.

Among them were several regiments: the Gbeto, meaning huntresses. The Gulohento, riflewomen. The Gohento, archers. The Agbalya, gunners. And Rin's regiment: the Nyekplohento, or the reapers. The deadliest and most feared.

"Do you remember your family, Rin?" asked Jinn after Iris translated their conversation.

At this, Rin stiffened. "It doesn't matter anymore, does it?"

The bitterness in her voice was palpable.

They stopped to rest only once, when nightfall made travel too dangerous. She'd heard of some French and Portuguese travelers disobeying the laws of their empire to still trade men, women, and children where they could, not only across oceans but within the very continent. It was, perhaps, the great luck of those filthy men that none had had the misfortune of crossing paths with her. Iris had heard stories of travelers who did as they pleased while here.

She thought of Lulu's song and wondered if some people might just deserve to die.

It had been easier when she was Hiva. Destroy and start again. Like Noah's flood in the Bible. Wash everything away and create something better. . . .

She thought of Adam but didn't recoil. Instead she wondered. Those who clung to Hiva simply wished for something new, didn't they? Of course, in all her many lives, the "something new" born from destruction was *never* any better. But it was only natural to keep wishing for such a thing. . . .

Iris caught herself and sat up. She held her sharp breath in her throat until her face flushed. And when she released it, she looked at her palms and realized that Adam's words no longer seemed so insane. The knowledge of that made her tremble with fear. It was like an out-of-body experience. Who was she becoming if she could identify with Adam Temple?

Her hands. They could bring about so much destruction, and yet wasn't there another side to the coin? Wasn't rebirth the twin of death?

In Iris's mind's eye she could see "Anne" flipping the coin in her hand. Night and day. Two Hivas . . .

Iris shook her head. She'd promised herself she wouldn't overthink anymore. But now she was wide awake. She needed something to occupy her, so she went to Temple's journal again. Above all else, it was an interesting piece of literature, albeit more than a little pompous. The way he documented his travels felt akin to many travelers who thought themselves divine for having stepped foot on land already trodden. He went on about leopards and musky crocodiles and other nonsense. But most telling of his arrogance was his musings on the king:

> He had made me wait many days before I could speak with him. Once I was finally granted an audience, surrounded by the company of his brutal Amazons, I came to notice that he was but a petty man sitting upon a throne of his

own making. I asked him many questions, which he did not answer. Or, more likely, he had no answer to them, but the arrogance of men often leads to dishonest shows such as this. I have my doubts that this was the man who commissioned the creation of a contraption such as the Forge. Or that this "Forge," which I learned of in secret inside the dark din of a tavern, even exists. Only upon witnessing this work with my own eyes will I acknowledge that they are capable of conducting similar research to that of the British Empire, who herself still struggles to manipulate the white stone in her own facilities.

Ingenuity wasn't a cultural trait. Temple's dismissiveness angered her. It was something that Adam, as heinous as he was, had over his father. But as she ruminated over the passage, she considered again if the wonders of the Forge were greater than even Temple had realized. To turn the supernatural to human . . .

No. She'd already abandoned that mission. She wasn't moving back. Only forward.

She sat hypnotized by the owls hooting and crickets incessantly chirping into the sky. The rhythmic breathing of her sleeping companions blended with the night's symphony.

It had felt good killing Slessor and his men. That was what she hadn't wanted to admit.

Mine eyes have seen the glory.

Forward. To where?

In Abomey, two children played marbles on one side of a straw fence while their mother, in a green wrap, talked to a bald man in a red dress. He recognized Rin immediately. Soon they began whispering to each other. Then the children sped off down the winding road past the thatched-roof houses.

"They're telling everyone," Rin told them. "I've arrived with the fabled Isoke."

While the man shyly kept his distance, the woman walked up to her, sizing her up more confidently. It was the woman who told her, "The king lies ahead. They're waiting for you, *Isoke*." The way she said Iris's old name was not with reverence. It was a challenge.

This is for Rin, Iris reminded herself, and walked ahead without backing down.

The palace complex sprawled across green grass and red sand. Circular clay huts with roofs of animal skin were surrounded by wooden fences to separate each compound from the other. Houses made of soil and stone were held up with sturdy poles and logs of wood. Hawks soared majestically overhead while the crickets chirped their choruses, welcoming them. But this was not in the least the only "welcome" Iris received.

They marched out in a line one by one: women with stern glares, unshaken by man or ghost. Iris knew immediately. They were warriors.

Dressed not in the prissy attire of European military men but in comfortable, sensible clothes. Pants in beige, red, or blue. Silver robes. Multicolored blouses tied with red sashes or brown rope. White headscarves and red beads around their necks. Sandals or bare feet upon the hot sand. Large and thin. Muscled and thick with swords, rifles, bayonets, and machetes.

Palace guards. They appeared one by one from behind a red clay house. Bare-chested men nearby fell to their knees and bent their heads low. A young woman leading the procession carried a little bell and rang it. The modest tinkling reminded her of a toy she'd heard in Whittles, but as Iris's memories flooded back, she knew that nothing about what was to transpire was child's play.

The kingdom was of interest to many merchants and greedy colonists, who sought the land's resources for their own. It was like that even when Iris was a member of this very military force. One could not just walk into the seat of power without being shown the strength of the formidable army guarding it. Usually, it was a warning. This time, it was a test.

A blanket was laid out in front of Iris. Jinn stood away, but Iris did not dare look at him. No weakness here. Just strength. She followed Rin's lead, sitting down upon the white cloth. The young woman with the bell stopped her ringing. Then an older woman, tall and built, with larger silver beads in her hair, stepped out from behind her, stretched out her arms, and bellowed loud for the congregation.

"The enemy is on the tip of the machete," she cried in Fon.

Out of the doors of a house, two women carried a heavy basket woven with strips of wood. Another basket placed on top of it obscured the contents within. But when they placed it on the ground before the white blanket, Iris heard a distinct grunt that stopped her heart. Rin stared ahead wordlessly.

"The enemy is on the tip of the machete," she said again.

"We're going to cut him into small pieces," responded the rows of warriors behind her, standing. Waiting.

The top basket was lifted off. There was a man inside, thin and hollowed out, likely from days of imprisonment. His hands were tied together with rope, his black hair shaven down to his skull. He said nothing. He only looked at Iris with contempt.

"Isoke! She Who Does Not Fall," cried the woman.

"Show us you do not fall!" shouted the warriors.

"Isoke!"

"Show us you do not fall!"

They cried this many times, a call-and-response that rattled Iris's nerves even as she tried to at least outwardly live up to the reverence that name had once had.

Yes, in those days, she'd been as fierce a warrior as any of them. And sitting here on this blanket, seeing Rin stand and take a machete from one of the women's hands and pass it to her with a bow, Iris knew immediately what was expected of her. She'd done it before in another lifetime. Watched others do it. Observed with interest, let events unfold as they would with a fearless heart.

But that was then.

Iris's hand trembled a little as she stood and took the machete from Rin.

"Show us you are who you say you are," said the woman.

Iris's knees wobbled beneath her.

"This man has violently defiled and murdered several young women in the city," one of the warriors said. "Now. Show us you are who you say you are!"

Iris didn't know why, at that moment, she thought of lying on a cold table in Cambridge University. She didn't know why, but she could picture each face of those academically trained scientists, laughing about having a drink later as they observed parts of her body through a microscope. Doctor Pratt's beady black eyes stared back at her. And when she saw this man, she realized that just like ingenuity, callousness knew no cultural boundaries.

Lulu's song began humming in the back of her mind, as quiet and defiant as the lack of remorse in this man's expression.

Some men *should* die. They all thought they had power, didn't they? And whatever little power they had, they lorded it over the weak, those disgusting fools. But they didn't know what *true* power was. Iris had almost forgotten: she didn't need to overthink. She didn't need to apologize. *She* was the powerful one here. And she had the right to use her power as she chose.

Iris dropped her machete.

Anima. Yes, their anima. She felt the warm life energy that flowed through all living things and connected all as part of this earth. Anima—that invisible yet still tangible force never changed, no matter the civilization that needed to be destroyed. She felt each of them, but zeroed in on the defiler. That similar buildup of panic as when she'd felt Slessor followed, with the same euphoric release when she burned that man alive with just her will. When she opened her eyes again, the basket was empty but for a pile of his ashes.

Silence. No one moved. The two women who'd carried the prisoner checked the basket. Then, lifting it up, they faced the other warriors and overturned the basket. As their prisoner's ashes fell to the ground, so too did the king's war-riors. They fell to their knees and began crying her name:

"Isoke, Child of the Moon Goddess! She Who Does Not Fall!"

"The legends are true after all. She has returned to the kingdom covered in glory!"

"Come," said the woman with the bell, her expression now gleaming with pride and awe. "We will take you and your servant to the king at once." Servant? She must have meant Jinn. "He's been waiting for you, Isoke." Then she clasped Rin's shoulder with an approving nod. "And you've done well, child. The king will surely reward you."

Rin bowed her head slightly in response. But when Iris turned back, Jinn was staring only at the ashes on the ground. He was scared.

The thought of Gram's horrible face paralyzed her. And when their eyes met, Iris felt a rush of shame that she resented Gram and Jinn both for.

Iris followed the women through the compound, bound for the king.

She noted Rin's small, tilted grin before leaving.

20

IRIS HAD NOT KNOWN THIS KING. She had served under Ghezo, a man whose throne sat atop the skulls of his enemies. This man, King Glele, seemed just as intimidating. Thin pink lips and strong graying eyebrows. A wide nose with a strong ridge, and a chiseled jaw upon which he tapped the brass handle of his pipe. He was a man who had come face-to-face with African leaders, American slave traders, and Western power brokers. He sat in a polished ivory chair that itself was placed upon a blanket, the cloth tied around his waist as sparkling a white as his studded sandals. The king was inside a palace complex walled off with red clay, under a vast roof draped in grass and animal skin, held up by strong wooden poles. He sat surrounded by princesses and wives, soldiers and servants, two white ambassadors huddled in the corner, and eunuchs carrying fans.

Iris knelt on a small carpet upon the sand for an hour, while the king said nothing. Waiting. It was a tactic to show his importance. Men like him always had a trick or two up their sleeve to conjure up an illusion of dominance. How tiring. Iris waited nonetheless, irritated but willing to play. How else to see where this little game led?

Then he lifted his hand. That was his order. "Show me your power," he said.

She smirked. Good. She wanted him to see. She wasn't one to be toyed with. With Rin and the *ahosi* standing behind her, she showed him. A new criminal. A new pile of ashes. Iris covered her mouth to hide her lips, for they were trembling into a smile. It was easier this time. Her heart was pounding from the thrill of it, though a tiny pinch of fear burrowed itself into the chaos of excitement—the kind of fear one had when dancing too close to a fire. These criminals were scum. Who cared if they died? That was what she told herself as sweat wetted her brow.

Iris's eyes welled up with tears from the overwhelming taste of her own power. And when her heart ached in misery, she chided it and threw it aside. She wasn't going to let her conscience ruin her. Not anymore.

The king stood and stretched out his arms, not to embrace her, but to acknowledge her.

"The legends of my fathers were true," he said, "and I've waited long to prove them to be so. Welcome back to your home, Isoke."

Cheers. Wails. Pandemonium whirled so frantically around her that no matter how quickly she turned around to catch who had just fallen to their knees, there was a new distraction behind her: Someone grabbing her feet. Someone trembling and shouting praises.

"Isoke! Isoke!"

The crowd had turned to shambles. It was the reaction one had when coming close to divinity. It arrested Iris.

It satisfied her.

"Come, Isoke," said a woman she didn't recognize, though the bone structure of her tiny face was angular and strong. "Come with us! Let us start the preparations!"

"Preparations? For what?" Iris said, but a group of giggling and cheering women grabbed her arms and dragged her away.

Inside a little house made of clay, women remade the braids that Granny had woven for her the night of the Astley's performance. Her hair had seen many rough days, the once clean lines overgrown and dirty. They washed her hair in a pot, dried it with towels, and then went to work, following the same expert tracks Granny had made, combing her long, thick black tresses. Three women at a time. Their hands worked fast and nimbly, and this time, despite the pain, Iris wouldn't dare complain, not in front of them, not the way she would have if it were Granny's hands tugging at her knots. Iris kept her shoulders back as a queen would.

After a while, when they'd almost finished, she heard Jinn's voice. "You're smiling."

Iris turned to the wooden door to her left. It was only upon seeing his worried expression that she became aware of the shape her lips were making. They drooped into a scowl as she turned away.

"What? Am I not supposed to smile?"

"They speak English so well," whispered one of the girls fixing Iris's hair.

"It's true they came from England, then," said another, nodding. "How fascinating."

"You always did like to get the princess treatment whenever you could." Jinn leaned against the doorframe. "Liked it a little too much. Back at the circus, you were always speaking as arrogantly as a real royal," he added quietly.

When she responded, "And who says I'm not one?" Iris noticed his stern expression softened into a sad smile. It was an exchange they'd had before.

Silence stretched between them. "Is this how you were treated in your other lifetimes?" Jinn asked.

Iris held her breath as her body seized up. So direct. She wasn't sure if he'd ever been this direct in asking about her other eras as Hiva, if he'd ever even asked at all. He waited patiently, but when she looked at him, she saw the vulnerability of a child searching.

"Kings once named cities after me." Her voice felt suddenly ancient, heavy with the eons she'd existed.

Jinn moved closer. "Because of what you can do."

Iris lifted her chin. The women fastened gold beads upon her long braids, still winding down the side of her face and pouring down her shoulder. And as songs of praises wafted in through the door and windows from outside, she wondered where that invisible punishing voice inside her had suddenly come from, the one that had frantically told her not to revel in her own glory. Hiva had been worshipped like this in many other civilizations of the past; why not this one?

The women were done. Iris stood from her chair and faced Jinn. "Yes, because of what I can do. Because of my power."

But she was caught off guard. She didn't expect him to touch the side of her face with his palm. The women gasped and muttered but said nothing.

"You should be treated like a princess," he told her. "But not because of how well you can kill."

Iris felt his fingers sliding off her cheek. She moved with them, unwilling to let them go, before realizing the women were watching her. She stood regally, like a queen. But she missed him the moment he left her.

Her heart was aching again.

No. It didn't matter to her. She refused to care. She wasn't the Iris who cared anymore. She told herself that as she let the voices of the Dahomey lift her up along with their hands, which draped her in purple lace. The servants of the king placed her on a silver litter and danced with her weight upon them in a square of red sand. The dancing lasted hours.

Iris lifted her veil of purple lace, and above the crowd she saw scores of humans singing her praises beneath fanned umbrellas used to shield them from the heat. Their jubilance drowned out the wails Iris heard in the night from the ghosts of the past. Their shouts suffocated the murderous, bitter hatred of Nyeth's final words. The venom and promises of retribution. They told her that she was not a monster to be defeated, but a woman to be celebrated. That she had been created for nothing less.

A ruler. Like Adam said. Her lips cracked into an awkward, uncomfortable grin.

"I used to be a dancer in Britain, you know," she told them once she noticed their arms had become tired from carrying her.

"A goddess who dances," said one man.

"Of course—now, all goddesses dance!"

Did they? Iris wasn't sure if it made sense. Or maybe it wasn't supposed to. In the midst of such jubilation, did anything really have to make sense?

"But she came from Europe? Does she dance like a white woman?"

Jeers and laughter. "So stiff like that?"

"No, no!"

Iris was laughing too, because she'd once seen the kind of dancing they were talking about when she and Jinn were hired to entertain a high-society party. The awkward jolts. The gentlemen too scared to ruffle their own suits. Iris laughed and laughed, a little too wildly, until she forgot what she was laughing about.

"Perform for us, Isoke!" said a young woman from the crowd, and the excitement was electrifying.

"Set me down." Iris felt half-drunk and lopsided from the buzz. She couldn't stop smiling. "Set me down, and I'll show you. Clear the area."

To cheers and gasps of excitement, she decided to perform one dance she'd choreographed herself many years ago, before Jinn had come to Coolie's circus. Back then, Natalya the fire-breather would light a circle of flames around her. Since she couldn't very well expose Jinn's secret, she asked them to bring torches.

They made room. Set the torches on fire. And in the unbearable heat, under the moonlight, she stripped down to only her white chemise undergarment, leaving Granny's skirt and peach blouse with Rin. Leaving behind the shackles called "embarrassment" and "timidness," she took two blades given to her by the warriors and danced.

"The Spirit of Fire," Coolie had called the performance back then, meant to show the unstoppable spirit of his company's "Nubian Princess." But unlike those shows in Europe, though she still felt eyes upon her, she did not feel frozen by them. Their gazes did not crawl upon her like spiders, nor did they grab at her body lustfully. Freedom. She could breathe. Tears leaked from her eyes. As her dancing became improvisation, as she twisted and turned, as she lifted her face to the heavens, she heard the voices of the dead, and for now, let herself be free of them.

She saw Jinn standing by a tree, apart from the crowd, his eyes filled with emotion she couldn't grasp. She saw his face wet with tears.

Jinn was crying.

Because of her? Out of happiness? Sadness? Fear? Her stomach flipped, and the heat rose to her face. And when that familiar misery burned in her chest, when the faces of the men she'd killed passed over her sight, she let out a warrior's cry as if to chase it all away. Some of the *ahosi* responded with their own battle cry, while others watched with interest.

But Jinn . . .

Their eyes met for just a second before Iris turned to her crowd and continued dancing.

The great feast that night left her fatigued but satisfied after days of surviving on moldy bread. Rice, beef, goat meat, beans, plantains, corn, yams. Her mouth burst with rich, hearty, spicy flavors. They gave Rin the biggest ceramic bowl Iris had ever seen, filled with food.

"Good job, Olarinde," said one military woman as a string of them came over to slap her on the back or clasp her shoulders. "You've done well. The king will reward you handsomely."

Maybe this was what Rin had wanted. Why she so desperately needed to bring Iris back to the king and complete her mission. Not just to avoid punishment, but to gain glory. Sixteen years old, with such an important task. Alone in the white man's land, but she'd triumphed and brought back She Who Does Not Fall. It was clear from the shouts of admiration that Rin was now the star of the Reaper Regiment.

Rin soaked it all in with her usual stoic nobility, though she spoke very little and kept to herself. Servants handed out food to everyone in the compound, generals and servants, rich and poor alike. No one was to remain hungry. This was a feast to celebrate the coming of Isoke.

"Be careful," Jinn told Iris. "All this praise is going to go to your head."

He was joking with her. It was a shy joke lacking all confidence, but a joke nonetheless. Iris didn't know what to think.

"Quiet, you crank," Iris muttered under her breath while she stirred her tomato-and-beef stew with a spoon. She wondered if his tears back when she was dancing had just been her imagination. It had to have been. After his joke, he reverted back to his surly self, but when he scooped up some beans and placed them in her bowl, he did so with a gentle expression.

"You don't seem as uptight as before," Iris told him before shoving the wooden spoon in her mouth. "I guess miracles really can happen."

"I've been thinking a lot lately," he admitted, as if that weren't already obvious from the time they'd reunited in Paris. "But back there with the Dahomeans..." He stopped. "Right now. You seem happy. Happy and"—he lowered his head, searching for the word—"free."

For as long as they'd known each other, every joyful moment had been tinged with the sorrow of the unknown. Who was she? Where did she come from? The agony of not knowing, followed by the agony of knowing. But now...

Turning, he gazed at her with an almost sheepish hesitance. He was seeing her in a new light. Iris could tell from the softness of his brown eyes. Or perhaps that was what she wanted to believe. His voice became very quiet. "Maybe that's all that matters."

Rin, who sat on her right, seemed to be watching the two of them. That made Iris even more nervous. With a slight jitter of her hand, Iris took the spoon from her mouth and rested it upon the bowl.

"Eat," he told her before scooping his own food.

Blushing, Iris turned from him.

She was a little surprised when Rin offered Jinn a small cup of alcohol, and more surprised when he took it graciously. Just like their chats on *La Daphnée*. Seeing the two interact with the kind of maturity that didn't seem to exist within in her relationships with either of them drew an indignant blush from her cheeks. She silently grabbed her own cup and began drinking. The alcohol tasted hard and bitter, shooting straight to her skull, giving her a sweet lull.

"Rin." She turned to the girl, who was drinking her alcohol quietly. "Now that I'm here, I am quite curious about the Forge. Would you take me to see it?"

Rin stiffened for just one second, her little cup halting in a tilt against her lips. But soon she relaxed her shoulders and sipped again. "Not tonight," she said. "The Forge is locked down. You'll likely be shown it tomorrow by one of the generals. Besides, I'm tired."

Jinn picked up on their conversation. "What are you talking about?"

"The Forge," Iris said, and then, realizing that she'd been using its Fon name, translated it into English. "It's the machine that gave Rin her abilities."

"The Forge, eh?" Jinn repeated the word in Fon. "I'd like to see it too. If it's similar to what gave us powers in London, then we need to study it. Maybe your plan can still work, Iris."

Iris answered with a noncommittal shrug. She didn't like him pressing. But then if he didn't press, he wouldn't be Jinn. There was something comforting about that.

To Iris's right, a few *ahosi* with particularly sensitive ears turned their way and looked at them. Even with the celebration raging around them, they stared suspiciously.

Rin leaned over discreetly. "Isoke, tell him not to speak of such things so lightly out in the open," she whispered as quietly as she could. "Even if they do not speak English, any mention of the Forge out of a foreigner's mouth will draw suspicion."

Iris nodded, but she wouldn't know just how seriously the *ahosi* took their secrets until later on in the night, when Iris went to find Rin, who'd been called to the nearby armory. Through the open window of the fortified tent made of animal skins, Iris saw one of the women who'd marched at the front of the procession earlier in the day. The older woman with larger, silver beads in her hair. Iris saw her slap Rin in the face so hard that the crack caused the birds perched upon nearby trees to fly off into the sky.

"First you tell that boy about our Forge," said the woman. "Now you say you want to go to Abeokuta? Have you lost your senses while overseas?"

"I'm sorry, General Sesinu." Rin spoke in Fon. "It's true that since leaving Abomey and going overseas, I've desired more and more to see my home." Iris had never heard her sound so timid. Her one good eye avoided her leader. She focused instead on the shelves of blades and rows of guns lined up against the tent.

"What home are you talking about?" said this woman, Sesinu. She was twice Rin's height and weight, but it was the contempt in her wide eyes that most intimidated Iris. "You are one of the king's wives. Do you hear me? You belong to the king. This is your only home. Since when have you said otherwise?"

Rin stayed quiet.

"Take inventory before you leave," the woman told her before exiting the storehouse. She saw Iris on her way out and bowed her head slightly. Whether or not Iris saw the display seemed to mean nothing to her. Perhaps it didn't mean anything to Rin, either; the girl seemed normal when Iris came in to check on her.

But under her breath, the young warrior said, "I've never said it because I never once believed I could. Not until now." Facing a flat shelf of machetes, Rin took the handle of one before whipping around and facing Iris. Though she said nothing, her expression was pleading. Iris didn't know what to say in the face of it. She only took the machete gingerly from Rin's grip and placed it back on the shelf.

"What do you believe your role on this earth is, Isoke?" Rin asked her quietly as Iris adjusted the machete to make sure it was perfectly parallel to the others. "Why were you born?"

"Now, how can I answer such a philosophical question while my stomach is about to erupt?" Iris grinned awkwardly because she knew this wasn't the time to joke, but her nerves had led her astray nonetheless.

"You have incredible gifts. If only I had them, I would know what to do with them."

Iris frowned. Rin was a warrior, but as young as she was, as innocent as she was compared to a death god, she had no idea of the kind of burden she was wishing upon herself.

"I wouldn't throw them away," Rin continued. "But I wouldn't let them languish, either."

Iris paused, thinking of her latest two victims. A swell of panic seized her chest for just a moment. "Then what would you do with them?"

Rin stared at the collection of knives and swords surrounding her. "Help an ally."

She didn't speak to Iris again that night.

21

"HURRY AND REMOVE HER CLOTHES!" SAID one *ahosi* the next morning. "Dress her in the proper uniform of a warrior. Then we will begin the test."

Inside the large tent she temporarily shared with Rin, women tugged Granny's clothes off Iris's body.

"Oi! I—I can change myself!" Iris told them, squirming as they shook their heads and steadfastly continued their work. For some reason, they thought it a sign of honor to act as if she shouldn't have to do the most basic of tasks on her own. She supposed this was what it truly meant to be treated like a queen no matter where you were.

They stuffed Iris into more traditional dress: a long, colorful sleeveless shirt, a red-and-brown wrap tied around her waist, and a long, thick cloth slung around her neck.

"Don't!" Iris yelled when one of the women snatched Granny's clothes and bunched them up carelessly. "Don't take those away. They're mine. I'll keep them with me."

The woman looked down at the raggedy English outfit with distaste, but with a shrug, she handed it over to Iris. They didn't know what the clothes meant to her. She wasn't about to let them toss them out or cut them up into scraps. With a sigh, she reluctantly placed Granny's present under the bed she'd been given to sleep in.

Jinn poked his head into the tent. He opened his mouth to speak to her, but his face froze when he took in the sight of her. Iris stiffened, suddenly too aware of her own body.

Catching himself, he cleared his throat. "They're calling for you. A-are you ready?" he asked her.

Even with his hue of skin, there were times when she could see splotches of red break through to the surface when he was flustered. Like now. Iris lowered her head, unable to find the words for a long time.

"Iris?"

"Jinn." She looked up at him, biting her lip. Grasping her hands tightly, she let a silent sigh escape from her mouth. There was so much that needed to be said between them. Misunderstandings to clear. But he was here. In the midst of all the madness, he was here with her. She couldn't ignore that. "Thank you," she told him.

"For what?"

"Being here."

She thought of Sesinu slapping Rin and wondered how alone the girl would have felt if she'd returned to Dahomey empty-handed. Excruciatingly so, she imagined. If Iris had come here without Jinn, it would have been the same. She couldn't deny that.

Jinn stared at her for a moment before leaning in. "Sorry, I didn't quite hear that."

"Oh, just shut up!" Blushing, Iris folded her arms in a huff. "I said it once, and I won't be saying it again!"

Even the tiniest of smiles could brighten Jinn's face. He swallowed, his hands gripping the tent covers. "It's strange," he whispered. "Why does it feel like no matter where we go and what you do . . . you're always still . . . just you?"

"Jinn . . ." Iris's chest squeezed as he turned to leave.

"Oh! Rin!" he exclaimed, because the girl was standing behind him. Silent. Watching. Neither of them had noticed.

"It's time, Isoke," Rin told her, giving the two another furtive glance before letting Jinn pass.

Rin led her out into the compound, which was surrounded by the clay walls of the palace. No one walked through the shadowy open entrances of the doors, guarded by women carrying long guns and wearing ivory horns on their heads. The *ahosi* warriors gathered in rows upon the red sand, wearing similar dress, but also white caps and dark sashes that strapped blades to their waists. Layers of blocky red beads adorned the dark brown necks of many: gorgeous and sturdy necklaces, sometimes thick enough to cover their chests. Rin wore her yellow wrap and a string-bead top that left her stomach exposed. It was easier, Iris imagined, to take out her sword that way.

As for swords, the *ahosi* provided them. Two *shamshir*, Iris was surprised to see.

This was another of the warriors' tests. Iris had proven her magic. Now she had to prove that she was a warrior.

"We were told you'd be comfortable with such a weapon," said Sesinu, folding her arms over her stocky body. She seemed different from last night when she'd reprimanded Rin. Her sternness certainly hadn't left her, but she seemed friendlier as two women threw the *shamshir* upon the ground at Iris's feet. She watched with an almost motherly expectation to see what Iris could do with them.

Behind Sesinu, many of the women began to chatter, but two particularly loud young and annoying voices pierced through the rabble.

"She won't take them," said one girl with a tiny face, squeezing one of the seven buns of black hair upon her head. "Look at her—she doesn't look like she even knows what she's doing."

Her friend nudged her in the ribs. "True, Aisosa. Hasn't she lived among the British all this time?" Four long, big braids peeked out from underneath her white cap. "Even if she fought well back then, how would she know how to fight now?"

They were not even older than Rin. They couldn't have been, not with their adolescent appearance to match their adolescent arrogance. Their talk was rapid and biting, like a couple of schoolgirls gossiping about a new exchange student. They made it very clear that they were specifically trying to wind Iris up. But it was when the girl with the buns said, "You're right, Natame, she's been overseas too long. She's practically white now," and burst into laughter that Iris's irritation truly flared up. Gritting her teeth, she bent down and took the *shamshir,* much to the encouraging applause of the group.

A little amused, Sesinu nodded with a satisfied grin. Unsheathing her own blades from her sash, she took on a battle pose. Iris gulped. She remembered how tough it had been to fight Rin when they'd first met. It wouldn't be any easier to take on her superior.

She was quite right. Sesinu disarmed her in two swift swipes. Iris fell on the ground, the woman's blade to her neck, much to the disappointment of the two young warriors.

"What is that?" Natame waved her hands incredulously while teasing jeers filled the air. "She Who Does Not Fall? But she just fell, now."

Aisosa giggled. "I don't even think I counted to five before she tripped on her own feet."

"Hush," Rin said. She'd joined the crowd and was standing next to the young girls. With a stern look, she softly knocked Aisosa on the head with her knuckles.

Iris wanted to be the kind of person who could bear indignity with quiet nobility, but she was rapidly losing her patience and felt *very* much like knocking a few heads.

"Come, Isoke." Sesinu flicked her fingers toward herself. "Your body surely remembers how to fight."

Your body remembers. Exactly what Rin had told her when they first met. And it did. Iris just had to relax and let the memory rise to the surface.

She closed her eyes and breathed in and out, dismissing the chatter, the trash talk, and the words of encouragement.

"Is she all right?" Annoyingly, Iris could hear still hear the two young girls' voices.

"She seems to be gathering herself, but I'm not sure. Why don't we ask her servant?"

If Iris had been drinking something, she'd have ended up expelling it from her mouth in that very moment. She looked over her left shoulder. There, standing at his usual recluse-like distance from the crowd, was Jinn in his loose, open white shirt and brown pants. As he wiped the sweat from his forehead with the back of his large, veiny hand, he blinked, confused as to why the women were suddenly laughing at him.

I should probably clarify that he's not actually my servant, Iris thought, but found herself chuckling brightly with the other women instead. On Jinn's occupational status, she decided to keep her lips shut. Besides, she liked the idea of having a manservant.

"He's handsome," Natame said. "Where did you find him anyway? Is he your lover?"

Iris blushed furiously. "N-no, that's not it! He's my partner at the circus. Grew up in Paris and—" Actually, she wasn't sure how to describe him.

"Why not? You can take any man you want now. Don't be so uptight."

"Natame! Why do you always need to talk so much? She's embarrassed, can't you see? Look at her squirming, poor girl," one of the women said, her lips curved into a smile even though she was supposed to be scolding her junior. Natame and Aisosa broke out giggling.

"Enough. Come, Isoke! Or else let me come to you." Sesinu launched forward.

This time Iris was ready, meeting her blade for blade, flipping in the air to avoid the woman's sweeping kick, knocking her back with the *shamshir*'s handle.

"Now that's what we want to see!" cried Natame, pumping her fists. With her arms folded, Rin watched with a discerning eye, swaying to either side. She didn't seem surprised when, after two minutes of battle, despite meeting Sesinu blade for blade, dodging her attacks and landing blows, the woman managed to disarm Iris once again, catching her off guard with an elbow to the chin and a kick to the chest. Iris landed flat on her back, the blades flying from her hands. But the battle had been fierce enough to satisfy the crowd. They cheered approvingly.

"Now we've seen your power and your prowess." Sesinu reached down for

Iris to clasp her hand. Pulling Iris up, she added, "Though you'll need more rigorous training if you're to be restored to your former days of glory."

"Isn't it frightening," Rin said, "that none of you have considered if she wants to be restored to her former days of glory? If she wants to stay here at all?"

The cheers stopped. The warrior women of Dahomey stared at Rin.

"She's the king's warrior; where else would she go?" a woman answered behind her.

"Home. Wherever she deems 'home' to be." And Rin looked very bitter as she turned away. She stared at the ground, touching her damaged eye. "Most of us have our own homes we were taken from too."

A true hush fell over the compound. Though Sesinu stepped forward menacingly, it was another woman, tall and lanky, who backhanded Rin. Iris gasped and readied herself to fly to the warrior, but Sesinu lifted up her arm, blocking her.

"How ridiculous," said the woman who'd struck Rin. "You were a tribute to the king, you know that. You are one of his warriors. This is your home. Why do you speak of things of the past?"

Natame leaned sideways to "whisper" to Aisosa. "What's this, now? And look at General Sesinu. It looks like she isn't surprised at all." She was quickly shushed.

Sesinu clucked her tongue and shook her head. "You haven't changed at all in the months you were abroad, have you, Olarinde?"

She seemed annoyed, or perhaps more precisely, disappointed. Natame was right. Though the other warriors seemed surprised by Rin's outburst, Sesinu didn't seem taken aback in the slightest. Something told Iris that the two had had this conversation before.

"We leave our families and our homes to dedicate ourselves to this cause," Sesinu continued. "Desiring to leave our duties and return is nothing more than a show of weakness."

"And there's nothing worse than weakness," said Rin.

"This is the law," said Sesinu with a point of finality. "And the king decides the law."

"The king decides the law." Rin's bottom lip shook before she bit down on it—hard enough to draw a drop of blood.

The warriors were frozen to the spot, watching this battle of wills unfold, glancing between the two women.

Sesinu chuckled as she looked around the compound. "See their ghostlike faces, Olarinde? You challenged me once about this in private. I never thought you'd voice your opinion in front of anyone else. This is precisely why I recommended you for the European mission. To test your loyalty."

Ghostlike, yes. Everyone was shocked. But there were a few pensive eyes and unreadable expressions. Iris wondered how many might have secretly agreed with Rin.

Even Iris had been taken in a raid. Other girls had been given as tributes. As fearsome as the group was, as much as Iris admired a military force made entirely of women, the means by which it came to exist was complex at best.

"The test is over. Come, Isoke," said Sesinu, "let me show you more of our armory."

As the warriors dispersed and Iris was led away, she looked back at Rin. She'd never seen Rin look so vulnerable—so different from the confident warrior who seemed so proud of her pedigree. A lonely girl left alone on the compound.

Later, Iris learned that it was to be a day of surprises. A curious delirium seemed to descend upon the earth in the heat of the evening. Iris, in a simple red wrap she tied under her arms, walked barefoot into the surrounding forest.

It was Jinn she found once again hiding from the crowd, this time behind a tree.

Jinn, behind the tree with a broken Rin, holding her gently in embrace.

22

NO, THERE WAS SOMETHING WRONG WITH this picture. Something strange.

Jinn was leaning into Rin, his knees buckled. His arms enveloped the young warrior, not in a lover's embrace but almost in an attempt to stay on his feet. His eyes looked red and unfocused. Rin, oddly stiff, was whispering something into his ear. Like an unfinished painting, there was something that felt wrong about them.

Was he drunk? But Jinn wasn't the type to get so inebriated he couldn't even stand. Unless . . .

Iris's throat dried. Was it because of her? Everything that was happening between them?

Rin began to drag him away. Iris felt like a coward hiding her presence from them. Like a coward . . . and yet she couldn't do anything more than watch. If her behavior had driven Jinn to the bottle . . . well, that wasn't on her. She wasn't doing anything wrong. She'd already made up her mind not to apologize anymore.

Why does it feel like no matter where we go and what you do, you're always still just you?

She just didn't know what to think.

Iris left them alone.

King Glele summoned her at nightfall. The palace was a sprawling, flat-roofed building in the compound, with two levels. She met him on a red clay balcony. Her fingers traced the railing. She could finally feel a little breeze here—not enough to sway the thick palm leaves that covered the moon from sight, but just enough to tickle the wispy hairs upon her skin.

"You're not so different from what I expected," Iris told him. "Are all kings so stern?"

He barely responded. He'd changed into a full white robe and green cap embroidered in gold, the colors of the ceremonial cloth draped across his broad left shoulder. At her words, he scoffed and barely spared her a glance. The confidence of a king who made war and kept slaves.

Iris had seen many such men before in her past as Hiva. There were some men whose sense of self-importance wouldn't allow them to show fear, even in the presence of someone they deemed a goddess.

"Western powers are gathering as we speak," the king said ominously. He was all business. "In Berlin, state leaders plot among themselves to take control of this continent. The tenuous arrangement we've had with the French will soon turn into an all-out power struggle that will last as long as my army can stand. But despite the power of the *ahosi*, I can't guarantee our victory in the long run."

"Do you know about John Temple?" Iris asked, because despite having decided to abandon her journey, a part of her still needed to find out. "About the Enlightenment Committee he was a part of? About why he was truly interested in my power?"

"The white men who welcome the end of days? John Temple was an arrogant fool, but he was a frightened one as well." King Glele flashed an unapologetically smug look. "He came to me not only to seek knowledge but to seek protection from those he aimed to betray."

"Betray?" Iris recalled Adam's story—he'd convinced the Enlightenment Committee that he'd murdered his father on their orders. But instead the man had fled, taking the Moon Skeleton with him. After losing it, they'd squandered their primary means through which to escape this supposedly doomed world.

"Unlike his murderous fellow club members, John Temple did not desire the end of the world. When he came to me, it was clear he certainly did not believe any world should be theirs for the taking, even if they had the machinery to take it. Like this 'Helios.'"

Iris watched the kinge. So he did know of the so-called "New World." How much had John Temple told him?

"Knowing of my country's military prowess and resources, he came to me offering information in exchange for protection. That there was more technology being built that exceeded all imagination. Together, we could destroy the Enlightenment Committee and all others who sought to use it for their own gain. But first, he needed possession of the greatest weapon of all—the one currently walking our earth." And the king looked at her. "You."

Iris scowled. Of course. John Temple suspected the true nature of Hiva. He and his son were the only members of the Committee who'd deduced it themselves. If he didn't want the world to end, sabotaging the Committee wasn't enough; he'd have to find a way to control her—or get rid of her. But . . .

"I'm not anyone's tool," she said resolutely. She was not as tall as King Glele, but she didn't shy away from his glare, which held the cold confidence of a king who ruled with an iron fist.

"You should not misunderstand me, Isoke. I have no care for another world. The one we live in is wondrous enough. Filled with possibility. And when there are too many powers that conspire to take my kingdom from me, defeating them is my first and only priority."

He looked out over the compound, over the homes and winding paths, over the forests and the hills in the horizon.

"Last I saw him, John Temple was afraid of his own child, who'd tried to murder him."

"Last you saw him?" Iris narrowed her eyes. Adam had tried to kill his own father only a few weeks before the tournament began. But that meant—

"You . . ." An incredulous laugh escaped from her lips. "You've seen him recently, haven't you?" And when King Glele nodded, a wave of excitement rushed through her. "He could still be here!"

"Not here. That man is looking for you. For your origins. As such, my kingdom was only a short stop, for even we do not know where you came from,

Isoke. Although I did tell him that it must not have been a coincidence that we found you in a village not so far from here."

Searching for her origins . . .

"That man was never able to rest, never able to enjoy the work of his hands, for he was cursed by the constant drive of his own greed and curiosity. He created as many enemies as he fled from. Perhaps he looked too far beyond his horizon. But I believe in what I can see, and I desire to keep what is owed to me. Isoke, you will fight for me again."

The celebrations, the food. The shouts and praises. They were for a warrior who had fought side by side with them in a bygone era, not her.

But who was she? Who was she supposed to be? She refused to care, but she couldn't stop caring, and that was her curse. Iris felt as if she were constantly rethinking it, reimagining and re-envisioning an identity for herself. And yet there was one thing she knew for certain.

"I told you," she said, unafraid. "I'm nobody's tool."

A quiet battle of wills raged in the stretch of silence, the tension between them cut only when Aisosa and Natame ran, breathless, out from the door-less shadowy entrance behind her.

"King Glele." Aisosa caught her breath and stood up straight. "We've just been given a report that there's been an attack at the Forge."

"An attack?" Iris pressed her hand against her chest.

The king stepped forward, alarmed. "Have you seized the assailant?"

"We have him surrounded inside the Forge, but he's fighting back," said Natame. "He tried to kill General Sesinu, sir. She's just barely alive."

"Sesinu?"

The utter shock on the king's face was warranted. Sesinu was a general. A powerful woman. A leader. Even in the short time Iris had been here, she understood how respected Sesinu was. She knew the Dahomey's customs. Whoever had tried to kill Sesinu was doomed to a painful death.

The king turned to Iris. "You see, Isoke? Even now we are under siege. You do not know Sesinu, but she's known of you and hoped for your return as we all did. As your king, I expect nothing less than to see you respond accordingly."

The expectant, pained expressions on the girls' faces affected Iris more than she thought they would. They were young, the two of them. They likely saw Sesinu as a mother figure.

"Who is the culprit? Tell me!" King Glele demanded.

The warriors hesitated before answering. They couldn't very well disobey the king's order. And yet the way they glanced ever so subtly at Iris was a bad sign. The stinging pit in her stomach told her she wouldn't like the answer. Dread washed over her as her thoughts drifted to the confrontation between Sesinu and Rin. The strange questions Rin had asked her afterward . . . the way she'd touched the blades in the weapons storehouse.

No, Rin was ruthless, but not careless and certainly not stupid. She wouldn't pull something like this, no matter how angry she was.

Would she?

Iris held her breath. The warriors confessed, and it wasn't Rin. But when they said the culprit's name, Iris's world lost all sense.

"It's the servant who traveled here with Isoke," they said. "The man called Jinn."

23

THE FORGE LAY INSIDE A FOREST that separated the city of Abomey from a nearby village. On the way, Iris saw four warriors carrying Sesinu's body on a stretcher. Her chest was stripped bare. The white bandages they'd wrapped around her stomach had turned red from her bleeding wound.

"Sesinu!" Iris cried as the stretcher passed, reaching out her hands but too scared to touch the woman's body. "She's going to be all right, isn't she?"

The warriors glared at Iris as they passed by but said nothing. Well, they had their job. Iris had hers.

Atop a hill, surrounded by tall trees, the Forge looked from the outside like many of the round structures built from clay, fortified by earthen materials, and topped with a thatched roof. A single room large enough to fit two or three families. But this was not a regular home. Smoke drifted out of a long black metal tube piercing through the tip of the cone-shaped roof, and the same metal tubes lined the ceiling, mazelike, above her head.

The tubes had been built to stabilize a contraption twice as tall as any one in the room: it looked something like the front of a train without wheels, brassy and rusted, or maybe like one of Uma's long fantastical engines with its hatches and gears. And yet at the same time, the way it lay flat upon the stone ground reminded her of a coffin: large, intimidating, and appropriately adorned. With the round hatch left slightly open, the smoke that didn't leak out through the attached metal tubes slipped out from inside the furnace.

Yes, a furnace. And Iris could see what they were burning: shelves of white crystal, the same material that her immortal heart was made of, collected from deposits left behind when she was reborn. Experiments on the detritus shed from her body—it was just like the Basement, except inside the burning furnace, through the smoke, Iris saw a glowing lamp. Was that where they placed the other substances they kept here, like those fetishes she spied: dried animal bones, kola nuts, palm nuts, and blood mixed with sand? There were men in robes who held divining tools, like small stone statues of gods holding trays upon their heads and long ivory effigies of gods. There were also those on stools who used metal rods to keep the gears of the furnace turning, to keep the fire inside burning and discharge from building up inside the structure. A combination of divination, knowledge, and creativity. So this was the Forge that had given Rin her powers. Human ingenuity was truly terrifying. It felt just as impressive and as dangerous as the Helios.

Iris lost herself in it only momentarily. While the diviners and scientists stayed huddled to one side of the furnace in the upper left corner of the expansive room, five *ahosi* warriors cornered a dazed Jinn with spears and rifles. His bloodshot eyes darted from warrior to warrior, but when he tried to take a step forward, he only stumbled back, hitting the wall.

"Careful of the fire that comes from his mouth," one of the warriors said.

"What's happening here?" Iris ran forward and launched herself through the group. "What are you doing to him—?"

But she stopped when she saw Jinn's hand covered in blood. It was as if he'd reached inside Sesinu's body himself. And the more he rubbed his face to wake himself from his stupor, the more the warrior's blood smeared all over his face. Iris couldn't stand to watch it. She grabbed his right wrist and yanked it down.

"Jinn! What happened?" She bent this way and that, trying to catch his gaze, but he kept turning his head from side to side and blinking as if trying and failing to recognize his surroundings.

"I-Iris," he stuttered. "What's going on?"

"That's my question!" Iris tugged his wrist pleadingly, but when she looked at his hands again, she noticed the bits of skin crusted in his fingernails.

Whose skin?

"Isoke, with all due respect, move," said one of the warriors with a shaved head: Izegbe. She gripped her rifle tight enough that Iris could see the blue veins through her brown skin. "We are here to capture this man."

Iris whipped around, her mind swirling with excuses. "Jinn would never kill someone in cold blood. You're all mistaken. Did you even see him stab Sesinu? All these witnesses—someone must have seen something!"

The warriors glanced at each other awkwardly but maintained their battle stances. They were ready to strike at any minute.

"It was during an inspection," answered Aisosa, uncharacteristically timid as she watched the situation fearfully. "That's why Sesinu was here. Usually, no one else is supposed to be here while an inspection takes place. . . ." She paused and looked at Natame, who shrugged.

Iris placed her hands on her hips and stared wildly from woman to woman. "So no one was around to see Jinn stab Sesinu?"

"We guards heard her scream and ran in—they did too." A warrior flicked her head toward the diviners and scientists. "They came in through the back, we through the front. And what we saw was this man with a bloody knife in his hands and one of our generals bleeding nearly to death on the floor. Exactly what are we supposed to think?"

Iris looked at Jinn, but his eyes could not even focus on her long enough to return her gaze. He was blinking, his breathing shallow. He could barely speak. Something was wrong.

"Jinn wouldn't do this." Iris was sure of it.

"You'll forgive us if we don't trust him. We don't know him," said a scientist.

"And the other day he was asking questions he shouldn't have about this place," added one of the guards.

Another scientist nodded. "How do we know he didn't accompany you as a spy? The French have employed all kinds of agents to learn our secrets. And from his strange abilities, it seems they've learned quite a lot already. Didn't you say he grew up in Paris?"

Iris remembered her off-the-cuff remark, and her stomach dropped at her realization that she could have damned him through her embarrassed rambling. She grabbed Jinn's sleeve so that he wouldn't fall over. "You may not trust him, but can't you at least trust me? I'm telling you, Jinn is not a spy, and he is not the type of man who would harm some stranger at random. He's—"

Iris bit her lip. He was an annoying crank. Always nagging at her, chiding her when she did something immature. When they first met, he'd spent most of the time annoyed when she messed up a routine with a slip or a wobble, before that annoyance slowly turned to concern. When she stumbled, even while dancing on the floor during practice, his hand would reach out to her almost instinctively to steady her: close enough to touch, but never quite committing to contact. It didn't take too long before his hands could touch her easily.

There were times when he infuriated her with his watchful, worried eyes, and other times when she wondered what they saw when they looked at her. She already knew, deep in her heart, what she wanted them to see, even if she couldn't admit it to herself.

"Besides." Gripping Jinn tighter, she gathered herself just as her chest began searing with an odd kind of pain. "Look at him. He can barely speak, barely talk! I think something's happened to him. We should investigate before jumping to conclusions."

"He became drunk, perhaps?" guessed Izegbe, her gun aimed straight for his forehead. "Or perhaps he has a taste for opium. Many foreigners have tried to smuggle it into our kingdom; it wouldn't surprise me."

"*What?*" Iris spat, infuriated by Izegbe's ridiculous assumption.

The women nodded to one another and began moving in.

"Stop it!" Iris said, letting Jinn go, standing in front of him defiantly. "I am Isoke. You know my power. Do not come near him."

Izegbe only lifted her head in defiance. "We *will* come near him. So what will you do?"

Iris was the one who almost took a step back, but the slight tremor of her foot in the air made her cognizant of her own momentary cowardice. Steeling herself, she stood firm.

"What do you *think* I'll do?" she answered, her chest swelling as she suddenly remembered her power. Millions of years' worth. More than any of them. She lowered her head, her dark eyes promising pain. "Leave, or I'll get rid of you all right here."

"You won't," Izegbe said simply, and when she turned to the girls beside her, they nodded in agreement. Frustratingly, bafflingly, they weren't afraid of her. *Nobody* was afraid. "We could see during your battle with Sesinu. You indeed have power, but not the cruelty to use it without damaging your own heart. Even when you burned our prisoners alive, it affected you. You became wild that night, laughing, throwing off your clothes and dancing like an unruly child. As if you were escaping from something."

Iris sucked in a sharp breath as if she'd been pierced. Her arms dangled heavily at her sides. How could this woman see so directly into her soul? Or was it because she was gifted with the hard gaze of a warrior that she could discern the weakness in others?

"You don't know me," Iris whispered. "Stop!" she added when they came closer. "I will fight you. And remember," she added with a smirk, "I don't fall. Not for good."

"As the legends say." Izegbe nodded. "So, then, how we seize our prisoner is clear."

Izegbe shot her in the chest.

24

"SHOW YOURSELF," SAID HIVA, SETTING DOWN the book she was studying.

In the quiet of the night, the figure who had been not so stealthily following her the entire day finally slunk out from around the tree.

It was not a Naacalian. Hiva had been among the humans for six months already. She knew the taste of their anima.

No. The anima of this being, wholly unique, felt familiar.

It felt like hers.

Hiva glanced up and saw him. Brown hair curled lusciously over his golden skin. A statuesque creature, like the sun god the Naacal had once mistaken her for upon their first meeting. The god they prayed to.

"Are you Helios?" Hiva asked him, watching flora peacefully bloom in his tresses. They were like the field of daffodils beneath their feet. Nature performed the work of covering his naked body, for he possessed no clothes. It had never done so for her.

He shook his head. "I am Hiva. Greetings."

Hiva sat up with interest. "But *I* am Hiva."

"Yes." He nodded and looked up at the stars. "There are many earths." He stretched out his arms in the cool breeze. "I've been to another before, briefly.

And then I came here. I sensed you. I came using the technology from my earth. I wanted to meet another like myself."

The Naacalians had mentioned a term before—something they called *Side Worlds*. This must have been what they had meant. Hiva observed with neutral interest.

"Nature bends to you," Hiva said, watching the daffodils sway next to him.

"Yes, it's curious." He crouched low and touched a petal. "Nature has been rather kind to me ever since I stopped my mission and began trying something new."

"Stopped your mission?" Hiva repeated.

"Yes. And began to question."

"Question what?"

The man smiled. "Everything. Nature . . . it's trying to tell me something. . . ."

"Nature is trying to tell you . . ." Hiva didn't understand, but the other Hiva didn't seem to notice her confusion. He tilted his head as if listening to the flowers.

With a sigh, she shook her head. "And so now that you are here, what do you wish to do?" Hiva picked up her book. It chronicled an abbreviated history of the rulers of Naacal. There was still much to learn about this civilization. She would not judge the world until she'd come to know everything. "Are you here to observe me? To judge me as we would judge humanity?"

But this Hiva was strange. He dug his toes in the ground, tracing a circle. He looked down upon the earth sheepishly. "Rather, I was hoping for companionship," he said, and gazed up at her shyly. "Is it all right, Hiva, if I call you sister?"

Iris awoke to find a diviner praying over her with a fetish. The smell of burning kola nut dragged her from death back into the land of the living. She groaned and put her hand over her chest, where the bullet had pierced her. Fragments of the bullet fell off her garments and onto the floor as she lifted herself up. The sun was rising. Jinn and the warriors were nowhere to be found.

"Jinn," she whispered, looking out the open window. The gentle light in the sky told her dawn was close to breaking. No one was outside. Nothing but forest for miles.

"Isoke," said a shy scientist behind her with a square nose and round chin. "It's true that we did not see what happened inside the Forge. We were outside." He flicked his head toward the back door. "But I do remember seeing someone rush out of this window and into the forest."

Iris whipped around so fast, the poor man jumped. "Did you see who it was?"

"No." He shook his head. "But there are not many people who know about this place."

At any rate, she needed to find Jinn, and fast. That wasn't hard to do. The king of Dahomey kept his prisoners within an open section of the palace compound, in a crowded cage made of thick logs of wood tied together with straw. The people of the compound surrounded the cage, jeering at the prisoners, who spat and jeered back. But underneath the unforgiving sun and the hot red sand, many of the men could do nothing more than shout for food or wait for their punishment. As the warriors had once told Iris, here was the worst of society: assailants who had targeted, harmed, and killed the most vulnerable in their community. Jinn, who looked gaunt and defeated, didn't belong here. Who else among this lot were unfairly accused?

Unfairly accused. Memories of euphoria sprang up from within her like water from a well, only to bring back the faces of the prisoners she'd killed for the Dahomey, twisted in horror. Her stomach churned with dread.

"Oh God." Iris covered her mouth, her breaths quickening before she shook the thought from her mind. At least, she tried to, but she couldn't rid herself of the vision of their bodies turning to ash.

And then she saw Jinn again. The sight of him trying to peer over the heads of the other prisoners in the cage transformed panic to frenzy. But before Iris could fly out from between the two buildings she watched from, a warm hand grabbed her wrist and pulled her toward the bordering trees.

"It's no use," whispered Rin. "Don't even try it."

Iris whipped around. She could see the girl sweating under the heat, more than usual. Rin's eyes darted around to ensure no one among the *ahosi* in the compound could see her.

"He didn't do anything to that woman, and you know it," Iris whispered from behind the prickly, rough bark of a palm tree. "He didn't even know her. He had no motive. And that's not who he is—"

"I realize that, but do you really think they'll care? This is one of the worst offenses anyone can commit against the king and the community. Sesinu is like a mother to everyone. She was wounded badly. We still don't know if she'll live in the end. . . ."

Her voice broke, and her hands shook. Rin clasped them together, but her usual calm was nowhere to be found. Iris had never seen her so disturbed. The young warrior gritted her teeth and shook her head, as if to snap herself out of her stupor.

"They'll want his head," Rin said.

Iris stepped back, slamming against the tree, her body numb. "His head?"

"Unless you stop them."

Iris's own head was spinning as Rin gripped her bare forearms. "This is not a normal offense. It's worse than any crime. They won't stop until they receive retribution for this." The words came out rapidly, as if she only had one breath left to spare for them. "You must kill the king."

"What?"

"Do it, Isoke! It's the only way you can stop Jinn's execution."

"Now wait a bloody minute!" Iris shook off Rin and placed a hand on her forehead as she tried to catch her breath. "Kill the king for this? That's insane. I'm not exactly his best friend at the moment, but he's not done anything to deserve being killed."

"*To you—*" Rin spat before catching herself. Iris stared at her. For a moment, she looked like a small, lonely child who had been found out by her mother. But Rin gathered herself once more. "It's not about what one deserves. It's about the power he wields. If he decides that Jinn must die—and he will—your lover is as good as dead."

Iris was taken aback. "My *lover?*"

"He *is* your lover, isn't he? You'd do anything for him. That's obvious."

Iris's cheeks flushed, and her throat dried. She thought of Jinn embracing Rin by the trees. He'd had the same dazed look as when he was inside the Forge.

Dazed and confused. As if he didn't know where he was.

Iris lowered her head. A light wind ruffled the grass on the ground, a cool whisper upon her own legs and feet. Silently, she raised her eyes to look at Rin. The girl was still young. A seasoned warrior, yes, but an impetuous child not nearly mature enough to understand the depth of the world beyond just herself.

"Do it," Rin said. "You must."

After a while, Iris shut her eyes and nodded. She could sense Rin's relief.

"The king wants to have a hearing with Jinn and the other warriors," Rin told her. "It should start soon. Jinn will be taken to see him."

It was already starting. From around the tree, Iris could see two men open up the cage, keeping the prisoners at bay with rifles. Two *ahosi* called out for Jinn, and after he was pushed to the front of the crowd, he was taken into custody. Iris was running out of time.

"Rin, go ahead. Try to stall them as much as possible. I need to check something first."

Rin gave her an incredulous look. "What could possibly be more important than this?"

"The scrolls, my clothes, and Nyeth's ring. I'll gather them up. We'll need them if we're to make a quick getaway."

Or so she said. But she didn't have time to gather those things; there was a place she desperately wanted to check: Rin's small one-room home they'd both stayed in. Then the servants' tent Jinn had slept in. But she found no evidence to confirm her suspicions. Iris wasn't even sure what she was looking for. She didn't know what could have been used to forcibly take away Jinn's senses. Opium was her first guess, remembering Izegbe's accusation. But she saw no pipes, no hint of white powder anywhere in either of their quarters.

"Alcohol?" Iris whispered to herself. She'd originally thought Jinn had indulged because of his complex feelings toward *her*. The gears in her head were turning in a different direction now.

Toward a different conclusion.

She ran to the open kitchen quarters where they made food. The rich smells of meat boiling in stew with onions, peppers, and spices titillated Iris's senses. There was no door separating the inside and outside; the women and men cooked outside, their tin pots boiling over wood fires, but they could just as easily walk through the threshold, over the wooden frame, and help with those slicing fruit upon clean tables. What kind of alcohol had they served at her celebration party or even last night's dinner? Iris asked a woman outside who was pounding yam with a stick in a large wooden mortar.

"It was basic rum," she answered with a little laugh. "Of course you shouldn't drink too much of it at a time, but unless you've had an ocean of it, I don't think it would have the effects you've described."

She was right. But there was something else she needed to know.

"Did you see Olarinde near the kitchens these past few days? Was she around the food?"

Everyone shook their heads. "She's a very serious girl, and fairly busy," said the woman. "Honestly, sometimes I wonder if she eats at all. She needs to loosen up a little."

"Well, it's not easy," said one cook. "She was such a young girl when she lost her eye in a battle against the Egba. She became even quieter then. It couldn't have been easy for her."

The others nodded in agreement, and immediately the chatting began.

"When she first began her training, didn't she get into fights with all the other children constantly? Even the ones who wanted to be her friends."

"I don't think she ever really liked being here."

Rin chatting with the doctor in Ajashe. The hatred in her eyes that burned whenever Iris mentioned the king. Iris couldn't deny what she knew in her heart as the truth finally settled.

"I agree," Iris said darkly, and stared out over the compound. She had to check Rin's room one last time. She needed to find the evidence before they did. Before—

Loud rumblings and a sudden chorus of shouts lifting into the air told her that she was out of time.

"I heard the king is overseeing the execution of a prisoner," said one man inside the kitchen. "The one who tried to murder Sesinu. Sesinu was always kind and encouraging when I started cooking here. I hope she heals quickly."

"So do I." Iris bowed her head a little, bidding them goodbye, and rushed to the central compound where King Glele was to decide Jinn's fate.

By the time Iris had rushed into the palace complex, a large crowd had already gathered in the space enclosed by the red clay walls. Someone had thrown Jinn, whose hands were tied in rope behind his back, in front of the king, who once again sat in his ivory chair underneath the imperial roof, surrounded by servants, warriors, and consorts.

"Wait!" Iris cried, pushing aside a guard and kneeling next to Jinn on the sand. "I know what happened to Sesinu is terrible. I know that. I know your community is hurting, but please, I'm telling you that Jinn didn't have anything to do with what happened to her!"

"Sesinu." Picking up on that word, Jinn bowed his head. "Iris, something's happened," he whispered. "But I don't know . . . I can't remember anything about that night."

"Quiet, you idiot," Iris hissed in English. "I'm trying to save you."

"But it's true. I think I heard them say Sesinu was hurt." He looked at her, vulnerable and afraid. "Is she okay?"

"What are they whispering to each other?" said one of the *ahosi.*

"Be careful," said Izegbe. "It is not just Isoke or Rin. That man too has a strange power. He breathes fire out of his mouth. We saw it inside the Forge."

Frightened murmurs. The king stared at the two of them, his finger placed beneath his bottom lip as he considered them thoughtfully. "Isoke. What evidence do you have that your servant did not commit this crime?"

"He's not my servant," Iris said, and touched his arm tenderly. "He's my circus partner. He came all the way here to a foreign land, understanding nothing of the language, the customs, but he came here anyway because he was worried about me. He's—" She paused. And because she knew Jinn couldn't understand him, she pursed her lips, shifted uncomfortably, and admitted, "He's someone I care about very much. Please don't kill him."

Though there were some confused whispers and sneers here and there, most of the crowd was quiet. To Jinn's left was a group of women Iris recognized. Aisosa and Natame were among them—their backs stiff and upright owing to the presence of the king, though their expressions betrayed their nerves—and Rin. As stiff as she was, her good eye remained on Iris and Iris alone, grappling with her silently, her fingers twitching in anticipation.

Rin had said that the only way to save Jinn was to kill the king. Iris had that power. She had the power to kill everyone here. Why shouldn't she? Whoever had power made the rules. Wasn't that the law of humankind, the law that governed the world? Whether one had earned that power or received it through the fortune of birth, it could be wielded at one's leisure. It was how the kings of Dahomey had built their famed military. How many standing with Rin were, like Rin, victims of a system of forced conscription that had taken them from their families? How many felt as Rin had?

The ones with power ruled the world.

Hold her down, gentlemen. Do not underestimate her. This beast is dangerous.

The sound of Doctor Pratt's voice rattling in her head drew her out of her own body and into the cold Cambridge lab where men who went on to be doctors, professors, and gentlemen of society had cut into her with scalpels and tools not meant for human flesh. Her soul chilled. The beat of her crystal heart slowed to a crawl.

Power. The Enlightenment Committee wielded it without mercy, and because of that, countless had died unnecessary deaths in the Tournament of Freaks.

Power. The family of that little girl, Lulu, would still be in the land of the living if not for those who'd used theirs against them.

And as Iris looked back at Rin with an apologetic look, at the girl who'd lost her community, her autonomy, her eye, all Iris could see were the men she'd killed just days ago.

And again on *La Daphnée*.

And again in the Library of Rule.

And again in the Coral Temple, and again and again until the bones had mounted up before her in a pile too high for her to see the top of.

What was she to do with the curse of power? Or was her conscience the curse?

Expelling a deep breath, King Glele held out his hand. On cue, a servant came to him and, genuflecting, handed him something Iris couldn't see until King Glele held it up in front of him. A little brown bottle.

Oh no. The bottle. The moment Rin saw it, she began to sway on her feet.

"It's called 'laudanum' overseas," said the king. "A drug. And it was found in Olarinde's clothes."

Gasps in the crowd. Iris lowered her head. Back when she'd noticed the bottle Rin had taken from the hospital in Ajashe, she'd let it slide. There was already too much for Iris to think about. But it was clear now why she'd been so interested in drugs and medicines.

A part of her still didn't want to believe it. She hadn't managed to find anything suspicious in Rin's room, after all. It could all have been a mistake on her part.

She didn't find anything because the king's men had found it first.

Rin's entire body trembled as the warriors around her glared at her in disbelief.

"Do you really think that I would take a man's precious life without thoroughly investigating the circumstances first? I'm so disappointed in you, child," said the king, drowning out the sounds of Rin's protests. "Bring her out."

"Wait!" Iris said quickly.

"Wait!" Rin cried at the same time, rubbing her hands together, as two women roughly grabbed her arms and dragged her in front of the king. "Wait, please, wait!"

But her pleas were lost among the jeers. Iris glanced from Rin to King Glele, frantic, eyeing the weapons the *ahosi* now pointed in Rin's direction. As the young warrior was thrown down next to Jinn, a few guards picked Jinn and Iris off their feet.

"Olarinde. You were seen offering this man alcohol last night," said the king. "This man is a stranger. He has no reason to kill Sesinu. Did you not think of something so obvious before you committed treason against your people?"

Rin covered her mouth and retched upon the ground before bending over, grasping the sand. Despite Iris's anger, despite her hurt from Rin's betrayal, seeing the girl begging for her life wrenched tears from her eyes. The king was wrong. Rin *had* considered it. But her use of Jinn was not to fool the king.

It was to manipulate Iris.

She'd known that Rin had had something to do with Jinn and Sesinu. She'd known it in her heart, though she'd lacked the evidence to prove it. Even if she had found what she was looking for, what would she even say in front of the king, whom Rin so desperately wanted her to kill? What could she say now that Rin was surrounded by the fiercest warriors, who'd now become her deadliest enemies?

"Why, Olarinde?"

"What did Sesinu ever do to you? What did *we* ever do to you?"

"We were sisters in arms! We battled side by side!"

"You're a traitor! Were you turned by the French?"

The accusations came as fast as bullets, as sharp as the edge of a blade. The king silenced them with a hand.

"Let her speak," he said. "I want to hear her reasons for herself. Olarinde, advocate for yourself. Help me understand why you've hurt Sesinu." And then he paused. "Ah, yes. Sesinu took part in the raid that brought you to me. Is that the reason, child?"

Sesinu had helped kidnap Rin? Iris held her breath. She looked around her at this group of hardened warriors, wondering who had come from where and which women had helped kidnap their comrades. That was when she remembered: she'd tried to do the same to Granny and Anne, under King Ghezo's orders. The cold truth of it made her quiver.

Rin couldn't speak. She didn't need to speak. The king should have already understood why. Her fellow warriors, too. Iris was sure that among the crowd there were some—even if it was just a few—who felt Rin's pain, the precise agony that came with the bitterness of loss.

"What's power without mercy?" Jinn whispered, surprising Iris, who remained frozen in fear and silence. "What's power without mercy?"

The jeers began again and grew louder. Jinn could not understand the king. Iris wondered if anyone could even hear him. He was speaking in English, but his words were not meant for them, the king, or even for her. His jaw set as he struggled to keep in his rage.

"I don't understand what's happening. But from what I see, it's always the same. There's always someone on the ground begging for mercy and someone who gets to decide whether to give it or not. Wherever I go. *Wherever* I go. Father . . . why are we like this?"

Why are they like this? It was a question Iris had asked herself many times before. Situations across the world were not identical. The way human beings in different lands structured their worlds and wielded their influence was not exactly equivalent either. But humanity always seemed to slip into the same pitfalls.

What was she to do with this world? With herself?

Iris opened her mouth. She wanted desperately to advocate for Rin, to express every convoluted thought looping around in her mind, but she couldn't.

"Please don't kill me," Rin said in a quick, hushed whisper. "Please don't kill me."

And she repeated it. Again and again, she repeated it until Iris threw herself upon her.

Such a simple plea, but wasn't it a plea that connected all forms of life? Trees and sea creatures, insects and land animals. Just as much as any human. All life was born to end, but that quiet plea was something each one shared. That plea, meek and fragile, slipped now from the lips of a small girl, a frail thing, and it broke Iris to pieces, until all she could do was weep.

"Please don't kill me . . . ," Rin whispered again, her voice weak, and then, together with Iris, she cried. She couldn't leave Rin alone to die. That much she knew.

Some of the congregation shifted uncomfortably. Some lowered their heads. Others, the older women, looked at Rin without mercy. Which among them would decide Rin's fate?

"Olarinde," began King Glele.

"I won't let you do it," whispered Iris, though she doubted anyone but Rin could hear her.

"Olarinde, your crimes—"

Iris rose to her feet. "I won't let you do it."

The *ahosi* were ready. King Glele stood firm. But Iris didn't care. The king lifted his chin in full authority, but the sound of Rin swallowing her own tears fortified Iris's body.

"Isoke," he said.

"Shut up!" Iris cried. "I *will* not let you kill this girl—"

An explosion rocked the earth, almost throwing Iris off her feet.

The crowd screamed, and the warriors held their weapons at the ready, but smoke had already begun to fill the air—a very odd smoke. It debilitated her. The moment Iris inhaled, it overwhelmed her nostrils. She immediately began to feel her strength leaving her.

"Iris?" she heard Jinn calling her before he devolved into a spasm of coughing. "Iris!"

Iris tried to stand on her feet, her hands grasping at Rin's arm, but she couldn't see the young warrior anymore. More explosions. More smoke obscuring the king and all the others from her sight. The very second she found her footing, she heard a familiar voice.

"Gather them up quickly. Make sure Iris remains unharmed."

Her heart gave a painful thump as her lips trembled open. "A-Adam?"

She passed out on the red sand.

25

HIVA PUSHED OPEN THE BARN DOORS. The journey across this continent had made her weary. She could only annihilate what she saw. And what she saw in front of her eyes was a group of Naacalians, young and old, huddled together by the horses, weeping.

Nyeth was among them. With a loathsome wail, he separated himself from the huddling masses and threw himself upon her.

"Hiva! My Hiva! My goddess!" Strands of his blond hair caught in his wet lips as he buried himself in her robes. "Spare me! Even if only me!"

She had already destroyed half of the Naacalians' greatest military forces and wiped out the clergy. Only he had escaped, using his cowardly wiles to swear fealty to her and help her access the secret temples, palaces, and facilities hidden from her so she could erase the humans found inside. She could only kill was what was in front of her eyes.

When he realized his usefulness had expired, he fled from her secretly in the night. It was no bother to her. She'd known that eventually Nyeth too would join the ashes.

And yet. "My goddess, I have information. Important information only I can give!" He clung to her. "Even now, my people conspire to flee from your wrath. They've built contraptions greater than even the Helios. Contraptions powerful enough to destroy you."

"None can destroy me," Hiva replied flatly.

But Nyeth wouldn't be deterred. "Are you willing to find out?" he pressed, because by now this was all he had. "They're aiming to launch these beasts from the four corners of the earth. The greatest of these inventions lies inside the Great Sea. I can take you. I know the way."

The Naacal had only survived this long because their technology was advanced enough to pose somewhat of a challenge to her. If they'd created even more fearsome machines to kill her, it would be better to get rid of them first. Starting with the most dangerous.

Hiva listened. "The greatest of these inventions. Where is it?"

Nyeth's blue eyes shimmered. "The Coral Temple."

"Hiva!" A little boy broke away from his mother and ran toward her as his parents screamed. Kneeling on the barn floor, he imitated Nyeth, gripping her hem. "Hiva, spare us!"

But ever since that day on the road when Nyeth had killed the old man, Hiva's judgment had been kindled against humanity. Once her decision had been made, there was no turning back. Thus it had always been, for eons unto eternity.

As the child, his parents, and the others in the barn burned from the inside out, Hiva could hear her brother's anguish ringing in her ears.

Even the children? Even the children, sister?

It was the last thing he'd said to her before parting.

Nyeth was trembling, still gripping her as if he'd been carried away upon the wind with the ashes. Once the dust had settled, he looked up. It was unmistakable—the flash of hatred etched upon his face as he gazed upon her.

"I'll take you," said Nyeth, shutting his eyes and turning from her. "To the Coral Temple."

There was no turning back.

"Iris. Iris, my love?"

It must have been my imagination.

The sound of Adam's voice dragged her from sleep. Groaning, Iris clasped

her throbbing forehead before trying to move her body. She wasn't strapped to
the wooden chair beneath her, so that was a good sign, but the effects of the
smoke hadn't worn off yet. Her mind needed time to settle before she could
freely move the rest of her.

"Rin!" The thought of the girl crying and begging before the king knocked
Iris's senses back into place. But when she gathered her bearings, Rin, the king,
the *ahosi*, the sand, and the blaring sun—none of them were to be found.

Now *this* had to be some kind of basement in England. She looked around
what seemed like a dirty old boiler room converted into a mad scientist's lab.
What else could it be? Glass tubes and liquid-filled pumps bordered the walls.
Long tables and desks filled with paper. But most striking were the light bulbs,
each as big as a balloon, placed on mounts and connected to electrical wires
that wound toward the walls and blanketed the ceiling. Iris was mesmerized
by the golden lights that flickered inside, before an acute sense of dread made
the hairs on her arms stand on end.

A lab. Her body tightened in panic. The sight of the tables and tools on
the shelf forced Iris barefoot out of her chair onto the cold, smooth blue-
and-sunset-red Tabriz carpet.

"You're not in any danger, Iris."

As if hit with a shock of electricity, Iris looked up toward the mezzanine
level. Dread turned into fury. Adam. With his back to her, he stood up from the
floor, a book balanced in his hand, and turned slowly. In his brown checkered
vest and white pants, he looked down upon her with the smug expression of a
man who'd just seen a plan fall into place—which meant nothing good for Iris.

"What are you doing here?" she demanded, backing up too rapidly; she
bumped into one of the tables, sending a stack of papers fluttering to the
ground. "Where the hell am I?"

"Not too far from Dahomey. You're in a munitions facility inside the Atakora
Mountains," Adam answered, as if it were a simple question she should have
known the answer to. "Bosch Munitions Factory 7A, I believe it's called."

"A facility inside . . . inside a mountain?" Iris gaped up at him and then
stared at the wooden floor in shock. A munitions factory in Africa. Yes. Yes,
Benini had mentioned that there was one in West Africa he'd intended to go to.

But inside the mountains? Suddenly paranoid, as if the walls would cave in on her any second, Iris wrapped her arms around herself.

"You've been asleep for a few days, Iris."

She hadn't imagined anything. It truly was his voice she'd heard among the Dahomey as smoke had exploded around them.

"I thought you'd drowned in the Seine," she said, and added with an extra dose of venom, "Really made my day."

Adam chuckled, and she remembered, with slight disgust, that he seemed enamored with her hatred of him. "Is that the way to treat someone who just saved your friend's life? Rin, wasn't it? She would have been executed, as far as I could see, if my colleagues and I hadn't gotten there when we did."

"Your colleagues?" Iris shook her head, incredulous. "You and your 'colleagues' snuck into the king's palace?"

"I didn't say it was an easy feat."

He'd known they were on their way to see the king, but Iris didn't think he would follow her all the way here, even if he'd managed to survive. She'd underestimated the depth of his obsession.

But if he had saved Rin, then where was she? Where was Jinn?

The heels of his shoes clicked against the wood as he began descending the stairs. But when she ran to the table and picked up a scalpel, he stopped halfway down.

"If you wanted to kill me, you could always just burn me alive," he reminded her with a little smile.

"Believe me, I'm tempted."

"But you lack the will to act. That's always been your problem, Iris. You think too much." He sat down on the stairs. "Or maybe you care too much. And that's why the world is, regrettably, still standing."

What if Adam had been present when she'd burned Slessor's men alive? Iris bit her lip at the thought. How satisfied he would have been to see her morals slip off her like a nightgown. How smug he'd be if he'd known that for one moment, she'd considered his words—actually considered them—actually wondered if they could be true.

"You're a goddess, Iris," Adam said, and the ruthlessness of his gaze frightened her. It was as if he could read her mind. "Don't tie yourself down to the rules of men."

"Goddess? More like an accident of nature."

This was a voice Iris had never expected to hear, not in this place. But when she turned, the door to the lab slammed closed as in walked Madame Bellerose, dressed from head to toe in a demure, high-necked red dress that reached down to her black-heeled boots. With her red hair wrapped up in a bun, she'd tied white flowers into a wreath and placed it upon her head as if to show the people here what true royalty was. As always, her vicious expression both enhanced and struck down her beauty in a single blow. She glared at Iris as if looking at an escaped mule and sneered.

"I really couldn't believe it when Lord Temple told me you were the Hiva," she said, as if it pained her to do it.

That was right. The Committee knew. Bellerose had sent Jacques and Gram to lock her up in a cage, and now the woman had decided to come in the flesh. But Iris would be damned if she'd let herself be kidnapped again.

"I'm surprised you stepped out of your mansion to venture a voyage to chase me, Violet." Iris folded her arms. "Last I saw you, you were crying and cowering in a corner next to the corpses of your fellow psychopaths. You've grown a bit of a spine since then, I see."

Madame Bellerose growled viciously like a cat about to strike. Adam seemed to love witnessing it. "Wench. If I hadn't seen the rest of Temple's research for myself, I never would have imagined a savage like you would be so . . ." She huffed. "So . . ."

"Integral to the fate of humankind?" Though the thought of it had long tortured her, in this instance, she felt a tinge of pride saying it, and more than a little satisfaction in shoving her importance down this horrid woman's throat.

"*You*," Bellerose snarled, before gathering herself and hiding her snarl behind her white-gloved hand. She looked at Iris, still dressed in the wrap given to her by the Dahomey, with the utmost contempt. "Indeed, life likes to play little tricks here and there. No matter. Now that we have you, you're never escaping. We once believed the world's end was inevitable. Now that we know *you're* to be behind it, we have more options. I, for one, don't care to throw this world away, especially when I can have it and so much more."

At that, Adam's dark gaze slid to her for just a moment. Madame Bellerose didn't notice.

"Even if you do have the power to unleash the end of days, you never will," Bellerose continued. "You'll spend your eternity here."

After taking off her right glove, Madame Bellerose stuck her fingers between her lips and whistled. A group of guards traipsed in on cue, armed with guns; it wasn't them but the scientists in black coats who'd followed them inside that sent Iris's pulse into a panic.

"Perhaps," said Iris, lifting her head with a defiant snarl. "Or I'll just murder you and escape?"

"You won't." Madame Bellerose tilted her head slyly. "Even a beast has its weaknesses."

Bellerose signaled to one of her guards, who dropped two shoes onto the floor—not a pair, but Iris recognized them immediately: Jinn's dirty brown boot and Rin's black strapped sandal. Gritting her teeth, Iris glared at the woman.

"Where are they?" she demanded. "Tell me, or I swear—"

"Please swear. Kick, shout, howl, do whatever you'd like. This is a very big facility—and quite cleaner, I've noticed, than the Basement." She looked around, half-impressed. "Your friends are very well guarded and nicely subdued. But," she added quickly, once Iris took a threatening step toward her, "I've given their handlers strict orders. If they don't see me every half hour, they're to assume something unfavorable has happened to me—and kill them. Unlike you, they can't come back from hell."

The realization that this horrid woman had her beat tasted like poison. Iris's shoulders slumped, a bitter chill paralyzing her.

"Without John Temple around, we don't have the Moon Skeleton. We don't have any means to power the Ark or the Helios. Well, we'll just have to rely on our own research." Madame Bellerose twisted a strand of loose hair that had curled down her cheek. "Once our men have pinned you down and torn out your crystal heart, I'm sure there will be quite a bit we can do with it. Bosch will be pleased to have it. Men!"

With the sound of a clap, they sprang into action. Iris's fury rumbled hopelessly inside her as half the guards stalked out of the room with a laughing Bellerose, and the other half accompanied the scientists, snatching Iris up by the crooks of her arms and forcing her onto an experiment table.

Iris kicked and screamed, but she saw out of the corner of her eye that Adam just watched. Her heart beat in her throat. He was so close by. Was he going to sit back as his precious goddess was mutilated? Was this the grand plan he had for the world? Why wasn't he helping her?

Her fury did have somewhere to go after all. It crushed inward as she began hating herself for her own weakness. The men strapped chains around her wrists. It was all too familiar. The icy burn of metal against her skin. Her lungs struggling for breath. Her chattering teeth and locked jaw. Terror gone unnoticed by her assailants, who looked at her through the cold, calculating gaze of science and progress.

"You know what to do, Iris." Sitting on the staircase, Adam spoke with an air of calm as he sucked in a deep breath, lifted his head toward the dark ceiling of wires, and shut his eyes, almost as if in silent prayer. "No one believes in you, but I do. You know exactly what to do."

She thought of how free it'd felt once she had decided not to care any longer.

"Ah . . ." She let out a desperate breath of release. Maybe it was her imagination, but for a second, she began to think that she could *smell* their anima. The life force of others had begun titillating more of her senses. A fresh, but ultimately bland and hollow, scent slipped through the barrier of her skin.

She hadn't even begun to consider its taste before she realized that she was alone in the room with Adam and a pile of ash.

Even the children? Even the children, sister? A familiar howl, like hands wringing her throat. The dying eyes of a child who'd begged her for mercy.

"Oh no." She did care. "Oh no . . ." The throbbing pace of her heart sent her mind spiraling. After Adam freed her, she threw off the unclasped shackles with a frightened yelp and grasped her arms, shivering. Her thoughts stuttered out excuses. They were enemies. They were going to hurt her. So what if she'd killed them? They were evil. They'd deserved to die.

They'd deserved to die? As if seeking vengeance, a bit of ash wafted into her throat, choking her. Were they the ashes from the barn? Or from the Library of Rule? From the Naacal? The Atlanteans? Slessor's men? She coughed and coughed, panicked, frenziedly beating her chest, but her throat wouldn't clear. Who was this? Who was this inside of her?

As if on cue, as if only Adam had the power to peer into her mind and discern her darkest thoughts, he began laughing.

"You're alive," she said. It was as if she'd just realized it. "Why did I keep you alive but kill everyone else?"

"Because inside, you know: you need me. To guide you. To keep you on the righteous path." His eyes glinted. "Because inside, you know I'm right."

He lifted his hands to the heavens. "'For thou hast smitten all mine enemies upon the cheek bone; thou hast broken the teeth of the ungodly.'"

"Stop it!" Iris cried, covering her ears and shutting her eyes. But out from the darkness came little Lulu—her bright smile and her unforgettable tune, carrying with it her innocent rage.

Mine eyes have seen the glory . . .

Iris let out a tortured groan, only for her to feel strong, ivory-smooth hands on her wrists, tearing her own hands away from her ears. Before she knew what was happening, Adam was upon her, pinning her to the table. Someone else looking into the sensual expression of such a handsome man, a boy who'd grown up with a demon-like beauty to match his twisted heart, might have been stirred, but Iris only felt disgust—at him, at herself, so much so that she did not struggle when he leaned in. She felt his breath upon her ear.

"That," he said as she bit her lip and turned her head from him, "is exactly who you are, Iris."

"No!" She saw herself reflected in his eyes and for a moment felt as if they were joined. No, she would never be joined to him. She wasn't him. She wasn't Gram. She wasn't Hiva!

"Embrace yourself. Embrace *your* glory."

She pushed him off her and slapped him in the face, a desperate shudder thundering through her body. "You let them die. Whose side are you on, anyway?"

"A ridiculous question." As he sought to catch his breath from his sudden fit of passion, he adjusted his vest and ran his hands through his messy black hair. "Yours. Always yours."

Iris wanted to throw up. She wanted to cry.

"That's why," Adam continued, "I'll tell you where they are."

Iris sat up, her hands clasping the cold table. "They? You mean Rin and—"

"Your precious Jinn, yes." Adam gave her a very dark smile. Though one of his eyebrows was raised in amusement, Iris felt that if she could touch his words, they'd sting like acid. "They're both in the east wing. Rin, poor girl, still frazzled from her near execution. She's on the third floor of the building, fifth door around the corner to the right. And your Jinn is in the basement's cold dungeon inside the vault. A torture chamber, really. As for why Bosch would have one in the first place, let's just say the man is thorough and doesn't take kindly to information leaks."

Rin on the third floor. Jinn in the dungeon. Iris gripped her wrap with her fingers.

"You won't miss it," continued Adam. "At least, I should *hope* you won't, for their sake. They're being tortured on Madame's orders as we speak."

Adam took two steps back from her and, surrounded by the buzzing light bulbs, bowed cordially and stretched his hand out toward the door. Something was wrong. Iris could feel it in her ancient bones, but there wasn't any time to consider it, not with her companions in danger. Holding herself back from hitting Adam again, she made for the door.

The more she killed, the more arrogant Nyeth's voice inside her became.

You have a taste for it now. The scent. Why not just kill them all? It'd be so much easier.

316

If Iris were the Hiva of old, this munitions factory would have been one of her prime targets. Countless men and women with sooty faces and in old, raggedy clothes scurried about in workshops, creating weapons of destruction. Iris saw them as she snuck through the many hallway levels of the endless building. In one hot room they were casting bullets in molds, and in another, cannonballs. Shells littered the floor of another workshop. Or were they naval mines? Rows and rows of them stretched out between the workers, spaced equally down to the centimeter, polished to shining perfection, a metal field of deadly flowers.

Whether these workers were imported from Europe or lived in neighboring towns, and regardless of gender or age, they all had to wear the same dull gray uniform as they casted, melted, and welded. They didn't have the face of villains—only people desperate for shifts and pay. And yet what came out of their hands . . .

Iris gasped and slipped behind a corner as two women wearing gloves and scarves tied around their hair passed by her with prim steps. Now was the time to push everything else aside and concentrate. She needed to find Jinn. Get to the basement, rescue him. Together they'd find Rin and escape whatever trap Adam had—

A damp hand clasped around her mouth. Shocked, Iris tried to rip it off her, only for more hands to grab her limbs and pull her away.

"Shh," said a man's voice. English. "She wants to see you."

She? "Bellerose?"

"No."

Iris turned to look at her captors: all very tall white men in clean black jackets. None of them carried a hint of malice as they ushered her along discreetly, forming a wall around her to more easily conceal her presence.

What are they playing at? Narrowing her eyes, Iris turned and let the men lead her.

It was a tiny room tucked in the far corner of the factory. The left part of the ceiling sloped down into a diagonal slant. Light bulbs hung by wires down the ashen walls. Men sat on stools near a pulley hanging unused from the ceiling. Brass tubes and beakers filled with blue fluid littered the already cluttered desk near the back, and if it weren't for the puff of smoke billowing from the glass atop the Bunsen burner, Iris would have recognized the woman standing behind it immediately.

Iris balked as the men let her go and shut the door behind her. "U-Uma?"

Behind her desk, Uma Malakar straightened up, raised her goggles, and grinned.

26

G OOD, YOU'RE HERE." UMA PATTED HER dusty hands on her dress and waved Iris over. "There's something I want you to take a look at."

But Iris could barely move. She shook her head as an iron ball by the boiler, connected to electrical wires, glittered dangerously. "Uma? What are you doing here?"

No, that wasn't the question she'd wanted to ask.

"You." Her expression darkened. "Are you working with Bellerose and Adam? Did you help them kidnap me?"

She could taste the venom on her lips. It seemed Uma's men could sense her vitriol, because the moment she squeezed her hands into fists, their guns went up.

Uma stayed them with an indifferent wave. "No, of course not. Believe me, I was as surprised to hear they'd brought you to this facility as you probably were when you woke up here. Sorry about that, by the way. Must have been tough."

"Then why are you here?" Iris stayed on the alert, watching the woman pull that same brass pipe out of her sari and begin to smoke. "What do you want with me?"

"I was already on my way here on Bosch's orders." Uma let out a puff. "Too many weapons, too little time. I travel far too much for my own liking. Bosch, the poor man, trusts only me to get certain projects up and running."

More weapons. Iris grimaced. She should have expected nothing less from Bosch's main developer, but it still left her restless and strangely irate. Did Uma really not think anything of what she was helping Bosch to do?

Apparently, the genius had more pressing matters to attend to than her conscience. "Once I heard that you'd been brought here," she said, "I knew I'd have to seize the opportunity before you eventually escaped. And I know you'll escape."

Uma gave her a wink. Then, from behind a pile of books, she pulled a tin plate off her desk.

Iris's breath left her body. The meridian. Hiva's meridian. The one she'd used to send him spiraling through time and space for several lifetimes. She could feel him. She could feel his hatred all over it.

Trembling, Iris glanced up at Uma. "You've seen him, haven't you? You've seen the other Hiva."

"To think there is another Hiva . . ." Uma scowled in annoyance when a man behind her tripped over a stool. "Watch it, you fools. Unless you want this room to explode. Seriously." Shaking her head, she turned back to Iris. "It really can be bothersome being the smartest one in every room."

"He's in London. Oh God, what did he say?" Iris took a hesitant step toward her. "Did he say anything to you?"

Uma stroked her chin. "Other than the fact that he seems to want your head? No. But judging by the look on your face, you apparently already know that."

Iris remembered his whisper of hatred, his promise back in Paris to destroy her. It was only a matter of time until they met again.

"Before I set sail from England, I asked him many questions, and to my surprise, he told me many things. He was quite forthcoming . . . perhaps because he didn't see me as any kind of threat?" Uma pursed her lips at the thought. "I wanted to know about the nature of Hiva. Who created you and why? He didn't know much about the 'who,' much to my dismay. But he certainly knew the why."

To destroy the world. That was their only purpose. Uma gave her the tin plate. Hiva's emerald crown glittered beneath the lights.

Uma folded her arms. "You're in a bit of trouble, girl," the scientist said. "Without the Moon Skeleton, the Committee is looking for another source of energy to power the Ark. A source of energy that could power weapons beyond our imagination."

Iris nodded lifelessly. "My heart."

"Yes, your heart. That crystal heart holds many mysteries." Uma almost stared at her chest greedily before catching herself. "Of course, I don't want you to die for good."

"You don't?"

Uma seemed a little ashamed to admit it. "Well, of course not. What a waste that would be." She turned away, embarrassed. "But I had my men bring you to me so I could let you know that the other Hiva seems convinced that you *can* die for good. And that he knows how to do it."

Iris almost dropped the tin plate. Die. For good? How? A pang of fear Iris had not known before sprang up inside her. The fear of a permanent death. It shouldn't have been possible.

"Alas, he never told me. When I asked, he simply gazed off into dreamland. A strange thing, he is. Lost in his own mind. His own memories. I'll bet he can disappear like that for hours. Maybe that's why he seems so emotionless." Uma smirked. "A tin man in a body made of flesh."

Permanent death. Iris covered her mouth with a shaky hand. Frantically, she searched her memories, but she couldn't recall if it had ever been a possibility.

"He told me this meridian is broken. If it weren't, he would have been able to teleport to you by now. But I could see it in his eyes. He's after you, Iris. He won't stop until he finds you."

In the chaos of the past few weeks, she'd almost forgotten. Hiva was still a threat.

Uma tapped her pipe. "Hiva told me that he could sense your life force, your anima, particularly through objects related to you. That he could track you by following your scent." She smirked. "Like a police dog being given a piece of bloody clothing torn off a serial killer. If that's the case, you should be able to do the same." She jerked her head toward the meridian. "It's useless to him, so he barely budged when I took it off his head. I plan on studying it, but now that you're here . . ."

Uma seemed to battle with herself for a moment before she sighed and shrugged. "Yes, take it. Go on, take it."

Iris glanced up at her, shocked. "You're letting me have this?"

"You can use it as a tracking device to make sure he isn't around—or know when he is."

A tracking device. It was then that Iris remembered the Coral Ring, that tiny device Nyeth had once planned on using to "clip a god's wings" inside the Coral Temple. *Her* wings. Iris still didn't know how it worked. Why would a ring be integral to taking away her powers? The secret lay in Nyeth's shattered bones.

She'd once assumed the anima trapped inside the Coral Ring would be enough to find the Coral Temple. It never worked. Every time she touched it, all she could feel was Nyeth's hatred in his final moments. At any rate, Nyeth's body lay in the British Museum, so perhaps it never would have led her to the temple anyway. Only a few short weeks ago, Iris would have done anything to find that ancient place. To bring the technology found inside to Uma so the genius could engineer some kind of reverse-freakery machine. Now, Iris didn't know *what* to do.

Not that it mattered. The Coral Ring was rotting somewhere in the king's compound.

"Don't just stand there." Uma shooed her. "Go on, take the meridian and go about your business escaping."

Iris didn't know what to say. She didn't want to admit her gratitude, but there was something about the way the older woman rolled her eyes that made her smile a little. Adam had once tried to manipulate Iris into using John Temple's journal to find his father. This felt somehow more sincere.

"Thank you, Uma," she said. Uma shrugged again, trying very hard to look noncommittal.

Iris touched the meridian. Indeed, she could feel Hiva's anima through and through.

But she could feel so much more. A quiet darkness.

And the more she touched it, the deeper she sank into it. Into a cosmos of memories. Buried deep inside Hiva's hatred was the kindness he'd once had. For nature. For humanity. The stump from his missing arm bleeding. His pleas before she'd sent him away from this world. Lifetimes of pain turned to numbness, turned to a thirst for vengeance. Iris couldn't stand it, but she couldn't let go the meridian, either. She couldn't let go of his pain. . . .

And then:

You had forgotten. But now do you remember?

Out of the darkness. A voice. A familiar ghostly hymn.

"Anne?" Iris's heart began to race. The tin plate clattered to the ground as she gripped the meridian with both of her hands.

Not Anne. The One. She appeared once again in Anne's image, her little brown body buzzing with light. And once again, she held out a coin. Day on one side. Night on the other. Day and night. The sun and its shadow.

The truth shall always be. . . .

The meridian shattered. Iris had held it too hard. It fell to pieces on the floor, along with trickles of her own blood from her palms.

"What is it?" She hadn't noticed Uma's hands clutching her shoulder. "You were standing there for twelve minutes and thirty-two seconds. I counted it! What did you see?"

Iris glanced down at the broken meridian, shaking. Her head was throbbing. Her mind fogged up like a window in the middle of a misty night. She didn't know what to tell Uma. All she knew was that she never wanted to touch the broken crown again.

"Iris!"

Iris backed away from the woman and shook her head. "Don't tell anyone I was here." It was all she could say.

Uma straightened up. Iris didn't know what she expected. But relief washed over her as the woman nodded. "I won't, you have my word. Go."

Stumbling back, Iris sucked in a breath and ran out of the room.

—<><>—

Iris still had a job to do. She couldn't let herself dwell on what she'd seen, though the memories still pulsed through her nerves. Jinn and Rin. She had to find them. She forced the last few jitters out of her system and focused.

The basement was not nearly as well-lit as the rest of the facility. Iris took down a torch from its place on the wall to lead her way through the darkness. The stone steps stung her bare feet with cold. She gave a slight shiver. This deep underground was very unlike the sweaty workshops above. But she was inside a mountain. There had to be a way in and out. It was just a matter of—

"Finding it." Bones of the dead, perhaps the remains of workers long gone, lined the walls, spreading out into tunnels on her left and right, cobwebbed and undisturbed. They framed the giant vault within the frigid brick walls. She could hear a muffled moan on the other side of a Gothic arched wooden door. Bellerose said Rin and Jinn were being guarded.

Another soft, hopeless moan. It wasn't the guards.

"Jinn?" She couldn't hear any other voices. She could barely hear his voice properly. The door was thick, without windows. But if he was being tortured . . .

Remembering Madame Bellerose's and Adam's taunts, Iris blew out and dropped the torch, then flew to the door, grabbed the wide brass handle, and shoved it open with a heave.

"Jinn!" she cried, stumbling into the room before she could properly get her bearings. She nearly tripped over her own feet, but her grip on the handle kept her standing. After she stabilized herself, she looked up and exclaimed in confusion: "Wait. Rin?"

Yes, it was Rin chained to the wall with two heavy iron rings, her lowered head twitching at the sound of Iris's cry. There wasn't a single guard in sight. What was this? A trick? The dungeon had to be seven feet high, but as for its width and depth, there wasn't much wiggle room for the young warrior. And with her hands tied, there wasn't any way for her to free herself.

"Rin." Iris ran to her and lifted up Rin's head with both hands. "Are you okay?" She tilted it to both sides and checked the rest of her body, but there were no signs of torture—at least none that she could see. Not only Bellerose, but Adam too had clearly lied in more ways than one. Why tell her that Jinn was here when he wasn't? "Rin!"

She slapped Rin awake. A pitiful groan escaped the warrior's lips as she squeezed and opened her good eye, which widened a little at the sight of Iris.

"Oi." Iris gripped her chin and shook it rather ruthlessly to knock the rest of the sleep out of her. "Are you okay?"

"Iris . . ."

Iris wasn't sure what to make of the ashamed and defeated Rin chained to the wall in front of her. Her hands high above her head, Rin couldn't draw out her sword even if she wanted to, but it didn't seem like there was any fight left in her to begin with.

"Rin. We've been kidnapped."

"The king . . ." Rin looked from left to right, her body groggy and sluggish. "I've been drugged, haven't I? My limbs feel weak." Her cracked lips curved into a wry smile. "I guess it serves me right, after what I did."

The sound of Rin's quiet, derisive laughter upset Iris for reasons she couldn't understand. But there would be time to discuss everything later. "I'm going to get you out of here. Just wait."

"Do I have any choice?" Rin smirked.

As Iris searched the dark dungeon, the torture tools, and underneath the cold gray table, she tried to ignore Rin when the girl suddenly let out a single, clear chuckle. But the low, nearly imperceptible strangled voice that followed, a stream of air that could have been giggles or sobs, made her turn and face Rin once more.

"I'm disgraced," Rin whispered. "If the Committee hadn't kidnapped us, I would have been executed on the spot."

"You don't know that," Iris said, unable to watch her friend's head bobbing up and down as she struggled with herself. "The king wanted to hear your story, your reasons. He was willing to give you a chance."

"What was there to say? I wanted to kill the king. It's as simple as that."

"Rather, you wanted *me* to kill the king for you—by framing Jinn."

Rin remained silent. Iris continued searching.

"You stabbed Sesinu." Iris searched through a pile of hay in the corner.

"I deliberately missed her vital organs. She should survive."

"And that makes it okay?" Iris whipped around and gave her an incredulous look. "Is that what you had planned all along when you tried to force me back with you?"

"No." Rin's braids dangled to her hips; they shielded half her face from Iris as her head drooped. "Not until I saw with my own eyes what you could do."

"Why didn't you just kill him yourself if you hated him so much? You had the chance all these years. Could have done it without bringing me and Jinn into it."

"I was scared."

"Scared," Iris repeated under her breath.

"Yes, scared." Rin snapped her head up. "Am I not allowed to be? Of course you wouldn't know what it's like. She Who Does Not Fall. You can't die, why would you ever be scared?"

It was a simple question. Honest and to the point. What right did Iris have to pretend she understood the true pain of fearing for one's life when she couldn't die? Iris stared down at her hands, suddenly ashamed of herself.

"*I* was taken from my *home*," Rin continued. "How could you ever understand my pain, you who have no home? You told me yourself that you emerged fully formed from the earth. A great goddess with no family. Who are *you* to judge *me*?"

Rin's cries echoed across the high, dingy ceiling. For a while, only the torches flickering on the wall filled the silence. Iris's hands felt numb. And it was in that moment of shame that she suddenly remembered how ancient she was. A being disconnected from the rest of life. Created to judge it despite sharing none of its concerns. A pang of hatred aimed at herself made her lips shut. Iris turned her back to Rin.

"Well, there's nowhere for me to go now." Rin sucked in a breath and exhaled it loudly, letting her breath carry some of her panic and pain as she moaned. "I've betrayed everyone. The *ahosi*. And you. You must hate me. I used your precious Jinn, after all."

"Why does everyone keep calling him 'precious' like he's some kind of rare metal?" Iris picked up an ax hanging on the wall. "It's very annoying."

Rin's eyebrows rose as Iris strode toward her. When Iris lifted the ax above her head, the girl flinched. But the blade came down squarely on the thick clasps chaining her to the wall.

Crack. The sound of steel against steel. "Well, I've killed plenty in my lifetimes—even in this lifetime. If there's anyone to judge you for stabbing someone in the gut, it isn't me." *Crack.*

"I forgive you, Rin," said Iris, concentrating on applying just enough pressure to free the girl, not cut Rin's hand off. "As for Sesinu and the others, I don't know. But *I* forgive you. I don't blame you at all."

Rin was baffled. "W-why . . . ?"

Because Iris had committed much worse atrocities. Having lived so many lifetimes, she knew: being hurt by the world made one want to hurt others in return. She already knew that. She'd seen it with her own eyes. And she understood.

Didn't Bellerose say she'd be making the rounds? Iris had to hurry. The first clasp came off and eventually the second. The chains came down just as Iris heard hurried footsteps coming toward the slightly open door. She couldn't understand what they were saying. Was it German? Either way, she lifted her ax, ready. At first Iris wasn't sure if Rin could fight. When the three guards in their blue uniforms burst into the cell with guns, Rin's arms remained at her sides. It wasn't until Iris swiveled the girl around with one arm—and, with her hand, blocked a bullet meant for the younger girl—that Rin snapped out of her stupor.

Another bullet pierced Iris's right shoulder. Just as Iris gasped from the searing pain, Rin called her sword. The swirl of white crystal made the guards pause in shock just long enough for Iris to toss the ax to her left hand and bring it down on their guns. Rin dispatched of the rest of the guns, elbowing the final man in the jugular.

"We're not to kill them, then?" Rin looked to Iris, this time with a soft, searching gaze, and waited.

327

"No." Iris looked at her hands. The taste of anima stayed with her, stuck to her tongue like melted sweets. It made her sick. "No more killing."

Rin looked down at her sword. "I'm proud of being a warrior," she admitted, and as Iris moved close, she could see the two of them reflected on the blade's surface. "I'm proud of the women I've fought beside. But I don't think . . ." She bit her lip. "But how the king builds his army. I don't think it's right."

Perhaps only Rin could condense years of sorrow into just a few simple phrases.

"Me neither." Iris placed her hand on Rin's shoulder. "I'm sorry, Rin."

Rin looked at her and nodded.

"Come on," Iris said. "We've still got to get Jinn. He's on the third floor."

"Then let's go."

It should have been simple enough to find him. Adam's directions to the dungeon had been accurate. But he'd lied about the prisoner she'd find there. The question was why. A sense of dread lingered as they escaped the dungeon.

The east wing was truly a labyrinth. Iris should have asked Uma for a map before leaving. She and Rin stuck out like sore thumbs, but luckily Rin was better at stealth than even Iris was. The workers and guards never noticed.

"Boris Bosch's munitions factory," Rin whispered as they hid around a corner. "Whatever devices they used to smoke us out of the palace compound must have come from here too. Along with other weapons."

Iris had already seen her fill of them, along with those building them. But this was Bosch's company. He would sell these monstrosities to heads of state and mining magnates to secure land and power while pocketing the money. She wouldn't have been surprised if some of the money made here had helped fund the tournament that had cost so many lives. But how many more deaths was he responsible for?

Iris and Rin bent down low beneath a window that looked into another workshop room. Iris hadn't meant to peek through it. But when she did, it was all she could do to cover her mouth before the workers inside could hear her gasp. A glowing orb took up the entire center of the room. Suspended in air by three chains tied to the ceiling, it was a wonder it didn't crash to the ground with its weight. It had the appearance of a cannon so large it could fit an entire adult man inside it. But it wasn't made of metal. It was made entirely of white crystal.

There was a small shard of it upon the open window ledge. Taking it, Iris inspected its surface. It was like staring into her own soul. A part of her that she'd left behind.

Iris dropped back beneath the window. After placing the little white shard into her dress, she nudged Rin in the ribs, and together they snuck up the stairwell.

"So if we escape, where will you go?" Rin asked suddenly as they climbed. "Back to England?"

Iris hesitated. To live in peace. That had been her goal the day she fled London. But the creation of Hiva did not allow for peace. Death and agony followed that name. Too many wanted to use her or rid the world of her. And as for her—

She stared at her hands. She couldn't afford to lose control. She was already losing it.

She grimaced the moment she remembered Adam's lips against her ear. "No," she said with a tone of finality that felt right. "I'm getting rid of these powers. I'm getting rid of Hiva for good. I don't have Nyeth's ring, but I do have a lead on where John Temple might be."

"I see." Rin sounded disappointed. "Then what will happen to me, I wonder?"

Iris couldn't be sure what kinds of thoughts were swirling in that pretty head of hers, but seeing her friend so miserable, she felt compelled to give Rin a punch in the arm. "Just forget about what happened, you hear me? Everything's going to turn out all right. Okay?"

Rin said nothing.

East wing. The third floor of the building. Fifth door around the corner to the right. Iris and Rin hid in a broom closet, waiting for the hallway to clear before they burst in.

Jinn was strapped to something akin to a black barber's chair in the center of a room not unlike the one Iris had woken in. Smaller, yes, and with fewer light bulbs, but this was indeed the domain of a mad scientist. Experiments could be done here with the tubes of bubbling green liquid and the live wires, generators, and Bunsen burners. A leather gag kept Jinn's fiery mouth closed.

And behind his chair was Adam Temple, grinning at her.

Iris wished she'd kept her ax, but it had been too heavy to carry with her. "What are you doing here?"

"I wanted to see for myself just how far you'd come. It's why I dismissed Bellerose's guards and left Rin alone in that dungeon."

So this was all another one of his games. Iris wanted to scream.

Adam leaned over Jinn's chair with his arm dangling on the chair's shoulder. Jinn was wide awake, struggling against his straps—harder, once he saw Iris and Rin.

"Hello, Rin." Adam waved his fingers. "Before we left, we made sure to leave a message for the king of Dahomey as to your whereabouts."

Iris froze. "What?" She looked over to Rin, who understood only when he repeated it in French. Rin went rigid.

"He'll send his best warriors," she whispered to Iris.

Iris frowned at Adam. "You're really okay with them coming here?"

"Why not? This isn't a secret facility but for a few rooms off-limits. Bosch has invited world leaders to do business here for many years. And with the French threat looming, I'm sure the king would love a chance to get his hands on a mass of useful weapons so advanced that no army in Europe has them yet—oh, and capture a fugitive for good measure."

Each time he spoke, he made sure to translate for Rin, and he seemed to relish seeing her precarious calm slowly but surely crumble.

"What is this about?" Iris demanded. She now saw that wires were draped down from the ceiling and attached to a metal cap strapped to Jinn's head. Nothing about this spelled anything good.

With confident strides, Adam walked over to the leftmost wall. Among the tubes and electrical apparatuses was a lever: a metal square within an empty space inside, like a light switch Iris had seen before. He placed his hand upon its wooden handle. That was when he began speaking to Rin in French. Iris's frayed nerves were screaming. Finally, so did her mouth.

"Stop it! Speak in English!" she demanded, because Rin's expression had hollowed out as if she'd seen a ghost.

"I'm only offering her protection. She's a phenomenal and feared warrior, but up against a regiment of phenomenal and feared warriors, I'm not sure how long she'll last. She's up for execution, you know. If she runs, they'll chase her. She knows a lot of their secrets and has connections with the French. It's a very dangerous situation she's in." Adam didn't exactly look broken up about it. "But we can negotiate a trade. The most wondrous weapons King Glele has ever laid his hands upon, for a very minimal fee—as long as we get to keep Rin with us. Safe."

Iris couldn't believe his audacity. "You're full of garbage, aren't you? You expect me to believe that?"

"Well, Bosch isn't going to let us give his weapons out for free, so of course I'd have to add a small charge—"

"I mean Rin," Iris spat. "You're not really offering Rin protection."

Adam looked confident. "I've heard quite a lot about King Glele from my father. He's a pragmatic man facing many issues more pressing than a traitorous brat. Not to mention, he's a very wealthy man. Bosch has been seeking to forge a connection with the king. Giving away some samples may be just what he needs. Between the great Boris Bosch and John Temple's son, I'm sure we can secure a deal with the king."

Then why was Rin's body shaking? Why were her eyes bloodshot? Why did she shiver at Iris's tentative touch?

And then Adam's smile turned wicked. "If she allows me to kill Jinn, that is."

Silence. Iris's hand slipped from Rin's arm. She stared at both of them in disbelief, but all she could see were shadows.

"W-what . . . ," Iris stuttered. "What . . ."

Adam's hand was still on that lever. He tapped it thoughtfully. "I'll do what she says and *only* what she says," he said. "If she tells me to kill him, I'll kill him. If she tells me to spare him, I'll spare him—but she'll get no protection from me."

"You won't do any such thing—"

But the moment Iris took a step forward, Adam put up his hand and quickly added, "And if you take one more step, I'll kill him anyway. It's a very easy lever to pull."

"You're mad," Iris growled, even more infuriated over the fact that he seemed to be enjoying himself.

"Life is about choices, Iris," he said darkly. "You still don't understand yours. But maybe others can make the choice for you."

"You pampered, evil little prat. I'm sick of you thinking you can toy with me!" But she couldn't move. Not with Jinn thrashing against his bonds. Not with Adam so close to the lever.

"Then kill me," Adam offered simply. "Use your power."

Iris gulped. "I won't kill you."

"You've done it before. You've killed for millennia."

"I won't do it. Never again." As she watched the madness blossom in his eyes, the thought that he'd once made sense to her, even in the slightest, made her skin crawl. "Never again!"

Never again? What a laugh. How many times had she killed since awakening? How many people? She kept making that vow, and she kept breaking it when it suited her. Until when was she going to deny how good it felt to let herself go?

She could kill Adam. She *should* kill Adam.

She tasted blood on her lips.

"You're Hiva!" Adam cried. "What will it take for you to understand what you must do to blot out humanity's transgressions? More murder? Bloodshed? War and devastation? You. Are. Hiva!"

That was right, she was! Iris gritted her teeth. But when she saw Jinn, when she saw the distorted reflection of herself on the side of a metal generator, her jaw stiffened and the anger inside her subsided to a kind of self-hatred that made her want to collapse.

"I don't *want* to do it. I don't want to do it ever again."

She didn't. But what did it matter how many times she said it? She needed to take action.

The truth was, she would never stop killing so long as she had these demonic powers.

The only way to stop herself from killing ever again was to have her powers taken from her.

She looked at her hands, trembling harder until she finally burst. "I won't be Hiva," she declared. "I won't do it! Not for you!" She grabbed Rin's arm. "*Please*, Rin, we'll find another way. I'll keep you safe!"

But Rin did not meet her eyes.

Stillness descended upon the four of them. Iris's throat was hoarse from yelling, so she could barely whisper Rin's name. She called to her instead through a gentle tug upon her arm.

And then Rin looked at Adam. "Do it," she said in English.

Adam pulled the lever.

27

NO!" IRIS SHRIEKED. *"No!"*

Click. Both she and Jinn looked up at the wires connected to his deadly helmet. Nothing. A flaccid spark and nothing more.

"Oh dear, I forgot to turn it on," said Adam, and he turned the knob of the generator next to it. "I guess we'll have to start all over again. By the way, Iris, it's true that if Rin tells me to pull this lever, I'll do it. I'm giving you one more chance. With one word, I'll do it. Unless you kill her before she speaks again."

With her chest shuddering and heart pounding, Iris gripped her scalp through her hair. *"Adam . . ."*

"It's your *only* chance, Iris. Kill her, or she kills Jinn," he said quickly.

Iris hadn't time to think. The generator connected to the wire made a whirring noise that told her it was on. The temperature gauge was alive with movement. If she took a step, Jinn died. But Rin . . .

"Rin!" she yelled, and grabbed her just as Adam bent over, placing his hand next to his ear and leaning forward meaningfully.

"Désolé, je ne t'ai pas entendu," he said.

Rin sucked in a breath. "Do it—!"

"No!" Iris grabbed Rin and threw her to the floor. Rin punched her in the face. Blood spurted from her mouth.

"Do it!" Rin screamed. "Do it!"

"I said *no!*" Iris returned the punch square to Rin's jaw as the two continued to tussle back and forth. Rin grabbed Iris's braids and cracked her forehead against Iris's. It felt as if her skull had just shattered. Iris cried out in pain, holding her head, rolling over. And out of the corner of her eye she could see Adam, that ever-infuriating madman, the same dangerous child who'd tried to murder his own father, lying back against the wall, watching them fight with an intrigued boyish grin.

"Ladies, the clock is ticking," he said, and made a show of tapping his foot.

"Adam, you bastard!" Flinging Rin to the floor, Iris jumped to her feet with every intention of breaking Adam's teeth, but he was alert, his back straight, his arm up and ready to pull down the lever in a flash. "Why are you doing this—?"

Rin tackled her. And yet even as they fought, even as they threw punches and blocked kicks, Iris could still hear Adam preaching above the din.

"Because so long as you hold on to your misguided notion that you require the bonds of love and family to live in this world, you will never understand what you must: that this world is evil. It's not the earth's fault. It's what humankind has done with it. You've seen it with your own eyes. You're seeing it now: the tragic failing of humanity that is within all of us."

Rin pressed her knee down on Iris's back, pinning her to the floor. Groaning in pain, Iris looked up just as Adam grabbed his vest where his heart was—or should have been. Then again, when he spoke next, what Iris heard in his voice could only be possible if one had a heart.

"I knew it the moment I saw my siblings' brains splattered upon the ground. Children. Can you believe it, Iris? Just children. My mother went mad. And my father was too busy pillaging his way through someone else's continent for glory and accolades at home to witness their deaths as I had. So busy, in fact, that he couldn't spare the time to visit their graves or speak at their funerals as I had. As *I* had. Where was my father? Where was he for me?"

Anguish. Hopelessness. His hand trembled precariously on the lever. Jinn watched his hand, beads of sweat dripping down his jaw.

"You've wandered the world, Iris. Tell me, are men different anywhere? Is there goodness *anywhere*?" And Iris knew in that moment that it was a genuine question. He truly wanted to know, just as she had once. But unlike

Hiva, who saw the world through neutral eyes, Adam had no such good fortune. He observed the terrible world that destroyed him and had come to the same conclusion that she had throughout countless civilizations in countless lifetimes.

"'Wherefore, as by one man sin entered into the world, and death by sin; and so death passed upon all men,'" Adam whispered. "My father wasn't there, but my mother always taught me—even in those dark days before she took her own life—that God was watching us. And I knew as soon as I saw you. You were sent by God, Iris: a god yourself, crafted by the heavens to do what has always been written must be done."

"Adam . . . ," Iris began, but she didn't know what to say. Rin's knee bit into her spine. The pain was so precise and acute that it snatched the breath from her lungs.

"Kill her, Iris. Kill me, too, if you please. Whether you do it to save him or just for fun. It's all the same, because all of humanity is the same, and thus we will share the same fate. Murder isn't wrong if it is done for a just cause."

She didn't know what to say. So she spoke to Rin instead. "I know you're scared, but this isn't the way," she said quickly in the language only the two of them in this dark room of horrors could understand.

"Quiet," Rin hissed, but she sounded so tired, so crushed from the inside out.

"I know you think you have no choices, but you're wrong. Jinn is my family. My granny is my family. I have a goose named Egg. And you can be in my family too, if you want. I'll add you. Only if you want, but why not? We can protect you. We *will* protect you."

"*Quiet!*" Rin barked again, stepping off Iris's back and gripping her by her clothes, lifting her up until they were both on their knees, both looking into each other's eyes. Both tearing up.

"We will love you and take care of you. I promise," Iris said. "You will always have a home with me as long as you want it."

Each of them breathed heavily, because each was fighting her own separate battle. Jinn's eyes darted between the three of them, his body suddenly very still upon the chair. Adam watched the two women for a moment, then gradually, and with increasing fury, doubled over. His hand squeezed the lever.

"You never listen," he whispered. "You never . . . *listen*." And then he snapped his head up. "I'll have to make you listen!"

His hand moved the lever down just as Rin's sword pierced the wall through the empty square space inside the lever, stopping it in its tracks. Adam grunted in surprise and tried to pull it down again, but Rin was on him in a flash. One high kick to the face sent him crashing to the ground. Shoving the lever back up, Rin pulled her sword out of the wall and stomped down on Adam's chest.

"Rin, don't kill him!" Iris cried, because she had seen enough death.

So Rin didn't kill him. She stabbed his hand with her sword instead.

Adam coughed out blood, crying out. Iris couldn't understand what Rin told him in French as she gazed down upon him writhing in pain. It didn't matter anyway. Iris ran to take the helmet off Jinn's head. Ripping her sword back out of Adam's hand, Rin swung at the wires connected to the helmet, severing them, then cut through the leather straps binding him to the chair. Iris took Jinn by the hands and lifted him up to his feet. He barely stumbled forward before Iris launched herself at him, wrapping her arms around his wide back and crushing him to her with all her strength.

Jinn coughed at the ferocity of her embrace. And when she let him go, he looked dizzier than he had after being drugged by Rin. "I-interesting few days," he stuttered.

Iris smiled. "Isn't it always?"

"Jinn," Rin started, but closed her mouth and lowered her head. Of course, she didn't know what to say. It was more than just a language barrier. How could she explain her actions over the past few days? Iris thought she could advocate on Rin's behalf. But Jinn only placed a firm hand on her shoulder.

"You've got some issues. Welcome to the club."

Rin blinked, confused, looking to Iris like a lost lamb for a translation. Iris only cracked a smile.

"We can talk later. We've got to get out of here first," Jinn said, and looked behind him. Adam had lifted himself up into a sitting position, groaning and spitting blood as he held his damaged left hand close to his chest. Jinn took a menacing step toward him.

"Stop," Iris said, holding him back. "Like you said, let's get out of here."

He blew a stream of smoke from his nose like a dragon. Even if *she* didn't burn Adam alive, Jinn still could. But she wouldn't let him do that. She felt it now, more clearly than before: the weight of a life. The responsibility of power. She saw it reflected in the one eye Rin was still able to use.

But it didn't take too long for Adam's grunts to become laughter, quiet, beautiful, and melodic like music, perhaps, except for the definitive tone of hatred poisoning it. "You haven't won." He shook his head. "You haven't won anything. This is just beginning." And as he tilted his head, he pointed his amused glare at Jinn in particular, his lopsided smile haunting, as if he knew something they didn't. But didn't he always, this Adam Temple? "Run off then," he told her. "Run, Iris. And see what's in store for you."

The three glanced at each other and escaped the room, leaving Adam to chuckle and bleed by himself.

28

"WHERE THE HELL IS THE EXIT?" Jinn asked as the three descended the stairway as quickly as they could.

"I don't know, Jinn, I was unconscious when they took me here."

"Well, so was I."

"So we're all in the dark."

"Except you've been sneaking about this whole time, and you never once thought to see if you could find the exit?"

Iris scoffed. "I was a bit busy trying to find you and save your life!"

"And even then, I have Rin to thank for that, really."

"Excuse me?"

"There!" cried a guard, spotting them the moment they left the stairwell and turned the corner. "Get them!"

Damn it. Iris had known their luck was bound to run out sometime. Here on the main floor of the munitions factory, the guards attacked with batons rather than guns, likely to avoid setting off an explosion. What the guards did not seem to understand as Jinn, Iris, and Rin plowed through them was that Iris was trying to keep them alive too. Their anima flowed more freely into her with every brutal contact; but even without touching them, she could smell it, feel and taste it: each human being's shocking vitality. The essence that all life shared on this earth. And the more she waded through the filthy hate, greed, and darkness, the closer she came to touching what might have been at the core of all anima: potential.

For harmony. For balance. For something *better*.

But something so ephemeral was hard to grasp, certainly harder when the guards kept streaming through each hallway, blowing their whistles to alert the others. They saw in front of them the enemy. Skulls to crack. Business to protect and accolades to gain.

The trio rushed toward what looked like a possible exit. TRANSIT DEPARTMENT NO. II was written in big white letters on the black top frame of the doorway, but it was so heavily guarded that it'd be hard to pass through the bodies, or even the barrels of gunpowder and wheelbarrows of shells being pushed through the threshold.

Jinn's mouth began to spark.

"Are you crazy?" Iris grabbed his sleeve. "This whole place will go up in flames! This way!"

She pulled him into another hallway—a familiar one. Bosch's torture chamber under the factory.

A draft flowed out from the tunnel to the left of the vault. Rin walked in that direction, stretching out her hands, her fingers reacting with a twitch when she felt it. "There's a path here," she told Iris, flicking her head to it.

"If there's a draft, this might be another exit," Jinn guessed.

Well, they couldn't go back up to the main floor and risk getting caught, could they?

Lamps hung on the walls above the metal track on the ground, lighting their path. As they rushed down its length, soft voices wafted toward them, carried along with the breeze.

"Someone's down there," said Iris. But they had no choice but to keep going.

The corridor eventually opened up into a vast cave, big enough to fit *La Daphnée* several times over. They must now have been deep in the Atakora Mountains. Iris had seen many strange sights even in this lifetime. Human invention constantly bewildered and at times beguiled her. But she was not prepared for what she saw stationed in the cavern below.

A warship.

Bigger than Slessor's, bigger than any Iris could have ever imagined; big enough, surely, to fit several decks and pack in thousands of people. And yet it carried no sails. Where the mast should have been was a machine in the shape of a whale, to Iris's eyes. Long steel wires attached it to various points of the ship and more still to the meshwork of steel lining the ceiling of the cave, keeping the monstrosity in place.

The machine was a vessel unto itself—no, a floating device. Iris could see that it had its own sails, rudders, and even propellers. The combustion system looked so much like Adam's hot-air balloon, yet several times larger. It had a massive propane burner.

The contraption stretched so high above them that it made every human standing near it look like an ant. Still, Iris could see them clearly: men and women standing on high wooden platforms inspected the creation from each side. A small group of ahosi warriors stood in two rows close to the ship, behind King Glele himself. Iris recognized Izegbe, this time with a white cap to cover her shaved head. All the ahosi wore the same uniform; the front row carried spears, and the second had guns.

Uma was there too, smoking her pipe. And next to her was a white man who stood in front of the king with his arms folded. He wore hunting gear, from his round, sturdy beige cap to his brown khaki pants, vest, and boots. Iris recognized the white objects dangling on his string necklace as teeth, likely from an animal he'd killed himself. He seemed the type—his hands were large and sharp like an eagle's talons, shrewd as his hooked nose and blue eyes. Shaggy blond hair had colonized the bottom half of his face, and when he turned his head to the side, Iris could see a thick red scar stretching down his left cheek.

As the trio stayed hidden at the edge of the wooden corridor, the voices of those below echoed through the hollow cave. The man in hunting gear spoke in a low voice. Iris couldn't hear him, but an interpreter standing on his other side translated into Fon.

"He's asking you to remember that this is a rare opportunity, King Glele," the interpreter said, a white scarf tied around his thin neck. "Not just anyone can look upon the Ark. His fellow members in the Committee would be against it. But this is his way of thanking you for your interest in a long-term contract with his company. He hopes that this vote of confidence will help secure your continuing patronage."

"The Ark . . . ," Iris whispered behind her hand. The ship that was to take only those the Enlightenment Committee deemed worthy to the New World. Now that they knew she was Hiva, the purpose of the Ark had changed. With her, they could conquer the New World like they'd conquered so many other lands and lay claim to both.

Workers on the ground were fitting the ship with the cannons she'd seen made in the workshops above. Several crates filled with explosives were scattered around the cave, spaced well apart from each other, but bound for the ship without a doubt, each labeled with BOSCH GUNS AND AMMUNITIONS in thin black writing.

The Committee was preparing for interdimensional war.

"King Glele seems impressed," Uma said to the man, amused, as she took another puff of her pipe.

The sight of her nonchalance made Iris grit her teeth. Did Uma care or didn't she? She couldn't tell anymore. Was scientific discovery—knowledge for knowledge's sake—truly enough to justify to her the crimes that were about to be committed?

The king listened to the interpreter and considered his words silently before nodding. "I have already been aware of your Committee for some time, thanks to your former colleague, John Temple," he said. "I have no interest in otherworldly schemes. Your Ark means little to me except as proof of the usefulness of your weapons. But it seems we each have our enemies: for me, the French. And for you, the might of your own colleagues."

When the hunter grinned, it looked wrong, unnatural. His teeth were tinged with yellow and seemed to be stained with the blood of animals he'd hunted mercilessly.

"King Glele," started the hunter as his translator began interpreting. "The Enlightenment Committee is an antiquated faction based on the idea of shared precariousness. If the world did end, then we elite would have to figure out how to survive together. But the world isn't ending. And I don't like to share. War sells my wares, and the war to come will make me a very, very rich man."

"What a greedy man you are," said King Glele. "But perhaps that is why they call you the merchant of death, Boris Bosch."

Bosch. Iris shivered. So this was the man they had barely seen at all during the tournament.

"Iris." Jinn nudged her in the ribs. "Look."

Now, this was a problem. The path they'd been following diverged into two ahead of them. The first, a narrow, rocky ridge, continued high along the cavern walls toward another tunnel, the only one visible in the entire cave. The exit? They wouldn't know until they reached it, but they wouldn't reach it unless they stayed on course. The second rocky path wound down toward the congregation on the ground gathered around their alien technology. The choice was clear, but both roads would leave them exposed. There was nothing to hide behind.

"We'll have to move quickly," he said. "Come on."

The exit. Iris sucked in a breath and followed the lead of the other two. There was so much commotion with those working on the Ark and the discussions down below that Iris prayed it would cover their escape. They rushed nimbly upon the narrow path. Iris put all her skills as a former warrior and dancer to use. It didn't even matter if they were seen. All they had to do was make it before—

Iris's foot slipped. *How could her foot slip?*

Her heart stopped as the rocks underneath her began to crumble, taking Iris down with it. Alarmed, Jinn reached out for her, grabbing her hand, only for gravity to make fools of them both. The two became the gathering's main attraction as they rolled down the side of the cave.

Uma stared in shock for a moment before burying her head in her hands, shaking it. Both Bosch and King Glele yelled something, sending two sets of guards chasing after them. The *ahosi* got to them first. Iris and Jinn had barely managed to crawl out from under the fallen rocks before two women pulled them up by the arms and another two pointed their rifles straight at their heads.

"We meet again, Isoke," said Izegbe, the mouth of her gun upon Iris's forehead. "I've already killed you once. Get up, Olarinde!"

Because Rin had slid down after them, perhaps in a show of solidarity; a kind gesture, but a foolish one. She couldn't fight all of them off. But, Iris noticed, she didn't try to. Rin lifted her hands in surrender and let herself be led back to the king. Bosch's guards kicked Iris and Jinn to the ground while two *ahosi* warriors forced Rin to kneel before her king.

"I, for one, had no idea they were here," Uma lied with a shrug, tapping her pipe.

"Olarinde, I was told you were here," said the king. Iris could not see him, but a kind of measured scorn had entered his steely voice. "Our last meeting was interrupted. You never explained to me why you betrayed me."

Rin remained silent. Iris could feel every eye upon them. The Ark loomed ahead. When Iris looked behind her, King Glele was gazing up toward the narrow ridge where they'd fallen.

"You came down from there of your own free will. And you came to me without fighting." The king sounded surprised and maybe a little curious as he considered it. "Why? What is it that you wish to say to me, child? Or are you ready to come back to the palace to face the consequences of your crimes?"

"Iris."

Iris seized up at the sound of Bosch's voice, calling to her in English. When she turned, she met his malicious eyes, as clear and blue as a river one drowned in.

"He can do what he wants with the wench. But you? You belong here." He stretched out his arm toward the Ark. "Your womb will birth weapons never before seen in this world. Your spine will become the backbone of progress. The weapons I sell here will push humanity to new heights. And the profits will flow."

Uma flinched, her lips pursed. But even the confident weapons developer couldn't seem to push back against her boss, the man who'd given her carte blanche to sate her scientific curiosity. She narrowed her eyes ever so slightly but said nothing.

Meanwhile, Bosch's thin pink lips, nearly covered by his beard, curved into a smile. "Your crystal core will be the very heart of our enlightenment, girl. Be proud."

This was the man who'd made his fortune selling war across the globe. It wasn't enough to bring weapons to distant lands. He would use whatever conflict the Committee aimed to launch in the New World as a stream of never-ending profit. The Enlightenment Committee. The Crown. The Dahomey. And whoever he might find in other dimensions. It didn't matter to Bosch who he sold his wares to—as long as conflict never ceased.

"I've seen men like you in other lifetimes," Iris said. "I've killed men like you."

"So why not kill me now?"

For a time, Bosch's question went unanswered, but Rin's words filled the silence.

"I did not come here to submit to you, my king, but to apologize. What I did was wrong. But taking me to become your warrior was wrong as well."

King Glele lifted his head. "Is that so?"

Rin was breathing heavily. Iris could feel her fear. But from where she was, Iris silently encouraged her. And Rin spoke on, her voice trembling, but firm.

"Yes. One day, I will make things right with Sesinu. But I will not be yours any longer. I respect the *ahosi*, but I want something else. Myself. I want to discover who I am. To live as Olarinde without fear. A new path. My path. I want to find it. I *need* to find it."

Her words pulsed in Iris's veins. Iris stared at her hands. And she understood. She understood so terribly it made her tremble.

"Interesting . . . ," Iris could hear Uma whisper. "Very interesting . . ."

Shooting his developer an annoyed glance, Bosch grunted with impatience and turned back to Iris.

"I asked you, girl, why don't you try to kill me?" he repeated, egging her on, but the smile on his face told her he believed as others did—that she didn't have the will to carry it out.

They might have been right.

But the truth was clear, underlining Rin's courageous confession, beating deep within Iris's soul. And it was very simple.

Iris placed her hand on her chest. "Because *I* need to find who I am too."

"Oh my, I feel dizzy." Uma suddenly wobbled too far to the right and collapsed. The guards stared at her, baffled.

A needed distraction.

Iris jumped up and kneed Bosch in the groin. As the man doubled over and cursed in German, Iris caught Uma's eyes. The woman winked and nodded before letting herself fall into the arms of the men struggling to pull her back up.

Iris smirked. Jinn beamed at Iris with unmistakable pride just before he elbowed Bosch's guard to his right, grabbed the gun from the man's hand, and aimed at one of the crates of explosives. This time, Iris gave him her blessing.

The explosion rang out. A dangerous gamble, but he'd chosen the crate farthest from anyone to minimize the damage. The fire and smoke sent workers and guards alike scattering.

"Protect the king!" Izegbe said, coughing, while the *ahosi* closed ranks. The smoke filled the area, so thick it was difficult to see through. Iris kept her eyes on the back of Jinn's head and held on to Rin's hand to make sure she didn't lose them. That was why, when Rin paused, she felt it. Someone had tugged Rin back by the arm. Someone who'd leaned in close enough for even Iris to hear. Was it Uma?

"The false door in the northwest corner. Go and find your true path, Olarinde."

"Izegbe . . . ?" Rin's whisper was almost childlike. The woman shoved her forward before she could linger too long.

Iris coughed the smoke out of her lungs and turned back, thinking of the two women who'd helped her. They'd make it. Iris had to believe it.

"Let's go," she hissed, and they were off.

While the guards and workers dealt with the smoke and fire, Rin led the charge, following her former ally's directions.

"Search for the false door," Iris instructed Jinn, and they began feeling along the cave wall. Iris's palms slipped over the rock frantically; all the while, she could hear Bosch screaming in German. As the smoke began to clear, Iris heard the slow rumbling of a slab of stone sliding.

"I've got it," Jinn said. "Here. Help me!"

Iris and Rin helped him push. With all their strength, they managed to move the stone just enough to squeeze their bodies through the narrow opening. A stream of fire from Jinn's mouth warned the guards not to follow. Rin slashed at the rocks above them until they came crumbling down, closing off most of the entrance behind them. The only way was forward.

In this dark, winding tunnel, there was no light. They followed the direction of the breeze fluttering their hair and brushing their skin, until the bright sun and open air welcomed them.

"What a view," Iris said with a little gasp as they finally escaped the cave, stepping outside onto a terrace on the side of the mountain—hundreds of feet in the air. Reminding Iris of a garden gazebo, it was made entirely of white wood, expertly crafted with a railing to protect wanderers from falling off to their deaths. Beyond the terrace was a vast expanse of terrain: green hills and forests, dusty dirt paths and white birds flapping their long, majestic wings toward the blazing sun. But they were too high up; it was a long drop from where they stood to the valley below. Inspecting the terrace, Iris saw it was attached to some kind of vertical railway and pulley, a structure that stretched down into the valley.

"Is this the way down?" Iris asked the others.

"I should have known you'd find your way here. But cockroaches always find a way to survive."

Iris whipped around. Inside another terrace to her left, Madame Bellerose lowered her binoculars, pointed her gun at the duo, and without so much as another taunt, began shooting. The three ducked for cover.

"The lever!" Jinn cried with his hands over his head. "Pull the lever."

"Lever!" Iris repeated in Fon, because Rin was the closest to the metal handle on the pulley. "*This* lever you can pull!"

This time, Rin didn't hesitate to grab it and pull it down, as Madame Bellerose's bullet nearly blew off her fingers. The wheels of the pulley began turning. The terrace began descending. But soon, Madame Bellerose's aim shifted—from their heads to the ropes that kept them from plummeting to the ground.

"Oh, don't worry, *Hiva*," said Madame Bellerose above them. "We'll be sure to retrieve whatever pieces of your body we find in the jungle."

Iris heard a snap. The terrace shook. So did her heart. She began screaming as ropes snapped and the white wood contraption plummeted down the side of the mountain, taking them with it. Each of them gripped the railing to keep from being tossed into the air. Iris's insides felt suspended, and if they didn't do something quick, they'd end up splattered all over the luscious green grass. But her mind blanked. She shut her eyes and held on tight, her voice hoarse, the air snatched from her throat.

"Tree!" she heard Rin yell in English. "Tree!"

It was all Rin could say and was not much to go on, but Iris understood when she pried open her eyes and noticed the forest trees surrounding them. There wasn't any room for error. Before the terrace could descend any farther, they leaped out of it, grasping the branches of the nearest tree, leaving the terrace to crash into the ground below.

For a moment, all Iris could do was hang there, the wind knocked out of her.

Then Jinn was kicking as he struggled up onto a branch. Iris had found the same branch, and Jinn pulled her up next to him while Iris heard Rin clamber onto a branch above them.

"Well . . . that was . . . quite the escape." Somehow Iris had managed to squeeze in a chuckle while wheezing, an act that earned her annoyed groans and irritated grumbles in two different languages.

29

S O WHERE ARE WE HEADED?" ASKED Jinn, ducking underneath long, twisting vines as they made their way through the opulent, exploding greenery of mahogany and ebony trees.

"We? Are you sure you want to come with me?" Iris teased. "Don't see me as a monster anymore, do you?"

"Not that again." Jinn let out an exasperated breath.

Iris could tell she was in for some kind of nervous explanation. By now she didn't need it. A lot had happened between the time they'd argued on *La Daphnée* and now. Still, for some reason, a part of her wanted to pick on him for doubting her in the first place—and she enjoyed seeing him squirm.

"I never did," Jinn continued. "I was just . . . spooked. Confused." He searched for the right word. "Afraid."

"Afraid that I was what Gram said I was?"

Jinn considered it before shaking his head. "Afraid that you'd one day not be you anymore."

Jinn had already lost so much at one monster's hand. If he had lost Iris too because of the monster called Hiva . . .

She squeezed his shoulder. "There's nothing to worry about. I'm me. Whatever name you want to give me. I'll get rid of these powers and be who I want to be. You'll see."

And Jinn smiled back at her. It drew a blush from Iris's cheeks.

As for where they were headed to next, there was only one place Iris could think of. "When I met King Glele, he told me John Temple had seen him recently," she told him, pausing with surprise because a brightly colored snake had slithered out from behind the trunk of a tree.

"Recently?" When she stopped, he did too, almost as if by instinct. "So the man could be around here somewhere?"

Though Rin kept walking forward, unperturbed, Iris waited for the snake to pass before continuing. "The king specifically said John Temple had only gone to Dahomey as a 'short stop' because he was looking for my origins."

"Your origins." Jinn swept the sweat from his forehead. The sun had gone down, but even the night couldn't stave off the brutal humidity. "Which means—"

"The place I was born—or reborn. I have a feeling I need to go there. Something tells me John Temple was looking for the same thing I am."

Iris couldn't get his journal entry out of her mind: *If what the king told me is indeed true, I'll find my divine intervention in the place where heaven dwells.*

John Temple was a man who knew more about her than she seemed to know about herself. His obsession to learn about the Hiva was matched only by his son's own, although their reasons diverged in the starkest way possible. If only Iris had John Temple's real journal—or something else of his she could use to track his anima. It would take a lot of the guesswork out of this journey. Alas, it was in Uma's lab, somewhere underneath the Crystal Palace.

But she had something else.

The idea struck Iris like a lightning bolt. She reached into the folds of her wrap and brought it out: the white crystal shard she'd taken from Bosch's factory. As thick and long as a finger, and yet with a quiet strength that had kept it from shattering. The amount of resources it must have taken these scientists just to manipulate it into the forms they wanted . . .

Whatever force had called her forth again to destroy humanity wove her, skin, flesh, and bones, deep within the secret places of the earth. It was during that process that her crystal heart was re-formed, but shards of it remained, deposits left behind as she climbed out of the dirt and began walking the earth once more. The Oil Rivers area near the Niger region—the place where she'd been reborn—had become a mining site controlled by the British Crown. John Temple had been there before; he'd detailed his trip in that book he wrote for the bored British bourgeois, *A Family's Travels through West Africa*. What if he'd returned there recently?

"I'll use this." Iris stared at the white crystal. "It's part of my body. It has its own anima within it as well. If I concentrate hard enough, maybe I can find the mine."

"And if you find John Temple there?" Jinn watched her carefully as she turned the white crystal around in her hand. "What then?"

Iris didn't answer. The periphery of palm trees before her opened up into a clearing under the moonlight. She could hear the rippling waves of a waterfall tumbling down a rocky cliff into a small lake below, see the moss-colored stone through the vines in her path. Rin had already gone on ahead of them, but Iris remained where she was.

"'The place where heaven dwells,'" she said. "Did he ever find it? I'd like to know where it is too. I think I need to go there. Yeah. I can find it there. The way to truly become *me*."

At the edge of the clearing, Jinn slipped in front of her and grabbed her shoulders. His touch made her feel secure and safe. His large, familiar hands gripped her firmly but gently. "I want you to be happy, Iris. With Granny."

"I want to be happy too. With Granny. And with you."

Jinn blinked, taken aback. His handsome face took its turn to flush.

"Hiva's existence alone has given too many people too many ideas. I don't need that name or these powers. I want to live *my* life with the people I care about." She lowered her head shyly. "As long as they don't mind living their life with me."

The boy who'd once known only loneliness cleared his throat nervously. "Oh, is that so?" Jinn's voice was as soft and tender. "Is there anyone mad enough?" he added under his breath.

"Excuse me?" She hit him on the shoulder, pouting. But the little smile playing on his lips drew a relieved smile from hers.

The leaves of the shea trees behind them began to rustle. Iris thought it was a partridge, but soon she could hear giggling and the whoosh of bodies dropping down behind them. Jinn and Iris turned around. The young women standing ready before them with their blades drawn seemed to notice their flirting—and it made them grin even more widely.

"See, I told you they were lovers. They're sweet, aren't they?"

"We were going to let you finish, but we got bored and decided to jump down now. Sorry!"

"Natame! Aisosa?" Iris shoved the white crystal back into her dress quickly, gaping at the sight of them.

Indeed, there the two young woman were, Natame with her braids dangling underneath her white cap and Aisosa with her buns perfectly spaced upon her head. Aisosa carried a brown sack behind her, strapped to her with rope. Natame had extra blades held to her hips by her sash. Even with all the extra baggage, Iris hadn't heard them following her at all.

"The king ordered us to scope the perimeter, just in case," said Natame.

"We're good at that sort of thing." Aisosa winked, and on cue, the two girls raised their blades. Gulping, Iris looked at Jinn and reluctantly allowed the girls to march them into the clearing, where Rin was already sitting on a log.

"Ah, Natame. Aisosa. How have you been?" Rin asked as casually as if passing a friend on the street.

"Um." Iris stared incredulously as Rin brushed her braids behind her shoulders. "Aren't you the least bit concerned?"

"She knew we were following you," said Aisosa.

"What?" Iris whipped around, only to be met with the tip of the girl's blade.

"I knew they were following us," Rin confirmed, stretching out her neck. It looked like she took this as a good opportunity for a rest.

"Then why—?"

"Because they mean no harm." Rin dipped her foot into the small lake and breathed in calmly. "Isn't that right, girls?"

At first, Natame and Aisosa stared at Iris very menacingly, their blades glinting with starlight. Aisosa cracked first.

"She's right!" The girl smiled, and lowering her weapon, she ran to Rin. "A lot of us have been talking since you left, you know," she told the older girl.

"Opinions are more split than you would think. Quiet as it's kept, there are a few of us who understand your feelings."

They wouldn't have escaped Bosch's facility if not for Izegbe. Iris could still remember her whisper.

"General Sesinu will be okay." Natame placed her machete blades behind her sash with the other blades and rubbed her neck.

At this, Rin stood, turning to her. "Is . . . is that so?" She looked hopeful and ashamed at the same time.

Natame nodded. "Make sure you apologize to her properly the next time you see her."

Rin lowered her head and obediently nodded. "Of course," she whispered.

"What are you two doing here?" Iris asked as Aisosa skipped over to the lake, then bent down and dipped her hands into the water. "The king still wants Rin back, doesn't he? He still wants *me* back."

"That's why we're going to keep this short," said Natame. "We'll give you this and then pretend we never saw you."

She threw a set of blades onto the grass at Iris's feet. *Shamshir!* The ones she'd danced with. Iris recognized the small chip in one.

"Wherever you're going," Natame said, "I have a feeling you'll need those, Isoke."

"These too!"

Aisosa tossed the bag she'd been carrying, and upon hitting the ground, the animal skin unraveled to reveal Iris's old clothes—the ones Granny had made for her. Iris searched them and breathed in deeply when she felt the familiar cold of a metal band. Nyeth's ring.

"Where are the scrolls?" Jinn asked, seeing none of the parchments Iris had taken from the Library of Rule.

Iris looked around the grass. "The scrolls!" Iris repeated in Fon.

Aisosa grinned a little devilishly. "We're not that generous," she said as Natame smirked.

But they had been generous enough. "Do you think you can do one more thing for me?" Iris said. "Send a message to a friend in Ajashe. His name is Max, and his sister, Berta, is staying with him in a hospital there. Tell him we'll be going to the mining site where Hiva was born. He'll know what I'm talking about."

After all, like Jinn, Max had witnessed the memories that the Helios had delivered to Iris in the Crystal Palace. The place where she'd been reborn, the way she'd dug herself out of the earth—Max had seen it all.

"That's fine. One more favor you owe us," Natame said with a shrug.

"What are you up to?" Jinn asked Iris.

"I wanted to come back to check on him, but I don't think there'll be enough time. I just want him to know why." Iris gathered up Granny's clothes and Nyeth's ring. "Thanks, you two," she said to the girls very seriously, gazing at them with the kind of respect owed to a warrior.

But by the water, Rin's body suddenly became rigid, her hand ready at her chest. "Natame. Aisosa. You still have a long way to go."

"What?" Natame cocked her head to the side, her cheeks burning with youthful rebellion. "And what is that supposed to mean?"

"It means *you've* both been followed as well."

The party turned toward the entrance of the clearing. Upon the tallest tree was a figure Iris had seen too many times before, one that made her heart race in fear and fury.

"Fool."

As always, his face was covered in his harlequin mask, his top hat and black cloak flowing even here in the tropics. Iris didn't know which Fool it was, but it didn't matter. She dropped Granny's clothes and picked up the twin *shamshir*, tossing one to Jinn, who caught it and prepared himself. Natame and Aisosa, who had never seen Fool before, stared as if he were an abomination.

As far as Iris was concerned, he was. "So you followed your master all the way here?"

"I come bearing tidings," he told them, his singing voice soaring over the trees. "From dear Lord Temple."

"He doesn't quit," said Jinn through gritted teeth.

Natame shook her head. "I thought I'd seen everything."

"What is this *thing* saying?" Aisosa tugged at Rin's arm, but Rin only shook her head.

"Fear not. I won't be long. Lord Temple has issued a warning to you, Mr. Jinn, that the dark specters of the past are never really gone."

Jinn's expression turned grim, his fists shaking at his side.

"And to you, Miss Iris." He said her name as tenderly as one would the lover of his master. Iris felt sick. "The fairy tale you desire for yourself is a dream. One cannot live without loss. But through suffering, you will be made strong—strong enough to summon divine wrath and do what you must for this fallen world and those of us who have fallen with it."

Cryptic. Iris wanted to respond with a witty retort, a chuckle, some kind of proof that she wasn't as shaken as she was. But the words "suffering" and "loss" continued to reverberate through her, plucking at her frayed nerves and mocking her insecurities.

"Temple has unleashed his final trump cards. And now I get to please my lord by giving him a boon in return: the potential whereabouts of his father, John Temple."

The mining site. "You heard everything." Iris bit her lip at the realization.

It was then that Fool spread his arms out wide to the heavens. "A great gathering is upon us! Isn't it poetic that it will be at the place of your origins—you, who began everything?"

"Does it make you feel good, Fool?" Jinn asked with a scowl. "To be the lapdog of a madman?"

"Ah, dear sir, truly there is no Fool as loyal as I, though I had rather be any kind of thing than a fool!" His cape fluttered in the slight breeze. "And yet I would not be *thee*." In the moonlight, only half of his mask glimmered, its frozen lips seeming contemptuous as he looked down upon them. "Farewell."

Fool disappeared back into the trees.

Rapture

AS NIGHT FELL UPON THE KINGDOM of Dahomey, shadows danced across Adam Temple's beautiful face, though his expression was not in the least lovely. His hand, dressed and bandaged, shook against the white terrace on the east side of the mountains. She was out there in the forests. With *him*. Thwarting Adam at every turn, mocking him with her continuous denial of her own greatness.

He bit into the corner of his lip so hard, it drew blood.

His mother had recited to him tales of God's wrath as one would bedtime stories. She'd sung to him Deuteronomy and Joshua like lullabies. The decimation of the Canaanites. The Baroness had returned to that particular tale often after the deaths of her smallest children.

Even as a child, Adam knew that only the destruction of the old could lay a path for something new. Something glorious. And standing here on the terrace, he felt fear, true fear, for the first time since he'd been left in the abusive hands of his uncle.

"What am I to do, Mother?" He gripped the terrace with both hands, letting the searing pain from his injury burn and fortify his body. "What in the world am I supposed to do now?"

His father had fled like a coward. He was of no help. But who else would take up this mantle? To create a new world—a better one, where no one else would have to suffer? Where innocents were not born to fall prey to the strong?

Where children like Abraham and Eva could live out their lives in peace?

"I'm not wrong." Adam thought of Iris's expression, dripping with disdain as she looked at him. "I'm not wrong." He fell to his knees and lay his forehead against the balustrade. "I was never wrong."

"You *were* wrong, dear, in one respect."

Madame Bellerose. Though Adam didn't bother to turn, he heard her heels upon the floor, each sharp click driving him further and further into his own self-hatred and frustration. Soon he could feel her arms sliding around his neck, her cheek pressed against his.

"You fell in love with a beast."

Adam shrugged her off. "Iris is the cataclysm."

"Then she's *the* Beast." Madame dusted herself off and stood. "Either way, aren't your standards a little too low, boy?"

Love. Was it love? Adam couldn't tell anymore. The obsession driving him was one of duty and righteousness, and within that girl's magnificent eyes he could see that same righteousness calling out to him. She wanted to do what was right. But the experiments of that vile Doctor Pratt and those ten years of wandering in the wilderness in her own amnesia had left her confused as to what "right" was. It wasn't her fault. In her defiled state, many had taken advantage of her, swarming her like moths. Her so-called Granny Marlow. Maximo. Rin. Jinn.

Are you that far gone, Iris? Maybe it really will take a war to convince you how evil mankind is. Adam gritted his teeth, and the fury within him boiled out of control. Balling his hands into fists, he slammed the terrace, the pain screaming as he wanted it to.

"Don't be so dramatic." Madame Bellerose's laughter only infuriated him further. "Whatever it is that you seem to want with her, she's already rejected you. Now you need to figure out what it is that you need to do."

Adam turned and glared at her. Madame Bellerose was a vision in carmine, the ruffles of her dress bunched at the back, her white gloves stretching up her arms even in this heat. He wondered if that little fan she waved back and forth did anything more than flutter her loose cherry-red hair.

"The Ark is nearing completion, and Bosch's woman, Malakar, is sure to find a way to power the Helios without the Moon Skeleton. Two worlds are within our grasp now. We just need that beast's heart. There's no greater source of power we have than the white crystal. Imagine what kind of technological wonders the source of it all will provide."

"You don't know that for sure." Adam said, though he knew well enough from his father's research and Pratt's vicious experiments that the power of Iris's crystal heart exceeded that of its residue. Madame Bellerose knew he was aware of this. She tilted her head to the side, answering him with a raised eyebrow.

"I've been around many stupid men my whole life, boy. My aging husband, who thinks his dear wife is off on vacation. My poor deceased, treacherous brother. Cordiero, Cortez. So many others of our Committee who killed each other in the Spring Day Massacre, all for this—a chance to rule. Van der Ven is a boorish man. I hate him." She spat and flicked back a strand of her hair with a huff. "Always trying to take control of everything. I'd rather see him dead than have him think he has the right to rule over us."

Van der Ven was certainly in his home somewhere planning a coup. Only a fool wouldn't see that. In his greed, he'd plan to join forces with Bosch for his weapons and rule both worlds.

"I've killed many in my day. But you, boy, are too smart to die."

And so was she. She was cunning, had many resources and connections. Getting rid of her without any repercussions would be difficult. She was much more useful as a chess piece to play. And like every other piece he'd procured, when the time came to move her, he would.

She approached him slowly, meaningfully, the back of her hand trailing his cheek.

"Don't you think we're stronger together as allies than as enemies? With Bosch's weapons. Against Van der Ven . . ."

As she drew her lips close to his cheek, Adam thought of Iris out there, searching for her own path without him. What he wanted was greater than the greedy desire of the Enlightenment Committee. He was after a higher cause. And Iris? The thought of her set his body aflame. Her beauty and daring mixed with his desire for the divine, creating a new kind of hunger that only she could elicit within him. He *needed* to be with her. To guide her. To be by her side at the end of days. His father's research had prepared him for the coming of a god. He'd witnessed her rebirth with his very own eyes ten years ago at the fair. And what had he done since then? The wound in his hand was a pitiful reminder of his failure—worse, his rejection. He was like Joshua without Moses to lead him.

He was lost. Alone. He ached for her to understand him. He *yearned* for her.

His hand reached up for Madame Bellerose's hair until his fingers were intertwined in her locks. Gripping her viciously, he yanked her head back. The gasp he drew from her lips was frightened but a little exhilarated. A beast. Bellerose was ridiculous. It wasn't Iris but the two of them here on this terrace who were more beast than human.

"We join hands," Bellerose said breathlessly, struggling only a little against his vice grip. "Against Van der Ven. We rule both worlds. We plunder and take as we please. We live like gods. So? What's your answer, boy?"

His answer was the same as it always was: the end. But his body was on fire. It ached for her. The more she eluded him, the more he ached.

He covered Madame Bellerose's mouth with a kiss. He pulled away from her, only to see her expression turn lustful. As she grinned, exhilarated, she gripped the back of his head and hungrily licked his lips. Then, throwing her roughly upon the terrace, he began to strip off her clothes and his own. A gasp of delight escaped her. He didn't stop, even as a man's voice called out to them from the shadowy doorway. A familiar voice.

"We'll soon be ready to leave," the gruesome man said, his voice low and furtive, the kind one used when whispering a prayer for blood. "We'll head to the mines. I'm familiar with such places."

"Good. Go. Do as I asked."

He had more than one card to play, and it was time to set both plans in motion.

The figure slunk back into the darkness just as Adam buried his face in

Madame Bellerose's neck and let his tongue taste her boiling skin, while she laughed.

As he hatefully plunged inside her, as she gasped and cried, he erased the unsavory sounds she made and instead let Iris whisper sweetly in his ears the kind of things he imagined she might say, if she would only let him give her the kind of pleasure her existence had given him. He was not wrong. He had never been wrong since the day his family died.

He imagined them in heaven, smiling down on him with approval.

HER BONES OF RUIN

THE TENT HIVA WALKED INSIDE SMELLED of goose.

"Ch-child? Is that you?"

The old woman sitting in a rickety chair dropped the quilt she'd been sewing and whipped around, hopeful.

What was this? Hiva had followed the trail of his *other* to this circus on the outskirts of town. But this old woman *couldn't* have been the other Hiva. Fables refused to believe it.

She jumped at the sight of them, her hand going to her chest, before her face fell. "Strangers," she said, more to herself than to them, before reaching for a little half-empty bottle on the table near a short stack of circus costumes. Medicine or gin? "Is there anything you want? Mr. Coolie's trailer isn't too far from here, so if you have business, seek it with him."

Her skin was wrinkled, her fingers frail, though they nimbly threaded her needle through fabric. Gray kissed the outer trim of her coarse black hair, and her narrow face looked sickly. This grandma wasn't a match for Hiva. He doubted that she could lift the white goose curled up on a pile of hay in the corner.

"What I'm looking for isn't here," said Hiva, looking around the tent. "Though her presence fills this place."

Well, clearly she isn't here. Fables tapped his foot, losing patience quickly.

Hiva, in the meantime, seemed particularly taken with the goose sleeping in the corner. For reasons Fable couldn't fathom, the divine being crossed the tent, squatted down, and began to . . .

Pet it?

Yes, he petted it. A god who seemingly had no regard for living things. He seemed taken with it. He drew the animal into his lap, wholly focused on the smoke-blemished white feathers he stroked.

The old woman must have seen the baffled expression on Fables's face, because she began to giggle. "You've got a couple of teeth missing, young man."

Fables immediately shut his lips together and, blushing furiously, shook his head. "Who are you?" he demanded.

"You're asking me? You're the ones who burst into my tent. Who are *you*?"

Taken aback by her feistiness, Fables glared at the old woman. She had an accent he'd never heard before, so it took an effort to fully understand her, which for some reason annoyed him. Her dark, velvety brown skin, wrinkled with age but still shining brightly in the light of the lamp she had on her table? That annoyed him too. The exuberant life in her eyes, dark as coal? That sure as hell annoyed him. It made him squirm and shift. When he looked at her, when he dared to look in her eyes, he thought that this was what his grandmother might have looked like, or his great-grandmother and all those before her. Then a tingle of insecurity shuddered through him. It was something about her quiet strength in the face of two strangers who very well could be robbers or thieves ready to kill her.

Fables thought, *How dare someone like her*— very quickly, and then caught himself before doubling down. Fables's ivory mask was a blessing. It saved him from all manner of evil, as ugly and awkward as it was. But if his blood weren't mixed with women like her, Fables wouldn't have had to run out into the streets, escaping his father. All because of a woman like her, who now dared to be stronger than he ever could be.

He eyed Hiva, still in the corner with his goddamn goose.

"Excuse me, young men." And to top it all off, the old woman had the audacity to look impatient with him. "This is the Coolie Company, and I'm the seamstress. They call me Granny Marlow around here. If you need Coolie himself, perhaps you can come back in the morning. He's gotten a lot grumpier these days, but I'd say after recent events, he's been thoroughly tamed." She laughed brightly. It made Fables's blood boil. "I'm sure he'd—"

"Quiet, you old n—" And then Fables said a word he'd heard his father say plenty of times, though it'd never escaped his mouth once—at least not that he could remember.

The old woman sat shocked in her chair for a moment. Then she stood up and slapped him hard in the face. The hit stung, and the pain reverberated through his screaming skull.

"Stop all that. You came into *my* tent, boy. You're trespassing," this Granny Marlow reminded him. "Dawdling around like a scarecrow in a storm. Hate yourself all you want, but don't take it out on me; I have nothing to do with it. I'm fine." With a dismissive wave of her hand, she sat down and picked her quilt back up.

"H-hate?" Fables stuttered, and let out an incredulous laugh. "Shut up, you old bag, I d-don't hate myself. . . ."

"Young people are so nasty these days." Granny let out a sneering noise like she was sucking her teeth and waved him off again. "Hurry and get on if you have no business here."

"Nasty." Over his shoulder, Fables caught a reflection of himself in a standing mirror in the corner of the tent. Dirty skin, suspicious eyes. A face stitched back together enough times that he could count every wound. He gave her a malicious grin. "Yeah, nasty. Well, the world's nasty. People like you and me don't get treated right. That's why it all needs to go."

Granny Marlow raised an eyebrow. "All of it?"

"Yeah."

"You mean everything? *Everything,* everything?"

"Yeah!" Fables stomped his foot before realizing it made him look like a child. The old woman seemed to find it amusing in a sad way. Exasperated, she continued sewing.

"Well, I've had my fair share of pain, I can tell you that." Her hands paused as she considered it. "Pain. Yes. I remembered the horror of that raid. The heat of the fires. Grabbing my sister's hand and running." She stared up at the ceiling. "And that demon woman," she said in a quiet voice. "That woman who fought on and on . . ."

Granny's hand crumpled around the unfinished quilt, a patchwork of browns, reds, and midnight blues. "But they weren't the only enemies to look out for. I was knocked out. And then my sister and I were on a ship. And we . . ." With a deep intake of breath, she swallowed the lump in her throat and lowered her head, shutting her eyes. "And when my sister died in the zoo, when they took her dignity from her, I blocked everything out. Who would have known I'd end up here with that woman—the woman who never aged, not a second, no matter how many years we spent together?"

Granny's face softened as she picked up her quilt and showed it to him. "I'm making this for her, you know. That silly child."

"Her . . ." And something clicked in Fables. "You can't mean . . . Hiva?"

"Yes, I think she mentioned that name once while we were in the zoo. Such a detached thing back then. No trace of life in her. But she changed. We changed." With a warm, motherly smile Fables himself had never known, she looked down at her quilt. "So many things have happened. I don't know where she is, but I'm sure she'll return one day. And when she comes back, I'll give her this. I'll tell her everything is okay and make sure to welcome her with a big hug."

"A hug . . . ?"

"What?" Granny cocked her head to the side. "Don't you have someone like that? Someone you want to hug in your arms so tight and never let go?"

Fables turned to Hiva, still preoccupied with his goose. He wanted to call out, but his throat was dry, his mind blank. There wasn't a single word he could think to say. It was then that he felt it: the inseparable, immeasurable gulf between him and this divine being, as uncrossable as the space and time that separated him from his family. But it was different from Granny and her Hiva. The warmth of their love was palpable. It was the warmth of *her* Hiva's humanity.

"Ah," Granny said sadly. "No wonder you want it all to go."

Hiva let go of the goose, and in the clothes Fables himself had ripped from the bloody corpse of a scientist, he stood. His fingers twitched, his golden eyes suddenly focused on the opening of the tent.

"I can feel it," he finally said after a time of silence. "The weapon. I know where it is."

Fables was ready for the conversation to end. But even as he left the old woman to her quilt, the memory of her words mocked him until all he could hear was the ringing silence joining him to this Hiva, who regarded him less than he did an animal.

It's fine. I'm fine, he thought desperately. The thought of those he hated dying horrifically at the hands of someone brave enough to do it was more than enough reason to keep going.

The words STAFF ONLY and UNDER CONSTRUCTION were painted on the doors in black letters. Inside the British Museum, Fables checked to make sure no one was around as Hiva unhooked the velvet rope shielding the doors.

Glass cases lined the wall inside this long, dark museum room. Plants and artifacts Fables had never seen. And inside the display in front of him, a human skeleton loomed overhead, whispering to him of an unfathomable tale that spanned eons.

Hiva's steps were heavy as he approached it. Touching the glass, he gazed upon the bones with a kind of reverence.

"Gods are gods because they cannot be taken easily," he said. His golden eyes glimmered in the moonlight. "Sister. It's time. I'm coming for you."

30

AFTER TWO DAYS' TRAVEL, IRIS ARRIVED to find the mining site in total pandemonium.

Shots were being fired at all sides on the ground and from the sky. Sharpshooters from the watchtower tried to pick off the girl who shot at the bevy of British guards of the National African Company from her horse. Another body flashed between them in a blink, slitting the guards' throats with a small white knife, while sooty-faced miners hid underneath the pavilion.

Iris's heart raced at the sight. What was happening? Who were they? On the way to the Oil Rivers region, Jinn's thigh had been bitten by a snake close to the Lagos Lagoon, and it'd delayed their journey by several days. If they'd come earlier, would it have made a difference?

There was no time to think about it. With her *shamshir* blade strapped to her side, in Granny's clothes and with Nyeth's ring safe in her pocket, Iris led the charge, running toward the carnage.

The guards couldn't seem to catch the two invaders, who picked them off one by one.

"What are you?" one guard cried. "Did those bloody locals send you?"

Iris couldn't see the attackers clearly until she was close enough to hear their voices. But Jinn had already come to the same conclusion she did.

"You've got to be kidding me," he said through gritted teeth as they headed for the raging cowgirl firing a pistol.

"Clear the space!" Berta ordered with a laugh, her blue dress flying up as the horse neighed and kicked his front legs. "Get all your Brit asses outta here! This is your last warning!"

The miners heeded it. No money in the world was worth this trouble. They'd likely been taken from local villages and were being paid pennies to work here anyway. The British guards, on the other hand, had the stolen property of the Crown to protect. Apparently they weren't ready to cede ill-gotten ground to the two siblings—but this was no ordinary duo.

"Berta!" Iris ducked a shot from the sharpshooters above, only to notice Max kneeing a guard in the stomach. In a loose red shirt too big for him and a pair of old, ripped brown pants, he turned to her with that wide, cheeky grin she was so familiar with, except this time it was tainted with splashes of blood.

"Iris!" After wiping his dirty face, he waved. "Hi!" And he punched another man so hard in the face that a tooth flew out of the man's mouth.

"Maximo!" Jinn shouted. "What the hell are you doing?"

The guards mistook them for Max and Berta's co-conspirators, because now their guns were trained on Jinn, Iris, and Rin. Iris dove to the ground as a torrent of bullets flew at them.

Max shrugged. "Waiting for you. Clearing a space. As soon as we heard you were headed here, we hopped on a couple of horses and rode like mad. Or what, were you just going to sneak into a carefully inspected, round-the-clock-monitored Crown-owned mine without a plan?"

Iris lifted herself off the dirt. "And *this* is a plan?"

Evening had just begun to come upon them, the sun's descent painting the sky in dark reds and yellows. The British had built a wooden framework around the cage used to lower men into the mines and lift up the white crystal. Iris recognized the little girl crouching inside it.

She gaped. "And you brought Lulu?"

The little girl crouched inside the cage, covering her head with her arms. This was madness. The child was traumatized enough.

Berta scoffed atop her horse. "I wasn't leaving her alone someplace dangerous!"

"And this *isn't* dangerous?"

Iris didn't have the time to argue with the psychotic duo. Something about the existence of Hiva seemed to inspire madness in others. Now that the guards were distracted, it was time to get what she came for.

Rin masterfully blocked some of the bullets with her sword, but they all knew they only had one shot. They charged for the steel cage, which was held to the scaffolding with chains and attached to a pulley.

"Lulu!" Iris scooped the child up once she jumped inside the cage, though they both yelped when a bullet hit one of the chains. "Get inside!" Iris screamed to the others.

Berta flipped off her horse, a wild breed that leaped forward and crushed the guards in its path. Rin threw her sword at the watchtower sharpshooters, knocking one of their guns out of their hands with expert aim. A warning spray of fire from Jinn's mouth caused the rest of the guards to back off. In the midst of the confusion, Max kicked the pulley out of joint. Just as it began spinning out of control, he jumped inside the falling cage and whirled down the long, dark shaft with them. It skidded against the metal scaffolding, which slowed their descent, the rattling of the chain battering Iris's eardrums. The rickety cage beat against the metal.

Iris shielded Lulu as they came to a rough, shaky stop against the solid ground. Max opened the cage in a hurry and tumbled into the dark cave, then immediately bent over and tossed his lunch onto the hard stone.

"Gross!" Berta kicked him in the behind. "I told you not to eat all those mangoes on the way here! Not to mention, we should have stopped when I said to, so you could digest."

"I was in a hurry. It would have been nearly four days on foot." *Retch.*

"Ugh!" Berta stomped her foot. "*Older* brother. I might as well be the older one. You're just as stupid as you were when we were kids!" Though she couldn't hide her little grin.

"You shouldn't have even come here." Jinn stomped out of the cage.

"Still with a stick up your butt." Max straightened up and wiped his mouth with his red shirt. "I'm fine as always, mate."

Jinn punched him quickly in the back, exactly where the Ajashe doctor had very recently removed the bullet that'd almost killed him. Max let out a yell, reacting with a violent arch, and stumbled away from him.

"Fine, eh, *mate*?" Jinn slapped Max in the back of the head. "You could have killed yourself, your sister, and Lulu. Not to mention that the bloodshed out there wasn't necessary. Then again, you've grown quite accustomed to killing, haven't you?"

Iris glanced nervously between the two men. Old rivalries hadn't died. They'd only gotten bloodier and more personal. But Jinn was right.

Iris squirmed as Max smirked. He'd come here to help her, and for that she was grateful. But seeing Max's cheerful grin now made her uneasy. At least before, he would have hesitated before pulling a trigger or swiping a knife.

Max noticed her trepidation. Defensively, he scoffed and folded his arms. "It got the job done, didn't it? And the girls can take care of themselves. Or so Berta insisted."

Berta certainly could. She'd already scurried toward a prominent fork between two diverging tunnels. "What can I say? I'm an active girl. I don't like staying in one place for too long."

Even Lulu had gotten over the shock quickly and was wide-eyed and smiling, trying to catch her breath like she'd just been on some kind of circus ride. Iris shook her head. The six of them were down here now. There was no other choice but to move forward. Who knew when Adam would show up with whatever "trump cards" he'd prepared?

The miners had certainly done some work here. The cave needed no lamps because bits of white crystal sparkled within the walls, illuminating the darkness with a white hue.

"This is you," said Rin, touching the walls. "Or at least part of you?"

Leaving Lulu to chase after Berta, who she seemed more comfortable with, Iris followed Rin to the wall. "Yes," she said, and rubbed her hands over the rock, feeling the sharp bumps, the life in them. *Her* life. She shut her eyes. "The white stone belongs to the earth, after all." As her palms grazed the white crystal, the jumbled memories inside her began sorting themselves into proper order. The white crystal was as natural as any mineral, but invisible to the eye—until it was time to bring forth Hiva. Then the mystic mineral came together and formed one heart, and from that heart a body. Deep within the earth.

It had all happened here in this place. She looked around the glittering mine. The stone seemed to be singing to her quietly.

"I don't like it," Max said, his fingers twitching into a fist. "The look of this, I mean. It reminds me of sugar."

"I love sugar," said Lulu, as Berta gave him a worried look. Perhaps he'd told her by now of everything that had happened to him on that cursed ship. "It's sweet."

"So is revenge. Which reminds me." Max turned to Iris. "Temple. He's not going to leave you alone, you know. No matter what you decide to do here."

"I don't care what he thinks." Iris felt the white crystal prickle her skin. "I'm here to decide my own fate. And if I fail—"

Iris caught herself.

"If you fail?" Max gave her a sidelong look. "Do you *expect* to fail?"

"No!" Iris said. "Of course not. I was saying 'if'—"

"So you're allowing an 'if' in this equation, then?" Max didn't yell. He didn't even seem all that disturbed. He only looked at her. Studied her as she squirmed.

Jinn grabbed his shoulder. "She misspoke, Max," he said.

Max glanced at Berta. His expression hardened. "But if that 'if' becomes reality—"

"It won't," Iris assured him, though the tremor in her voice didn't give off the confidence she'd hoped for.

"You once swore to me that you wouldn't become Hiva." Max lowered his head slightly, his eyes still on her. "That you wouldn't endanger us. You swore that in Ajashe."

"You have nothing to worry about," Iris said. "You, Lulu. Berta," she added, making Max scrunch his nose. "I know what the stakes are."

Berta was his top priority. He'd told her definitively. He didn't need to tell her again.

Iris sucked in a breath and gave him a reassuring nod. "I'll get this done, I swear."

But Max must have known. Anyone with a working brain would have known that this was all a shot in the dark. A wish driven by intuition.

Max gave her a cheeky smile and a gentle pat on the side of her face. "I trust you," he said, with an expression that told her he was at least halfway convinced.

Was her mission here just a fantasy? Maybe. Still, she had to try.

This was where her present life began. "The key is here," she said resolutely.

"The key to the Coral Temple, you mean?" Jinn looked around. "This anti-Hiva technology the Naacal built—?"

"It's in the Coral Temple," she said, and she knew it was true. Nyeth's venomous glare, always in the back of her mind, told her it was true. "I just have to find a way there. I just . . ."

Iris stopped. A sudden breeze filled her lungs. She rose and fell with it, letting her whole body expand and expel it out. No one else had felt it. Only her.

Iris looked at the right tunnel and, as if in a dream, began moving toward it.

"Iris?" Max said. Out of the corner of her eye, she saw him exchange glances with Jinn.

The tunnel's ceiling was too low. Even Iris had to bend a little to keep from having the top of her head scrape the rock.

The miners hadn't gotten too far inside this one. But they weren't looking for what she was. She dipped her hand into the pocket of her moss-green skirt and pulled out Nyeth's ring. Its power had presence here. It shuddered and whined.

Suddenly, Iris could see herself as Hiva in those old days, jumping from a high tower onto the roof of one of the most glorious Naacalian temples she'd ever seen. Built entirely of orichalcum, it was pearl-colored, sturdy, and gleaming, with sprawling towers and pillars. And an entrance only a chosen few could pass through because—

Iris stopped at the end of the tunnel and turned sharply to the left. The party stopped behind her, Berta nearly bumping into Rin.

"What the hell, Amazon?" she said, though when her breath suddenly hitched, Iris could only assume that one of Rin's death glares had shut her up. "H-hey, so, my brother told me we're on a mission to save the world." Berta continued after clearing her throat. "That true? That's what you guys were talking about back there, right?"

Max laughed. "She can't understand English," he explained when Rin didn't answer.

"Save the world, save the world!" Lulu chirped, ignoring him. "Max said this is where we gotta do it! It sounds important!"

"Oh please, I just brought you along so you wouldn't wander off and get lost," said Berta. "You don't even understand what we mean by 'save the world.'"

"I do so. This world needs changing. It needs *saving*. Miss Iris here's our angel, so of course she's gonna do it. She's going to make all our lives better. Right, Max?" Lulu looked up at him with her large brown eyes.

"Well, she's going to do *something*, Lulu. And that's why we're here." His voice darkened for just a moment. "To see what she does."

She caught the hint of distrust in his tone. Iris spared them a wary glance, but not for too long. Soon their voices disappeared into the empty space of silence that stretched on and on inside her. She placed her hand on the left wall and, with a deep breath, lifted her head with closed eyes.

She could see what it was *supposed* to be. The round, golden door rimmed with a solid ruby strip. The door's magic was owed to tiny Naacalian automatons near imperceptible to the eye, designed to take a bit of blood from only a chosen few and disperse it along tiny pathways inside the heavy door. Iris wasn't sure quite how the technology worked. She'd only heard the explanation once from Nyeth, who'd shown her this place one secret night and made her one of the chosen few in those days he mistook her for a goddess of good. By the time she'd begun her assault upon the Naacal, they were in such disarray that they'd forgotten to change the "locks."

Iris took a rock and began breaking apart the wall.

"Iris?" Jinn jumped back as debris flew.

"Help me. Everyone, help me!"

Eventually, they each grabbed rocks and aimed for the wall, but none as wildly as Iris. The words from John Temple's journal replayed in her mind, clear, pompous, and unyielding in his obsession to discover the secrets of the world.

To drag a god back down to earth required nothing short of divine intervention of a different sort. If what the king told me is indeed true, I'll find my divine intervention in the place where heaven dwells.

She'd memorized the passage. It bothered her when she slept, and she didn't understand why—not until part of the wall crumbled to the ground, revealing the golden door with its straight-angled indents forming a pattern like an electrical circuit.

"Iris." Jinn gripped her elbow as she moved toward it instinctively.

"It's here," she said.

As soon as she placed her hand on the surface, the entire wall began to shake until the door slid and remained open. But when she stepped through the threshold, her feet found nothing but air, and she tumbled down until her body hit the white surface of a cracked marble path, knocking the wind out of her.

"Iris, you okay?" she heard Jinn call above her.

"It's okay! A bit of a drop, but I'm fine." She rubbed her neck.

Soon she heard bodies falling and feet landing around her, some with nimble grace, others with heavy thuds and an unceremonious series of words.

Max had carried Lulu when he jumped. After he gently let her down, Lulu gasped in awe. "What is this place?"

The temple was not as it once was. Broken, grayed pillars. Heavy stalactites hanging down where the ornate high white ceiling used to be. Arched, dark shadowy entrances with Naacalian characters etched into the stone walls. And twisted, winding, narrow white paths suspended in the air, leading to three pairs of grand, gold-rimmed double doors in the distance.

As pure white sand trickled like a waterfall down a fountain into the bottomless pit beneath the white marble paths, Nyeth's curses sang to her.

"Where the hell are we?" Jinn's voice was barely a whisper.

Iris stared through the expanse of the ruins. "The place where heaven dwells," she whispered, holding out Nyeth's ring in her palm. "This is Heaven's Shrine."

31

"THESE ARE THE ROOMS WE'VE BUILT to pray to you," Nyeth told her, gesturing to the gold-rimmed double doors on their left and right, his red-and-gold robes of the clergy sweeping the white cobbled floor.

On the day the sun died, Hiva had appeared before the Naacal, rising out of the earth in front of a gathering at the Naacalian palace. Wearing no clothes, bathed in the light stolen by the eclipse, she'd declared her intention to live among them. And after she'd survived their attacks of swords and arrows, they'd fallen to their knees in awe and fear. This must have been the god they'd prayed to for many ages. The god of the sun: Helios.

"No," she'd told them. "My name is Hiva."

From that day on, they'd worshipped her even more fervently than their old gods.

"And this is where we would commune with you," he said, clasping his hands together politely. He'd trained his entire life to achieve oneness with their god. He showed her the set of doors at the very front of the hall. "The god birthed by the sun. Since the old days, those aiming to become clergy would have to undergo a set of trials to reach the Room of Murals and speak with the old god, back when we were unaware of you, the *true* god. Hiva, would you like to see?"

Nyeth's smile had been so dazzling in those days.

The days before she'd burned it out of him.

—∞∞∞—

"Iris?" Max touched her cheek.

In a flash, she jolted back into the present, her eyes refocusing. She shook her head. "The Room of Murals," she whispered in this wasteland version of the shrine's main hall.

Yes, this was Heaven's Shrine. Just as the scrolls had mentioned. That labyrinthine temple the color of beach clay. But now the temple was in ruins. The marble floor had broken, and the pillars had caved in. Only the orichalcum paths to each of the three sets of doors remained, leading them from the main gate, precarious in the air. How deep was the cavern beneath them? Iris could only see darkness and feel a strange draft of wind floating up from it—the soundless howls, perhaps, of the priests who'd once trusted in her.

"Well, this is a hoot." Berta laughed incredulously, her shoulders giving a sharp bounce, before she turned to Max. "You sure we should have come here?"

"Why not? Looks like a good time. Hey, don't get too close," Max added, for Lulu had bent over the path to look deep into the cavern below. If they made one wrong move, there was no telling how far they'd drop.

"The Room of Murals," Jinn repeated behind her, and gripped Iris's shoulder. "What do you mean by that?"

Iris hadn't even realized she'd spoken aloud. She'd been so wrapped up in visions of the past. . . . Squeezing her eyes shut, she pressed a hand against her forehead before turning to them. "The Room of Murals is where they prayed to—" She hesitated. "Their sun god." She didn't need to tell them everything. "But I remember hearing that once I became their enemy, they repurposed the room."

It was as the scrolls had written: *And so the sacred room to speak with God was changed into a room to clip his wings.* She touched the blade at her side almost instinctively.

"That's where they put it," Iris said without any doubt in her heart. "That's where we'll find what we need to 'clip my wings.' To make me . . . normal."

"Or *kill* you." Jinn grabbed Iris's elbow and tugged her closer to him. "We can't know exactly what we'll find down here."

He was right. Iris still wasn't sure what they'd find. She'd never discovered the grand machine they'd built to try to rid themselves of her. She knew they'd corralled all their scientists to work on it in their facilities on the earth and in the seas. But as for what it was, since she'd never given them a chance to use it, she never found out.

She was playing everything by ear with nothing guaranteed. From the corner of her eye, she saw Max pull a flustered Berta close to him.

"I'm going anyway." Iris rolled up her sleeves and hiked up her skirt to make it easier to move. "Anyone who wants to come along, feel free. If you'd like to turn back, go ahead. But I'm moving forward. That's all I can do."

"Forward. Well, that certainly sounds like you," Max muttered under his breath with an amused sigh. "I'm in. Berta, take Lulu back with you."

"What?" Berta scoffed. "Back where? To the British?"

Max huffed, blowing a few of his brown curls off his forehead. "Just sneak past them or something. Hey, listen to your brother."

"Oh, stop it. We haven't seen each other in damn near ten years. I'm not leaving you now. Plus, how would we even get back up there?"

"Berta—"

"Ugh, will y'all *stop* your hollering and get *on* with it?" Shaking her head, Lulu slipped through both of them and gave Rin a thumbs-up. "I'm ready."

Rin and Iris exchanged glances before Iris gave a heavy sigh, her shoulders slumping. This wasn't what she'd bargained for, but there was no turning back now. With a wary eye on the drooping pillars around them, Iris began her march.

The way up the long cobbled white path toward the gold-rimmed entryway was treacherous, least of all because of its narrow shape. Though the material had remained sturdy enough for thousands of years, when Iris's foot touched the sides of the path, bits of debris broke off and fell into the bottomless pit below. They marched in single file, Rin holding Lulu's hand and the Morales siblings bickering back and forth while Jinn held out a protective hand against Iris's back, just in case. At times the draft from below blew up with a soft, whining whistle; however, just as Iris approached the doors at the end of the hall, they began to bellow with madness.

Leave, Iris heard them say.

You're not welcome here.

You were a mistake. . . . You should never have been born.

"Who are you to say that?" A cold wind leached tears from Iris's eyes. "Who are you to tell me that?" Her fingers curled into a fist. "You don't get to say that!" she screamed.

"Iris!" Jinn yelled, gripping her shoulder, whisking her around and pulling her back to reality.

Suddenly, the cold wind rushed up all at once, knocking them off their feet. As Iris collapsed onto the cobbled path, she heard Lulu scream. Gritting her teeth, she turned her head just in time to see Rin catch Lulu, who dangled off the side of the winding path.

"Lulu . . ." Iris boosted herself up to her knees as the wind silenced. Catching her breath, she looked behind her. "Everyone . . . are you all okay?"

"Are *you* okay?" called Berta from behind. "Who the hell were you yelling at?"

Iris couldn't answer. Rin had pulled Lulu back onto the path. Max looked after Berta, who wiped her curls from her face.

"It seems like we're in one piece." Jinn stood, pulling Iris to her feet.

Nodding, she turned back toward the set of doors just as another gust of wind howled from beneath, more frantic, more bloodthirsty than before. Iris was blown off her feet.

She remembered Jinn screaming and reaching out for her, the tips of their fingers touching as she dropped into the abyss below.

It was hot.

The sting of her bones snapping into place. Her spine re-forming. Her lungs filling up with air once more. It was a while before she could feel her toes, before she could pry them apart and twitch her legs to the side.

It had been a long fall. She could tell because even with her eyes not yet fully formed, she could feel the results of her body painstakingly putting itself back together. Her curse and her blessing. Only she could have survived the drop.

The others. A sharp thump of her heart; she pried open her lips, and a rush of heat entered her lungs instead. She called out to them. No one answered. When she was able to open her eyes and move her neck, she looked from side to side. It was a relief that she couldn't see the remains of her friends anywhere, but where was *she* in the first place?

The ground beneath her was unsteady. The cave hazy from the heated air. She stretched out her arms but retracted them just as quickly. Lava. Beneath some of the broken stone, rubble, and debris was lava, thick and rumbling.

Sweat dripped down the edges of her hairline as she hoped beyond all hope that no one else would fall down here. They must have gotten to that entrance, right? Iris bit her lip and looked around. On the far end of the room was a square door, but she'd have to find her footing on the few patches of solid ground to get to it.

She tried the strip to her left. It wobbled from her weight but held firm as the lava slurped and bubbled around her. A lick of fire caught the hem of her skirt, singeing it.

"Damn it," she cursed, struggling to breathe in the heavy air as she flapped the flames off her skirt. It was the skirt Granny had made her. She wasn't going to let it burn away here. But the next leap almost took her into the fire. Whipping out her sword, she plunged it into the cave wall to steady herself.

Above her was darkness. But she could hear the air stirring and the wind up there howling.

In the old days, trials had awaited the religious hopefuls who'd desired a touch of the divine in the Room of Murals. Now that they'd turned Heaven's Shrine into a weapon against Hiva, what awaited her?

After one final mad leap to the front, with a desperate wail escaping her lips, she kicked open the door and prepared herself for the worst.

Stairs. White stairs in the darkness, one gleaming platform after the other, rising steeply, stretching endlessly. She plowed ahead, and as she did, the memories of her past judgments followed her. It was a Naacalian trick, a brain-warping device that forced particularly painful recollections to the forefront of the mind—recollections that elicited emotions of guilt.

She could see, deep within the crevices of her mind, each memory playing out one by one. Flying ships crashing into buildings that collapsed upon decimated populations. Guns the likes of which no one currently living had ever seen, shooting off rounds before the hands that grasped them turned to ash and the machines clattered to the ground. Whole armies disappearing into the air.

And him. The other Hiva sitting on the grass, surrounded by children.

"You know," he'd said. "On my earth, after so many cycles of living and judging, I'd begun to wonder what it was all for. Now I'm starting to believe that maybe I didn't understand. Maybe there's a choice for us. Maybe there's always been a choice."

"The choice is judgment." Iris's voice. "And the judgment has always been death."

Iris hated hearing herself. But she had to remember that this was all in the past. Naacalian scientific sorcery. For them, technology was a part of worship. Part of how they determined one's worth. She had to pull herself together.

"But does it have to be?" On the side of a green hill overlooking the ocean, the other Hiva in his beige robes let the children pluck weeds from his long, curling hair. "We're of the earth," he said. "Born to protect it from all that endangers its life. This living, breathing earth that loves and hates just as humans do. But if it is capable of such emotion, then why can't we feel the same? If we can hate, then we can love as well. And maybe forgive."

He gathered the children up in his arms. But Hiva shook her head.

"You misunderstand everything," she said. "It's not a matter of hate or love. There is no love and no hate. Only what needs to be done. The truth is as it shall always be."

You've misunderstood everything. The voice of "Anne" was but a whisper within her. *You misunderstand me still.*

Iris shut her eyes as she continued up the stairs, her legs pumping beyond the point of numbness. And off to her left, she could still see Hiva on the side of the hill, holding the children to him even tighter. And though he didn't want to show his helplessness, he trembled nonetheless. "You are the Hiva of this earth. This world is yours to judge. But sister . . . what about mercy?"

"Agh!" *Jinn*. He was screaming. She couldn't see him, but she could hear his voice echoing beyond the steps in front of her, and it was enough to snap her out of the memory entirely.

"Jinn!" She climbed faster, blotting out the voices from the past. The screaming was coming from the other side of a white door, and now Iris could pick out more yells—Rin's and Max's. Berta's too. The grunts of battle.

If we can hate, then we can love as well.

"Jinn, I'm coming!" And she reached for the door.

Cold, midnight-blue stone. The inner heart of a cave. Dark marble roads. Slender pillars erected long ago, reaching to the high ceiling. The creatures Iris saw scuttling across the earthen floor had all the makings of monsters engineered by the Naacal: tall enough to reach Iris's hips, the tops of their steel bodies had the shape and the icy blue pallor of the jellyfish that used to surround the Naacal's underwater labs. The thick symbols etched into their surfaces detailed the manufacturing name, plant, and development number of each creature:

SPECTER TYPE 0. MU NEFERIT. NO. 01X699

She counted ten. Fourteen. Twenty of them. All fighting Jinn and the rest. The specters' bottom halves had eight legs, four on each side. When they scuttled along the ground and opened the round blue glass at the center of their heads, a beam of pure electricity shot out, crashing into the pillars. It was all the others could do to leap out of the way in time.

"Careful!" Max screamed to Berta after crushing one's head with his foot. "Stay clear of those . . . um . . ." He struggled to find the words. "Fire Beams?"

"Cannon Lights!" Berta had her pistols out and was shooting, but the bullets just bounced off the specters' surfaces. "Cannon Lights, definitely!"

She'd clearly given Lulu her shotgun, but it wasn't doing much better. Eventually, the little girl began using the barrel to beat the specters away.

Rin had better luck, slicing them with her sword, then rolling on the ground to dodge more electrical beams bursting from the machines. Iris had seen these specters before. She'd fought against them before. Armies of them had littered the Mu continent, attempting in vain to destroy her. Many more had been waiting for her in Heaven's Shrine on her way back from the Coral Temple the day she murdered Nyeth.

A buried memory resurfaced: Nyeth clinging to her inside a barn of ashes.

The greatest of these inventions lies inside the Great Sea. I can take you. I know the way.

To the Coral Temple . . .

"Aim for the glass," Iris ordered, running toward them. "The blue glass on their heads! It's their weak point!"

At the sound of her voice, everyone turned and gaped, calling out to her. But there wasn't much time to celebrate. The specters were relentless. Far to her left, Iris spotted Jinn, his back against a pillar. After setting a row of specters on fire, he turned to her.

"Iris!" He lifted his hand to usher her over. "Iris, where have you been? What happened—?"

Out from around the pillar, a jaundiced hand grabbed Jinn's neck and slammed the back of his head against the stone. Jinn's lips opened in a wordless gasp. His whole body twitched in unspeakable pain as Gram slid out from behind the stone.

32

JINN!" HIS NAME SCRAPED IRIS'S THROAT and shuddered out of her as she ran.

Adam's trump cards. Iris screamed for Jinn while Fool's harlequin grin taunted her in her memories. *Mr. Jinn . . . the dark specters of the past are never really gone.* And of course, *a great gathering is upon us.*

Shots rang out. One pierced Rin in the arm, causing her to drop her gun. Another narrowly missed Max's head.

"You!" Max spat as Jacques aimed at him from a stone platform in the distance. "How did *you* get here?"

"The door was open," Jacques said.

Gram had no interest in the specters, or anyone else but the prey he had in his grasp. What he wanted was flesh and revenge. He dug his dirty nails into Jinn's throat, aching, no doubt, to rip out Jinn's jugular. But Jinn still had some consciousness left in him. He grabbed Gram's hand and bit down hard.

Feeling someone else's teeth in his flesh only seemed to rile Gram further. After he let go of Jinn's throat, Jinn crashed the back of his head against Gram's forehead, then gripped his arm and flipped him over.

Her *shamshir* blade out, Iris jumped atop a specter, crushing it with the heels of her boots and using it to propel her toward Gram. As Jinn wobbled on his feet, Gram rolled out of the way, dodging her.

"This . . ." Jinn took a shaky step forward. "This ends today, Gram!" Steadying his hands, he reached for the hilt of his blade, his eyebrows furrowing in concentration. "Iris, you ready?"

Iris nodded. "Ready."

Iris and Jinn fought, each with their weapon. Together, their blades danced. "The Bolero of Blades." Two *shamshir*, a pair made sacred by their partnership, striking at the head of the beast. But Jinn's movements weren't as graceful as they usually were and not nearly as precise. Gram, that monster, was nimble enough to dodge their sweeping attacks. With Jinn fighting off his pain, he and Iris were out of time, out of rhythm. Gram knocked Iris off her feet with a quick jab and grabbed Jinn's leg.

"You're the one I'm to kill first," he said, pulling Jinn forward. "To make the girl realize her place."

Adam's orders. How could that fool have rescued Gram from the river where he should have drowned? *You think you've won?* he'd said while bleeding in Bosch's factory. Iris's nails dug into her left palm. He wouldn't stop until she'd submitted to his will. He wasn't any different from Doctor Pratt. From the rest of the Enlighteners. From anyone who'd sought to define and own her. She hated him. She hated him with everything she had.

"Your place . . ." Jinn gritted his teeth as he tried to fight off Gram. "*Your* place, Gram, is where it's always been."

Explosions rang out behind them. Iris flipped over onto her stomach and covered her head as an electrical beam shot out from a specter.

Jinn gasped, his eyes wild. "Your place is in *hell*."

Iris dashed out of the way and crouched as a stream of fire burst from his mouth, enveloping both Gram and his own legs. Both men screamed out in pain together, a bloody symphony.

"Jinn!" With a rush of adrenaline, Iris jumped to her feet and pulled Jinn away from Gram by the back of his shirt, but Jinn wouldn't stop. He sprayed Gram until there was nothing left but fire.

Iris took off her blouse to beat out the flames. Once she'd extinguished the embers on Jinn's legs, she put her tattered blouse back on and dragged Jinn to his feet. He was unsteady on them, wincing with every step; then he stumbled back, the breath trembling out of him as timid as a whimper, as he looked at Gram's motionless, burning body, unable to believe his eyes. But Jacques's finger was still trained on them. Iris pushed Jinn aside, letting the bullet hit her in the shoulder instead.

"Iris!"

Iris wasn't sure who'd said it. Beams were still firing. Berta was hiding behind a pillar, aiming at Jacques, but she couldn't pick him off. Rin was shoving her sword into the glass eyes of the specters, taking them down one by one.

But all would soon go quiet.

As Jinn held Iris upright, footsteps rumbled in the distance. Slow. Deliberate. The floor trembled as if wanting to flee. What was left of the specters regrouped, scuttling back. Deep within Iris's ancient bones, she knew what was approaching them out of the darkness.

The minotaur.

It was the only way Iris could describe it. During those ten years in which she'd lost her memories, she'd filled up her mind with books instead, reading about different peoples, different cultures, wanting to see where she'd fit. She'd read some aloud to Granny while the woman was sewing her an outfit. But some were too gruesome and strange to share. She'd come across tales of gods and monsters that seemed distant, yet somehow so familiar. The monster of Crete, born with the body of a man and the head of a bull. The cruel "gift" of the god of oceans. The result of a monstrous union, who awaited Theseus at the end of his labyrinth.

This creature too was the result of a monstrous union: human brilliance, ingenuity, and greed. Like a hastily constructed wooden toy, Iris could see the dark lines in its body wherever limbs and joints were attached. A wide, brawny body made of dark brass and rusted steel. A monstrous bovine head with horns twisting up into the sky. And a seven-pronged spear in its hands, the staff and blades glowing with a haunting white hue. The Naacal had dreamed up their own creatures of myth and legend too. Humankind seemed to share similar nightmares across cultures and generations.

GOLEM TYPE 2. MU NEFERIT. NO. 04Y871 was written across its chest.

It attacked, charging with the force of a bullet as gunfire spurted from its back and propelled it forward.

Everyone dove out of the way. Iris had seen this thing before in the middle of its production inside a Naacalian lab, but she had never faced it. She didn't know how to stop it. She flipped over her blade anyway.

Max threw the broken remains of a specter at the golem as it rushed forward, but the smaller machine burst apart against its chest. Lulu and Berta fired their guns at the same time. Its glass eyes reflected each shot.

As the golem launched its great spear down toward them, Berta grabbed Lulu and leaped out of the way while Rin jumped upon the long rod and, running up it, began slashing at the monster's head.

A beam shot at them, missing Lulu's head by a few inches. Another one knocked the *shamshir* out of Iris's hand. The specters were still aiming to kill. A bullet crashed through the blue glass of one, shattering it, causing the machine to sputter with an electrical charge and explode. Iris looked toward the platform. Jacques. He lowered his hand, his deadly finger smoking as he mouthed something to her.

Protect the child.

Iris planned to. She planned to protect everyone, but how? The golem was fast, sweeping Berta, Rin, and Max away with one brush of its arm. Jinn was still limping from setting his own legs on fire. But the golem wanted her. The specters. The Naacal had created every machine to destroy her. She just needed to remind them that she was right here.

As Max slammed into a pillar, bits of debris fell down from the ceiling. She stared at the fallen pillars across the cave and realized what she needed to do.

First, she called to it. Raising her head, she reached inside the golem with her power and found that bit of anima that existed deep inside its wires and gears. Yes, anima. To build a machine such as this, the Naacal would take apart human bodies, disassembling them down to their cells and reassembling them into the fleshlike material that built up the golem's core. Iris wasn't sure how it worked—only that the humans sacrificed for science were not volunteers. They were the poor, the destitute, and the enslaved. One of the many reasons Iris had decided to destroy the Naacal long ago.

And this creature, this golem, seemed to sense her mind touching the spark of anima within its machine body. It trained its hollow white eyes on her and began to charge.

"Hide!" She pushed Lulu away and started running. *That's right*, Iris thought, dodging the golem while running toward the opposite end of the cave, away from the rest. The specters followed suit. *Come get me.*

Electrical beams trailed her, bursting apart the walls as she ran across them. Just as the golem aimed its spear, she flipped back, landing like a circus performer upon its head. She grabbed its horns, her body dangling down its back as it twisted around wildly, trying to throw her off.

The specters aimed.

A shot of lightning. The specters' beams crashed into the pillar above. As chunks of stone came toppling down, Iris kept the beast pinned and refused to let go.

"Iris!" cried Jinn as the specters crowded her. "Iris, get out of the way!"

No. Not until the last second. Not until there wasn't any time left. Not until . . . *now!*

She leaped away, running and hurling her body to the side as far as she could fling herself. The crushing impact of the collapsed pillar threw her body even farther. The specters were close enough that the massive explosion of one destroyed another, and another, and another. The entire cave shook. Iris rolled like a rag doll across the ground. She lay upon her back, covering her ears and curling herself into a fetal position as another explosion sounded and another pillar fell sideways and slammed into the ground. When the smoke cleared and the dust settled, the golem and the specters were nowhere in sight amid the flaming wreckage.

Iris snickered almost childishly as she watched the fires wafting up. Her mind drifted for a moment, and she passed out, only to be jolted awake by Jinn several minutes later.

"Iris. Hey, Iris!"

She was curled in Jinn's lap, his arm around her, shaking her. "I'm all right. I'm all right," she whispered, her throat hoarse.

"That was pretty gutsy." Impressed, Berta blew a curl off her face but winced right after. None of them could afford to look confident. They'd survived only by the skin of their teeth.

Max knelt down in front of Iris, inspecting her bruised and battered body, his head tilted to the side. He wasn't worried as much as he was intrigued. The old Max would have been worried. "You're serious about this, aren't you? This scheme of yours."

"It's not a scheme," she said, coughing the smoke out of her lungs. "It's a dream."

"All that power inside that little body of yours." Max stood, looking down upon her, and for a moment, Iris could see that devilish glare he'd given Slessor's men before killing them. "You could do whatever you wanted with it. Are you sure you want to give it up?"

"Max," Jinn warned.

"And are you sure you *can* give it up? What if you can't? What happens to the rest of us?" He flicked his head toward the flaming rubble. "Will we end up like that?"

Jinn scowled and gripped Iris tighter, though she noticed his hands trembled just a little. That was right. It was Jinn who'd told her not too long ago, aboard *La Daphnée*, that people couldn't always get what they wanted, no matter how hard they wished for it. If the situation called for it, with the world on the line, sacrifices could be necessary . . . could be inevitable.

"I'm warning you," Jinn said in a low, shaky voice.

But it was Rin who grabbed Max's arm. Iris wasn't sure how much Rin had understood, but her deadly glare told Max it was time to stop. The two sized each other up for a moment, Max with a dark, strange little grin on his face.

"It is not any of our choices, but the girl's and the girl's alone. I accept that now."

Jacques. He was so quiet that nobody had noticed him descending from his platform and approaching them. The fires that had enveloped Gram's body on one side and the Naacalian machines on the other raged on, the smoke still lingering in the air. He stopped in front of Lulu, who stood next to Max. Berta aimed her gun at him the moment Jacques reached into his pants pocket. But what he took out wasn't any kind of weapon.

It was a crucifix. He crouched down and placed it in Lulu's palm.

"Girl. What is your dream?" He was looking at Iris. "You have a strong will. Even if I bring you to the Committee, you will never let them keep you. I see that now. So tell me: What is your dream? What do you hope for yourself in this life?"

Iris sat up straight in Jinn's arms, the arms that were part of the very dream she'd told him about.

"I want to be me. I don't want to hurt anyone. Never again."

"And you're sure you can make that dream come true?"

Iris nodded resolutely.

Jacques stayed silent for too long before closing Lulu's fingers over the crucifix. He was mumbling something. Something Iris had heard before.

"For the sake of His sorrowful passion, have mercy on us, Lord, and on the whole world."

"You can trust me," Iris insisted, shifting to her knees. "You can trust me, Jacques."

"I have only one God. And I've decided to put my faith in Him." He turned his back to leave. "Oh. That's right." He stopped. "I have a message to deliver to you. From young Adam."

Jinn folded his arms. "Of course you do."

Jacques looked over his shoulder. "'The only ones who can truly hurt us are the ones who love us the most.' That is what he said."

"He saying he loves you?" Max said with a smirk. "Do assassins pass on love notes?"

Jinn was not nearly as amused. Iris grimaced, her skin crawling.

Jacques patted Lulu on the head. "You look like my daughter," he said, gazing into her deep, dark eyes. "Get home safely, child." Then he turned to leave.

"But I don't have a home . . . ," Lulu whispered, staring at the crucifix in her palm.

"We'll find you one." Iris forced herself to her feet. "When all this is over."

"When all this is over." Jinn's hand lingered around her waist for just a moment as their eyes locked.

They could do this. Together, they could do this.

They traveled through the cave and up another flight of stairs, which led them to a rather confusing room. It seemed as if thick white staircases were pouring in from every angle, at every direction and out of every wall. Each staircase led to its own dark entrance. The group stuck together, following the path they thought would lead them to where they needed to go. But each door they opened spat them back out again into the same room on a different staircase.

"Damn it," Berta cursed as they tried again for the fourth time. "Can't we take a break?"

"You want to set up a campfire?" Max muttered.

"You know, I remembered you were far nicer."

"Yes, but you see, that was in your pre-cowboy days."

"How long has it been?" Lulu slumped over and rubbed her stomach. "I'm so hungry."

Rin seemed to notice her slowing down. Bending, she gestured for Lulu to climb onto her back. It was an act of kindness that drew a blush to Lulu's cheeks. She wrapped her arms around Rin's neck and let the young warrior carry her up the steps. Or was it down? It seemed like they were going down now.

"You good?" Jinn asked her, turning behind him. Rin and Lulu nodded.

"This is never-ending," Berta said after a while. "What is this place?"

Iris remembered this room. It was more of the Naacal's perception-warping technology, part of the trials the clergy had to face. Thankfully this room hadn't been fitted last-minute with anti-Hiva murder machines. That didn't make it any less annoying.

The tiny black door in the corner below was their goal. She led them there just as the other Hiva had led her once, jumping off one flight of stairs to another. The right combination of doors.

"Got it!" Iris's hand finally reached the black doorway. She doubled over, breathing heavily, her body still smarting from her battle with the golem, while the rest of the party panted and cursed. "This is it."

It had to be.

Iris opened the door and walked inside.

The Room of Murals used to glitter white and gold. It was a long hall lit by standing torches perched upon its eggshell-white marble floor. The fires were now out. The room filled with cobwebs. But the mural was the same as she remembered. A mural that stretched along the front wall behind an altar, telling the story of the sun god's creation of the Naacal—and the red Naacalian symbols painted sloppily over it:

And in the same way, Hiva will rise again.

For it is Hiva's fate to destroy mankind forever and ever.

Misery unto eternity . . .

Bold symbols. The furious writing of the Naacal. Just as Iris had read in the Library of Rule. Her whole body stiffened. And perhaps it was because of the shock that she didn't notice the man sitting in front of the altar.

Iris instinctively reached for her blade, but she needn't have. His brown pants and white shirt were dull and tattered. Cobwebs stretched down from the ceiling, trailing from the mural to the sacrificial altar he lay against and tangled in his long black beard. Spiders crawled over his legs, shifting the hair on his bare forearms and climbing his rolled-up sleeve, but the man didn't seem to react to them at all.

He'd been sleeping. But he'd managed to pry his eyes open once Iris walked in. His shaggy, twisted hair stretched down past his shoulders. No one knew what to say.

He spoke first.

"A . . . dam? Adam?"

Iris stood in silence as the man said Adam Temple's name again and again, searching for him among the party. She shook her head. What was going on?

She opened her mouth, afraid to ask. But she had to. She pursed her lips together.

"Who are you?"

The man's neck was thin enough to snap, but he managed to turn it anyway, just to look Iris in her eyes when he told her, "My name is John Temple."

33

A ND HOW ARE WE SUPPOSED TO believe you?" Jinn prodded.
John Temple was no longer capable of laughing. The brown
water pouch tied to his waist was empty. The black stopper on the
floor was overrun with the critters slithering out of his bag where water
used to pour.

"God, he smells." Berta covered her nose. "This is beyond disgusting."

"Hey, you!" Max called to him, but seemed unwilling to take a step closer.
"Are you really John Temple? How long have you been here, mate?"

Berta whispered to Max, "I heard someone could last a whole three weeks
without food and a few days without water, and I mean, that's if they're *real*
stubborn," she said. "But the guy who told me was drunk at the time, so I don't
know how reliable that is."

Max frowned. "And just how often did you hang out with drunk men?"

Lulu shushed them both but continued to stare at the man in awe.

Iris had once bought a book called *The Life and African Explorations of
David Livingstone*, written by the explorer himself, because she'd wanted
to know more about the world she and Granny had come from. The first few
pages alone enraged her.

The kind of men who wrote these books cared nothing for people like her and Granny. They traveled for their own gain. Money. Acclaim. Validation of their own beliefs. And this husk of John Temple, with his dead children, dead wife, and sociopathic son?

"What have you gained?" Iris asked him in a whisper. "What have you gained by coming here? By studying me? By following Hiva's origins into the bowels of hell?"

"Nothing," he whispered. "Nothing."

John, once lauded as a baron and a scientist, once counted among the most influential in his world, simply sat there rotting for the spiders to take him. He parted his cracked, pale lips to say more, but no words came—only the wheezing of a half-dead corpse.

"Hiva," he said finally. "Are you H—?" His voice was hollow. "Hiv . . . Hiv . . . Hiva . . . ?" John Temple's faded eyes grew wide.

The number of years he must have spent poring over his research, writing about her body as a concept to be studied. This man didn't want the world to end. It was why he'd run from the Committee. He'd journeyed over land and sea to learn about her—to learn how to stop her.

To drag a god back down to earth required nothing short of divine intervention of a different sort. If what the king told me is indeed true, I'll find my divine intervention in the place where heaven dwells.

"Did you learn how to do it?" Iris asked him. The slight breeze in the hall disturbed the cobwebs over the torches. "Did you learn how to drag a god back down to earth? To clip her wings?"

"The place . . . where . . . heaven . . . dwells: Heaven's . . . Shrine." The more he used his voice, the easier talking became. "I found this place . . . and became lost. How long has it been? How long . . . has it been . . . ?"

Iris shook her head. Seeing him destroyed and disoriented elicited a kind of pity she hated feeling. She would have been more comfortable with hatred. Well, she felt that, too.

But she felt he should know.

"Your son Adam tried to kill you because you ran off with the Moon Skeleton. He wants to destroy it. He doesn't want anyone to escape the apocalypse. He wants the world to end. He thinks it *should* end."

At the sound of his son's name, his face seemed to brighten ever so slightly. "Adam. My son. How . . . how is he? My boy."

"Did you hear a word I said?" Iris took an angry step forward. "Your son is trying to destroy humanity, and I'm pretty sure it's because you failed as a father."

John Temple looked up for a long time, mumbling to himself. Iris wondered what he saw behind those clouded eyes.

"How many were we?" he suddenly whispered, each word sounding like scraped wood.

Iris shook her head. "What?"

"How many were we? How many were we, dear Charlotte? Adam. Abraham. Eva. Even Father . . ." His lips cracked into a dreamy grin. "'And two of us at Conway dwell. And two are gone to sea. . . . Two of us in the church-yard lie. Beneath the church-yard tree. . . . Their graves are green. They may be seen. . . . I dwell near them with my mother . . .'"

Where had Iris heard that before? It sounded like a poem. . . .

"Iris, he's gone insane," Jinn told her with a nudge. "There's no use in engaging him."

"Wait, how did he get in here?" Berta nudged Max in the ribs, and she was right. "Before we got here, the place was buried, right?"

Berta was right. There was something she was missing. A mystery Iris hadn't yet uncovered.

And then it suddenly made sense. "There's another way to get into this temple, isn't there?" Iris asked. "Or multiple ways?"

Why not? There were parts of the architecture she hadn't seen. There could have been more to Heaven's Shrine she didn't know. Other entrances, other weapons. Other secrets . . .

John Temple began to move. Iris thought he was convulsing, like he'd finally die right here in front of her. At her question, he nodded. But his head kept bobbing from side to side uselessly, because he was gesturing toward something.

"My . . . my jacket."

His tweed jacket pocket. Iris cautiously approached him, cringing at the sound of her boots crushing the insects crawling across the marble floor.

Brushing away the cobwebs, she quickly reached into John's pocket. Her hands felt the cold, smooth rod of the crystal, and when she pulled it out—

"I've seen that," Jinn said when she turned around and showed them.

"We've all seen it," Max concurred, turning to Rin, whose serious expression deepened.

During the Tournament of Freaks, their first task had been to steal skeleton keys from one another. Many had been killed during that first round. As Iris held this skeleton key in her own hand, the memories of bloodshed and mayhem flooded into her.

This key was an exact replica. Or perhaps the original. Two perfect rings interlinked. A small crown resting upon its head. A silver chain affixed. Iris remembered the pattern. It felt all too familiar to her.

"The sun and its shadow," she whispered. A phrase now familiar to her. Two overlapping circles, one dark, one bright. The Naacalian symbol for the Hiva.

But this key was neither ruby nor iron. It was not made of any of the materials the Enlighteners had used to commission their tournament trinkets. This skeleton key consisted of the pure white crystal that had created her.

The Moon Skeleton.

"This key . . . this key does more than power the Helios," John Temple explained. "It opens many of the Naacal's secrets. It's the key to many things." He paused and shut his eyes. "It's yours now."

Iris stepped away from him, staring at the long key in her hands, clinging stubbornly to it. "Why?"

"So that you can choose. Choose . . . life. Choose life in the place of me . . . who chose this. I failed them. Only here did I realize. I failed my family."

Bits of saliva dripped down from his mouth to his unruly beard as he spoke. He hadn't the energy to wipe them himself.

Iris shifted uncomfortably. This man had spent years chasing after her ghost. He'd kept her heart in his family safe as if it had been his to keep. Iris didn't particularly enjoy watching this man decay before her eyes, but she refused to feel sorry for him.

"That's ironic," she whispered. "You wanting me to choose life when you've never had any respect for mine."

"The Gorton Zoo was proof enough," he said. "Any event, if disastrous enough, can turn you at a moment's notice into mankind's foe. And then . . . then there will be no stopping you. It is written in the tablets. It's already happened once in this lifetime."

Anne. When Iris turned from him, she caught Max staring at her. Only at her. His expression was indecipherable. Two of his fingers were linked around Berta's wrist. Soon, John Temple called for her again.

"It wasn't until I became like this that I realized: the choice has always been yours. Regardless of what we men do with our petty ambitions. The choice . . . is yours, Hiva."

Iris squeezed the Moon Skeleton in her hand. "My name is Iris," she said.

"The future . . . the future . . . is yours to decide." John Temple coughed so hard, he drew blood. "But before you choose, listen to the voices of those whose fates are in your hands. Cross over to the other side. The others are waiting for you. They came through this place before you. Led by that man . . ."

Iris frowned. "Others?" she heard Jinn say behind her.

But John Temple did not elaborate. A sense of dread descended upon her as quickly as the insects scuttled across the man's body.

"We should try to get him out of the mines," Jinn told her. "Get him medical attention."

"Why? He's already half-dead," Max scoffed callously, folding his arms. "Besides," he added, "I hate Temples."

"Max," Jinn warned.

"He thought he was more important than he was and paid for it," Max retorted. "Now look at him. He got what he deserved. Just like his son will."

"Max." Berta tugged on Max's shirt, a little spooked. Max relented, though his expression remained unreadable.

"Leave me," John Temple said. He didn't elaborate. He only lay back against the altar, his body limp from the stress of speaking.

"What now?" Rin asked Iris, holding Lulu's hand.

"Well, we should get him medical attention whether he wants it or not," Iris said decisively. "But I don't like the idea of us separating. He got lost here by himself. It could happen to one of us. We should keep going and pick him up together on our way out. We shouldn't be long."

Perhaps he had gotten what he deserved, but Iris couldn't live with herself knowing she'd left this man here to die.

But there was something else to consider. Iris mulled it over for a moment. Then, inhaling a heavy breath, she gave Rin the Moon Skeleton. "Can you keep this for me for now?"

Rin stared at the key, taken aback. "What? Why?"

Iris smiled. "Because I trust you with it."

"What are they saying?" Berta whispered to Max. "Why is she giving her the key? What's the key do?"

Max shushed her. "We'll see how this all turns out soon enough."

Cross over to the other side. The others are waiting for you. Iris wasn't sure who he was referring to, but as she stood in the Room of Murals, as she let old memories untangle themselves and blossom within her, she understood what he meant by the "other side."

Iris walked around the altar. The mural, like the door, had been programmed to respond to "Hiva." It had been part of the Naacal's plan to lure her to that temple beyond it—the place where a god could fall.

She was ready for her wings to be clipped.

Iris placed her hands on the now-filthy mural. It shuddered and rumbled. And, like the gate to Heaven's Shrine, it lumbered and slid to the side. Beyond the wall was an elevator, supported by a brass framework that descended into the dark abyss.

Iris almost laughed when she saw the shocked expressions of the group behind her. Or maybe those were nerves. "If anyone wants to come along, now's the time."

As she expected, no one was willing to wait here with John Temple among the insects.

The lift had a little golden button, and after touching it, the outline of a door formed and popped open. She stepped inside the glass structure. It was wide enough to fit them with room to spare. Once they were all inside, the door closed, its demarcations disappearing until the glass was whole again.

The Naacal had truly been a creative people. If only they had used their intellect and imagination for better exploits.

Iris remembered standing on this very platform with Nyeth inside the glass lift as it descended into the darkness. It had been his final stand after witnessing her destroy his people.

Well, he'd murdered his own people with his own hand—the ones he'd deemed useless. All this technology and wealth, yet the Naacal had enslaved and brutalized many while leaving others to starve. Those with power hoarded it with an almost maniacal greed. Those without it were driven to beg or kill to survive.

Choice? Was there a choice? If she didn't destroy the world, then would she live in it ignoring the injustices around her? Was her own happiness enough?

Several hours passed. The lift took them in many odd directions under the earth. Lulu slept in Iris's lap. It wasn't until the pressure around them suddenly changed that she awoke with a start. But what she saw before her was a wonder few would ever see.

"L-look . . . look!" Lulu cried.

The glass lift had taken them into the ocean. The glass structure and brass framework were strong enough to withstand the pressure. The Naacal had many underwater facilities, and this network had been their main method of travel. Iris was surprised it was still intact.

The group stared in awe at the scenery around them. All manner of sea creatures big and small drifted by the elevator, gently repelled by the electrical force embedded within the glass. Seaweed, algae, seagrass— an entire marine garden stretched out before them, splashing the waters with reds and greens. Whales swam in the distance, singing a haunting song. And a large creature, with little black eyes and a hairy snout like a pug, flapped its fins as a school of bright yellow fish passed by. It was a miracle of life.

Every time she had destroyed the world, she'd never touched the flora or the fauna. Why was humanity the only creature with the willingness and ability to harm the earth? If only all could achieve harmony . . .

"It's beautiful, isn't it?"

Iris turned. A peaceful warmth had settled upon Jinn's face. His expression was calm, his body relaxed. His brown eyes were reflected in the glass.

"If my father were alive, I'd tell him everything. All these wonders I never thought possible. Everything I've been able to experience since I met you, Iris."

Iris's heart fluttered. "So you don't regret meeting me then?" She kept her tone light, but deep down she wanted to know. "Me, who dragged you into untold madness?"

"The world is madness," Jinn answered, staring into the ocean. "The world is beautiful. The world that my father and I once lived in together. It can't end."

"It won't." Iris touched his arm and looked up at him. "I swear that."

Any event, if disastrous enough, can turn you at a moment's notice into mankind's foe.

As long as you are unwilling to do everything it takes to stop the inevitable, we are all in danger. Innocents. My own children. No one else will be sacrificed to your selfishness.

Different voices from different memories. The words formed like icicles in her veins.

Why had it suddenly become so difficult to breathe? Her throat closed up. She took deep breaths. Then she buried herself in Jinn's chest. He hesitated for a moment before wrapping his arms around her.

Why did he hesitate? Or was she overthinking things again? She was always panicking when she didn't need to. It hurt her beyond words. She just wanted this to be over.

"Look, down below!" Lulu knelt. They could see it through the bottom of the clear floor: a round dome made of orichalcum, glowing the color of midnight blue and embedded inside a pocket of air brimming with light—a heavy contrast to the darkness of the sea. The symbol of the Naacal scratched onto its surface was clear, even at a distance. It wasn't very large—smaller than the Crystal Palace, certainly. But as a small hole in its roof opened to welcome the glass lift, Iris felt the same kind of dread as when she'd searched the Basement.

This was the Coral Temple—the underground facility where Nyeth and the other Hiva had conspired to bring her to her end. It'd become the site of Nyeth's end instead.

His ring felt hot in her pocket. Its time was coming. She could feel it.

The glass lift deposited them onto the ground and immediately retreated back up.

Nothing had changed. Light cascaded through the glass window in the domed ceiling. Dark blue pillars stretched up from the white marble floor. Iris and the others stood upon a platform under a pillar of light; beyond it, a spiraling staircase led down from the dais. But when Iris turned behind her, she could see the one thing that had eluded her memories.

A cube made of transparent glass balanced on one of its tips, held to the ground by some unseen magnetic force and washed in a faint golden light, its size so large that it stretched halfway up to the ceiling. It reminded her of the glass in the British Museum, the one that held her skeleton on display. It smelled of death. And the large symbol scratched in white upon its surface seemed to promise it: a circle with four points, crossed out as if it were a blight. A sun in chains. It was a symbol that she'd only seen once before, on one of the Naacalian scrolls she'd stolen from the Library of Rule. A symbol whose meaning still eluded her.

"Hiva's Tomb."

His emotionless voice sucked out every other sound around her. All she could hear were his steps. But she could feel his anima. Smell it. Taste it. A life force that wasn't a life at all, pulsing with emptiness and a touch of hatred.

She turned. Slowly.

"Hiva."

The word escaped her lips before she'd fully accepted his presence. But as he ascended the winding staircase, she recognized him. His long, curling brown hair filled with the flowers of the earth he'd once so loved. His chiseled features and those wide golden eyes that had never once seemed capable of deception until she, through her cruelty, had driven him to learn it.

He wore a black cloak that covered his body from head to toe. She couldn't see any part of his olive skin, but his face was as beautiful as always. His expression softened when he saw her. It was as if his body had released its tension the moment their eyes locked. He was serene. Determined.

But he wasn't alone. Behind him marched a procession of familiar faces, none of which greeted her with even a hint of a smile. Cherice, Jacob, and Hawkins. In Hawkins's hand was an issue of the *Evening Standard*. Under the light, Iris could just make out an image on its front page—an image of a mining site. This mining site. She shook her head and looked again. It really was. Just beneath it, Iris could see a photo of Adedayo, one of the African envoys who'd come from this region to London several weeks ago. She would know. Hawkins himself had helped her spy on him.

Why did Hawkins have that newspaper with him?

There was someone else among them, someone Iris had never seen. A lanky boy with brown hair and thin, awkward features.

"Twig?" Berta called out, incredulous.

"Fables!" Lulu cried at the same time.

This boy, Fables, looked up, surprised to see them, but then lowered his head again as if in prayer. In his hands, he carried something long wrapped in a gray blanket and bound up in rope. Though Iris squinted, she couldn't tell what it was.

Iris's group stood behind her. Hiva approached her, remaining at a distance. His group formed a line beyond him. No one spoke.

"M-Max . . ." Hawkins froze to the spot. "Max . . . is that you?"

"Maxey?" Cherice's pumpkin-colored hair swished as she searched for him. Once she caught sight of him, the tears began to bead on her eyelashes and drip down her cheeks.

At the sight of Max standing next to his sister, Hawkins's, Jacob's, and Cherice's expressions twisted in both joy and agony. Cherice fell to her knees, while Jacob laid his head on Hawkins's shoulder and wept.

"He's alive," Jacob said. "Lawrence, he's alive. He's alive. . . . Hey!" He cupped Hawkins's face with both hands and pulled it to him. "Are you listening to me? He's alive!"

Hawkins couldn't respond. The newspaper fluttered out of his hands to the ground. "Max . . . ," he started. Max stiffened, his bottom lip curling up. His jaw tightened at the sight of his orphan friends.

"Max?" Hawkins took a step forward. He didn't know how to react, and Iris could guess why. Club Uriel. His actions that night had caused Max's suffering.

Frantically, he picked up the newspaper and waved it in the air. "I did it, you know. I traveled through a photograph. I took everyone here. And I didn't get stuck. I got over my fear." He tripped over himself. "Isn't that mad? Isn't it amazing?"

Iris shivered as the crazed look in Hawkins's eyes screamed for forgiveness. She knew that what had happened to Max hadn't been any one person's fault. But when Max didn't move an inch, Iris couldn't help but wonder if Max didn't see it that way.

Hawkins took another hurried step forward, but Hiva lifted up an arm to stop him. No one was to leave their place until he told them to.

"I've come for you, sister," Hiva said. "Just as I said I would."

The "others" John Temple had warned her about. Led by "that man." The mural had been programmed to respond to "Hiva." There were two Hivas here. Warring gods, together again.

She knew she hadn't hallucinated their meeting in that spiritual realm outside of space and time. Now they were here. Together again in the place where she'd murdered Nyeth and banished Hiva to millennia of wandering through dimensions, anchored to nothing, being nowhere and everywhere for so long that he'd lost the humanity he'd once had.

"I don't understand," Jinn said beside her. "Who are you? How do you know Iris?"

Hiva's answer was devoid of the emotions she'd stolen from him. And yet perhaps it was her imagination when she heard, buried deep in the core of his words, a flicker of bitterness and a hint of the desire for revenge.

"If Hiva is the sun, then I am her shadow," he told Jinn before turning to Iris. "And this is your final judgment."

34

I HAD ALWAYS HOPED I'D COME BACK here again, he'd told her in the darkness. *That I'd see you, sister.*

To kill me?

To destroy *you.*

Iris trembled. Hawkins, Cherice, and Jacob somehow seemed like hollow husks of their former supernatural selves. Sunken eyes, dry lips. Scars wrought upon their bodies—at least the parts that she could see. They waited for Hiva to speak, but some weren't so patient. Jinn opened his mouth, ready to attack—

But nothing came out of his mouth. He coughed, holding his throat in confusion.

"The barrier surrounding the Coral Temple is powerful," explained Hiva. "Powerful enough to dampen preternatural activity. The Naacal employed such technological preventive measures in all the facilities where they experimented with powers beyond their control."

No powers. If they wanted to fight, they'd have to do it the old-fashioned way.

"Twig! What are you doing here?" Berta stomped her boots when the awkward-looking boy did not answer. "What's going on?" Her hands hovered close to her pistols. "I saw those guys in Oklahoma. Max, these are your friends, right? That's what they told me."

Max shut his eyes for a moment before letting his body relax. He smiled. "Yeah," he answered. "They're my friends."

He pulled Berta closer to him.

Hiva had begun to move. He took a step forward, his black cloak sweeping the floor. It was so strange, seeing his golden eyes without any trace of the life and mirth they once had. He who used to scoop Naacalian children up in his arms and give their furry pets loving kisses. He moved now like one of their unfinished machines. Seeing him like this made Iris's stomach churn.

He was another casualty of her existence as Hiva.

There on the dais, he began to tell his story.

"From the earth Hiva comes. And to the earth Hiva returns," he told them.

So cold. Under the light streaming in from the window, Iris wrapped her arms around herself. He sounded so cold.

"It was like that on my earth. Perhaps it is so on every earth." Hiva's golden eyes fixed on her. "The cycle of rebirth, judgment, and death. Once I tired of it, I sought other worlds. Surely existence was different elsewhere. Surely there were other ways to live. The technology of the new civilization that had bloomed upon my world made it possible. I began to travel."

And he had come to her earth during the era of the Naacal. Iris remembered meeting him by a tree in a field of daffodils swaying in the wind. She remembered his excitement at finding her—someone facing the same choices, the same dilemma of life and death. He'd asked her so many questions. How many civilizations had she destroyed in the past? Did it affect her as much as it did him? Didn't her heart break at the sight of lives burning to ash?

Even then she could tell that his naïve interrogation was directed toward a singular philosophical dilemma: Is there another way for us to live?

The Hiva before her did not waste so many words. "I have seen millions of civilizations far more advanced than your own come to a fiery end. Sister, you and I have struck them down ourselves. Despite my musings, I learned very quickly that so long as the cataclysm known as Hiva exists, mankind is doomed. As long as the woman standing before you draws breath, your world will die."

"That's not true!" Iris squeezed her hands into fists. "I'm here because I'm looking for another way. If you would just help me, maybe we can find it."

Hiva shook his head. "It is not what you believe, but what these humans believe, that matters now."

Silence.

"What if there is no other way?"

It was Jacob who had spoken. He was sincere, this boy. He held no real malice for her in his eyes, but he spoke honestly, huddling closer to Hawkins, holding on to Cherice's hand. These orphans from different backgrounds who'd survived on the streets together, depending on only each other. "Iris. What if it's inevitable?"

"John Temple said it too." Max. The warmth drained from Iris's skin. He pulled Berta to him still closer until there was barely space between them. "That it's happened before, decades ago. That it always happens . . ."

"*This* time will be different." Iris couldn't believe how empty that promise sounded. It was as if the confidence she had in her own desires simply didn't matter. She looked up at Jinn, her lungs able to breathe again when she saw him give her a reassuring nod.

Hiva tilted his head, considering her carefully. "You love life as I once did?"

"Yes," Iris answered stiffly.

"Then you should be able to sacrifice yourself on their behalf. You should be willing to do anything to fight for them, as I once tried to. Even if it means giving yourself up." With his right arm, he pointed to the vast, tilted cube behind them. "Sister. You know what that is."

"Hiva's Tomb," she answered, because she remembered it now. The way Nyeth's eyes had darted to it just before dying. The greatest of their inventions.

And it'd just been completed, too. . . . Damn it all. . . .

In the center of its flat surface, just underneath the Naacalian symbol of the chained sun, was a silver mold, the shape of a circle.

The shape of a ring.

"Hiva cannot be killed but subdued. That is what the Naacal believed. And so they created this machine. A machine that can be activated by the Coral Ring."

As Hiva spoke, everyone gazed up at the structure looming over their heads.

"Its purpose," Hiva continued, "is to disassemble Hiva to an atomic level. Though it cannot destroy her crystal heart, it will not allow her to gather the parts of herself together again. In this tomb, Hiva will exist, alive and conscious in name only, in suspended animation. And so she will remain here under the ocean waters, her cells unable to gather again, her body unable to rebuild itself, for all eternity."

A fate worse than death. Her mouth dried. It was so cold inside the Coral Temple. She'd never noticed it before, never cared. Now all she could do was shiver helplessly. She felt painfully alone. Her crystal heart thumped in her chest, and she wondered how the Naacal had been able to create such a terrifying wonder in secret. It was the perfect countermeasure to defeat an unkillable god. And maybe the fate she deserved.

"You have Nyeth's ring," Hiva said, looking down at her skirt. "I can feel his anima."

Iris gripped her pocket and felt the ring inside the cotton fabric. "Yes."

Hiva nodded. "Then you can do what needs to be done. As long as you live, no matter how hard you fight against your nature, there is a chance that you may destroy this world in the end. Knowing that this is true, will you choose to bring peace to this world once and for all?"

Iris gritted her teeth, shrinking back, though no one had advanced. "Don't act so concerned. You don't give a damn about peace anymore. You just want to see me suffer."

"Quiet, you heathen! Don't you dare speak to him like that!" It was the lanky boy who'd spoken: Fables. Though she'd never met this young man in her life, he looked at her with such venom, it made her toes curl. He clutched the mysterious object wrapped in cloth tighter to him.

Hawkins hesitated before speaking. "It's your move, Iris," he said. He, Cherice, and Jacob trusted Hiva more than they did her. "You can end this all here. Right now."

Everyone was watching her. They said nothing. They didn't need to.

"Is this how you planned to 'destroy' me?" she asked with a wry smile.

Hiva's golden eyes glittered.

Her Other had given her a simple choice and thus, so casually, plunged her into the void of confusion and despair. She stepped back, turning away from all of them, but when she looked up, she saw it: Hiva's Tomb. The Naacalian symbol, black as poison. A cage made for her and her alone. Another cage . . .

Iris took Nyeth's ring out of her pocket and traced its shining rim. The silver lock of the tomb called out to it. She could activate it. Right here, right now. She could end it all.

"All this time," Iris whispered, staring at the ring lying cold on her palm. "All this time, I'd been looking for a way to stop the 'Hiva' in me from destroying humanity. I traveled around the world—for this. For this moment."

"Iris!" Jinn called from behind her, and though she could feel him grip her elbow, he still somehow felt so far away from her.

How naïve had she been? Thinking that she could somehow find a solution that would let her get everything she wanted. It all seemed so absurd now. She couldn't hide from the truth anymore, not when Hiva had laid it out so clearly before her.

Ignoring Jinn's pleas, Iris wrested her arm from Jinn's grasp and walked toward the tomb. She faced it properly. The gleaming gold. The silver lock the exact size and shape of the round coral-colored plate affixed to Nyeth's ring.

She turned. Despite being unable to understand every word, Rin seemed to sense what was happening. The anxiety was written all over her face. Lulu and Berta waited wordlessly, Berta's eyebrows furrowed in confusion, Lulu grasping her skirt while pressing a fist against her heart. Max, however—Max simply waited. He waited to see what she would do.

And beyond them: Hawkins, Cherice, and Jacob. From their slouching bodies and sagging faces, Iris could see they'd been through hell. It was as if the kiss of death had caressed them more than once. Iris knew the despair all too well. She'd once had it herself after being locked up inside the University of Cambridge at the mercy of Seymour Pratt and Britain's scientific best.

Caged like an animal at a zoo.

It was why . . .

It was why she couldn't go back to confinement. Never.

Being stripped of her humanity. Her body parts disassembled. Living behind a glass cage for eternity. It was an unacceptable nightmare. She refused. And even if the world ended, she'd continue to refuse it. She was never going anywhere she didn't want to go again.

She touched the glass of the tomb with her hand and, shaking her head, finally collapsed to the floor. "I'm sorry," she said. "I'm sorry, but I can't do it. I won't. Not for anything or anyone."

"You bitch!" Cherice screamed, as if she'd been waiting to erupt. "Even if it means we all die, you still won't do the right thing? What about Maxey, huh? What about Berta?"

"What about Berta . . . ?" Max repeated just quietly enough for her to hear. He was wrestling with himself. Iris could hear it in his voice. "What about us, Iris?"

"Why do *I* have to do the right thing all the time?" Iris staggered to her feet. "Why do I have to die and go? It's not fair! Can't you see that?" She looked at Max, who looked away, his eyes lowered to the ground in thought. "I promise—"

"Promises mean nothing." Hiva turned his head to the side. "You've seen it for yourself: the cruelty of my sister is unchanging regardless of the times. Now you know what you must do."

As the flowers twisted in his hair, he held out his right hand. The boy, Fables, approached him and knelt as if for a king, holding up the object wrapped in gray cloth.

Hiva took it and, sweeping off its cover, showed Iris.

A blade. Beige with a tinge of yellow. Long and chiseled. At first Iris thought it had been made hastily out of some kind of strange wood.

And then she remembered. She remembered Hiva on these very steps, bleeding from the blade she'd used to wound him and kill Nyeth. . . .

"That blade," Nyeth said between labored breaths. *"We made it out of his . . ."*

Bones. A blade made out of Hiva's bones. And Iris could tell, without even sensing the anima in it, that the blade Hiva held in his hand had been made out of hers.

"Only we can kill ourselves. This knowledge has been with me since birth—since the One who created me first raised me from the earth," Hiva said. "It was the same for you. As expected, you had forgotten. You've forgotten many things, sister."

Iris shook her head, staring at the sharp point. Her own left arm, carved like a stake to kill a vampire. "Where did you—"

The British Museum. It was the only way. Iris's heart began thumping rapidly in her chest, her blood rushing from her face.

"Sister, if you'd aimed for my heart that day, you would have killed me," Hiva told her. "I wish you had killed me. How many millennia did I spend afterward wishing you had? You decided to show me 'mercy' then. But will they show you mercy now?"

Hiva's golden gaze passed over every other person in the room. "Let it be known: one *can* kill a god," he said. "Whoever wishes to kill this god, come forward." And then, after dropping the bone blade upon the dais, he stepped back.

At first, nobody moved. And then it was a mad rush to the blade. Hawkins, Cherice, and Jacob. Jinn and Rin. Max and Berta. Whether they wanted to save her or kill her, they didn't need powers to batter each other. The tangle of bodies, the shouts and screams were so severe that Iris could no longer differentiate them. She stumbled back until she felt her shoulder blades against the glass tomb, tears streaming down her face.

"Mere hours leading to this moment, I heard them quietly plotting." Hiva, in the midst of the chaos, had slunk up next to her. "They decided among themselves: they would take my life after they took yours, now that they knew the method. But it seems their hatred for you was so strong that they desired to kill you first."

Bitterness that knew no logic. Like Nyeth's own. Like countless others, because of her very existence. Was this what it meant for her to be alive? Iris struggled to breathe.

"Don't be sad, sister." With a serene expression, he stood next to her, watching the mayhem unfold. "For eons, we observed and exacted judgment upon humanity. Shouldn't humanity have the opportunity to do the same to us?"

"But you don't care about humanity," Iris said, sobbing. "Not anymore."

"I wished to see you betrayed, destroyed." He placed a hand upon her shoulder. The ecstasy of revenge murmured beneath his quiet, neutral voice. "And after the ones you hold dear deal you the final blow, I'll ruin this earth. Let that be the final thought you have as you go in despair."

Jinn punched Hawkins so hard that the boy went flying, along with one of his teeth. Jacob ran after him. Cherice tried to grip Rin in a headlock, but the warrior elbowed her in the stomach. Iris couldn't watch. She couldn't move. Maybe she *should* die. She buried her head in her hands.

"Miss Iris?"

Lulu. Fables wasn't the only one who'd stayed out of the chaos. Shakily, Iris looked down at the little girl.

"I don't understand. Aren't you an angel? Aren't you going to put a stop to everyone that's bad and protect weak people like me?"

Could she? What was her dream anyway? To live in her own peaceful bubble while the world suffered, knowing that at any minute she could turn into a mass murderer and begin her campaign of genocide? So many people wanted so many things from her. And through all their perceptions and desires, Iris had lost sight of herself.

"I'm sorry, Lulu," was all Iris could say.

All that Lulu had been through felt palpable in that moment, as Lulu looked up at her with the kind of disappointment and sorrow that made Iris want to curl up and die. Shaking her head, the girl turned away sadly, took Hiva's hand, and walked away from her.

"I'm sorry," Iris said, laying her head on the glass tomb. "I'm sorry." She just didn't know what to do. "I'm sorry." Who was she? "I'm sorry!" Who was she supposed to be? Why did it hurt so much? Why had she been born? What was she to do?

Who could she count on?

"Max!" Several people had screamed his name, but it was Jinn's voice she heard over all of them.

What happened next felt like a dream. Fast footsteps approached her while she cried against the tomb. Berta screamed Max's name next. Then Rin screamed out Jinn's. Jinn screamed. Max's growl sounded feral.

Then the sharp pain in her back. The glass of her tomb cracked. She looked down. It was the blade that'd cracked it. Its sharp point dripped with blood. She struggled to breathe, her hands grasping the bloody spot where her heart should have been, before she realized: the blade made from her bones had pierced it.

Her shaky, bloodstained hands slipped across the glass cage as she tried to straighten up, but the blade in her back had cut clean through her spine. With whatever strength she had left, Iris lifted her tearstained face.

And saw Jinn reflected in the glass. His sorrowful expression, his despair, fading like the dying sun.

She couldn't believe it, even as she shivered from the familiar contours of his chest against her back. She couldn't believe it, even as he laid his hand on top of hers, the hand that had thrown her up so many times into the air as they danced together atop their tightrope. She couldn't believe it, even as she felt his hot breath against her ear.

"I'm sorry, Iris," Jinn whispered. "I didn't . . . I'm so sorry."

And then finally, within the Coral Temple, Iris's crystal heart shattered to pieces.

To dream was futile. To search for one's self, vanity. Iris realized this as she watched the reflection of the man she'd loved fade from her sight.

It was the final death.

THE NEXT STAGE

IT WASN'T A PERFECT PLAN, BUT Adam had run out of the ability to care. It was a bloody one. That was all that mattered.

The conference room in Berlin carried the stench of power. Long tables lined up together with maps to trace, documents to read, and treaties to sign. Sturdy wooden chairs scuffling against the Persian rug, as European men of the highest status left their seats to give a speech by the velvet drapes or negotiate a territory with another dignitary. Next to the grand, expertly carved oak door hung a map of Africa, upon which the gentlemen in the room affixed their greedy eyes.

The Berlin Conference. No, the Congo Conference, Adam had heard King Leopold call it. It was the part of Africa that whetted the sick man's feral appetite the most. Leopold himself might have been here somewhere among this congregation, along with other such powerful men of ill repute. Germany, Austria-Hungary, Belgium, and Denmark. Spain, France, Britain, and many others. Elites from fourteen different countries had gathered here to formalize their claims to various territories across the central continent. Claims they had no right to, but such was the evil of men.

Among the dignitaries were a few men who had once belonged to Club Uriel. Van der Ven, having finally arrived after weeks of delay, sat with his Belgian colleagues. Adam's pedigree and family history allowed him to sit with the Brits and witness history unfold. The explorations of his grandfather, Isaac, and father, John, had already done so much to help the Crown, they told him. And they were always looking for an edge. Tensions with the French were already high. But there was barely a country here that didn't have tensions with another.

Evil men wanted to conquer, and they wanted to conquer before others could beat them to it. In a way, staring at these men scurrying about in black jackets, their white beards fluttering as they argued with one another, reminded Adam of the Enlightenment Committee. A lust for power. Tenuous alliances held together by string. Their agreement not to destroy each other was undermined by an unspoken distrust and a propensity for shedding blood that slept dormant like a powder keg.

All it needed was a match.

"Sanford." Adam leaned over to the diplomat sitting next to him. "I wanted to bring in one of my father's books, but I believe I left it in another room. Would you mind—?"

"Oh, don't worry," said the man. Henry Sanford. A fan of John Temple as much as he was of King Leopold. Seemed he had a type. "I was going to get up anyway."

"Thank you."

"Ah, Van der Ven. Come here, will you?" Otto von Bismarck spoke in German, but he knew the military man would understand. To Adam's eyes, Bismarck was a sad-looking man, his thick white eyebrows and mustache drooping at perfect forty-five-degree angles. Adam had only heard stories of the German chancellor from his father. But even in his tight military garb, he was smaller in person. He was an important man. Integral to Germany's ever-quickening development as an imperial power.

He would do.

Adam cleared his throat. The person they assumed was "Van der Ven" caught his eye. A slight nod was all it took for "him" to understand.

The dignitaries at the Berlin Conference had made a gentlemen's agreement to leave all weapons at the door.

But Adam and Lucille had formed an agreement of their own.

"Van der Ven" shot Bismarck in the head. His blood splattered across the map of Africa.

Shouts of shock and horror broke out across the room.

Adam was astounded at how well Lucille had kept her poker face. She was terrified. Her eyes gave it away. But the face of the fake Gerolt Van der Ven remained steadfast and arrogant, so like the man himself.

She was quite good, this shape-shifter.

"What is this monstrosity?" cried Clemens Busch, a younger German diplomat, who caught Bismarck in his arms as the man fell. "What have you done?"

"Van der Ven" answered by shooting a man from Austria-Hungary. Emerich something. Adam had never bothered to learn his name; it was too long.

As screams of confusion shook the rafters, the doors opened. Seven marbles rolled through the entrance, unnoticed by the howling men.

Right on cue.

Ah, Henry's toys, Adam thought pleasantly as the marbles exploded. Henry hadn't designed them to kill but to distract. The thick smoke allowed Lucille to change from Van der Ven to Henry Sanford, who by now would be lying dead in another part of the building. *Bang.* As the smoke cleared, "Sanford" took down Courcel from France.

Just as he expected, the men didn't run. They cried out for vengeance. One of the military men had decided to use his ceremonial saber to stab "Sanford," who grunted and fell to the floor.

"Where is Van der Ven?" they cried. "Belgium! What have you done?"

Someone was screaming horrifically in French. A struggle ensued. Adam dragged a bleeding "Sanford" out of the door. The Spring Day Massacre had begun like this. Once one domino fell, it would be easier for the others to follow. That massacre had culled half of the Enlightenment Committee. *How many will die today?* Adam wondered.

In the midst of the chaos, Adam managed to pull "Sanford" into another room. There, a wilting, pale Mary laid her hands above Lucille's chest and quickly began to heal her. Hopefully she'd pull through. Lucille was all too useful a card to play.

"What the hell was the purpose of all that?" Henry Whittle demanded, grabbing Adam's collar. "What did you just make us do?"

"So you asked me before. And when you did, I warned you not to ask questions."

"You blackmailed us, threatened us, into committing assassinations," Henry hissed. "I want to know why."

Adam closed his eyes. The alliances between greedy men were indeed pathetically breakable. All it took was a match to set the world aflame.

And then she would see. Iris would see the wickedness of men. The atrocities they were capable of when pushed to the limit. The boundless nature of their bloodlust. The reason the story of humanity needed to come to an end.

Perhaps it really would take a war for her to understand.

A world war.

Iris should have been dead.

Or were life and death nothing but two sides of a coin to the One, to be flipped and overturned on a whim? No. She was dead. She was gone. Iris was sure of it.

What was happening?

Out of the darkness, a specter appeared, a haze of light buzzing around her brown body as softly as a firefly.

"Anne," Iris said. "Did you save me? Did you . . . bring me back from the dead?"

But of course it wasn't Anne. The creature with round white eyes, cracked lips, and graying skin was the One who would summon her from the depths of the earth, who had called out to her so many times before, in her previous lifetimes that had spanned decades. Now here, in the underworld, she called out to her again.

I've done as I always have after your final death: salvaged your soul. And the One overturned her hand as if she held Iris's soul in her palm. *Your body has decayed. Turned to dust.*

Iris imagined her corpse disintegrating in the Coral Palace. A pitiful end. A horrible end.

And then she imagined Jinn's satisfied grin. His relief at the sight of her demise. And at that thought, a frightening emptiness opened up inside her. An expanse of grief.

Of rage.

But you have died before fulfilling your purpose. I can change that. If it is your wish, I can make you live again, she said.

A cosmos of memories. Eons of cataclysms.

In her hand, the One carried with her a coin.

Night.

And Day.

And now, both faces were Iris's.

What was the purpose of humanity? Why did such brokenness seem to follow people wherever they went? Were suffering and anguish endemic to them? Or was there another way?

She'd asked herself countless times before. And now she knew: there was no other way.

Shutting her eyes, Iris let it seep into her: the agony of civilizations past, combined with her own. It made her whole. She could see again. Ah, she could see so clearly.

It is time once again, the One said, holding out her coin. But Iris did not look at it. It wasn't necessary. She knew her answer.

Iris nodded. "They all must die."

And she opened her eyes.

ACKNOWLEDGMENTS

I am a wacky girl with wacky stories in my head. I want to thank everyone who keeps encouraging me to write them. Seriously, writing is not an easy feat. There are so many road bumps along the publishing path, and some feel like they were put there by some unseen forces that have been around long before I've been alive. So having people on my side to encourage me means so much. I'm going to do the typical award-show thing and thank God and my family first, because boy, I went through it writing this book and the last. I'm so thankful for my agent, Natalie Lakosil, and editor, Sarah McCabe, for their encouragement and patience while I got my shit together. My editorial team (Nicole Tai's copyediting notes are so thorough, you guys, and I loved it!) and the whole Margaret K. McElderry crew (thank you for the mug!).

I want to thank Michael Strother, my first Simon & Schuster editor, who really opened the door for me as an author by picking up *Fate of Flames* from the slush pile and deciding he wanted to buy it. It became a trilogy, the Effigies Series, which led to *The Bones of Ruin* and now *The Song of Wrath*, and I'm not done yet.

But most of all, I want to thank the fans who continue to support me from book to book. The ones who've been here since *Fate of Flames* and the new ones I've picked up along the way. I'm especially thankful for those who are supporting the Bones of Ruin series and are ready to see it through to the end. Your support and enthusiasm give me a reason to write another day. Thank you, always.